FIST OF DEMETRIUS

More William King from Black Library

• THE MACHARIAN CRUSADE •

Book 1: ANGEL OF FIRE
Book 2: FIST OF DEMETRIUS
Book 3: FALL OF MACHARIUS

• TYRION & TECLIS •

Book 1: BLOOD OF AENARION
Book 2: SWORD OF CALEDOR
Book 3: BANE OF MALEKITH

• SPACE WOLF •

SPACE WOLF: THE FIRST OMNIBUS
Contains books 1-3 in the series: *Space Wolf,
Ragnar's Claw* and *Grey Hunter*

SPACE WOLF: THE SECOND OMNIBUS
With Lee Lightner
Contains books 4-6 in the series: *Wolfblade,
Sons of Fenris* and *Wolf's Honour*

• GOTREK & FELIX •

GOTREK & FELIX: THE FIRST OMNIBUS
Contains books 1-3 in the series: *Trollslayer,
Skavenslayer* and *Daemonslayer*

GOTREK & FELIX: THE SECOND OMNIBUS
Contains books 4-6 in the series: *Dragonslayer,
Beastslayer* and *Vampireslayer*

GOTREK & FELIX: THE THIRD OMNIBUS
With Nathan Long
Contains books 7-9 in the series: *Giantslayer,
Orcslayer* and *Manslayer*

A WARHAMMER 40,000 NOVEL

THE MACHARIAN CRUSADE

FIST OF DEMETRIUS

WILLIAM KING

BLACK LIBRARY

A Black Library Publication

First published in Great Britain in 2013.
Paperback edition published in 2014 by
Black Library,
Games Workshop Ltd.,
Willow Road,
Nottingham, NG7 2WS, UK.

10 9 8 7 6 5 4 3 2 1

Cover illustration by Raymond Swanland.

A CIP record for this book is available from the British Library.

UK ISBN 13: 978 1 84970 643 8
US ISBN 13: 978 1 84970 644 5

See Black Library on the internet at

blacklibrary.com

Find out more about Games Workshop
and the world of Warhammer 40,000 at

games-workshop.com

Printed and bound by CPI Group (UK) Ltd, Croydon, CR0 4YY

It is the 41st millennium. For more than a hundred centuries the Emperor has sat immobile on the Golden Throne of Earth. He is the master of mankind by the will of the gods, and master of a million worlds by the might of his inexhaustible armies. He is a rotting carcass writhing invisibly with power from the Dark Age of Technology. He is the Carrion Lord of the Imperium for whom a thousand souls are sacrificed every day, so that he may never truly die.

Yet even in his deathless state, the Emperor continues his eternal vigilance. Mighty battlefleets cross the daemon-infested miasma of the warp, the only route between distant stars, their way lit by the Astronomican, the psychic manifestation of the Emperor's will. Vast armies give battle in His name on uncounted worlds. Greatest amongst his soldiers are the Adeptus Astartes, the Space Marines, bioengineered super-warriors. Their comrades in arms are legion: the Imperial Guard and countless Planetary Defence Forces, the ever-vigilant Inquisition and the tech-priests of the Adeptus Mechanicus to name only a few. But for all their multitudes, they are barely enough to hold off the ever-present threat from aliens, heretics, mutants - and worse.

To be a man in such times is to be one amongst untold billions. It is to live in the cruellest and most bloody regime imaginable. These are the tales of those times. Forget the power of technology and science, for so much has been forgotten, never to be re-learned. Forget the promise of progress and understanding, for in the grim dark future there is only war. There is no peace amongst the stars, only an eternity of carnage and slaughter, and the laughter of thirsting gods.

Exhibit 509-H. Extract from transcript from xenos artefact recovered on Procrastes 4. Warning – this translation
is heretical and spiritually contaminated. Access partially
de-restricted as part of ongoing investigation into possible
beatification of Lord High Commander Solar Macharius and
related trial of former High Inquisitor Heironymous Drake
for heresy and treason against the Imperium.

These records will be interpolated with the testimony of
former sergeant Leo Lemuel (missing, presumed deceased)
to provide a partial narrative of the Procrastes campaign and
the events surrounding it.

PROLOGUE

I bathe in the sound of their screams. Their pain renews me. The scent of their fear fills me with joy. Such pitiful things they are. I had hoped, against my better judgement, for the smallest of challenges, something to drive away ennui for this brief moment of eternity, but what I got were mewling animals, barely fit to sully my blades with their blood.

I stand here, surveying the field of battle from atop a mountain of corpses. I would think it a waste of valuable slaves, save for the fact that there are plenty more humans where these came from. They breed like vermin, filling the universe that was once ours with their squalling progeny. It is good to teach them their place once again.

One of the humans raises its crude weapon and points it at me. The creature is so slow. I spring to one side and the las-bolt strikes the corpse on which I had stood. Flesh sears. A stomach bloated with charnel gases explodes.

It matters not to me. I am nowhere near any more.

I see fear written on the human's clay-made, brute features. There is no appreciation of the beauty of my movements. It does not have any sense of how blessed it is, to be killed by my hand, to give up its life to feed me.

I leap, crossing thirty strides in a suspensor-assisted bound, and land beside it. My blade flickers. It looks at me dumbfounded. It has not felt anything yet. It looks down and sees that its coarsely woven tunic has fallen apart where my blade cut. It looks relieved for a second, in its last few painless moments of life, then it sees the blood starting to leak from its flesh. It wonders what has happened. It has no concept of how to kill with artistry or die with dignity.

I smile and move my blade again. Delicate as a haemonculus's scalpel is my movement. I peel back the flesh like the cloth of the tunic. Muscle is revealed, then vein, then the white, white glimmer of bone. The human's mouth goes as wide as its eyes. It gurgles then clamps shut its lips, trying to hold in its whining.

I am careful not to break anything, to sever anything. It has all happened too quickly for the human. Its sluggish nervous system is just starting to register the first glimmerings of true agony. I feel myself flush with a small jolt of pleasure. Its mouth opens again, a fish out of water, drowning in air. A faint trickle of saliva glistens on the corner of its lips, catching the wan sun's light like dewdrops on a leaf.

I pause for a moment to consider the loveliness of it, and

as I do some of the creature's oafish companions blunder into view. Their faces are distorted with animal rage. They have interrupted me in my meditation, and I resolve to quench their anger with their blood and fan the flames of their fear until it is a sun-hot blaze.

I reach out with my free hand to caress the dying human's face with the razor-sharp fingers of my gauntlets. I insert a blade into an eye socket and listen to the scream. It is a simple pleasure but one I always enjoy.

The humans stand their ground. One of their leaders bellows orders. Its harsh speech offends my ears, so I draw my pistol and fire. My shot is not intended to kill, so it does not. It sears the tongue and stoppers the creature's offensive grunting, changing a bellow to a gabbling whimper. The humans continue their slow, slow movements, raising weapons to their firing positions.

I pick up the dying creature and twirl it like a partner in the Tarentina of Skulls until its body is in front of me. I make sure it has a moment to realise what is happening, to bring its one good eye to bear on the weapons of its comrades. Something wet squirts down its leg; whether blood or urine I do not care.

It stiffens, knowing what is happening. It faces a firing squad of its own companions. Its form partially obscures mine for all the moments I need. It screams, thinking it is going to be a barrier between me and its comrades. It does not even have the wit to realise it is merely a distraction.

I leap as the dying human's skin sizzles under a storm of las-bolts. The greasy smell of frying flesh penetrates the nasal filters of my armour. I make a note to see that my artificer is suitably punished for its laxity before it dies. One thousand hours of screaming seems appropriate.

My leap carries me to the cornice of an ancient temple building above the squad of humans. They continue to fire, responding to the wails of their dying compatriot, cheering and grunting, somehow under the pathetic delusion that they are harming me. I take a second to look at their jester caperings. Overhead, the huge face carved into the side of the mountain looks down mockingly. I laugh, and the amplifiers in my armour project my mirth thunderously.

They look around, their bestial minds confused, lacking the wit even to look up. I could kill all of them in this moment. It would be simple. One grenade would do the trick, but where is the artistry in that?

There are twenty-seven of them, a figure divisible by three, which has always been a fortunate number for me. I decide to spare every third one of them, to let them survive to face the torturers. I will kill one-third of them cleanly, to give the survivors something to regret they did not receive, and I shall make one-third of them chorus their screams unto the heavens.

I spring among them, a carnivore among a herd of plant-eaters. For a moment I am amid the press of their bodies, surrounded by so-rippable flesh, looking upon meat puppets made to mock the shape of the eldar. I feel a delicious tingle of utter hatred. I stand stock-still for a moment to appreciate it before springing into action.

They still have not realised what has happened. I strike

one down from behind, applying a careful measure of force so that the skull does not break. I snap another's neck. I punch blade fists into the stomach of one who turns, and pull out the ropes of entrails. They squirm like sticky purple serpents. I see the pulsing of the thing's heart within its chest cavity and I resist the urge to pull it out. That would be too quick. I loop a rope of intestines around the throat of another and pull tight. It is not intended to kill, merely to mock. I vault over the shoulder of the squirming soldier. My kick snaps the neck of another.

I handspring as they try to track me, panicked, squeezing the triggers of their weapons. Their clumsy crossfire burns each other. I send a razor's edge flashing into the throat of one, then shoot another. I kill them before they can accidentally slay those I have chosen to let live. I do not wish them to spoil the symmetry of my creation.

I shoot and strike and lunge, killing one, sparing another, maiming a third. They are too slow to stop me. One of them at last realises it and draws a grenade. I see the delicious fear in its eyes and I know what it intends to do. It is so frightened that it thinks it is going to drop the grenade where it stands and die taking me with it.

The grenade begins its slow, slow fall to the ground. I snatch it from the air, grab the human by the head and force the bomb into the creature's mouth, then down its throat. I backflip away, suspensor-assisted, soaring into the air as its head and chest explode in a fountain of blood.

In the confusion, the humans have lost track of me again. I pick three at random and execute them with headshots.

They mill around, leaderless now, knowing something is killing them but unable to strike back. They are a rabble, not even worthy of contempt.

Sudden boredom strikes me. I am tempted to end the game and simply kill them all, but that would be undisciplined. One must finish what one starts. One must keep to one's purposes. The true artist never loses sight of his goals, even though the agony is its own reward, as is the terror.

I catch the pheromonal trace of something new, a human scent that, surprisingly, does not speak of fear or horror, that carries an icy tang of calmness and control. I swivel my head, seeking its source.

A human in a long black coat advances on the rabble as they turn to flee. It looks cleaner, more austere and disciplined than the rest, which is like saying one mon-keigh looks less idiotic than another as it flings its excrement at the bars of its cage. It shouts instructions but is ignored by the panicked mob. It draws a pistol and executes one of the fleeing humans. I feel a faint flicker of annoyance. The newcomer threatens to disarrange the symmetry of my work. There is only one way to prevent that, which is to make it take the place of the man it has killed.

I drop to the ground in front of black-coat.

'Xenos scum,' it snarls, marginally quicker on the uptake than the others. 'Die!'

The translation engines give its voice a flat, metallic ring. It raises its pistol to shoot me as it did its fleeing species-mate. I enjoy the way it froths at the mouth as it tries to bring its weapon to bear as I move. I am glad I decided to spare this one for later, because breaking its will and teaching it to worship me will be more amusing than simply killing it out of hand.

I reach out and snap its wrist before it can pull the trigger. I strike a nerve cluster that I long ago learned will immobilise a human, and then slap it unconscious with the sort of contempt I am sure it will understand when it comes to contemplate it. All around, the rest of its pack continues to flee. I pick them off, one by one as suits my purposes, taking a few extra moments to ensure that the corpses fall in a pattern that is pleasing to the eye, that the blood spatters are random but beautiful, and that there is more than a suggestion of intelligence at work amid the havoc.

I pause in contemplation at the centre of the artwork I have created. It has been a pleasant few minutes of relaxation, but now there is work to be done. I allow the communications channels to open again and listen to my followers as they go about their business.

It seems that they have encountered no more resistance than I have among the so-called defenders of this once sacred site. In a way, it saddens me. There are so few challenges left in the universe, so little of interest. I hear reports of captives being taken and that cheers me. Soon there will be feasting and gladiatorial contests and sport to be had with our new slaves. It is good.

This petty world is ours now. We have a secure base. Soon I will open the Gate of the Ancients and claim their lost treasures. I have taken the first step on my long road back to Commorragh and eventual triumph over my enemies.

* * *

Reports are coming in from all over this pathetic planet. The defences are every bit as poor as our scouts suggested they would be. Cities have fallen. Citadel towers are under our control. The population of most of this continent is subdued. We are masters of this valley now and will soon have access to its ancient secrets. The humans cannot stop us.

Of course, these valleys have some significance in their primitive faith. It is only natural. They are looking upon the work of their racial superiors, and no matter how weak our ancestors were, those eldar were still as far above humans in the great scheme of existence as a human is above a puke-lizard.

I push such thoughts to one side, unsure as to why I am even bothering to contemplate them. I confess there is something mildly disturbing about this place. The temples of our ancestors rise above us like the tombs of forgotten gods, which is, I suppose, what they are. I stride up the hill, acknowledging the respectful salutes of my warriors. Discipline is lax, a few have already begun to feast, flaying alive their still-living prey to consume the delicious agony. I make a note of the miscreants' names. I will see that some suitably subtle penalty is enforced later. They will get the message.

I stand in the shadow of the Temple of the Night-Dark One. I have come a long way to find sanctuary here, in a place where none of my enemies would think to look. My rivals are still back in Commorragh, enmeshed in their endless schemes. Can it be that I am really the only one who has read the ancient books of lore? It seems unlikely. I have learned to mistrust good fortune. Too often it is a smiling mask that covers the schemes of one's enemies. It is always wise to look closely when the universe offers you a gift. It proffers many a poisoned chalice in a form that looks like a victor's cup, as I have learned to my cost. The price of failure in the intrigues of Commorragh is very high.

I inspect the great entrance to the place. Above me stands an enigmatic stone giant. Its face is somewhat like mine, long and lean and beautiful, with pointed ears. Its shape is tall and slender compared to that of the disconsolate human corpses it looks down on.

I pass through the entrance and into the cool interior. This cave was once a spot sacred to my soft ancestors, back when they believed in their milksop gods. There are niches and alcoves with many small shrines where once offerings were left, flowers and incenses and such. I remove my helmet and make an offering of spittle on the face of a deservedly forgotten deity. A human, robed as one of their priestly caste, makes a shocked sound. My lieutenant, Sileria, digs her finger-blade into a nerve cluster and it screams.

'The forgotten ones have found new worshippers,' she says. She sounds amused.

'Deserving ones,' I say, and she laughs. There has always been an understanding of sorts between her and me. 'Monkeigh who have no understanding of what they abase themselves before, who do not even know that the things they worship are themselves long dead, devoured by She Who Thirsts.'

'I have secured the shrine as you commanded, Lord Ashterioth. No one has approached it, or will until you have inspected it yourself.'

She wears a questioning look. Clearly she is wondering why we are here and not pillaging the human cities of this world, taking slaves for the Dark Feast. I consider taking her into my confidence, but I am not suicidal. She might try to buy her way back into favour in Commorragh by betraying me to my rivals. She will learn what she needs to know when she needs to learn it. I wonder if she has sneaked into the inner sanctum herself to gaze at what we have come so far to find.

Of course she has, and she is confused because she has found nothing of value.

A beautiful creature, Sileria, but one lacking in both understanding and imagination. For her, if it does not glitter or scream it can have no value. She does not understand what else might be found in an ancient, empty shrine. I can see she is nerving herself to ask me a question, so I nod encouragingly.

'Is it true that you intend to desecrate all of these shrines, my lord?' She gives the word lord a faintly submissive erotic twist. I remember her writhing beneath my lash in bedchamber games of dominance and submission. Surely she is not so simple as to think I would let such memories influence me. But, of course, there is value to be had from encouraging her in such a false belief.

'In a sense, Sileria,' I say. In a sense it is true as well. If the ancient texts are to be trusted, I will be committing an act of desecration when the gate opens. I will take what the ancients built and twist it to my own purposes, which, most assuredly, were not theirs. She nods as though I have told her something significant; possibly it is something significant as far as her limited understanding is concerned. No matter how much she schemes, Sileria will always be a follower. Some are born to lead and others to follow, even among the Pinnacles of Creation.

'I go within,' I say. 'Make sure I am undisturbed.'

I leave her absent-mindedly stroking the human with her blades. Its whimpers are a mixture of pleasure and horror and pain. She will keep her new pet alive for some time, I am sure. I turn my mind to higher things as I descend into the long darkness beneath the temple complex. I have a long way to go before I find what I am looking for.

It looks like nothing. Even I, who know its significance, cannot suppress a feeling of disappointment. This is what I have come all these long light years for? For this I have travelled through the webways, absented myself from the intrigues of Commorragh and lost my high place among the Exalted? This?

I stand in a large chamber, surrounded by defaced statues of extinct gods. Before me looms an archway large enough to fly a skimship through, except that it would be impossible. There is nowhere to go. The arch looks as if it is a carving emerging from the wall. It leads onto nothing but blank stone laced with shimmering crystal. Is it possible I have made a mistake, I wonder, that the ancient texts are wrong, that I have become the victim of some gigantic, cosmic hoax?

I look at the archway again. On it are carved the faces of the twelve forgotten gods to whom this temple-site was once sacred. Even if I could name them, I would not. She Who Thirsts expunged their weakness from the universe when she took them into herself. They do not deserve to be remembered by the strong. We do not need such deities now, certainly not such feeble ones. We have become like unto gods ourselves.

I strip off my gauntlet and touch the cool stone, feeling at those mask-like visages. I do not know what I am hoping for. There are no secret buttons or pressure plates to be depressed.

I run my fingers over the deep veins of crystal within the arch, hoping despite myself for some response, some glimmer of ancient archeotech to come to life beneath my touch. Nothing happens.

I glance around. For a moment, I have a sense of being watched. I wonder if it is one of my warriors, spying on me, hoping to learn something; Sileria perhaps. I see nothing, and my senses are keener than most. The sense of ancient, shrivelled presence remains. Perhaps the tattered wisps of the ghosts of dead gods still cling to this place.

The time has come, I tell myself. I walk to the altar and place my hands on the ancient psychotropic crystals. They tingle beneath my hands, still responding to the ancient power of the place. I invoke the rituals I learned in ancient books stolen from the forbidden library. I feel a faint shudder in the crystal as the old powers awaken. Lights flicker. The earth quivers as if it is a giant beast whose sleep has been disturbed by an old nightmare. I have started the first pebble of an avalanche that will eventually bring the full geomantic potential of this place into focus and open the gateway. If all goes correctly, the seal will be broken and the ways beyond will become accessible within mere weeks.

There are rituals that I must still perform, powers that must be invoked, but I have begun. I am one step closer to achieving what I have planned all these long centuries.

I stand and contemplate the gateway arch, wondering whether I will really find the key to ultimate power beyond it. The texts hint as much. In this place, at this time, the ancients struggled to create a device that would be the ultimate weapon and the ultimate defence. The hints suggest that the Fall came before it could be tested but that they were close. If that is even only partially correct there is much I could do with their work.

I smile, alone with the ancient ghosts, thinking that for once I have stolen a march on my rivals. No one else knows of this place. No one will come here before the gateway opens.

If they do, I will destroy them. After I have taken my pleasure upon their broken bodies, of course, and taught them that there are worse things by far than the death they will beg for.

CHAPTER ONE

Exhibit 107D-5H. Transcription from a speech imprint found in the rubble of Bunker 207, Hamel's Tower, Kaladon, containing information pertaining to the proposed beatification of Lord High Commander Solar Macharius and to the investigation of former High Inquisitor Heironymous Drake for heresy and treason against the Imperium.

Walk in the Emperor's Light.

The huge warship rocked under the impact of a glancing hit from the planetary defence batteries. I could tell the *Lux Imperatoris* had only taken a glancing hit because I was still alive. The hull was still intact. My cold corpse was not floating in interplanetary space. For a moment, there was utter stillness, as if a quarter of a million men, the crew of the ship and all the Imperial Guard warriors it carried, held their breath.

Above me, through the armoured crystal dome of the warship's command chamber, I could see a world burning. Demetrius had been a globe of giant forests and ancient temples. Orbital strikes had set those forests on fire. As the wings of night swept over the visible face of the planetary orb, continents glowed fitfully. Occasionally the glittering contrail of a weapon blast leapt across my field of vision as the command ship added the fire of its own batteries to the assault. It had a terrible beauty to it.

Demetrius was not the first world I had seen burn in the ten years since I had joined Macharius's bodyguard, and I felt certain it would not be the last.

All around us huge holoscreens showed three-dimensional topographical representations of this sector of the galaxy, across which the gigantic war machine of the crusade rumbled. Beneath each holoscreen were tables on which scribes and tech-adepts moved representations of armies and fleets. I had no idea exactly what was going on, but then I did not need to possess such a thing. The man for whom I was a bodyguard already knew all of that and more.

The ten years since Karsk had not changed Macharius physically. He still looked like a warrior god. Some of the other generals were starting to show the signs of easy living and the spoils of victory on a galactic scale, but not him.

The juvenat treatments still worked better for him than any other man I have ever met. He quite literally did not look a day older than when I first saw him inspecting the troops before we began our assault on Irongrad. His hair was still golden, his figure was still lithe, his eyes still resembled those of some great predatory beast. But there was a hardness about his features that had not been there when I had first seen him, a grimness that had grown since his encounter with the daemon that waited at the heart of Karsk. He had seen something during that encounter that had transformed him into an even more relentless conqueror of worlds, made him more determined to reassert Imperial control over all the sectors lost to schism.

As he walked around the command centre he projected the same air of confidence that had been so striking when I first saw him. If anything, he seemed even more certain than he had back then, and he had every reason to.

For ten years the crusade had enjoyed almost uninterrupted victories. It had reclaimed hundreds of worlds, bringing them back into the Emperor's Light and restoring the true faith to countless billions.

I doubt that I had changed much either. Since being inducted into Macharius's personal guard I too had been given access to juvenat treatments, and they appeared to work pretty well for me. I did not feel any different from those early days on Karsk. The same was true for Anton, who stood nearby scanning all of the assembled personnel for any threats to the Lord High Commander. He still looked as tall and gawky as a fisher bird in the deltas of the Great Black River. His green uniform with the lion's head insignia of Macharius's family hung on his body as loose as hand-me-downs on a scarecrow. The juvenat treatment had done nothing for the old scar on his forehead. It still writhed like a centipede whenever he frowned or squinted.

Ivan watched everything with a cynical glitter in the human eyes that peered out of his partially metallic face. His grin revealed sharp metal teeth, razor-edged. The juvenat treatments had not worked quite as well for him, possibly because his body was riddled with mechanical parts and this interfered with the technical magic of the serums. Of course, the quality of his augmetic systems was much higher now, as befitted one who was the guardian of the highest warlord in existence. They obviously did not cause him quite so much pain as the older versions had, and he did not drink quite as much as he used to, at least not when he was around Macharius.

We had come a very long way from our homes in the slums of the hive-world of Belial.

The Undertaker watched everything with his strange, empty glance. He too was unchanged from Karsk. Of course, back then, he had been changed more than any other man I have ever known by the events we had witnessed. He had gone from being a junior officer on the crew of a Baneblade to the commander of the bodyguard of one of the most important men in human history, and it had not changed anything. Nothing ever seemed to. He watched everything with the same cold, blank expression he had ever since the days when the lieutenant's brains had been splattered all over his uniform.

We were not the only ones present responsible for Macharius's security, of course. There were some who had been there longer, retainers of his family, summoned from his home world to replace the casualties of Karsk and beyond. They looked somewhat like Macharius. All of them had the same golden skin and golden hair. All of them looked like smaller, inferior copies of the great man made from a slightly degraded mould. There were men drawn from a hundred different worlds and a hundred different regiments, all of whom had fought for a position in the service of the supreme warlord of mankind. There were Catachans and Hemorans and Mordians and Telusians. All of them were joined in one brotherhood by their loyalty to Macharius and his crusade.

The *Lux Imperatoris* rocked again as another blast came close. I offered up a prayer to the Emperor and wondered if He could hear me from His throne on distant Terra.

A scribe approached and spoke to Macharius with the mixture of precision, formality and reverence that Macharius inspired in those around him. He was doing his best to ignore the shuddering of the ship and the possibility of instant death as he brought news of another victory. The worlds of the Proteus system had surrendered, bringing another three planets, ten hive cities and nineteen billion people back into the Imperial fold. Macharius nodded an acknowledgement, turned and said something to another clerk, recommending the general in charge of the campaign for some honour or other, and walked on.

Two more uniformed clerks approached and saluted. Before they could even open their mouths to speak,

Macharius rattled off orders, sending instructions to commanders who were five star systems away, instructing them on which cities to besiege, which worlds to offer alliances to and which governors to bribe. He had no difficulty dredging up any of this knowledge. It was all there in his head, all of the details of an infinitely vast campaign the like of which had probably not been fought since the Emperor walked among men. He ordered more reinforcements sent to aid them and kept on walking towards the furthest tables.

Sometimes he looked up and gazed upon the surface of the burning planet with a look of longing in his eyes. I felt a certain sympathy for him then. Macharius was a warrior, born to fight. He loved commanding this great force, but I suspect he missed the thrill of physical conflict, the feeling of danger, of taking his own life in his hands. His thoughts were drifting to those final battles taking place on the world beneath us.

I could tell that he wanted to be there. I could tell also that he had something else on his mind, something to do with his current obsession with prophecies and divinations and ancient relics that so exercised his mind when he talked with Drake. It was a topic that drew the two of them together, it seemed, although Drake has never struck me as a superstitious man. Quite the opposite, in fact.

Here on the galaxy's furthest rim, superstitions were common. These worlds had been far from the Emperor's Light for a hundred generations; all manner of strange, deviant and heretical faiths had sprung up, and all manner of weird beliefs had infected the populations. Some had even taken root among our own soldiers, although you would have thought they would have been immune to it. Clusters of prophecies had begun to gather around Macharius himself. That was easy enough to understand. The Lord High Commander appeared invincible, gifted with near-supernatural powers of foresight.

There were some who claimed he was blessed by the Emperor. There were others who thought he was a supernatural being himself. Reports had started to arrive of shrines being set up to Macharius on dozens of worlds and not just by those unbelievers whose temples to false prophets had been overthrown.

The ship shook. We looked at each other for a moment before we went back to pretending that nothing had happened. An officer in Naval uniform walked over.

'A glancing strike to the void screens, Lord High Commander,' he volunteered. 'Nothing to worry about.'

'I am not worried,' Macharius replied.

'I doubt they could possibly know this is the Imperial command vessel,' said the officer. He clearly was more disturbed than Macharius as the possibility that they did occurred to him.

Macharius nodded and the officer pulled himself together, clicked his heels and saluted. As Macharius strode by, his mere presence seemed to reassure people. Worried frowns disappeared from the faces of scribes and star-sailors. Command must always look confident and that was something that Macharius managed supremely well.

We made our way towards one of the great command

tables with utter casualness. Indeed, so relaxed was our approach that I knew that we were approaching the spot in which Macharius had the greatest interest. I had learned to read the subtle signals of his moods by then. Or perhaps I delude myself. Few men ever truly knew what the great general was thinking.

Ahead of us was the command sphere for the world we currently orbited. On its flowing surface was a representation of the continent we could see through the dome above us. Instead of being lit by the fires of burning forests, this showed representations of armies as glowing patterns. Ours were green. The enemy forces were red. Various runes indicated the composition of the units, ours glowing steadily to show we were certain of their composition. The enemy forces pulsed with varying speed to indicate the margin for error in our scouts' reports on their position and strength.

Around the table stood a variety of ranking commanders and Drake. He was in theory an observer but stood with the air of a man who was actually in charge, at least until Macharius arrived. The High Inquisitor was tall and slim, with a pale, cold face and dark hair which now had a tinge of grey in it. Obviously the juvenat treatments had not taken so well with him, or perhaps he was simply much older than he had appeared when we first met and the drugs' effects had started to weaken.

I did not know much of the inquisitor's personal history, and he never volunteered anything to anyone in my hearing, even Macharius. He was a man much more used to asking questions than answering them. Uneasiness radiated from his person to those around him, in the same way as confidence emanated like solar rays from Macharius.

The High Inquisitor looked up as Macharius approached and smiled. I suspect that Macharius was as close a thing to a friend as Drake ever had, if friend is a word you can ever use in the context of an inquisitor. I had seen too much of his business in the past ten years to believe that he looked at the world with any more humanity than the Undertaker did.

Macharius nodded a greeting and went over to stand beside the inquisitor. The two men were of a height but otherwise were as different as two people could be. Macharius was physically powerful, Drake slender and ascetic and deceptively frail looking. Macharius wore the gorgeously braided uniform of the highest ranking Imperial Guard officer. Drake wore a plain black tunic and a scarlet cloak with cowl. Around him, a group of storm trooper bodyguards lounged like attack dogs. They eyed us as warily as we eyed them.

Drake nodded to me, which was not something calculated to make me feel any easier in my skin. He had taken an interest in me since Karsk, as he took an interest in all those close to Macharius. Often I had been summoned to his presence to answer questions about the general's moods and health. I had reported these conversations to Macharius, of course, and he had told me to answer truthfully. He clearly believed that I had no secrets about him to reveal to the Inquisition that they did not already know, and I suspect he was right.

Macharius turned to the tech-adept who stood by the command altar. 'Give me a view of sector alpha twelve,' he said. 'Close magnification.'

'In the Emperor's name, Lord Macharius,' the adept responded. He intoned a litany and moved his hands in some ritual gestures over the altar. We looked now at a three-dimensional map of a strange city. All around it was a clear, flat zone, where the forest had been burned early to provide a firebreak. The buildings were ziggurats, sheathed in metal, glittering in the light of twin suns. They looked as much fortresses as temples. They bristled with turrets and blister-bunkers and other fortifications.

War raged. Men in the uniforms of the Imperial Guard fought with fanatics in the green and purple robes of the local temple wardens. Blood flowed in the streets. The natives fought stubbornly, with the courage of zealots prepared to die for their misguided faith.

They were going to. So much was obvious. Inexorably, Imperial Chimeras and Basilisks and Leman Russ tanks pushed through the streets surrounding the stepped pyramids, moving in the direction of the gigantic central temple. Macharius looked at the colonel who had been liaising with the ground forces.

'My orders have been conveyed?' he said. There was a question in his voice, which was not like him. Normally Macharius gave a command in the full expectation of it being obeyed and then moved on. He did not check on subordinates unless something had gone wrong, in which case he moved swiftly and ruthlessly to correct the errors.

'The ground commanders have been specifically instructed not to bombard the central temple. The soldiers know there is to be no plundering on pain of death and that demolition charges and heavy weapons are not to be used within its precincts, Lord High Commander. I made your orders very clear on those points. There can be no misunderstandings.'

'Good,' Macharius said, and the man seemed to swell with his praise. Like everyone else on the command ship, he knew Macharius would not forget his efficiency or forgive his failures. He had gained credit in the eyes of the most important man in the crusade, and rewards would eventually and inexorably be disbursed.

The ship shook again, more violently this time, as it took another glancing strike from a planetary defence battery. It made me uneasy. I did not like to feel that any moment I might be vaporised and that there was nothing I could do about it. This was a battle fought with weapons so gigantic that ships with the populations of small cities could be destroyed in an instant, and an individual warrior could have no influence on his fate. Give me a ground battle or even trench warfare any time. At least there you can take cover and a few enemies with you.

The glow-globes flickered. A smell of ozone filled the air. Somewhere in the distance someone screamed. Someone else shouted an order. I suspect the screamer was being clapped in irons or assigned to a punishment detail.

'It seems that the enemy might be finding their range,' said Macharius. He chuckled and everybody else around him did the same. It was not that what he said was particularly funny, but when a general makes a joke, no matter how feeble, his subordinates laugh. It did dispel the tension.

Drake had ignored the near miss. He had been staring at the battle-map with total concentration, as if he could achieve a spiritual revelation if only he looked hard enough.

'We must have the Fist,' he said in a voice so low that only Macharius and those standing close to him could have heard it.

'Do not worry, my friend,' said Macharius. 'We shall get it.'

'We must,' said Drake. 'It may be one of the Imperium's most sacred artefacts – a relic from the time when the Emperor walked among men, a thing perhaps borne by one of his most trusted primarchs, a worthy gift for potent allies.'

Macharius smiled. He appeared to be considering something for a moment, which was unusual for him. Normally for him to think was to act, and to act with a decision and correctness that most ordinary men could not have achieved with hours or days of contemplation.

'In that case, I believe I shall secure it myself.'

Drake shook his head like a man hearing something he had feared but which he had hoped not to have to deal with.

'Is that wise?' he said. It was phrased like a question, but it was really a statement. Drake was one of the few men who would have dared question Macharius. It was a thing that was happening more and more in those days, as if a rift were slowly opening between him and the Lord High

Commander; as if he, so seemingly secure in his faith, were starting to have doubts in Macharius. In this case I was with him, for I could tell from the rare and slightly crazed grin spreading across the general's face that Macharius was serious. He really had decided to go planetside and lead the assault on the temple.

Drake knew as well as I did that once Macharius had made up his mind there was no possibility of deflecting him from his purpose, but the High Inquisitor was not a man to easily admit defeat.

'You should not put yourself at risk, Lord High Commander,' said Drake. I suppose he was thinking that he would be in trouble with his superiors if anything happened to Macharius. After all, he seemed to have taken on some responsibility for Macharius's safety after the events on Karsk.

'I have no intention of putting myself at risk,' said Macharius. He was already striding towards the exit arch of the command centre, though, and all we could do was follow in his wake, like the tiny satellites of a gas giant or a cometary halo whirling around a sun.

Anton shot me a look that I knew well. A grin that was considerably more crazy than Macharius's flickered across his face and was gone before anyone but me could have seen it.

Drake shrugged and began to stride along beside Macharius. His storm troopers moved in his wake, some of them even surging ahead as though they suspected danger might lurk in every corridor of the command vessel.

'I shall accompany you then,' said the High Inquisitor. 'You may need my services down there.'

'As ever, I welcome your company,' said Macharius. 'But admit it, you are just as keen as I to get your hands on the work of the ancients.'

A cold smile appeared on Drake's face, one of the few I had ever seen. He was a forbidding man in a position of fearful power, and I doubt anyone ever mocked him the way that Macharius did. Perhaps he enjoyed the basic human contact. It must have been rare in his life. 'I am certainly keen to know whether it is the thing we seek.'

The command ship rocked again under the impact of another planet-based weapon. I was suddenly glad that we were on the move, heading towards the shuttle bay. It would be good to feel ground beneath my feet again, and air in my lungs that had not been recycled through a ship's fallible systems a thousand thousand times.

It struck me then that for all his courage perhaps Macharius felt the same way. Even for a man as brave as he undoubtedly was, waiting on a ship under attack, when any moment its walls might explode and you might be cast into the chill vacuum of space, must have been a nerve-wracking experience. I asked myself if it was possible he was just as nervous as I and just hid it better.

I dismissed the idea as ludicrous.

CHAPTER TWO

'I told you this was a bad idea,' said Inquisitor Drake.
We were pinned down behind a low wall while heretics
poured autogun fire down on us. Bullets whined overhead
and ricocheted off the brickwork. The cloud of lead was too
dense for anyone to dare attempt to return fire. Merely sticking your head up would have seen it reduced to bloody pulp.

Behind us, an ancient tree, part of the temple gardens,
was so riddled with metal slugs that it threatened to topple.
The leaves had been stripped from all of the ornamental
bushes. The ancient runic stone standing in a fish pond was
chipped and splintered. A sundial cast a pockmarked dou-
ble shadow on the ground.

I wondered if Macharius had finally made a fatal error.
Perhaps his keenness to get his hands on the Fist of Demetrius would be the undoing of us all.

'Nonsense,' said Macharius with his infectious utter confidence. I looked over and saw that he was smiling. He was enjoying himself more than he had in weeks. His uniform was dirt-stained, blood was dripping from his cheek, a blister that marked the near miss of a las-bolt had started to rise on the back of one of his hands, and yet he looked like a man who could think of no place he would rather be.

One of his wild moods was on him. He had led from the front as soon as he had arrived on the scene, heading charges, striding across the field of battle as if las-bolts would swerve around him. Of course, Macharius had an uncanny ability to always be where las-bolts were not. He seemed to know instinctively when to step aside, when to take cover in a doorway, when to throw himself flat. His reflexes were almost inhuman. And if his reflexes did not save him, I suspect the High Inquisitor's psyker powers did.

Drake did not look like he was enjoying himself. He saw no humour in the situation. He was a man who considered himself too important to throw his life away in a small skirmish on the side of a minor temple on some backwater world.

'Nonsense?' he said. I could tell he was coldly angry and keeping his anger on the leash. It was a novel experience for him. Macharius was one of the very few people who did not quail at the sight of his wrath.

Macharius said, 'In approximately two minutes Alpha Company of the Bjornian Snow Raiders will appear on that rise over there...' He pointed off to the south, where some burned-out stumps of trees marked all that was left of one of the gardens that had once covered the sides of this temple. 'In one hundred and fifty seconds, Crimson Company of the Nova World Regiment will take up position on the roof of that observation bunker...' A nod showed us where Macharius confidently expected the troops to appear. 'They will pour enfilading fire on the heretic position, and we shall sweep forward and take the gate.'

He spoke with utter certainty that would have been mad in anyone else but which was justified in his case. I had seen him do this before and ninety-nine times out of a hundred he would be right. He seemed able to foresee the twists and turns of combat amid the chaos of a battlefield.

Of course, not even Macharius was right all the time. I sometimes wondered at what he did, the way he courted death. He was one who needed to put himself in peril. It was only then that he was fully alive. It was a dangerous trait for an Imperial general to have and possibly Macharius's only weakness.

'Lord High Commander, the heretics are advancing on us,' said the Undertaker. He might have been reporting the fact that our lunch had just been delivered from the field canteen.

The storm of fire had slackened over our heads. I could hear the shouts and battle-cries of the oncoming fanatics of the temple guard.

Macharius nodded as though he had expected this all along. Perhaps he had. You could never tell with him how much was skill, how much was knowledge and how much was just a superb bluff. 'Now all we have to do is hold our ground until the reinforcements arrive.' He checked the chronometer on his wrist. 'We have approximately ninety seconds.'

With that he stood up and snapped off a shot with his customised pistol. A heretic went to meet his false god. I looked at Anton and Ivan. Anton held the sniper rifle he had picked up on Dolmen. He had become quite proficient with it. Ivan still carried his standard-issue lasgun. As one, we moved into the kneeling position and saw a wave of fanatics rolling towards us as inexorable as the rising of the tide on the third moon of Poseidonis.

I did not need to aim. There were so many of them packed so close together that I could not miss. I just pulled the trigger and pumped the combat shotgun. It tore men apart, but still they kept on coming. The others fired their weapons. They could not miss either. Men fell, robes on fire, flesh seared to burned meat.

Drake stood as well, an eerie glow surrounding him and extending itself to cover Macharius at his side. I shuddered. I had never adjusted to the sight of a man using those inhuman powers, even if they were sanctioned by the Imperium in Drake's case.

Of course, there were other things with the heretics. Their priestly caste had guardians. They looked like great white apes with heads resembling those of wolves. They looked twice as tall as a man, stronger than an ogryn and about as intelligent. Local superstition claimed they were inhabited by the spirits of warriors chosen by the forest gods. A tech-adept had assured me the transfer was achieved by means of ancient spiritual engines.

To tell the truth, it did not matter to me in the slightest at that moment. The sight of them, with their arms three times as thick around as my thighs, their huge claws and their massive fanged mouths, was almost enough to make me turn tail and flee. Perhaps the most horrific thing about them was the near-human intelligence in their eyes. It was strange to see it gleam out of such savage, bestial faces.

'Hold your ground,' Macharius said. 'Not much longer now.'

One of the huge ape-wolves bounded forward in a spring that covered thirty strides in a heartbeat. By instinct or design it had somehow managed to pick out Macharius. Possibly it sensed who was the dominant figure in our ranks.

It landed on top of Macharius, bowling him over. It bellowed and screamed and rose, covered in blood. I aimed a shot at its head. The shell tore away flesh and fur, leaving only bone gleaming. I looked down expecting to see Macharius's torn form, but he was unscathed except for some rips in his uniform where those massive claws had torn.

I looked at the stomach of the great beast as it roared and tottered and stretched towards the sun. I saw that its chest was sheared open, flesh rent and bruised in the distinctive pattern that a chainsword leaves. There had been no need for me to shoot it. Macharius had somehow eluded its grip and struck a killing blow.

I had no time to brood on this idea. The wave of heretics hit us. The only barrier between the two forces was the wall we had been hiding behind, and that was so low a fit man could leap over it with ease. I found myself grappling chest to chest with a burly heretic. Somehow I managed to break out of his grip, knee him in the groin and then bring the butt of my shotgun down on his head with an audible crunch. I turned and caught another man in the stomach.

The fighting was close and deadly. Ivan bludgeoned around him with his metal fist. Retractable studs and blades had emerged, turning it into something far worse than simply an ancient mace. He used his arm to block incoming bayonets. I think his foes were surprised by the nature of his shield for none of them managed to land a telling blow.

I looked around to make sure Macharius was safe. Anton stood near him, sniper rifle in hand, still shooting. His speed and accuracy were impressive. No one managed to get close to him and somehow in all the chaos he managed to pick his targets well. Of course, the shimmering glow of Drake's shield protected Macharius and the inquisitor from any accidental hits, and he could unleash death with complete confidence that he would not mow down the very people he sought to protect. It was a small advantage, but in that sort of combat you take any you can get.

A heretic pointed a slug-gun at me. I threw myself to one side and twisted. Idiotically, I aimed the shotgun at him and pulled the trigger. The weapon's kick almost dislocated my shoulder. The shell did a lot worse to the heretic's stomach.

One of the great ape-wolves bounded towards me, enormous muscles bunching under its fur, great clawed hands flexing as if it intended to rip me apart. Its mouth was open in a howl. Saliva glistened on its yellowish tusks.

I pumped the shotgun, knowing I was only going to get one shot. I took aim at the open, screaming maw. I tried to ignore the fact that it was almost upon me, that all it had to do was reach out and it could crush my head with one enormous paw. I pulled the trigger. The shell passed through the roof of its mouth and took off the top of its head. The impact was enough to send the corpse toppling off-balance onto the heretics behind it.

I let out a long breath and something hit me with the force of a sledgehammer. My arm went numb. I was spun around like a rag doll tossed across a room. I fell, sprawling, as pain seared my bicep.

For a moment, I had those horrible suspicions you always have when you take a hit. Was this it? Were these my last breaths? Was everything about to go black?

I struggled with the pain, trying to fight off the darkness, determined I was not going to let myself fall forward into the grave if I had any say in the matter. Out of the corner of my eye, looking up at the purple-tinged sky, I saw something. The Snow Raiders were exactly where Macharius had said they would be. They were firing down into the flank of the heretics from their elevated position. I hoped they had enough sense not to fire their heavy weapons into a melee. The same thought had occurred to Anton. He picked up the fallen banner of Macharius and raised it as high as he could, obviously intending to remind the newcomers exactly who was down here.

I heard screams from the other side now, and I realised that for once Macharius had gotten something wrong. The

Nova Worlders had not taken up their assigned position but instead were swarming forward to take the heretics in the flank and rear. Under the circumstances it was a better thing than firing into the melee, but it was going to cost them in blood. They would have been better off maintaining their distance and pouring on the fire.

But, of course, they had seen the lion's head banner and realised the general was in peril, so they had leapt to aid him with no thought for their own lives. It was the sort of loyalty Macharius inspired in all those who encountered him. The general responded like the hero he was, charging forward, chainsword flickering, killing everything that got in his way as he moved towards the newly arrived Nova Worlders and away from the flanking fire of the Snow Raiders.

I picked myself up, shotgun in one hand, unable to move my wounded arm. I looked down at it. It was bleeding but not heavily. I let the shotgun fall at my feet, knelt and fumbled for my knife with my good hand. I peeled away the bloody cloth of the sleeve and looked at the arm. There was bruising and blood and mangled flesh. I was going to have to slap some synthi-flesh on it.

Just as the thought crossed my mind, a heretic leapt at me. He had an ancient curved bayonet attached to the barrel of his rifle, and he intended to skewer me with it. I threw the knife at him. It was a bad cast from an injured man, and all that happened was the hilt of the weapon smacked him beneath the eye. I had just effectively disarmed myself. I thought I was doomed, but at that moment, Ivan hurled himself between us, blocked the stab of the bayonet with his mechanical arm and then leaned forward. I was tempted to look away, knowing what was coming.

Ivan's mechanical jaws clamped shut on the man's windpipe. He shook his head, tearing out the man's throat. Blood spurted as an artery ripped, spraying Ivan's face. Droplets of blood ran down the metal half of his features like red tears falling on a mirror. I felt someone loom over me and turned ready to strike. Anton took a step back as if scared I would stab him. I asked him if that was the case.

'You don't have a knife,' he said with his idiot grin. 'It was a nice trick disarming yourself like that. Really lured the heretic into your trap.'

He moved closer, eyes scanning for trouble. Ivan was on top of the heretic's corpse now, still tearing at it like an attack dog. The fulcrum of the combat had moved away. The melee swirled around us but we were in the clear, surrounded by corpses and those who would soon be corpses.

Something sticky hit me on the arm, and I realised Anton had slapped synthi-flesh on my wound.

There was cheering. Macharius's banner flowed back towards us, borne by a tide of newly arrived Imperial Guard. I realised Anton must have let it fall or given it to someone else when he had come to aid me. Ivan looked up. All around his mouth was red gore. His metal teeth were red too. It looked as if he had been in a terrible accident but, of course, all the blood belonged to the man whose throat he had bitten out.

All three of us moved towards Macharius. Inquisitor Drake gave us a long hard look. I wondered if he thought

Anton and Ivan should have stuck with the Lord High Commander. There was a chilly moment while his cold blue eyes rested on me, then he turned away. His storm troopers kept looking, though, as if they had noticed their master's gaze and decided that they needed to pay special attention to anyone it studied so. It was hard to tell. I could not see their expressions through the face masks of their helmets.

Macharius himself did not seem to care. His face was alight with triumph and the pleasure that victory in physical combat always gave him. I was sure that he had noticed everything, though. He always did, and he never forgot.

A field medic came rushing up. First he went to check on Macharius and Drake. I saw Macharius point in my direction, and the adept came over and began to patch me up. In minutes he had adjusted the synthi-flesh sealant. My arm was cool and numb. For the moment I could not use my shotgun, so I hung it over my shoulder and drew a sidearm.

More and more of our troops came into view. Valkyrie troop-carriers were starting to drop storm troopers on the roof of the central step of the ziggurat now that all of the anti-aircraft weapons on the structure had been silenced.

Ahead of us lay the massive ebonwood door of the complex and, beyond it, the ominously silent halls within which the ancient wonder Macharius and Drake sought was said to lie.

There was still resistance within the temple, but it was sporadic and all the heart had gone out of the defenders. I suppose that even they knew it was hopeless now. Their sacred wolf-apes were all slaughtered. Their elite guards had given their lives to no avail. The priests themselves did not appear as keen as their soldiers to go and greet their gods. We caught sight of a number of them scuttling off into the distance as we approached.

Once again Drake had come well prepared. The layout of the temple interior already seemed familiar to him. His spies must have briefed him well or fed records from the local datacores into the technical slate he carried. He strode along confidently with Macharius at his side. They did not appear at all troubled by the thought that they might encounter enemies. I wished I shared their confidence. My arm was starting to lose some of its numbness, and I felt the first faint twinges of pain. The shotgun felt heavy and useless on my back, where Anton had helped me strap it.

From different corridors came the sounds of combat, and it began to sink in what was happening. We were moving through a zone that had already been cleared by soldiers of the crusade.

They were creating and expanding a perimeter within the temple, driving back the heretics, taking them prisoner or executing them. As we walked, groups of woebegone unbelievers were herded past us. They had the look I had seen on the faces of the defeated on a hundred worlds. It's always the same: a compound of fear and sorrow, and just the faintest hope that they might still be allowed to live or might somehow be able to turn things around. Hope is a weed that springs up in the human heart at the slightest opportunity, even in our cruel age.

We entered a vast cathedral nave. In the centre of the

room was an enormous altar. A massive metal gauntlet shimmered above it. Ancient technical sorcery made it float in the air. The gauntlet looked as if it had been made for something the size of one of those ape-wolves. It had monstrous articulated fingers with what appeared to be talons at their tips. About it was an air of tremendous antiquity and something else, perhaps holiness. Runes had been etched on its surface that were not like any I had ever seen before.

A glance at Macharius's face showed keen interest. Drake's features were a mask, but cold excitement glittered in his eyes.

Under the guns of some of Drake's storm trooper bodyguards stood a group of ancient-looking men. They were robed in green and purple. Their heads were shaved except for a long topknot, and their beards were bound into two forks. All of them wore torcs on their arms and metal gauntlets on their right hands. One of them, obviously the high priest, carried an incredibly ornate staff, carved with runes in a similar style to those on the gauntlet.

As Macharius strode forward, one of them attempted to break free from the storm troopers and throw himself at the general's feet. Macharius nodded for the man to be allowed to rise. He was not afraid of some ancient priest. He even helped the man to his feet. It was done with his usual magnanimity.

Macharius put an arm around the man's shoulders and together they walked towards the great armoured gauntlet. He stood there for a moment looking down on that incomprehensibly ancient artefact.

Macharius said something to the priest in a voice so low that not even I could make out what it was. The priest shook his head. He looked like a confused old man who did not quite understand what was happening. He leaned heavily on his staff. I wondered if he was just the figurehead of the local clergy and whether real power in the temple hierarchy lay elsewhere. I looked at the other priests. There were certainly some sharp-looking characters there. They watched the proceedings with keen eyes. One of them even said something to another in the local language, perhaps a comment on Macharius's treatment of their superior, before being knocked to his knees by a storm trooper.

Macharius made a chopping gesture to indicate there should be no more of that. The storm trooper's mirrored faceplate tilted to one side, and I sensed he was looking to Drake for confirmation. The High Inquisitor gave the slightest of nods and the storm troopers relaxed a little. I doubt the significance of the exchange was lost on the Lord High Commander, but he gave no sign of taking offence.

Macharius went over and helped the stunned man to his feet. He did not seem bothered by being surrounded by former enemies. I suppose they had already been checked for hidden weapons by Drake's people, but it was still an impressive display of nonchalance. I could tell the locals were impressed despite themselves. Macharius had that effect on people. He used it as well as he did any other weapon.

Drake was already giving orders to a group of servitors who had entered the chamber with a mechanical trolley, and they began to manhandle the Fist onto it. The priests set up a wailing that would not have been out of place at a bereavement ceremony on Trask.

Macharius raised a hand and stared at them in his best parade ground manner. Slowly they fell silent. 'I regret we must relieve you of this sacred relic, but it is necessary that we do so. The Imperium of Man has need of it.'

'But your excellency…' said the old high priest in his quavering voice. 'The Fist is a treasure passed down from the time when the Emperor walked among men, left in this temple as part of a sacred trust by Saint Leman Russ himself.'

It was gibberish, of course, but the old man clearly believed it.

'It may well be that the trust is about to be fulfilled,' said Macharius. 'And it shall be returned to its rightful owners.'

'You will be cursed for this blasphemy,' said the priest. His voice was cracked and there was a disturbing look of madness in his face. He pointed his finger directly at Macharius and screamed, 'Cursed!'

The storm troopers beat him down and this time no one intervened. Macharius did not look troubled, but the words seemed to echo eerily around the chamber.

Bored. I am bored. The waiting hangs heavily on my hands. I seek entertainment. It is easy enough to find in its simplest form. I watch the slaves being transhipped to our cattle-carriers and select out a few choice morsels on which to feast. Their obvious terror provides some simple satisfaction in and of itself, but such rustic pleasures cannot long distract me. I find myself brooding on the nature of the gate and what we have found here. The idea that I might be wrong gnaws away at me like a boreworm in the bowels of its victim.

I work upon my symphony using a polytonal synthe-siser and an auto-wrack. The screams of the flayed humans mingle with the flurry of notes I improvise on the multiple keyboards, but it remains unsatisfactory.

Sileria comes to my chamber and I while away an hour teaching her the pleasures of obedience. I think in her heart of hearts she really desires to be a slave. It is often the secret fantasy of the strong. I make her confess as much under the pleasure lash. She sounds convincing, but it all may prove to be part of the role she has assumed. Sometimes, I see a look in her eyes that spells out the fact that she believes that one day I will assume her part. In this she is sadly deluded, but it hardly seems sensible to tell her this.

I study the maps of the world and order my warriors to strike almost at random. The idea is to keep the humans guessing, to let them project their own patterns on what they perceive, to make plans based on incorrect informa-tion and their own fears and prejudices. It will keep them tied down while my true plan unfolds. And, of course, it keeps my warriors sharp and blooded, and swells my cof-fers with the flesh of the slaves they take.

How much longer must I wait? The gate should open soon. Then we shall see what we shall see.

CHAPTER THREE

Anton looked at the Fist of Demetrius where it lay in pride of place on a great marble slab of a table. He flexed his fingers experimentally and held up his hand in front of his face as if measuring its size against that of the ancient gauntlet. I could tell he was thinking about slipping his hand inside it. He was still that kind of idiot.

'Don't,' I said.

He glanced around. We were alone with the Fist, back on the *Lux Imperatoris*, in the cluster of luxurious chambers surrounding Macharius's own rooms. Ancient maps of a thousand systems decorated the walls. Captured banners and pennons spoke of hundreds of victories. Magnetic clamps held the Fist in position. Macharius seemed to like to contemplate it.

We were standing guard, just outside the main chamber.

Inside, the inquisitor and the general discussed the next stage of the crusade or, for all I know, debated the finer points of Imperial theology. Of late, many small points of conflict had arisen between them. The ship was making its way to the transit point in preparation for the jump to Emperor's Glory.

Ivan said, 'You think this thing really dates from when the Emperor walked among men?'

'How would Leo know?' said Anton. 'Even he's not that old.'

I looked at it. Macharius and Drake had certainly treated it with reverence. It had that strange old-new look of archeotech, that lack of ageing that only the works of the ancients showed. 'I don't know. It looks old, though.'

'You think it really belonged to Russ? That it might have been in the presence of the Emperor himself?' There was a hunger in his voice that I recognised, a desire to experience the presence of the infinite, a wish to touch that which had once touched the divine. We are told to take so much on faith, but this might be a physical manifestation of that faith, an artefact of ancient times. Certainly Macharius thought so.

'How would I know?' I walked around it. It was a power gauntlet of some sort, made for someone larger than a man. I would have struggled to lift it with both hands. How could anyone have worn it? Maybe it had something in it that made it lighter or amplified the wearer's strength when it was worn. Many of the weapons of the ancients were magical that way.

'What does Macharius want it for?' Anton was doing it to needle me, I felt certain, piling one seemingly naive question upon another, trying to provoke an answer.

'Why don't you go and ask him?' I said. 'Say you're having trouble sleeping at night and you won't be able to rest until you know. I am sure he will listen to you.'

'There's no need to be sarcastic.'

'There's every need to be sarcastic,' I said.

Ivan pinged his metal jaw with his metal finger. His gaze went from his artificial hand to the Fist. He held his hand up, palm towards him, fingers spread. One by one, he moved his fingers; I heard the whine of servo-motors as he did so. He was looking at the moving rods and pistons visible in the joints of his hand. I looked at the Fist and saw that they were there, on a larger scale.

'He's been collecting a lot of this stuff,' said Ivan. He was not looking at either of us. 'Maybe he wants to start a museum or a collection of relics in the palace back on Emperor's Glory.'

'Maybe,' said Anton. 'But would he really risk his life just to add one more thing to his collection?'

'Who knows why he risks his life?' Ivan said. 'I think sometimes he does it because he is bored.'

'The idiot is right,' I said. 'He particularly wanted this one, and he wanted it now. He came here personally to supervise the attack on Demetrius. There was no need for that. He could have ordered it just as easily back on Emperor's Glory.'

'Maybe it has magical powers,' Anton said. 'They say

many of these relics do – that they can heal the sick, cure the lame... smite daemons.'

Those last words hung in the air uncomfortably. None of us really wanted to be reminded of the daemons we had seen back on Karsk. And yet, once again, I could not help but feel that Anton in his idiot way might have stumbled on something. Macharius had been amassing his trove of holy relics since that time. What he had seen in the Cathedral of the Flame had altered him. He had looked into the eyes of a greater daemon back there, something that would have broken the sanity of a lesser man.

Certainly since then Macharius had been changed inwardly if not outwardly. He had become more driven, and much more fanatical than the man we had followed across the treacherous, rebellious hives of Karsk.

'You think he wants all these ancient holy artefacts so he can fight daemons when he meets them?' Anton asked. He was looking from face to face now, like a child afraid of the dark seeking reassurance from his parents. The difference was that Anton knew there really were monsters out there in the night.

'I don't think that's impossible,' was all I could find to say. The doors to Macharius's inner sanctum opened. Macharius emerged. 'Best get ready to depart,' he said. 'We will soon be making the jump to Emperor's Glory.'

I wondered if he somehow knew what we had been talking about.

* * *

We were in our stateroom when the signal for the jump was given. Warning lights started to flicker red then blue. Klaxons sounded one long blast then one short blast then one long blast. There was an interval of a few heartbeats before it started again.

'Here we go,' said Anton. He looked sickly. He had never liked warp jumps. I could hardly blame him for it, no sane man does. I looked out of the great stained armourglass porthole. Already a massive blast-shield was sliding into place over it, like the black disc that takes a bite out of a sun during a solar eclipse.

'Interstellar jumps,' said Ivan. 'I hate them.'

'You always say that,' I said.

'Because it's always true,' said Anton. He sounded nervous. It was the only time you were ever likely to hear him so. More even than Ivan he detested this part of space travel.

'It never gets any easier,' Ivan said. 'How many jumps do you think we've made? Two hundred, two hundred and fifty?'

'I've never counted,' I said.

'Me neither,' said Anton.

'That's because you can't count over twenty,' said Ivan. 'And if you ever lose a finger or a toe you won't even be able to count that high.'

'Ha-bloody-ha!'

He moved towards the couch and was starting to strap himself in. I began to do the same. Even as we did so, the last of the stars and the blackness of space vanished behind the metal transit shutters. The lights stopped flickering and became steady, and yet it felt like we were sitting in the dark, waiting for something terrible to happen. I could remember a similar feeling during my childhood in Belial, when the gangs used to fight outside in the corridors of our building and there was only a thin thermaplas doorway between us and them.

You always hear stories about ships that go missing: ghost ships lost in the warp for centuries, crewed by dead men, and those that have suffered catastrophic, inexplicable disaster in the endless darkness of space. People dismiss such things as mere tales, but they crop up with remarkable regularity anywhere star-sailors gather and the crews of the great interstellar ships come to drink. And there is no one, no one at all I have ever met, who does not sense the sheer wrongness of it when a ship makes the jump into that terrible sub-realm beneath the skin of the ordered universe, where they go in order to travel the vast distances between stars.

I never really know what to expect. All jumps are different. Sometimes they happen so smoothly that you don't even know they have taken place. Sometimes entering the warp is like being in a shuttle as it hits atmospheric turbulence on its way down. Sometimes it is a lot worse. This time, there was just a weird sensation of falling, a momentary nausea and then nothing much at all for what might have been heartbeats, or might have been millennia.

'Is that it?' Anton asked. He sounded shaky but relieved. His words had an odd sound to them, though, as if they were coming from a great distance away and subtly distorted.

'Well, we're still here,' said Ivan. 'Wherever here is.'

He had put his finger on it, of course. We had no real idea where we were, and we were not going to have until the ship reached the exit point of its transit. Only the Navigator guiding the ship had any ideas about that. We were cut off from all sight of our surroundings by those huge armoured blast-shields. No one aboard the ship would talk to us about what was taking place, and I suspected that few of them actually knew. It was one of those things we were discouraged from asking questions about when we were common soldiers, and we had never gotten back into the habit of doing so when we became attached to Macharius's command.

'How long do you think we're going to be here for?' The note of worry was back in Anton's voice. It was one of those things that was strangest and most difficult about warp travel. You never knew how long you were under. The ship existed in a bubble separate from normal time as it passed in the universe above. Your wrist chrono and the ship's clocks might say one thing, that you had been away for a few days or a few weeks, but when you reached port and consulted with the Imperial standard timepieces maintained there, you might find that days or months or years had passed instead. There were tales of people who had been gone for centuries and did not look a day older when they returned.

'Who knows?' Ivan said. 'And I mean that most literally. I doubt even our captain and his pet Navigator have the answer.'

Slowly, things started to settle, Anton's voice sounded

normal. It was as though our minds were becoming accustomed to their new surroundings.

We settled down for the journey.

I do not know how long we were in the strange realm but somehow it felt too long. The days seemed stretched. There were odd gaps in my memories. My dreams were troubled. When not on bodyguard duty all of us spent time prowling the endless corridors of the ship, exchanging words with the crew. They were tense, as a crew always is when crossing the warp. They were all too aware of what could go wrong.

Then it happened, the thing that every star voyager fears. Warning lights flared. A terrible vibration passed through the hull of the ship. Weird moaning cries filled the air. I sprang upright in my bunk and reached for a weapon.

'What in the name of the Emperor?' said Anton. He pulled himself upright, tugged on his gear and reached for a weapon. It was as instinctive for him as it was for me, although the chances were that there was nothing for us to fight out there.

'I don't like this,' said Ivan. It was understandable. No one likes to hear alarms going off on a starship, particularly not one under way.

'Really,' I said. 'Why ever not?'

'It makes it difficult to sleep,' he said and wrinkled a nostril.

The ship started to vibrate as if it were being impacted by a shower of giant meteorites.

'That's not good,' said Anton. His fingers were white where

they gripped his sniper rifle. I nodded. I knew we were all thinking about those tales of ships that had sailed off into the dark between the stars never to be seen again. Maybe we were about to find out what happened to them.

All of the lights flickered and went out for a moment. My mouth went dry and my stomach lurched. The thought that without power a starship is just a gigantic coffin entered my mind. No air getting purified and circulated, no heat to drive back the cold of space. No void shields to ward off enemies. It was so black in the cabin that I could not see my own hand, let alone the faces of my companions. I thought of tombs. I thought of ships full of frozen corpses floating through the infinite void. I thought of haunted vessels uncovered a thousand years after they last set out by terrified Imperial explorers. I took a deep breath and told myself not to panic.

It was hard. I could feel my heart pounding against my ribs. I closed my eyes, though it made no difference to the amount I could see. The knowledge that each breath might be my last filled my mind and brought with it a primitive, animal fear. I told myself to breathe, then to take another breath and then another. As long as I was doing that I was still alive. Every breath was a small victory over death.

'Leo,' said Anton. There was an undercurrent of fear in his voice.

'Yes?' I said. I was proud of the fact that my voice came out level and strong.

'Any chance of you paying back those five credits you borrowed on Glory?'

'Not till next payday.'

'Guess I'll have to wait then.' The ship began to shake, violently, like a hive in the grip of a quake. I could feel the vibration passing through my body. The whole floor seemed to be moving up and down. My head hit something hard, and stars flickered across my field of vision. Something wet ran down my brow, blood most likely. I grabbed the support strut of my bed. Muscles twisted in my arms as I tried to maintain my position. I felt the ache of my wound return redoubled. I was not healed well enough for this. I bit back a shout of pain.

The vibration increased. It was far worse than anything the *Lux Imperatoris* had endured from the planetary defence batteries back in the Demetrius system. I heard a groan from across the room and the clatter of metal hitting metal, and it came to me that Ivan had been tossed right across the chamber.

There were great groans from the hull as if the metal were coming under enormous stress, and the shuddering and bucking of the ship reached a crescendo. Suddenly, everything was silent and still. For a moment I heard nothing save the sound of my own breathing. It was not a good sign. The last thing you want to hear on a starship is silence. It might be the last thing you ever hear.

I was uncomfortably aware of all the sounds that were missing: the rumble of the drives, the whoosh of the great air-circulators, the low humming of the lights, the hundreds of small noises that signalled that the ship and its crew were alive and well. I held my breath, wondering how long it would be before all the systems failed and we died. At that moment, the lights flickered back on. I looked around the cabin. Ivan lay on the ground nearby. Anton was hunched up in his lower bunk, glaring wildly around, fists wrapped round the support stanchions he had been using to hold himself in place. With a groan Ivan raised himself from the floor and said, 'Someone should have a word with whoever is piloting this ship. I think he still needs to learn a few things.'

'He got us through whatever it was,' Anton said.

'We don't know that yet,' I said. They looked at me. I mopped blood off my face with a rolled up shirt and wondered what was going on.

Along with Macharius we stormed onto the bridge of the *Lux Imperatoris*, pushing through corridors that teemed with uniformed crew members performing urgent repairs. Hundreds of officers bustled around, reacting to incoming data, barking orders into speaking tubes, saluting as they took orders in turn from their superiors. Half the holo-screens looked dead. Tech-priests moved around them intoning technical liturgies as they performed the rituals of maintenance and repair on cracked command altars. The air stank of incense, rising above half-melted machinery. It made me nostalgic for the old days, for riding in the belly of a Baneblade.

The ship's captain was sitting there on his command throne, surveying his officers as they went about their work. His face was darkened on one side by some kind of flash burn. Men limped and nursed injuries. Medical adepts inspected bodies stretched out on the floor between command altars.

'What happened?' Macharius asked.

'We were caught in a warp storm, Lord High Commander,' the captain said. 'It came upon us suddenly as we passed through the immaterium. It separated us from the rest of the fleet. We could not remain in it without being destroyed. Our Navigator plotted an escape course that brought us up in this system. It was the only thing he could do, otherwise we would have been destroyed.'

'And where exactly is this?' Macharius asked. The captain steepled his fingers and let out a long breath. He looked at one of the officers who wore the uniform of an astronavigator, a grizzled, grey-haired man with his arm in a sling.

The astronavigator said, 'I will need to take sightings and plot our position on star charts to be entirely certain. My initial observations lead me to believe that we are in the system marked as Procrastes on old charts, but I would like to confirm that. When a warp storm strikes you can be driven a long way from your initial destination. We are lucky our Navigator managed to bring us out at all.'

'I'm aware of that fact,' Macharius said.

'It is a relatively rare occurrence, Lord High Commander,' said a smooth new voice. We looked around. A member of one of the great Navigator Houses had entered the command deck. He must have come from the sealed chamber from which he guided the ship. He was a mutant, but the third eye which he used to look out into the warp was decently concealed by a thick brocade scarf bearing the emblems of his House and calling. He did not wear Naval uniform. Instead, he was dressed in the sort of formal court clothes that one associated with the great merchant Houses of the Imperium. 'The main thing is that we have survived. Many do not.'

The captain looked up from the divinatory altar that he was studying. 'We have suffered some damage to the ship as we exited the warp. It will take us a few hours to perform repairs.'

One of the officers rose and turned to his captain, clicked his heels, saluted and made a report. 'Sir, we are picking up considerable comm-chatter. It seems that there is a human inhabited world in this system, and it is coming under attack by xenos.'

That got Macharius's attention. 'Record those communications and relay them to me. I wish to know what is going on here.'

If the Navy captain was offended by that peremptory instruction he give no sign of it. 'Of course, sir,' he said. 'But there is nothing we will be able to do until we restore the main power cores and get our engines back online again.'

'I want you to keep me informed of every development,' Macharius said. 'I want to know everything that is happening here. If those xenos make a move against us, let me know immediately.'

'It will be so,' the captain said. We followed Macharius off the command deck.

* * *

We looked out the huge circular viewport at the dark, dark curtain of space beyond. Macharius had returned to his chambers for the moment, leaving us to our own devices. We had chosen to inspect the damage to the ship from the nearest vantage point to our berths.

The armoured shields had been rolled back. I could see the great pockmarks in the ship's sides and the small human figures moving along them, checking for flaws in the hull. From here I could see exactly how huge the ship was, a self-contained worldlet, larger than a dozen parade grounds, large enough for an army to march across. There was a suggestion of mountainous hills in the way the superstructure rose over the plains of the lower hull.

'Think they'll find anything?' Anton asked.

'If the hull had breached while we were in the warp we most likely would all be dead now,' I said.

'Not if it got holed at the last moment, as we emerged. Something might have broken in then,' he said.

'You've been listening to too many sailors' stories,' I said. 'Next you'll be saying that a hundred years might have passed since we left Demetrius.'

'Well, they might have,' said Anton.

'Yes, they might have, but what difference would that make to us? We're still alive. That's all that matters.'

'We might have missed the crusade.'

'We could not be that unlucky,' said Ivan.

'I doubt any more than a couple of weeks has passed,' I said, not at all liking the direction this discussion was taking. None of the others seemed to have realised that all of the things they secretly feared had already happened to us. None of us would ever be going home. All of us were marooned in time and space. All we had left was each other and the people we knew. The Imperial Guard was our home now. It had been for many years.

'Any idea where we are?' Ivan said.

'Not where we're supposed to be, that's for sure,' I said. 'This isn't Emperor's Glory. The sun's the wrong colour.'

'Another hellhole in the back of beyond then,' said Ivan. 'Some things never change.'

'You think we're lost?' said Anton. There was a faint note of panic in his voice.

'We might be,' I said, just to wind him up. It was Ivan who chose to break the suspense.

'Even if we are, they'll soon find a way to get us home.'

'Did you see that bloody mutant, that Navigator?' said Anton. I looked around to make sure none of the crew were close enough to overhear him. The crews of ships are strange. They spent a lot of time locked in these durasteel coffins. They are loyal to each other, and they have no love for outsiders. Not that Anton ever paid much attention to such things.

'He's a mutant who has the blessing of the Imperium,' said Ivan. I could tell the words were making him uneasy even as he said them.

'Gives me the creeps,' said Anton. 'They say they have an extra eye in the middle of their foreheads, that's why they keep them wrapped. They say it looks into other places, let's them see things that are not there.'

'You've seen things that weren't there, when you've drunk enough,' I said. I watched a tiny figure clamber over a gargoyle on the hull. He seemed to come unstuck, like a fly taking off from a wall and began to drift off into space. I wondered if I was watching a small, distant tragedy about which I could do nothing. It would not be for the first time in my life.

I could see Anton's features reflected translucently in the armourglass. He sucked his lower lip thoughtfully. The scar flexed on his forehead. He was uneasy. 'It's bad enough having to get on these ships,' he said eventually. 'Now we don't even know where we are.'

'Not much different from usual in your case then, is there?' said Ivan.

'You think there might be some sort of curse on the Fist? You think it might be responsible for this happening? Those priests weren't too happy about us taking it.'

There had been a time when I would have laughed in his face for suggesting such a thing, but I had seen too many strange things since we left Belial. We all had. I watched the drifting crewman. He was tugging himself back in on a line. Maybe he had drifted off deliberately to get a better view of the hull section. In any case I felt relieved.

'You think some heretic priest's curse is stronger than the blessings on this ship?' Ivan asked. 'It's as venerable as a Baneblade and served the Emperor just as long as *Old Number Ten*.'

Anton appeared to consider this. 'No, probably not.'

'Good,' said Ivan. I wondered at the vehemence in his

voice and suspected he was just as uneasy as Anton. He just hid it better.

'Don't worry, we'll get home in one piece,' I said and added *eventually* in a murmur too low for the others to hear.

CHAPTER FOUR

'Lord Ashterioth,' Sileria says. 'There is something you should see.'

I look at her, mortally weary of existence, and I say, 'I am already looking at you.'

She smiles at the flattery but says, 'A ship has been detected.'

'Eldar?' I ask, wondering how my enemies could have found me. What mistake had I made that they picked up the trail so quickly?

'Human,' she says. 'It emerged into real space from the translocation point some hours ago.'

'A trader?' I say. It seems the most likely explanation. I know this world is not part of any of the human political blocs in this part of the galaxy.

'The energy profile fits that of a warship, lord,' she says.

'Just one? Not a fleet?'

She nods. 'It could be a scout. It is not progressing in-system. It is holding a position near the translocation point.'

'You think it some form of advance guard?' I begin to play back our invasion of this place in my mind. When we seized this world, no distress signal was sent on any of the channels we monitored, and we could not have missed anything the human's primitive systems could broadcast. I know they do not have any of the psykers the humans are foolish enough to use, the so-called astropaths.

'The energy profile is unusual,' she says and hands me the vision-slab.

I see instantly what she means. 'Very low emissions for a warship of that displacement. It is damaged, a straggler from a fleet perhaps, or survivor of a warp storm washed up here.'

She nods again, and I smile coldly. 'Muster the fleet,' I say. 'Let us go and take a look at this unexpected prize.'

'It could have been worse,' said Drake. He was sitting in one of the massive leather armchairs in Macharius's state room. Macharius sat across the table from him. There was a regicide board between them. Neither had touched it in hours.

'By this you mean we could be dead,' Macharius said. His face was grim, and I thought I understood why. There was nothing he could do here, the repairs of the great warship were outwith his area of competence. He was just as helpless as the rest of us, and he did not like it in the least little bit.

'I mean things could be worse,' said Drake. His voice was

patient. He seemed a man much more used to being patient than Macharius at that exact moment. I knew this was not entirely the case. Macharius could be as unflappable as a stone idol when waiting on news from a battlefield. Then he was never flustered. This was something different.

'I must be on Emperor's Glory soon and with this cargo intact,' said Macharius.

'We have suffered very little temporal displacement according to my chronometric readings,' said Drake. 'Once the repairs are done we shall be back under way. We will not have lost much time.'

'If our crew can locate where we are and plot a course home,' said Macharius. 'Something went very wrong on our way out.'

And there it was, the thing that was on all of our minds. Something had gone wrong and none of us were sure what it was. If we had been on a battlefield, Macharius would have known and understood any setback. Here we were just sentient cargo.

It never fails to worry me exactly how vulnerable all starships are. In the event of the Navigators going mad, getting killed or being taken out of action, there was no way of a ship getting home. No normal man could look out into the warp and pick the ship's path through that strange sub-universe. On the back of this fact, the Navigator Houses had turned themselves into one of the great powers of the Imperium. It was possible to argue that without them there would be no Imperium at all. Without starships, how would the great armies move?

The air flickered and a holo appeared in the air above the table. It presented a picture of the ship's command deck.

One of the watch officers suddenly stood up at the divinatory altar he was supervising, spoke something to the ship's captain, who gave an order to his subordinate, then spoke to Macharius.

'Lord High Commander, I must report we have picked up signals from multiple incoming ships. Xenos.'

'Hostile?' said Macharius. There was little chance they would be anything else.

'We must assume so.'

'I will need access to command echelon sub-nets of the ship's vox systems,' said Macharius. 'And I will need it now.'

The captain nodded. Macharius strode over to an altar and called up internal schematics of the ship. Being who he was, he had most likely memorised all of them earlier, but he wanted access now. He put a comm-bead into his ear and slipped a microphone under his jaw just as the battle-stations warnings echoed through the ship.

Ignoring them he began to speak commands, gravely, precisely and with a certain relish.

Our ships spiral gracefully out-system towards the contact. I sit at the helm and study the vision crystal. All around ancient power sources hum. The crew perform their duties in the long oval chamber, its ruddy light turning them into bloody phantoms. For a moment, I contemplate the beauty of the intricate mechanisms that keep me alive and move me across the face of the void.

The human ship has not moved, and its energy signature has not changed. It appears to be just sitting there waiting, as if daring us to come closer. I ask myself could this be a trap? Is it merely pretending to be crippled to draw us into combat? Certainly the profile of the ship makes it look powerful enough to provide a challenge were it in a proper state of repair. It is a battleship, massive and armed with multiple batteries of primitive but potent weapons.

I measure the strength of my fleet against it. Even if the vessel were at full power they would be sufficient to ensure our victory. I am certain of it. Nonetheless, I am uneasy. Once again the universe presents me with what looks like a gift. Once again I wonder what lies beneath the mask of reality. I push doubt aside. Even if a human fleet were to emerge from the daemon-haunted wastes they are foolish enough to traverse, we would simply retreat.

There is no real threat here. I give the order to assume attack formation.

'How many xenos?' Macharius asked. There was no tension in his voice, no sign of any unease. He was doing something he had been born to do. A sense of calm competence flowed out from him as heat flows from a fire. We had relocated to the bridge of the ship. The whole time we had moved Macharius had kept up a stream of communications with the commanders of his bodyguard regiment, deploying them to critical points around the ship, setting them in readiness for any boarding action. He seemed to have no doubts about his knowledge of where the best positions would be. He was almost certainly right in this.

'A dozen ships, Lord High Commander,' said the captain. 'None of them of more than half our displacement, but that means nothing with xenos. They may each have firepower equal to an Imperial ship of the line, and carry a complement of warriors equal to our own combined force.'

A faint frown flickered over Macharius's brow. 'Are our weapon systems back in commission?'

'Void cannons and main batteries are powered up. If we had another few hours we could simply have made the jump out of this system and avoided any conflict. General repairs are almost complete.'

'How about your Navigator – has he calculated our position and course?'

'He is working on it.'

'Perhaps you could suggest to him that he work a little harder.'

'Of course, Lord High Commander.'

Drake studied the flickering runes hovering over the altars. 'The xenos vessels are eldar.'

The captain rapped out an order to one of the crewmen. A partially translucent image hovered in the air above us, showing a long, shark-like vessel, whose sleek lines bore no resemblance to any human craft. The image shimmered and shifted as other eldar ships sprang into being. All of them were subtly different but were obviously the product of the same alien sensibility. There was something strange about the way they flickered, as if they were not quite present in our space. Sometimes they grew indistinct and vanished entirely, leaving only areas of darkness behind them. Our auspex systems were clearly having difficulty pinning down their position.

'Tell me about them,' Macharius said. His tone was conversational.

'They are most decadent and repulsive creatures, given to enslaving and torturing their victims. They exist outside the Emperor's Light and are our eternal enemies.'

Macharius's eyes narrowed. 'Slavers. We can expect a boarding action, then.'

'They will try and cripple us first,' said Drake. 'Destroy our drives, erode our void shields, silence our weapons.'

'Then they won't have much work to do,' said Macharius, not without a certain sardonic humour.

'That's true.' Drake seemed to hesitate for a moment.

'And?' Macharius said.

'And what?' Drake replied.

'You look as though you want to say something else.'

'It would probably be best not to be taken alive,' said Drake. 'These creatures have a reputation for tortures of the most heinous sort. They take pleasure in it.'

There was something in his tone that suggested he was understating the extent of their cruelty, and that just made it all the more frightening.

'If they want to take us alive, they will need to board the ship,' said Macharius. 'If they do, we shall teach them the error of their ways.'

He sounded confident, but then he always did. 'Let us go

to the command deck and see if we can encourage our Navy comrades to more speed.'

We are within range of visual pickup. I order ultimate magnification on the vision crystal and the human vessel leaps into view, a mountain of metal against the velvet backdrop of infinite night. It has the crudity of all human work, and I wonder again at the indifference of a universe that can allow such a species not only to exist but, apparently, to thrive.

Of course, it is not indifference. Long ago the cosmos proved itself to be actively malevolent, but still… The fact that it allows such beings to go on existing is proof positive that it has no taste.

Consider the human warship. The least gifted eldar child could create a vessel far more beautiful. This is a slab of metal covered in gargoyles, bristling with weapons. The lines are as blunt as a gulbak's club. It is as if the humans are so afraid of the cosmos that they feel the need to present what they consider a frightening face to it. It is a vessel designed to intimidate children. It shows no understanding that the truly dangerous creature has no need to show how dangerous it is.

It appears damaged. The thick armour looks pitted and wrecked as though the claws of some gigantic beast have swept along its length scraping away ribbons of metal. There are flickers of light where primitive chemical flame welding devices are used to patch the incisions.

'It does not look like a trap,' I say. Sileria glances up at me.

'It looks like an idiot's attempt at sculpture,' she says. We both laugh.

'Nonetheless, it is armed,' I say at last.

'What is it doing here?' she asks. 'It shows the markings of the human Imperium. They are not supposed to be within a hundred light years of this system.'

'Some new migration, no doubt,' I say. 'The barbarians are on the move once more, looking for new worlds to conquer.'

'Why here, why now?' Her words echo submerged thoughts floating through the under-consciousness of my own mind. She is wondering if the ship's presence has anything to do with our own or is mere coincidence. It is a weakness all of the eldar have, this solipsism. We believe the universe rotates around us. The more intelligent of us are aware of it, of course.

'We shall, no doubt, find out soon enough,' I say. 'Once we have taken a few new slaves and feasted on their agony.'

'I look forward to it,' she says, looking up at me and licking her lips.

There was a faint vibration as the ship's engines flared, and once again we were under way. The crew had laboured mightily over the past few hours and it seemed that their efforts had been rewarded.

The astronavigator looked up from his charts, set aside his astrolabe and glanced around as if noticing all of the activity surrounding him for the first time.

'I believe we can make the jump, captain, now that the ship's generators are capable of powering us.'

'How long and how far until the insertion point?'

'Roughly half an Imperial astronomical unit,' said the astronavigator. 'It should not take more than two hours, but it places us on a convergent course with the xenos.'

The captain was obviously making some calculations of his own. 'The eldar will be upon us before then. We will still have to fight.'

'Shall I begin pre-jump preparations?' said the Navigator. The captain did not look at Macharius. 'Yes,' he said.

'Now all we need do is survive the next couple of hours,' said Drake. 'And hope the ship takes no more damage before we can make the jump.'

Macharius looked at the enemy ship on the screen, staring at it as if he were looking on the face of an enemy.

'Xenos,' he said. 'Have we come so far from Imperial space?'

The Navigator looked at him. 'We are within one hundred light years of the boundaries of the Segmentum Pacificus.'

'They are very close to the crusade,' Drake said, obviously following the line of Macharius's thoughts.

'Scouts, perhaps, come to observe us,' Macharius said.

'Who can tell how xenos think,' said Drake. 'They may just be raiding here, or combining their raiding with scouting.'

'They will need to be dealt with,' said Macharius.

'Most assuredly,' said Drake. Neither of them seemed to have any doubt that they would survive to see that done. For myself I was not so sure. I did not like the sleek, cruel and confident lines of those oncoming alien ships.

I study the vision crystal. The human ship is moving now, drive power apparently restored. It still appears just huge, ugly and ungainly amid the darkness of space, but in movement it has taken on an aspect of menace. Gargoyles clutch the durasteel of its hull as if prepared to fly into battle. The scarred maws of primitive destructive engines emerge from its weapon bays. They pulse with energy, clearly being made ready for battle.

Sileria looks at me, awaiting my decision. Eagerness is obvious in every line of her body. She looks like a lash-hound straining at the leash to begin pursuing its prey. She runs her tongue over her pouting lips. Her pupils are expanded. Her breathing shallow. She is contemplating the banquet of pain that will present itself when we board the vessel and use its crew for our pleasure. If I decide that we should do so.

Command decisions are rarely so simple. Primitive as the human vessel is, both the divinations and its harsh lines speak of destructive power. It is no longer crippled and immobile. I do not doubt for a moment we can overcome it, but we may ourselves take damage in the attempt. Is it worth risking ourselves when we are so close to my ultimate goal? In a few more days the gate will be open…

'Lord Ashterioth, the human vessel is changing course. It is positioning itself for an attack run,' says the helm. I smile, astounded and oddly pleased by the arrogance of the humans, that they would dare attack us rather than flee in terror when they had the chance. It is this more than anything else that makes up my mind. We do not flee from our inferiors, not unless the odds against us are overwhelming.

'Order the fleet to attack,' I say. 'Let us teach these apes a lesson. Prepare the Impalers! We shall board them and take some slaves for the Dark Feast.'

The ship shuddered again as the eldar weapons slammed into it. Somewhere in the distance a generator whined and threatened to overload. Was it just my imagination or was there a tang of ozone in the air? All around us the bridge seethed with activity. Officers shouted commands into vox-communicators and relayed reports from weapons batteries and turrets. Ships' engineers bellowed incomprehensible catechisms of technical chant. The captain listened tensely and occasionally gave an order that sent crewmen scurrying.

I looked at Anton and Ivan; we were standing close to the commanders on the bridge along with the rest of the green-tunicked bodyguards, but we were not within earshot. Macharius, Drake and the others seemed to be too involved in preparing for a possible boarding action to pay any attention to us.

'They are hitting us pretty hard for creatures who supposedly want to take us alive,' said Anton.

'What would you know about it?' I said. 'For all you know they could be hitting our shield generators.'

'Hark at the expert on ship to ship combat,' said Anton. 'When did you join the Imperial Navy?'

'About the time your brain shrunk to the size of a nut.'

'Looks like we're going to find a new sort of xenos to kill,' said Ivan. The servo-motors in his fingers whined as he flexed them.

'Can't wait,' said Anton in a voice heavily laced with irony. 'Just as I was looking forward to some rest on Emperor's Glory, this had to happen. Trust these Navy boys to get even something so simple as a jump wrong. And they did not manage to just get us to the wrong place, no! They managed to drop us right into a proper little wasp's nest of decadent slavers with a liking for torture. I must congratulate them on that, sometime – with a bayonet.'

'Don't worry,' said Ivan. 'I'll make sure you don't suffer a fate worse than death.'

'Who's going to save you,' Anton replied.

'Leo will,' Ivan said. I glanced up at the image of the eldar ship. It was at once sinister and strange. I wondered at the sensibility of a people who could build something like that. I had been told that in space, the size, shape and structure of a vessel do not matter all that much as long as its basic framework is able to endure acceleration. That being the case, the predatory lines of those eldar ships did not say anything good about their builders, or the creatures within them.

Drake was studying the ship just as closely. His eyes were narrowed. A look of concentration was on his face. I wondered what was going on inside his mind. I doubted he was afraid, but he did not look entirely happy either.

Macharius continued to receive reports and calmly give orders. Occasionally he too would glance up at the image of the ships closing with us, as though he were trying to divine the exact nature of his opponent from that visual manifestation. Sometimes he asked a question of the captain and was given a terse response.

He steepled his fingers and closed his eyes. In his mind the whole ship had become a battlefield and he was laying out his forces according to the plan he had formulated.

'One hour until jump,' said the astronavigator.

Even I could see that it was taking too long. We were never going to get away.

The human ship comes closer. The vision crystal stays focused on it, so the distance appears to be the same. Only the vectors on the augury arrays have altered, lengthening to show the vessel's increased speed, darkening to show it is preparing its energies for warfare.

Dots on the board indicate our own ships, accelerating into attack positions, preparing to strafe the warship, to soften it up for boarding.

In the crystal I see the glint of energies in the enemy's weapon bays as its armaments power up. I feel a faint flicker of excitement. It is always possible that a lucky shot might destroy my command ship, or even simply kill me, allowing my vessel to survive. What of it? It would not be the first time I have died. The haemonculi can always rebuild me if even the faintest fragment survives. But then, for that to happen they need to be able to find the fragment and, even if they do, who willingly gives themselves into the hands of the masters of pain?

Reports begin to pour in over our communication channels. Our ships are opening fire, carefully, calculatingly, aiming for weapons and void shield generators. They seek not to destroy our enemy but to neutralise its weapons and defences. That ship and its crew represent a prize to us so they are careful not to do too much damage to their future property.

The enemy feels no such compunction. They unleash their potent, primitive weapons. Blades of energy stab across the void; lines of fire, brighter than the stars, seek our ships, which even now slide into evasive positions, the dark ripple of their shadowfields concealing their position from the foe.

There are certain small pleasures to be had in witnessing a battle in the airless deeps of space. There is the swift-moving beauty of the vectors on the table, the eerie glow of plasma contrails in the infinite darkness, the slowly spinning stars that glare down on the battle with the cold eyes of eternity.

That said, the combat is too distant and impersonal to be truly pleasurable. It lacks the ecstatic communion of predator and prey, the heady, intoxicating agony of the victim as they fall to the blade. No eldar can truly enjoy such battles as they do the swirl of melee.

I give the order to take us in close. I want to board this arrogant interloper's vessel and make its crew suffer. I want to look in the face of my kill as it dies writhing.

I order Jalmek to take the helm as I prepare to lead the boarding party. I smile with anticipation as I make my way to the Impaler.

CHAPTER FIVE

I stand on the boarding ramp of the Impaler, surrounded by my personal guard. They grin and smile, readying themselves for the hot joy of battle. I keep my face cold and distant as a leader must, but in my heart I know what they are all feeling, for I feel it too.

In my mind I picture the ebb and flow of the ship to ship combat. I see our vessels whirl and spin and feint, a cloud of fire-wasps stinging at a running sabre-tiger. Some aim for the weapons, some for the sensor eyes, others dive and swirl and spin, seeking only to distract the humans, to keep them from guessing where the killing thrust will come. All of this concentrated action exists only to prepare the way for this boarding action, for the swift joyous launch of the Impalers as they race to make contact with the enemy vessel.

I picture our assault craft racing towards the enemy ship, a swift, sleek sliver of crystal, hurtling on a contact trajectory that will lead to inevitable victory.

Divinatory scans have revealed the weak points in the human hull. They have been matched with memory crystal records of other attacks on similar human ships, which have been downloaded into the biosystems of my battle-armour. These will be matched against the actual layout we encounter, providing predictive maps to show us where to go. Half a dozen forces will advance from their separate entry points, spreading terror among the human crew, making surgical strikes against all resistance.

We are aiming for the armouries and the power cores of the vessel, to cripple its defences and its ability to resist, to leave it floating helplessly in space for our ships to destroy at will. I slide my helmet into position. I allow myself to smile. This is what I live for, to prove my superiority once more in the crucible of battle.

A sour feeling settles in my stomach. Of course, these are only humans. There is no glory to be gained in overcoming such, only a certain crude sustenance to be fed on. Still, it is better than nothing.

A faint vibration passes through the ship as the hulls come together. The boarding spikes engage. External cutters swing into place to prepare our route into the human vessel at the airlocks, the weakest point.

I glance around at my followers now, all as armoured as I, all as ready to do battle. Row after row of warriors prepare to leap into the gap. They raise their weapons in salute.

The enemy hull gives way. The massive leech mouth of

the forward orifice dilates to reveal the interior of the vessel beyond. I catch the strange scents of alien air, laced with the pheromonal patterns of unfamiliar emotions, tiny exquisite hints of past agonies, products no doubt of old battles and recent accidents.

I dive forward into the revealed breach. The faint tang of human life and emotion pervading the thick air envelops me.

Long, tense seconds passed. The ship shook. It felt like an earthquake rumbling through the giant hull.

'Lord Macharius,' said the captain. 'Our hull has been breached. The xenos have boarded us.'

Macharius smiled. 'We will engage them then.'

The captain did not look up from the tactical screens. 'By all means, Lord High Commander, please do. I must remain here and supervise this battle. There are emergency suits in those lockers. Please take them. You may find yourself in places where our life support systems have failed.'

Macharius glanced around at us. 'Let us go and kill some xenos.'

I checked my shotgun and got ready to fight.

We suited up. It was merely a matter of donning the void-hardened armour from the lockers and putting the rebreather helmets in place. It was all done according to the ancient drills. Macharius had patched himself into our own networks. Our troops were ready to engage, but so far he had restrained them. Knowing him, it was all part of some plan.

We made our way out into the corridors beyond the command level and dropped down a grav-shaft into the body of the ship. All the while, Macharius kept murmuring commands into the comm-net, telling our troops to remain steady, to wait, that our time would come.

Whatever he was going to do, I hoped he would do it soon. The xenos appeared to be making their way unopposed into the very heart of the ship. Even as the thought crossed my mind, Macharius spoke with calm authority. 'Begin the counter-attack now.'

The human ship is crude, sheets of metal riveted together, primitive mechanical systems that reflect their simplistic view of the universe. Lights flicker. Great horns pulse warning howls through the ship, no doubt letting them know that an enemy is aboard.

I race through the grey-metal corridor, following the predictive map, surrounded by my warriors. All are keen to encounter prey, to grab their share of glory beneath the gaze of their commander, to bolster their status in my retinue by outshining their rivals. Of course, all ultimately seek my place, but at this moment in eternity they must vie for my favour and I, like every other leader in eldar history, will use this to my advantage.

Massive metal doors are shutting in place. They are simple enough to override as we make our way into the depths of the ship. Ahead of us, our first group of humans emerge into the corridor. They turn as they see us, doughy features twisted in animal fear. They fumble stupidly for weapons.

I spring forward, blades whirling – sever a head, expose a spine, remove a limb before ever my feet touch the deck. I roll forward, putting myself below the line of fire of my bodyguards, whose shooting scythes down the remainder of the humans.

Good. So far my presence has ensured restraint. No one has yet made any attempt to over-gorge on agony. They are doing their best to simply remove the obstacles between us and our objectives, which is just as well, for there will be plenty of time later for nourishment, once this vessel is ours.

We race on, heading towards the core of the vessel, to the place where the ship's primitive engines lie. More uniformed humans loom ahead of me. I chop them down so that I can admire the pattern of the blood spurts on the wall.

Normally I would not be so spendthrift of slaves, but we have a world behind us and these primitives represent just a few thousand more lives. I can give vent to my contempt and disgust without thought of the cost.

I listen to reports on my helmet channels. Sileria informs me that resistance is light. Bael claims that the humans are too scared to stand and fight. Everywhere across the ship it is the same story. I suppose it could be that the humans were just taken so completely by surprise that they can mount no resistance, but I do not like it. Something feels not quite right here. I inform Manali's force to remain in reserve and ignore her disappointed grunt. It does not matter to me how much she wants to claim her share of the spoils, she must do as she is told or face the consequences. It would not do to be taken off-guard by these primitives.

As that thought occurs to me, I hear a shout and sounds of fighting behind me. It seems we have opposition here after all.

Uniformed humans begin pouring down the corridors. They are dressed in green tunics with some sort of golden feline's head embossed on them. They are not like the other humans in simpler uniforms, who I now perceive must be servants or ship's crew or both. They lay down a curtain of fire with their lasrifles that is dense and difficult to avoid.

I spring into a doorway and consider what is happening. Nearby, Drakin falls in a withering hail of fire, armour cracked, crystal flaring with a greenish chemical glow in the heat.

Reports flood in over the communications channels. All of our forces are now encountering resistance. It cannot be coincidence that this all happened simultaneously. Somewhere on this craft is a mind capable of a primitive form of tactical thought.

Judging by the points from which the reports are coming in from, it has deduced our likely objectives and chosen to allow us to advance deep into the ship before mounting a real defence. That being the case, it is only logical that forces will be moving into place behind us to cut off our retreat. Perhaps I am overestimating the mon-keigh mind of my opponent, but better to do that than walk into a trap from which there is no retreat.

I dispatch squads to the rear to check and clear our exits,

and I order the remainder of my force to begin flanking the beasts who oppose us. I shall leave some squads here to create the illusion that we are making a serious attempt to break through while we move around.

There is no way these primitives can match the mobility of eldar. We shall achieve our breakthrough; it is merely a matter of concentrating our firepower where they are weakest. Soon this ship will be ours.

We headed for the hull levels where our forces were already engaged and came to a vast open rampway, strewn with the bodies of the crew, many of them hideously mutilated. Amid them moved lean and sinister alien shapes that looked like spindly humans with enormously elongated heads. It took me a moment to realise that this was merely their armour.

At rest there was something insectile about them. You expected their movements to be swift but jerky with the machine quality you see in mantises. It was not so. In motion, they possessed eye-blurring speed and the grace of dancers.

There was only a comparative few of them below us, and they were confronted by a full company of Macharius's bodyguard, but they did not pause for an instant. They did not flee. They attacked, springing forwards like predatory beasts. Their weapons made little sound but men died, flesh stripped, bones glittering, throats wrenched into agonised screams. Perhaps the bolts that hit them were poisoned, maybe the weapons were designed to inflict the maximum pain, but I had never seen men suffer so as they expired.

'Stand your ground!' Macharius roared. We stood. When the Lord High Commander gave an order, you obeyed, no matter how awful the death you faced.

The eldar raced towards us. We laid down a curtain of fire that drove them scurrying backwards, seeking cover in doorways and corridor mouths. A ragged cheer went up from our ranks. Macharius did not acknowledge it.

'Squads one and nine, cover our flanks. They will attack us from there next.'

No sooner had he given the order than I heard more shooting start. The eldar had very swiftly regrouped and attacked from other directions with terrifying swiftness and ferocity.

Macharius rapped out more commands, steadying our boys. He dispatched the Undertaker and Anton and another squad to the right flank. I wondered if I would see either of them again. He kept speaking into the comm-net, ordering companies and squads into new positions, talking with the unit commanders, keeping himself abreast of the developing situation on the ship and interjecting words of command and encouragement to the soldiers around him.

I stood next to him, wondering even after all those years at his demeanour. I clutched the shotgun in my grip and kept my eyes peeled in case more of the eldar attempted a frontal assault. To my eyes, there was no pattern to anything, only chaos.

A wave of them surged forwards suddenly, breaking towards us. Individually the xenos were a match for a dozen Guardsmen, and they fought with a fluid, swift-moving ferocity that constantly probed our position for weak points. They would seem to fall back, morale broken, only to come surging ahead again with renewed ferocity. There were feints within feints, bluffs within bluffs.

The eldar died hard. We had the weight of numbers and we had Macharius. That should have been enough, but somehow it did not feel as easy as it ought to have.

As the reports of enemy counterattacks came in, Macharius ordered men forward to meet the threat and to neutralise it. His commands not only sent reinforcements to our embattled soldiers, they put units in flanking positions. He seemed to understand instinctively what the eldar would do, and know how to deal with it.

As the minutes ticked away, a grim smile played over his lips, and I realised that he was enjoying himself. These blood-soaked corridors were like a game board to him, and he had found a challenge worthy of his talents. The fact that his life and all of our lives were at stake was immaterial to him. He paused for a moment and looked around.

Drake stared at him. 'How goes it?'

'The xenos move constantly,' Macharius said. 'They use their mobility to probe and strike and search for weak points. They are overconfident. They are not used to being outmanoeuvred. I am building a net with multiple strands, ringing them round with layers of force. Moving our men to where they will need to strike next. I leave some weaknesses in the pattern so that they do not realise what is happening. They have nothing but contempt for us. They think they fight this battle on their own terms. I will beat them before they are aware they have been defeated. By underestimating us, they defeat themselves.'

He said it with his usual confidence, and I believed him. With Macharius, war was as much a matter of psychology as it was strategy and tactics. He had looked into the minds of those xenos and understood them, at least the part that related to fighting, which was all he needed to understand. Their assessment of his gifts was unflattering but that meant nothing to him. It was just another factor in the cold equations of combat that ran through his mind, an advantage that would give him victory, or so he believed.

I was correct. The humans cannot match our mobility. What I did not take into account is that they don't have to. They can rely on their superior numbers. I have moved my forces along alternative routes, but wherever we go they are waiting for us. It seems that the mon-keigh opposing me has deduced the most likely routes of our attack and moved his forces there to meet them.

Were the humans able to move just a little bit faster they would be overwhelming us. As it is, we are holding our own but getting bogged down in the conflict with their superior numbers.

I can see the realisation is starting to filter through into the minds of my underlings. They no longer joke and make confident predictions of the number of slaves they are going to take and devour. They are starting to take this conflict seriously. It is no longer a leisurely amusement to them. They are beginning to respond with increased aggression, to take less time over the small cruelties and indignities they like to heap on their foes, and work at simply killing them. They are very good at this.

I am starting to wonder who is organising this. Could it be that some of these humans are like orks, with an instinctive gift for warfare?

At times we fought silently. At other times screams like damned souls in torment told us that the xenos had claimed another victim. I have fought many foes, human and xenos, in my time. I have even stood against the servants of Chaos, but I don't think I ever hated anyone the way I hated those eldar. Mostly the Emperor's enemies are the Emperor's enemies, and I kill them – sometimes coldly and sometimes driven by the rage and fear that strikes a man in combat. But there was something unutterably loathsome about these xenos.

I listen to incoming reports on the channels. The humans are fighting back hard now, and our warriors are beginning to encounter much fiercer resistance. The other commanders still sound confident, but I am liking this less and less. My forces have yet to reach a single one of their objectives. This whole ship is turning into a gigantic death trap. My own force has been driven far from my original line of attack.

Perhaps it would be best to cut our losses, withdraw and destroy the humans at a distance. Letting the killing lust take possession of me was an error. I can see that now.

Suddenly, nearby, I catch the faint pheromonal spoor of something I have not sensed in a very long time. The tang of something other than a mere human, of beings who were worthy foes, who could endure agony far better. I catch the scent of a Space Marine. Perhaps this explains the difficulty we are having. If that is the case, there is a simple way of dealing with it. We need only find him and kill him.

CHAPTER SIX

We moved squad by squad through the corridors. In the distance I could hear screams and the sounds of weapons being fired. I caught the scent of burning flesh and an odd spicy odour that I did not recognise at all. I saw no pattern. There was nothing I could grasp, only the random-seeming ebb and flow of combat.

Macharius kept giving out instructions, shooting and chopping as he went. Another wave of eldar came at us, more numerous and ferocious than the last.

'Hold your ground,' he shouted. 'Reinforcements will soon be with us.'

I prayed he was correct. The eldar fought like daemons, slicing through companies of green-tunicked Guardsmen. These ones were different, even faster and more deadly than the previous bunch and possibly even more degenerately cruel.

I dreaded getting to grips with them. My wound still gave me a little pain, enough to slow me at a critical moment. If Macharius felt the same fear he gave no sign. He spoke calmly and, as if from nowhere, more squads threw themselves into the combat, catching the eldar in crossfires, pulling them down by sheer weight of numbers, for in the confined space their superior agility counted for less.

Something dropped from above me. I threw myself backwards and heard a scream as a blade pierced the chest of one of the other guards. Something blurred past me, hit the floor and bounced into an upright position, bringing a gun to bear on Macharius. Drake raised his hand and the air between the xenos and Macharius shimmered. The shots were deflected somehow. The xenos made an odd trilling sound that might have indicated frustration or perhaps some utterly alien emotion I would never grasp. I aimed the shotgun and pulled the trigger.

I would not have hit if the creature had not, for a heartbeat, stood frozen in place. Normally it would have been too eye-blurringly swift for me to draw a bead. The shotgun blast caught it on the backplate of its armour, shattering it. Alien blood emerged from the cracks. The creature still would not die, though. It flipped backwards, moving towards me, as though it knew who shot it and was determined to get revenge. I pumped the shotgun and tried to get a fix on it.

Another shot clipped the eldar as it twisted through the air. It landed awkwardly. I saw Macharius standing behind it, still giving commands even as he squeezed off another shot. It caught the eldar in the back and sent it spinning.

I could see Macharius had hit the weakened armour and torn through it. The eldar kept coming, slower now but still seemingly determined to kill me. I stepped to one side, hoping to be able to shoot from an angle where there was no danger of hitting Macharius or anybody on our side. It was almost at a distance to use its blade on me.

Ivan came barrelling towards it. It slashed at him but he deflected the blade with a sweep of his mechanical arm. Sparks flickered. Ivan twisted and caught the weapon between the bicep and forearm of his bionic limb. I stepped forward and smashed the eldar on its helmet with the butt of the shotgun. It somehow sensed my presence and tried to twist to avoid being hit, but Ivan partially pinned it. There was a terrible crunch as my weapon connected with its helmet. The helmet did not break but the eldar flopped to the ground. I had broken its neck with the force of impact.

I was glad.

I bound along a corridor, cutting down another human. I peel away part of its cheek with my finger-blades then throw it into its companions, blood spouting to blind them. As they howl with rage and despair, I move among them, killing the ones I choose, crippling others, letting some live to wonder why they were spared. They do not wonder long as my personal guard overwhelms them. They lack my artistry, caring only for the pain they can inflict and devour. In a way they are as feeble-minded as the humans. What can they find to feast upon in the petty gobbets of pain they cause here? Granted, create sufficient havoc and you have a banquet of agonies, but it is chaotic and unrefined and lacks savour. My followers are gluttons not gourmands. Of course, that is why they are my followers.

I pass through an open bulkhead door into chambers that are luxuriously furnished in a primitive human fashion. I sense the Space Marine is close. The aura is stranger now that I can catch more of it, ancient and unliving. I glance around and locate the source. It comes from a gauntlet, pinned to a marble slab by some sort of restraining clamps, displayed as if deserving of reverence.

It is an ancient object, curiously fascinating. Unlike so much human work, there is a sense of craftsmanship about it, primitive but functional. There is a trace of the aura of ancient battles, of old bloodshed and pain, a tang unlike anything I have savoured before.

What is it doing here? It seems there are no Space Marines aboard this ship after all. It has been guarded like a treasure and presumably it is worth something to the humans. More to the point, it may be worth something to me. I lift it and take it, passing it to one of my guard. As I do so I hear a warning come in over our comm-channels. It is from Jalmek, the pilot of my boarding craft.

'Lord Ashterioth, we have ascertained from the vector and angular velocity that the human craft is preparing to enter the warp. It looks like they are planning on escaping us through the forbidden realm.'

Is there a hint of gloating in Jalmek's voice? I feel a sudden lurch in my stomach. The humans are mad enough to travel through the realm of the soul devourers. If I am still aboard the vessel when it makes the jump, all that I am will be lost to the ancient enemy of our kind.

For a moment, I picture Jalmek giving the order to pull away, leaving the attack force stranded in this most terrible of all predicaments. If that is the case, there is only one way to forestall such a fate: cripple the human ship's engines before it can make the jump or take over its bridge and force the conclusion of the jump attempt that way.

I ask for reports from my sub-commanders. They are making progress towards their objectives but very slowly; too slowly. I consider ordering them all to concentrate on driving towards a single objective.

It might work – but then again the human commander has shown himself perfectly capable of understanding and responding to our attacks. He will merely regroup and concentrate his forces to prevent us from achieving our objective. He could slow us long enough to ensure we are trapped aboard the vessel while he makes the insane leap into the forbidden. Pure terror at that prospect begins to flare in my mind, the unreasoning fear that all eldar have of confronting She Who Thirsts.

We don't have time. We don't have time. The panic beats on my brain in waves. I am filled with the nauseating fear that we will be trapped aboard this primitive vessel as it makes its leap into the realm of madness; that our beacon-bright souls will attract the attention of the devourers.

The prospect of abandoning some of my bodyguard on the ship to achieve exactly this saunters into my mind. I imagine the fear of the stranded eldar and the fate of the humans as their vessel is warp-lost. It is a prospect not without appeal but I would not be there to enjoy it, and nothing would be more likely to spark a mutiny among my troops than the suspicion I had done this.

I bark out orders to begin the withdrawal. We will return to our ship and destroy this vessel at our leisure.

I sense disappointment among the stupider of my followers who wish to continue to fight and feast. The wiser heads understand the reason for my decision. I sketch an ironic farewell to the human commander in the air. Enjoy your petty victory while you can. It will be short-lived.

I take the gauntlet with me. It will be an interesting souvenir of this encounter.

I saw the body of one man, partially flayed, skin stripped away from his flesh to reveal muscle and vein. He was still alive, paralysed by poison but in terrible agony as the venom slowly destroyed his nervous system in the most painful way. In the heat of combat, amid the fury of battle, what sort of sentient being takes time out to torture a victim, to peel them like an epicure consuming a drugged black grape?

There were too many examples of that sort of thing for me to imagine that the first was simply an accident. The eldar killed in an unclean fashion, caused pain for the pure pleasure of it, showed no more regard for life than a small boy tormenting a garbage scuttler. There were times when it seemed they would rather torture than fight. No – it did not seem that way, it was that way. For the eldar, pain was like a drug to which they were addicted. They craved it the way a dried-out boozehound craves his next drink.

In the midst of chopping their way through a company of men, they would suddenly pause, stand stock-still save for their helmeted heads, which would swivel from side to side, surveying everything as serenely as a man inspecting a garden.

At such moments, if you glanced around, it appeared that there might even be a pattern in the way the corpses had fallen, some strange symmetry in the lie of the severed limbs on the floor and blood spatters on the walls. It sounds bizarre, but that's the way it seemed to me; that if I looked long enough I might discern some sort of structure underlying the flow of carnage. I strongly suspected that I would no longer be sane as humans measure sanity if I did.

I race through the corridors, listening to the chatter of small pockets of our troops who have been cut off. They are surprised to find the tables turned on them. They are having difficulty in understanding that they are no longer the hunters but the hunted. They pay for their lack of swift understanding with their lives.

I bound along the corridor, using ceiling and walls as easily as floor, scouting ahead of my own troops, keen to get off the ship and begin cleansing the universe of these human vermin.

Even as I do so, I sense the presence of humans ahead of me, moving to close the gap. I smile. The human commander misses nothing. He must be supervising the battle as closely as I. He realises that things have turned, although I wonder if he realises why.

Up ahead I suddenly see a massive wall of armed men. It looks like I underestimated my foe. The force we had been fighting had been merely there to slow us down, while he assembled a small army to cut us off. The humans are flooding into the area where our ship had penetrated theirs. We are going to have to battle our way through. I speed forward into the fray.

I aim a shot at the approaching humans, killing one. I dive into their midst, cartwheeling, kicking, slashing and shooting. The human leader may have planned for victory but he could not have planned for me. I unleash the full fury of my attack, in a way I so seldom do. A smile twists my lips as I bound among my targets, slaying every one with a stroke. Now is no time for artistry. We are mere minutes away from this ship making its jump. If we are to get away we must do so soon.

The remnants of my bodyguard smash into the human lines behind me. I have left very little for them to do. They merely have to kill the few humans that somehow squirmed beyond my reach. They do this with pleasure. Some of them are laughing. I wonder whether it is mirth or simply relief that they think we will be able to escape this craft before it makes the leap into the forbidden realms.

We fit ourselves into place as the boarding craft pulls away. Through the portholes I can see bodies being blown out into space as the air rushes into the vacuum, flesh already chilling. Some of the humans are still alive although not for much longer. I glance around and notice that we have some human faces among us. It seems some of my warriors have taken captives after all.

I am not as displeased as I ought to be. I am curious about the human who led this army. I have a few questions for them before they die.

And then suddenly it reached a climax. We advanced on the enemy. A horde of howling Guardsmen emerged from the side corridors, killing as they came. The eldar were suddenly caught between the hammer and the anvil.

Macharius had deployed our troops in such a way as to cut most of the eldar off from the hull breach they had been retreating towards. The corridors were packed with armed men, bristling with a density of weapons that was too much even for the xenos. Fast as they were they could not dodge every las-beam, there were simply too many of them; as well to try to dodge drops of rain in a typhoon. I think that then, at last, the eldar realised what had happened. I am not sure that even then they believed it. They seemed baffled.

Not that it mattered.

When they saw they could not escape they turned on us with a redoubled fury. Something had driven them to a frenzy of suicidal ferocity. The surviving eldar punched backwards towards us with the fury of daemons who know they are going to be destroyed and are determined to take as many victims to hell with them as they can. They came at us in great leaping bounds, weapons blasting, killing or crippling a man with every shot. Even then, at the last extremity, some of them could not resist causing pain rather than killing.

They charged across a junction, got caught in crossfire from both sides as well as from behind and from our position. It was a density of fire that Macharius had arranged. There was no way they could move through that blizzard of las-bolts without being hit. Their armour blistered and peeled and ran. They kept moving anyway, slowed perhaps by pain, but still determined to rampage and kill.

One reached us, slashing out with its long circular blades. It was shot in a dozen places, its beautiful, chitinous armour cracked and blistered. Its movements were slower than they had been but still almost too swift to follow. Macharius killed it with a blow and met its companion chainsword to blade. The teeth of his weapon screeched on the eldar's carapace and one of those long inhuman limbs flew in a different direction from the body it had been attached to. The fallen eldar still stabbed a Guardsman, the reflexive killing stroke of a dying sand-scorpion. The man went down. I stepped away. It kept trying to roll closer, all grace gone, just a furious daemonic engine of death.

Anton blasted it with his sniper rifle, sending a heavy calibre slug right through the visor of the helmet. Even then it did not stop flailing its limbs until heartbeats later. Even in death it tried to claim another victim.

More eldar slammed into us, close combat weapons slashing at our men. Again blood spurted, bone was revealed, part of a lung flopped out from a ribcage that had been somehow sheared in two. I aimed the shotgun and pulled the trigger but my target simply was not there. In the time it had taken me to aim and pull the trigger it had sprung out of my line of fire and my shell passed beneath. A moment later it was poised in front of me. All I saw of its strike was a blur. I knew in that moment my death was on me.

I flinched, but the blow never connected. Macharius's blade intercepted it. The eldar sprang back too fast for me to react but not too fast for the general. He followed it with a spring just as swift, and the xenos desperately tried to defend itself from a predator even more lethal than itself.

A second eldar was cleaving its way through our ranks when suddenly a bolt of strange lightning struck it, melting its helmet. A second later, Macharius had stepped forward, chainsword in hand. There was a raucous screeching as the xenos's armour gave way under the force of the impact. I noticed that Drake was standing behind Macharius then; it had been his psionic bolt that had taken the eldar down.

I took a quick glance around, looking for the last surviving eldar. It had realised what was going on now and was fleeing as fast as it could, moving swiftly through a glittering net of las-bolts, somehow managing to avoid the bulk of them while its armour shimmered and ran from the effects of the few that connected. Anton raised his sniper rifle and sighted. His shot smashed into the eldar and it tumbled, still graceful, but hurt now. When it rose to its feet, some of its eerie grace had been leached away. Anton fired again and this time his shot hammered into its head. It fell flat. Some of us ran towards it.

'Wait,' said Macharius, his words coming out somewhere between a snarl and a shout. The men who had been moving forward, led by Ivan, stopped and the Lord High Commander advanced. Once he was within reach the eldar struck, still almost too swift for the eye to follow. Macharius stepped to one side and decapitated it. I realised that the xenos, heavily wounded as it was, had been playing dead, hoping for some of us to come within reach so that it could take more victims with it. It would most likely have succeeded if Macharius had not been there.

I think they were overconfident those eldar, or we would have taken more casualties than we did. It seemed that not one of the Guardsmen wounded, no matter how lightly they were scratched, had survived. Macharius inspected the sword. A look of contempt flickered across his face.

'Neurotoxins on the weapons,' Macharius said. 'Kill you painfully. Very painfully.'

I looked around and suddenly it was silent, one of those eerie moments you sometimes get on all battlefields, when just for an instant, by some strange coincidence, there are no weapons being fired, no screams echoing, no battle-cries pounding in your ears. The silence itself hisses and you are aware of your heart pounding and the taste of bile in your mouth, and you look around at your companions and you realise that they are all as pale-faced and wide-eyed as you, with that strange unblinking stare that the survivors always get when the thunder of battle has passed overhead and is gone.

It lasted only a few seconds and then everyone started to cheer, a release of tension that went on until we started to count the cost.

CHAPTER SEVEN

Reports kept coming in. I could tell just from what Macharius was saying that we had taken heavy casualties, but it looked as though the ship was clear of eldar. Their attack had failed. It had cost thousands of lives from among our own troops, and the Emperor alone knew how many tens of thousands from among the crew of the ship, but the eldar were gone, driven off.

Warning klaxons blared.

'What now?' Anton asked, still so high on the fury of battle that he forgot how close Macharius was.

'We are about to make the jump,' Macharius said. 'The ship is being made ready.'

'Sir, there are huge bloody holes in the hull where the eldar came through.'

'The emergency bulkheads have been sealed and the

screens are being ramped up to the maximum. It's all we can do. It's either make the jump or let the xenos blast us out of space.' He smiled grimly. 'I don't think they will be inclined to spare us after the bloody nose we have just given them.'

It was too late to abort the warp jump even if he had given the order. The ship was already starting to shudder and vibrate, and I had the strange falling sensation I always got when we passed through into the warp.

I give the order to attack. Our ships swarm on the human craft, but it resists the fury of our assault. I order our ships to aim for any vulnerable point they can find, hoping to take out its drives. The human vessel smashes through the storm of fire and keeps accelerating. Its shields shimmer as it prepares to make its insane leap into the beyond. It occurs to me that we would, perhaps, be doing them a favour by destroying them, that instant death might prove to be a mercy compared to what may happen to them next.

I dismiss the thought. They may well survive – who knows what the probabilities are? No eldar has ever made a survey of them, but enough human ships move between the worlds to suggest that the odds are in favour of their madness, at least in the short term.

I wonder if there are any of my warriors still alive on board. My sensors say no, but there is always the possibility of error. I try to imagine what it would be like to be still aboard that ship as it crashed towards the forbidden. I wonder, do the humans really know what they are doing, entering a realm where the most evil beings in creation or below it lurk?

We begin another attack run. It may just be possible to cripple or destroy them before they make the jump. There is a certain pleasure to be gained from that.

We race closer again. The human weapons blast out at us but we are too swift for them, although evasive action slows our approach.

'We will make it, Lord Ashterioth,' Jalmek says.

'Would you care to wager on that?' I say. I am no longer convinced. Whoever is on board that ship has luck on his side, at least for today. Luck is always a fickle mistress, careless of whom she bestows her favours upon and when she withdraws them. Something tells me that today she smiles on my foe.

Jalmek looks at me. He has long ago learned the unwisdom of wagering against me. 'I think not, sire.'

Nonetheless, he continues to give a stream of orders and course corrections designed to put us into attack position and, just for a moment, at the end of a long twisting and snaking run, I think he has done it.

'Torpedo away,' he says, and our vessel spits out the missile and sends it streaking towards our intended target.

At the moment of impact there is a blinding flash, so dazzling that the viewer turns shadowy as it filters the coruscating energies we are witnessing.

When I look again, the human ship is gone.

'We destroyed it, sire,' said Jalmek. I can tell he is wishing he had made that bet now. I study the space where the human ship was and I am not sure if he is right.

Once again the lights flickered. Once again there was a hideous sense of dizziness and nausea, as if I had suddenly fallen from a cliff into an infinite void. Near me some of the soldiers were being noisily sick. Men who had marched through the worst horrors the eldar had inflicted on us could not keep their food down now.

Everyone around me swayed; in the strobing warning lights their faces went from greenish and pale to red and bloody-looking and then back again. I leaned against a wall, supporting myself, trying to get a sense of what was happening. Fear filled my mind. We were making a jump with a ship that had been patched together after one failed flight and whose hull had been breached by the eldar. At any moment, I expected it to buckle, for all the daemons of the star-sailors' ghost stories to start making themselves manifest. I stared at my companions as if any second they might be transformed into creatures of nightmare. Their features were oddly distorted.

Macharius stood there, glancing around him. 'Take two minutes,' he said. 'Your bodies will adjust.'

After the battle was over Macharius went to inspect the wounded, for his presence among them was always a comfort. He found what I had been expecting, and I am sure what he had too, that there were far fewer of them than there ought to have been, and this was not good news.

A battle is a bloody affair but normally far more men take wounds than are killed outright. Often those wounds will kill far more of them than combat in the long run, but that is neither here nor there.

You expect to see mangled bodies and bleeding men. You expect to hear the cries of pain and see wounded warriors wrapped in red-stained bandages and splattered with synthi-flesh. It is simply the way things are. Only this time, it was not.

There were plenty of dead. There were plenty of mangled bodies. There were plenty of dying. Far too many, in fact. Almost all of those who had taken even the slightest wound from the eldar were passing away, slowly and in great pain. A few were not, but there was no rhyme nor reason to it. It was as though the xenos had spared some victims on a whim.

Perhaps the poison on their weapons had run out, or perhaps it was something completely different. I just know that I have never seen so many wounded men who were so obviously going to die after any previous battle. And I had never seen so many bodies that had been mutilated in ways that showed a malicious intelligence at work. Even in the heat of battle, the eldar had taken time to work terrible harm on a selection of their victims.

Macharius's face was a mask. I knew he was furious. He was a man capable of great cruelty himself, but it was always in the service of something, the ideal of the Imperium he served. This was something else. It was a sign of sickness of soul somewhere. It was not the innocent malice of cats playing with rodents; it was calculated, the product of intelligences who had simply decided, for whatever reasons of their own, to cause as much pain as possible to whatever they encountered.

He stalked back towards his chambers, and we were silent, for he was wrathful.

The holding bay is crowded with prisoners and with warriors. The ranks of those who boarded the human ship are sadly depleted. Their armour is pitted and scarred in many places. Some are wounded and are receiving the ministrations of haemonculi.

All of them are glaring at me in a way they simply would not have done a few hours before. They can count the number of the missing as well as I can, and they blame me for the absence of every comrade who is not here. Each death is a mark against me, a signifier of failure. We have taken what they believe to be needless casualties fighting against our inferiors. I have, temporarily, lost the aura of invincibility that is so necessary for those who would lead the eldar. There is a sense of menace in the assembled gaze that I force myself to ignore. If my subordinates wish to challenge me, let them. I do not fear any of them.

I stare at the assembled humans and try to read the emotions on their faces. It is not easy. Their features are slack and witless, not mobile and expressive like eldar faces. Their small bestial eyes glare around with a mixture of fear and horror. I have switched off the translation engine for the time being so I can only hear the loathsome grunting that serves them as speech.

'Not the best of hauls,' says Sileria. She looks smug, as most eldar do when contemplating another's misfortune. I can tell she is measuring our losses against the number of slaves we have gained. In her mind, as in mine, the balance comes down heavily on the debit side. I wonder if she is contemplating a move against me while the warriors are disenchanted. 'I wonder how much nutriment they will provide. Very little most likely.'

'We shall not consume them... yet,' I say. I glance around. I have got all of their attentions now. They are curious as to what I have in mind.

'They do not look as though they would be much use for anything else,' Sileria says.

'I would question them,' I say.

'You wish to converse with these beasts?' Sileria says, unable to keep the astonishment from her voice.

'Yes, Sileria, I do,' I say, and I let a little of the lash sound in my voice. It is time to remind all of them who rules here and why. 'There was a human of unusual skill on that ship. Surely you noticed how they countered all of our attacks and prevented us from taking the prize. Or were you too busy sweating your way through the battle?'

Sileria looks huffy. She is not unaware of her lack of finesse in combat, but the accusation of sweating is the one that upsets her most. I can see she would challenge me if she dared, but she does not. A direct physical attack on my person could only end one way, and we both know it. She gradually relaxes as she realises that I am prepared for any assault she might make.

No, I think, if there is going to be any move against me by Sileria it will come indirectly through one of her many lovers, Bael perhaps, or as part of some cabal. She forces herself to smile, but it just makes her look petulant.

'Also there is the matter of this… thing,' I say, indicating the Space Marine artefact. 'It is a device belonging to one of the human elites, but I saw none of them aboard. I am curious as to why it was there and to what use it may be put. It was obviously of some significance to them, perhaps part of their primitive religion.'

She looks at the clawed mechanical gauntlet with contempt. I can understand why. It looks primitive and ugly, but there is something about it that speaks to me. It is ancient, and an aura of something clings to it. 'I do not see what possible interest it could hold to an eldar of your intellect,' she says, as if scoring a point.

Of course you don't, I think, and that is one reason why I am the leader here and you are not.

'The humans placed some value on it. It might prove useful as bait,' I say. A few of the warriors nod. This is the sort of thinking they understand. They are calming down a little now, but I can see that in every heart a desire for vengeance has been kindled. 'It may be the humans will return seeking it.'

'If they do we will make them regret it,' says Veldor.

'No doubt,' I say, letting a note of irony show in my voice. I gesture to one of the servants to bring me my flaying tools. It is time to start asking some questions. I open the casket and produce a curved flensing knife with a bulb of tomb-worm venom in its hilt. I turn to the nearest human, one who wears the over-elaborate garb of one of their leaders. I switch on the translation engine.

'You there,' I say. 'Come talk to me.'

Macharius looked at the Guardsman grim-faced, then he looked at the slab where the Fist had lain. Of the ancient artefact itself there was no sign.

'It is what?' he said. I think it was perhaps the first time I had ever really seen him lose control. In the past he had acted it for the benefit of an audience, but at that moment he looked genuinely shocked.

'It is gone,' said the Guardsman. He had the dazed, shocked look of one who had somehow against all odds survived an overwhelming attack by the eldar. 'The Fist of Demetrius is gone.'

I looked at the bodies of the dead. They were strewn everywhere, and they bore the markings of those who had died at the hands of the eldar. They had not gone cleanly into the Emperor's Light. Macharius's eyes narrowed. He walked over to the last resting place of the Fist and stared in, as though he could not quite believe it was gone, despite the evidence of his own eyes.

'I want the ship searched,' he said. 'Every compartment. Make sure the Fist is not still aboard.'

Drake looked at him askance. 'The eldar were here. It seems logical that they took it.'

Macharius nodded. 'But we cannot just assume it. I want every avenue explored.' Sailors and soldiers alike ran to carry out his orders, leaving only the two great men and their bodyguards alone in the chamber.

Macharius's fist clenched. He spoke with controlled anger. 'I want the Fist found.'

'We only just escaped the eldar,' said Drake, not unreasonably. 'We are lucky to get away with our lives.'

'Nonetheless, I will have it returned. I do not wish to see a sacred relic of humanity left in the hands of those xenos.'

'That is understandable,' said Drake. 'We put an enormous amount of effort into locating it. We spent lives recovering it. And if it is what we believe it to be then they cannot be allowed to have it.'

There was something else in the air here, hovering between them. I could sense it.

'The meeting should be happening soon,' said Macharius.

'If Sejanus managed things properly,' said Drake.

'Sejanus knew what to say. He will do what needs to be done.'

'We both know that the Adeptus Astartes are unpredictable and those ones most of all,' said Drake. 'Who knows how they will respond to your overtures? I would not care to predict that myself.'

Macharius smiled. It was a bleak expression. 'You still do not approve of this course of action, my friend.'

'It is a gamble that might be misinterpreted by those who watch over us.'

'I have considered that,' said Macharius.

'I don't doubt it. You consider everything.'

'But... I hear a but in your voice.'

'Imperial politics is not a battlefield, Lord High Commander,' said Drake. 'On the field of battle you are all but invincible. This is something else.'

Macharius looked around. There was something conspiratorial in their manner now. I felt this was something they had talked about in private during those long enclosed sessions with no one else present. What had they been discussing, I often wondered – the most powerful man in the galaxy and the inquisitor who had taken upon himself the role of counsellor and spiritual advisor. They were in the process of reforging an Imperium shattered by schism and civil war, of reclaiming thousands of worlds that had fallen from the Emperor's Light.

The faces of those the eldar had killed stared at us empty-eyed. I wondered about the place the Fist of Demetrius might have in Macharius's plans, and how they might be affected by its disappearance. Judging by Macharius's expression, the answer was not good.

Replete, I look at the mess of bodies on the tables. The interrogation was a surprisingly satisfactory experience. It gives me a simple pleasure to exercise my skills even on such beasts as these. And, of course, as part of the experience, they talked, willingly answering all of the questions I put to them. Not many can resist the flaying knife or the eye-gougers when they are wielded by an expert such as myself. Most of them would have talked willingly enough when they saw what happened to the first of them, but I see no reason to deny myself the small pleasures in life.

I consider what they have told me. I have a name for my foe now, Macharius. It seems to me that I have heard that name before in other places. He is the human associated with this new tribal migration they have under way. He is their leader. I am pleased with this knowledge. This Macharius is exceptional by the standards of the humans, a beast with an innate gift for warfare almost worthy of an eldar, one with a talent such as might emerge every hundred generations. It does not make my failure sting any less, but it does explain it.

Perhaps more interesting is what they told me about the artefact. It appears it is sacred to the humans. One of them, better informed than the rest, told me that it may have belonged to one of the ancient saints or primarchs, or whatever the humans call their primitive heroes. It is not the first time I have come across references to this Leman Russ. He is revered as the founding father of their Space Wolves tribe. Such beings were said to be gifted with near godlike powers. It comes to me that if this is truly the case, it is well worth investigating. I doubt it will come to anything but there was once a time when the humans were far more advanced than they are today, and it may be that analysis of the genetic helix will reveal something worthwhile. I am not hopeful, but it is an avenue worth exploring.

In any case, I have learned all there is to learn from the primitives and can return to our new base to continue my investigations. I have a foreboding that the humans will return. It seems this Macharius made considerable efforts to obtain the Fist. He will most likely do so again, if he survives.

That would be good. I would welcome a chance to humble him. Our defences must be made ready.

We waited tensely. We hoped and we prayed to the Emperor. The crew did a little more than that. They moved around the ship, reinforcing the bulkheads and checking all of the areas around the eldar breakthrough zones. Macharius had sentries stand guard with them. I don't know what he was expecting, perhaps for monsters to break through and take over the ship. My own fear was simply that the weak spots in the hull would give way and the stuff of the immaterium would come roaring in, or all our air would go roaring out, but I am an ignorant former factory worker from Belial and what do I know of the horrors we avoided?

I know that after the initial tense period of waiting after the jump we settled down into a parody of the usual shipboard routine, although we were more wary and more afraid even than usual. Macharius really did have the whole ship searched for the Fist and was disappointed to find that it was not aboard. After that he paced his chambers and studied star charts and planetary maps, but I could tell that he was disturbed. There were times when there was a tightness about his eyes and a grim twist to his lips that spoke of a controlled fury that only those of us who knew him very well would have noticed. At those times, we walked very quietly around him.

What could it be that was troubling him? I had seen Macharius sleep like a baby the night before a battle in which a million men died. I had watched him smile when we were surrounded and outnumbered by a thousand to one. Why had the loss of this one ancient artefact upset him so?

Granted it might have been a sacred relic of the time when the Emperor had walked among men – but we had seen no evidence of it. It had worked no wonders in our presence. We had marched triumphantly through the galaxy without it, and I fully expected to march triumphantly again. Macharius did not need sacred artefacts to march behind. He was his own banner and his own guarantee of victory. He had won every war he had fought. Still there was an unease in him, as if he sensed forces gathering against him, unseen as yet but coming. He was a man who liked to prepare for all contingencies, was Macharius, but what contingency was he planning for now? And why had Drake mentioned the Adeptus Astartes?

I pushed such thoughts to one side. The answers would become clear in time, I felt sure. And so we emerged from the second leg of our ill-fated jump. This time we arrived at our intended destination, Emperor's Glory.

'You refuse to aid me?' Macharius said.

'I do,' said the fleet admiral. 'With a heavy heart, but I do.'

As soon as we arrived in the Emperor's Glory system Macharius started making preparations to reclaim the Fist. He spoke to the fleet admiral in orbit over the new capital of the crusade on the vox-channels, but it seemed others had already been in touch with that august personage.

'Why?'

'I have spoken with your Navigator and his brethren in the fleet. They all believe that Procrastes, the system you escaped from, is unreachable at this moment in time.'

'I see,' said Macharius. He stared at the admiral. If he had looked at me in that way I would have acquiesced to his requests, but Fleet Admiral Kellerman was made of sterner stuff.

'I do not rule out sending the fleet there in the future. It is just that now is too risky. To send any of our ships into the jaws of that storm would be to place them at unacceptable odds of loss. Once the storm dies down that will no longer be the case.'

'Tell me, admiral,' said Macharius. 'How long can these storms last?' It was clear that Macharius already had a clear idea of the answer. He merely wanted the other man to be on record.

'They can last for decades, Lord High Commander,' said Kellerman. 'I would not get my hopes up about this happening any time soon.'

'Thank you, admiral,' said Macharius and cut the connection. He turned to Drake and said, 'It seems the Navy is being obstructive.'

Drake studied him coolly. 'I think he merely told you something you did not want to hear.'

Macharius shrugged. 'That he did, but nonetheless, I suspect he is being deliberately obstructive.'

'He would not be the first Navy commander to be so,' said Drake, who obviously did not want to argue the point. He had chosen a more subtle line of defence.

'This has been happening more and more lately,' Macharius said.

'A man in your position generates enemies,' said Drake. 'It is inevitable. I warned you about antagonising the magnates. I warned you that the lords of the Administratum would start seeing you as a threat. It looks like the first moves against you have begun.'

'I want the Fist reclaimed,' said Macharius.

'I strongly suspect you will need to do that without the Navy's help.'

'They are not the only people with ships,' said Macharius.

'You will need a warship, and a very powerful one, if you intend to return to Procrastes.'

'I believe I know where I can find one,' said Macharius.

'I was afraid of that,' said Drake.

CHAPTER EIGHT

Emperor's Glory looked exactly as you would expect such a world to look. The sky was clear and an astonishing shade of blue. The sun was bright and golden. Where there were no cities, the lands were as pristine as a park. The cities were studies in imposing beauty.

The buildings had gleaming marble facings, and gigantic statues of saints and Imperial heroes filled the streets. At least in the upper city everything was clean and gilded and perfect looking. The people were richly dressed. Perhaps in the undercity, things were different, but we had not yet had either the opportunity or the desire to look. It was beyond a shadow of a doubt the richest planet I had visited, and it was getting richer by the day.

A fantastic stream of wealth swept in, borne on the tides of war. The spoils of a hundred worlds and a thousand ongoing campaigns were stored in great warehouses, piled in the halls of palaces, worn on the scabbard belts and chestplates of victorious Imperial soldiers.

The world was the sector capital now, standing at the hub of a cosmic crossroads where the supply routes of the crusade met. Men and materials flowed in from the Imperium. Tribute and loot accumulated until it could be shipped back to the heart worlds. In the meantime, everyone of any importance was taking a tithe of it. I suspected that several new ruling dynasties would be funded by the profits of this war.

You could see the evidence of the wealth when you set down on the space-field. It was as big as a city and crammed with ships of every shape, size and classification. Enormous warehouses lined the edges or lay beneath the blast pads of the landing zones. I watched one huge treasure argosy being unloaded as we marched down the ramp from the sub-orbital shuttle. I had seen several more through the portholes in the ship's side as we waited to disembark.

Emperor's Glory was the first world on which I had stood in a long time where the sky was blue, the sun was bright, the air was fresh and no one seemed all that keen to kill me. In the air at the space port, you could just smell the odd metallic tang I have come to associate with docked sub-orbital ships, a compound of cooling metal, drive ozone and recycled atmosphere being released from the locks to mingle with the local air as you emerged from the hatch.

I did not need my rebreather mask. Even after all this time, the fact that I could think that still stunned me. I was born on a hive-world, where pollution was everywhere in the sealed corridors of the city. The external air beyond the hive was even more deadly. The idea that there was a place where you did not need to make sure your protective filter-mask was always available was still little short of miraculous to me. I could tell from looking at Ivan and Anton and the way they looked around with wonder that they felt the same way. Macharius just looked as if it were normal. His home world had most likely been like this. He certainly seemed at ease here.

A highly ornate airship descended on our landing zone. It was as big as a small orbital shuttle. and you could see that beneath all the gold-plating it was heavily armed and armoured. Even here in the new sector capital, seat of Macharius's power in these conquered worlds, no one except the general himself was taking any chances with his safety.

We went down the ramp ahead of Macharius, weapons drawn, as if we were making planetfall on some rebel world. It was mostly for show, of course, but it meant we kept in practice. Drake and his storm troopers followed us down the ramp.

From the airship a horde of attaches and executive officers emerged, all moving towards Macharius, all carrying reports and petitions and missives that must be delivered only by hand. They swarmed together, almost elbowing each other out of the way as they moved forward. We stood our ground as they came towards us like charging orks.

They appeared almost surprised that common soldiers would not get out of their way. We had done this before.

'Make way for the Lord High Commander,' the Undertaker said, in his flat, strange voice, and they halted. Almost any sane man would when confronted by his vacuum-empty eyes and emotionless manner. 'He will speak to you in order of rank when he reaches the palace. Now stand aside and do not obstruct the Emperor's business.'

His manner made it quite clear that he meant what he said. It seemed perfectly possible that he would order us to shoot if these office boys did not get out of our way. They sensed it too and our way parted. They fell into line and followed us back onto the airship, though. I could already see them jockeying for position, claiming precedence, forming small cabals and alliances.

Suddenly I missed the cold violence of the war front.

The palace that Macharius was building would be one of the wonders of the sector when it was complete. So much was obvious as we made our approach. It was the size of a small city, built in a shape that suggested the aquila when seen from overhead. Hundreds of thousands of workmen swarmed over the sides of the structure: painting, sculpting statues and gargoyles, working on the enormous victory masks of Macharius worked into the walls.

Once, I had walked across a completed section of one of the roofs. There were hundreds of statues of Imperial angels there, regiments of them, ready to storm heaven at Macharius's command. It had seemed to me to be a colossal waste. I was probably the only person who had looked upon them since the sculptors had departed for a new sector of the palace. I might well be the only person to do so until the end of time. Yet someone had seen fit to order them built. I wondered if it was some bureaucrat growing fat on contractor's bribes, or an architect swollen with megalomania from being commissioned to build this monument to one man.

I wondered about all of it sometimes. What made Macharius sanction the construction of such a monument to his vanity? He was already the most famous man in the Imperium save the Emperor. His name would ring down the millennia for as long as mankind endured. What did erecting this titanic palace add to its lustre?

It was indicative, though, that something monstrously proud was growing within the Lord High Commander, something that needed this confirmation in plascrete and ceramite of his importance. Or perhaps I do him a disservice. Perhaps it was being built because that is what was expected of him. He was hardly the first Imperial commander, or indeed the first great conqueror, to leave monuments littered about the galaxy. I doubt that he will be the last.

Still, it made me uncomfortable as the airship swung in towards the landing tower and made its final approach. Beneath us I could see the great geodesic dome of the Hunting Grounds. It was full of exotic jungle plants and great carnivores brought from across the sector to provide sport for Macharius and his chosen guests. It was a place of death and danger, as I would find out for myself one day.

'Gentlemen, you are dismissed for the moment,' said Macharius as we stepped across the threshold of the palace.

A new detachment of his personal guard stood ready to greet him. They were spotlessly garbed in their green lion's head tunics, drawn up as if for review.

The words were spoken with a pleasant, comradely smile, and their tone made it clear that he valued us greatly. I felt almost embarrassed by the thoughts I had been having about him just a few minutes ago on the airship. We stood at attention, though, until he was gone and Inquisitor Drake with him. After that, the Undertaker said, 'You're not on duty any more. There's no need to just stand there.' Taking himself at his word he strode off into the palace. The bodyguard split off into small groups and I was left standing with Anton and Ivan.

'How is the arm?' Anton asked, slapping it roughly.

'Better,' I said, 'or you would be spitting teeth right now.'

'Where are you going to get ten extra men in a hurry?' Anton said.

'Is that how much help you think you'd need?' I asked.

'No. I meant you would need them to…' His words trailed off as he realised what he was saying. He let out a long sigh, then stared off into the distance, back in the direction of the airship. Servitors were already starting to unload huge trunks full of plunder and wargear.

People in the green tunics of palace servants lounged nearby. They watched us, just as they had watched Macharius depart. 'How many of those guys are spies, do you think?' Ivan asked. His voice sounded slightly better since his mechanical parts had been upgraded, but it could still not remotely be described as normal.

'All of them,' Anton said. 'That's what Lady Patricia says.'
Lady Patricia was his latest flame. A highborn lady from
Emperor's Glory.

'She would know since she's one herself,' Ivan said.

'No, she's not,' said Anton, a little too quickly.

'Yeah, she would tell you if she was,' Ivan said.

'She's not.'

'Yes,' I said. 'She's just interested in your good looks and
personal charm.'

'That's right,' said Anton.

'Funny that,' said Ivan. 'Since you don't have any.'

'Look who's talking,' said Anton.

'So before you became Macharius's bodyguard, how many
highborn ladies threw themselves at you?' I asked.

'I think we all know the answer to that,' said Ivan.

'I had a few,' Anton said.

'I don't remember any,' I said.

'I don't think you're in any position to criticise me,' said
Anton. 'I'm not the one who fell into bed with an Imperial
assassin.'

'Hush!' I said. I always regretted the drunken time I had
told the pair of them about my involvement with Anna,
back on Karsk. 'That's the sort of fool statement that could
get you killed. It could get all of us killed.'

I smiled as though I were making a joke and I kept my
tone very light, but I was looking around to see who was
listening. Nobody seemed to be, but, of course, that meant
nothing. All of these people were adroit at appearing to
notice nothing while noticing everything, and that was not

taking into account the possibility of all manner of techno-
logical eavesdropping devices being focused on us. The very
powerful found it useful to keep even such minor members
of Macharius's retinue as us under surveillance. After all,
you never knew when someone like Anton would let something slip they shouldn't. Someone like me too, I suppose.

Even Anton had the good grace to look abashed. He had
learned something in our time with Macharius after all. He
considered his words for a while and said, 'Look, I know
what the Lady Patricia sees in me.'

'Nothing,' Ivan suggested, a little cruelly under the
circumstances.

Anton continued with an air of mock dignity, as though
he had not been interrupted. 'But you've got to remember,
I am using her as much as she is using me. How often does
a common soldier like me get to bed down with a highborn
bedroom acrobat like her?'

'She teaching you some new tricks, is she?' I asked.

'I am teaching her some, actually. Anyway, I don't tell her
anything she does not already know.'

'How do you know what she knows?' Ivan asked. He
looked quite genuinely curious.

'She tells me.'

'And no woman has ever lied to you,' I said.

'You leave me to worry about that. You worry about your
own women. I suspect you're in much more trouble than
me.' He reached out and picked a goblet from a tray being
carried by a passing servant girl, swigged a mouthful of the
yellowish nectar in it and walked on. He did it as though

it were his right, which it was. Everything was available to one of Macharius's bodyguards within the palace, and I do mean everything. It was a life of staggering luxury compared to the one which we had grown up with on Belial. In this palace, even common soldiers like us could live like merchant princes on our home world. It was one of the advantages of being there.

Anton let out a sudden loud whoop that had everyone looking at him, including Ivan and me. He just grinned his idiot grin and said, 'Did you ever think we would be living like this, lads?'

It was infectious. I found myself grinning back. 'No,' I said.

'Best thing that ever happened to us was running into Macharius,' Anton said. He believed that right till the end.

My chambers were in the same sector of the palace as Macharius had his. They resembled what I had always imagined luxury to look like, until I caught sight of the way the generals lived. It was not a barracks room. It was a suite with a living room and a massive four-poster bed in the centre. There was a naked woman in mine when I entered. I recognised her too. 'Anna,' I said. It was not her real name, of course. I never found out what that was. It was the first one I had known her by, though, all those years ago on Karsk. It is the name I still think of her by now.

'Leo,' she said. She was a good-looking woman, no doubt of that: compactly built, hair very short, large, deceptively trusting eyes. Her beauty could not be compared to the striking, surgically enhanced glamour of the local noble-women – she would barely have been noticed among them, which was the whole point, of course – but she was lovely. Her face was the same today as it had been when I first met her. It did not have to be, she could change it as she liked, but she knew I had a sentimental attachment to that look. Maybe she did too.

On the dresser beside her sat a large, custom-made pistol. I had no doubt there were half a dozen other weapons within easy reach. She was not a woman who ever entered a room without being prepared to fight her way out of it. 'I saw the reports that said you were back in one piece.'

I very carefully unbuckled my belt and placed my hol-stered sidearm on top of the chest of drawers. Her reflexes were much faster than mine. She was much stronger too. Somewhere, sometime, the strange archeotech of the ancients had been used on her, transforming her into some-thing other than human.

No, let me rephrase that. She was still a human. If she had not been, our lords and masters in the Imperium would have terminated her. She was an augmented human in the same way that Ivan was, although she had been changed in ways invisible to the naked eye and with much greater sophistication.

'I confess, I am surprised to find you here,' I said.

'No, you're not,' she said. She tilted her head to one side. 'You expected that we would meet again. We always do.'

There was some truth in that. I did expect to meet her at unusual times and in unusual places. We had encountered each other off and on a dozen times since the start of the crusade. We had occasionally been lovers. I suspected it was part of her job to keep tabs on Macharius's security contingent, but I like to think there was something more to it as well, that it was within the realms of possibility that she liked me.

'Why is that exactly?' I asked.

'You know why,' she said.

'Apparently I have hidden the knowledge from myself.'

'I am here to question you, to pick your brains.'

'I thought it was because you find me attractive.' She smiled with genuine amusement.

'You see, you did know the reason after all.'

'I find that hard to believe.'

'I both like you and find you attractive, and I am still here to pick your brains.'

'And that works better while you are naked,' I said, sliding onto the bed beside her.

'I thought we might amuse ourselves before I interrogated you,' she said, kissing me. I ran my hands over her flesh. There were areas beneath the skin that were harder and heavier than they ought to have been. She was still very lovely.

Afterwards we lay on the bed. She studied me, head tilted to one side, cat-like. 'What are you thinking?' she asked, reaching out to touch my cheek.

'I am still wondering why you are here?'

'You are not the soul of romance, Leo.'

'Nor are you. Let us not pretend otherwise.'

She shrugged and her face was for once mask-like. It was most unlike her.

'Is someone going to die?' I asked.

'You know I would not tell you even if someone was.'

'No. You would just leave me to find the bodies, like on Masara.'

'You are still angry about that, I see.'

It was difficult to keep the anger out of my voice, even with this very dangerous woman, who could read me all too easily. 'You killed two officers in Macharius's guard.'

'They were in the pay of the Autocrat of Absalom,' she said. 'They felt they had been overlooked for promotion and that their honour had been insulted.'

'I know. We found convincing evidence of that afterwards. Very convincing.'

'Too convincing is what you were going to say, Leo.' She held my gaze steadily.

'Can there be such a thing as evidence that is too convincing?' I said.

'Sometimes things need to be spelled out in such a way as there is absolutely no doubt. Particularly when the criminals are well connected, with relatives who have considerable influence in the high councils of humanity.'

'This was spelled out in such a way that a child could have no doubts about it. Diaries, journals, letters, decrypted communications protocols, all pointing in only one direction.'

'All of them authentic,' she said. I rose from the bed and turned my back to her. If she was going to kill me I would not have been able to stop her anyway, and I did not want her to be able to look at my face and read my expression.

'I can read the tension patterns of the muscle groups in your back as easily as I can read your facial expressions, Leo,' she said, as if she knew what I were thinking, which I suppose she did. 'It is one of the things I was trained to do.'

'What is going on?' I asked, turning to face her again.

'I am here to be certain things go as they should with Macharius.'

'He is still alive and the crusade rolls on,' I said.

'There are those who want him dead,' she said.

'Heretics have tried to kill him before. He is still here.'

'It's not just heretics, Leo. There are those in the Administratum who wish to see him fail.'

'Why would they want that? He has added more worlds to the Imperium than any man since the time of the Emperor.'

'Precisely because that is so.'

'What?' I turned to look at her.

'Powerful men make powerful enemies, Leo, and Macharius is the most powerful man in the galaxy at the moment, with the exception of the one who sits in the Golden Throne on Terra.' Her voice was flat but still she managed to communicate a surprising amount of reverence when she mentioned the occupant of the Throne. 'There are some who fear what he might do with that power, now that he has accumulated so much of it.'

'Macharius is a loyal servant of the Emperor,' I said.

She shook her head almost pityingly. Her voice was very soft. 'Leo, Leo, Leo.'

'He is.'

'I do not doubt it for a moment, but it is not me he has to convince. Macharius makes enemies just by being who he is. He demands efficiencies in the supply chain for his armies, that arms and supplies appear where they should when they should and with the minimum of spoilage.'

'What is wrong with that? It is merely sound generalship.'

'The wealth of merchant dynasties has been built on making sure those supply chains are not efficient. What Macharius sees as inefficiency, powerful men see as sources of revenue.'

'Powerful, corrupt men,' I said.

'I do not disagree. The word to place the emphasis on is powerful, with money to spend and friends in high places. And Macharius is giving even the High Lords reasons to mistrust him.'

'Really?'

'He has been reaching out to the Adeptus Astartes in subtle ways. That is not something the Imperium encourages in its generals. It likes its various military arms to be separate.'

I thought about the Fist and the potential uses Macharius might have for it, and all the time I was aware of Anna studying me. Doubtless she was learning one of the things she had come to learn. 'Why are you telling me this?'

'Because you are part of his bodyguard, and you will be in the line of fire when his enemies move against him.'

'They would be foolish to do that if he is as powerful as you say. He could crush them with ease.'

'He would be fighting with shadows. Macharius has one sort of power, they have another.'

'I think you will find that Macharius is adept at all the uses of power.'

'No doubt, but so are his enemies. It may be possible for them to find those among Macharius's followers who would replace him. They have armies too, great warlords whose soldiers are loyal unto them.'

'They would never turn against Macharius.'

'The same was once said of the Emperor himself. His greatest generals rebelled against him.'

'That is close to blasphemy, Anna.'

'Have I shocked you, Leo? Are you going to report me to the inquisitor?' Her smile was mocking.

'You already know the answer.'

'I could report you for not doing so.'

'There are many things you could have reported me for. You have yet to do so.'

Her smile turned pleasant. 'I am serious, Leo. Some of Macharius's own generals will be encouraged to plot against him. Perhaps it is already happening.'

'Why would they do that?'

'You are not so naive, Leo. You have seen some of these men up close. They are great generals in their own right. They too wish to write their names in the Imperial histories. Right now, they are merely moons reflecting Macharius's solar glory. If Macharius were gone…'

She let the words hang in the air and I could see she really was serious.

'You want me to tell him this.'

'He already knows. Macharius is not a stupid man, and as you have pointed out he understands the uses of all kinds of power. He also understands men who are motivated by glory. How could he not? He is first among them.'

'I sometimes think you do not like the Lord High Commander.'

'It does not matter whether I like him, Leo. It matters whether I serve him.'

She was a woman with a very firm grasp on what was important, was Anna, and had a gift for the precise use of words, as I was to find out.

'I do like him,' I said. I was surprised to hear myself saying that.

'It is in your self-interest to,' she said.

'I would like him anyway, even if it were not.'

'You have an unswerving loyalty, you and your friends, I envy you that.'

'And you don't?'

'I am loyal only to the Emperor.' She said this very distinctly, as if giving a fair warning.

'Does He give you His orders directly?'

'I am loyal to what he represents.' We were looking at each other warily now. I was not quite sure why she was telling me this. Perhaps she wanted me to understand finally at the end of things, and perhaps I did when it came. 'You are too.'

And then as sudden as a summer squall on the sea of storms, her mood changed. 'Do you remember Xenophon?'

I nodded.

'I remember the islands and the beaches,' I said. It blazed in my memory, bright with sunshine. I remembered giving her some seashells I had collected. They were polished to a sheen by the action of wave and sand. I wondered whether she still had them or whether they had been dumped along with all the other detritus of her life when she travelled.

'Me too,' she said. 'I was happy there.'

She said it as if happiness were a concept that she did not quite understand, a strange intrusion from somewhere alien, a wonder which she still needed to try and grasp.

'You will be guarding Macharius during his triumphal procession?' she said.

'Yes.'

'Be very careful, Leo,' she said. 'I would hate to see any harm come to you.'

I looked at her. I almost reached out but she was already in motion, rising from the bed, garbing herself in her robe. She dressed with grace and speed and no wasted effort, but when she stopped she was suddenly as clumsy as anyone else, wearing normality as a disguise, hiding what she was by pretending to be one of us, pretending to be only human.

She was good at that, as she was at anything she put her mind to. What she was best at was deception.

CHAPTER NINE

'As ever, Helicon Blight is at your service, your excellency,' the rogue trader said as he bowed to Macharius. I studied him closely. He was a tall, sparelooking man with a lined, sunburned face, craggy features and a sprinkle of grey in his hair. His clothing was of the finest fabrics, but it was not local manufacture. It was from some distant system still far outside the scope of the crusade, a reminder that not so long ago these worlds had been outwith the remit of the Imperium, and that we were still very close to the new frontier. Rogue traders were among the few citizens licensed to trade beyond its borders. They had other reasons for existing as well.

I knew Blight for an ambitious man and a spy. I had seen him reporting to Macharius in private on multiple occasions over the past decade, whenever he returned from one of his trading trips. His eyes were like chips of blue ice, and they stayed focused totally on Macharius as if they could divine the future by the study of the expression on his face.

'Can you help me, Blight?' Macharius asked. There was no sign of the eagerness he had shown about this matter in his discussions with Drake. He was once again a cold, calm Imperial general. 'I wish very much to return to Procrastes and free its inhabitants from the scourge of these xenos.'

'From what you have told me, it is a tricky passage, Lord High Commander,' said Helicon Blight. 'The fact that Admiral Kellerman flatly refuses to order his fleet to do as you have requested confirms that.'

Behind him, through a vast crystal dome, I caught sight of the blue shimmering orb of Emperor's Glory. Blight sat in an ornate throne. He smoked some char-weed from a hookah. It was no way to greet an Imperial commander, but here on his own ship Blight was ranking and perhaps he wanted to make the point. Macharius did not seem in the slightest bit disturbed. 'The Procrastes system is between two of the great warp storms and there are constant chronal flux streams emerging from there that can easily pull a ship off course. As you have found out to your cost.'

Macharius raised an eyebrow. The merchant prince said, 'I am not haggling, Lord High Commander, nor telling you how difficult it is just to raise my fee. You know I am your man and would do this for nothing. I am telling you the way the thing truly lies.'

'Difficult then, not impossible,' said Macharius.

Blight took a puff on his hookah and offered the

mouthpiece to Macharius. The general accepted it.

'Exactly so. With a sufficiently skilled Navigator we could make the passage, although I am not sure I would advise you to risk it. If I may be so bold, commission me to acquire what you seek and I will return with it or die in the attempt. My life is far less valuable to the Imperium than yours.'

'I have already made up my mind that I must personally supervise this operation.'

Blight shrugged as though the matter were settled. 'I would advise you to speak to Raymond Belisarius then. His kinswoman Zarah is in port now and is the most skilled Navigator in the sector. She also has some experience with those warp currents.'

'You do not feel your own Navigators could handle the matter? The less people who know of this the better.'

'I have every confidence in my people, but in cases such as this, with yourself as super-cargo, I would want the very best. Why risk anything else? Of course, it would cost the ransom of a planetary governor to hire her away from her present job.'

'I have the ransom of a thousand planetary governors,' said Macharius. 'Such questions are immaterial.'

'Very good then, sire. I will open negotiations with House Belisarius.'

'I wish to meet with them myself when you have concluded your arrangements.'

'That too can be arranged,' said Blight. 'Anything can, for a price.'

'I will meet any price that is likely to be asked,' said Macharius.

'I do not doubt it, your excellency,' said Blight. 'I do not doubt it at all.'

There was something strange about being in the presence of a Navigator. The strangeness was magnified when there was two of them, but that was not what held all of our attentions. It was the man who was with them, standing immobile as a statue behind their thrones.

He was tall, taller by far even than Macharius, and very broad. His ceramite armour made him seem broader still. His eyes had a peculiar canine quality in the way they reflected the light. Long whiskers drooped from his lips, huge sideburns concealed half his face. In his hands he held a bolter I would have struggled to lift. For all the life he showed, he might well have been a statue, but you just knew that he could come explosively to life and kill everything in the room if he chose to. This was one of the Wolfblades, one of the legendary wardens of House Belisarius provided by the Space Wolves Chapter of the Adeptus Astartes. He was bodyguard to the Navigators just as I was to Macharius, but on his own he was probably a match for the score of us.

Raymond Belisarius was a thin man, with a long face and cold, watchful eyes. He had a scarf wrapped around his forehead that bore the sign of his House. It hid the mutated third eye that was the mark of the Navigator and which in his case was said to be hideous beyond belief. According to the dossiers, he was some sort of cripple as far as his House was concerned. His third eye did not function as it was supposed to and let him guide ships through the perils of the warp. Instead, he had other gifts: a tremendous understanding of the workings of finance and trade, and an astonishing insight into the corrupt workings of the human heart. He was not only in charge of his House's business out here with the crusade, he was their spymaster and their chief merchant.

Like Blight, he had previously had dealings with Macharius. I had known the two of them to hunt together in the Great Dome in the palace. There were always times when they were apart from others and no one could overhear their discussions. Looking at the Wolfblade and knowing what I now did, I was beginning to have my suspicions about those talks.

Zarah Belisarius was a lovely, ethereal woman, who did not appear to be much older than twenty, although she was at least ten times that. Her face was that of a tranquil saint, her form willowy rather than full. She studied Macharius in a way that showed a good deal of interest. I supposed he was used to it, being who he was and all.

'Helicon Blight has told us of your request,' said Raymond. His speech was formal and seemed entirely for the benefit of his cousin. I wondered how much the other members of his House knew about his dealings with Macharius. 'He has not told us why you wish to go to this dangerous place.'

'That is my business,' said Macharius. 'I am willing to pay a good deal of money to see that it stays that way.'

The Navigator nodded as though he understood. He ran one long, narrow finger along his thin lower lip then touched the dimple on his upper lip. 'It is not just a question of money, it is a question of risk,' he said. 'We need to know what we may encounter when we get there in order to best decide whether to attempt it.'

Macharius looked at him, looked at the Wolfblade and then at Zarah. He smiled his most charming smile. 'You know as much about the Procrastes system as I. I have given you the information we have. I wish to free those under the xenos yoke and return them to the Emperor's Light. I will also avenge the insult of their attack on my ship. They stole something of great value to me and perhaps to people I wish to befriend.' A flick of his eyes indicated the Wolfblade.

I was not surprised at how circumspect Macharius was being. Navigators had their own culture going back past the dawn of the Imperium, and Belisarius was one of the oldest of their Houses. They also had connections with the Space Wolves Chapter of the Adeptus Astartes dating back to the Great Crusade. 'Are you interested, or should I take my business elsewhere?' Macharius said.

'Lord High Commander, it is up to my kinswoman. She may decide whether she wishes to take the contract or not.' He looked at Zarah. She looked at Macharius.

'I have some business to conclude here, and if I must break contract with my present employers then penalty clauses will be invoked and compensation called for.'

'I will cover those,' said Macharius.

'Those will be at a premium, when the reasons are known,' said Raymond.

'Perhaps it would be best if the reasons were not public knowledge then,' said Macharius. 'Our association has been mutually beneficial in the past, and it would be wise on both our parts to ensure that it continues to be so.'

Macharius was giving a polite warning not to try extorting too much.

'It shall be as you say, Lord High Commander.'

'Good,' said Macharius. 'When can we expect to depart?'

Raymond looked at Zarah. She said, 'One standard week if Helicon Blight's ship is ready.'

'Very good,' said Macharius. 'It means I have time to conduct business with my commanders.'

I could tell he was disappointed, though. He had wanted to depart immediately if he could.

CHAPTER TEN

The day was warm. The sun was shining, as it always was on Emperor's Glory, bringing another perfect day to a perfect world. The only things that looked out of place were the grim gunships standing on the plascrete of the space-field and the countless smaller commercial vessels coming and going.

Macharius stood on the landing ground. Inquisitor Drake was with him. They watched as enormous ramps were attached to the side of a massive military shuttle. They talked constantly, scoring points off each other with gusto. They were both clever men with strong views, and I think they saw such contests as a challenge, the way some people play regicide or spar against each other with wooden swords.

I listened to them as I watched our surroundings for

threats. 'You need to be more tolerant of the failings of the Administratum,' Drake said. 'It is a great machine. It works very slowly, but it works.'

'My men's lives depend on getting the right supplies in the right place at the right time,' said Macharius. 'All armies depend on this as much as the courage and faith of our soldiers.'

'I would not presume to contradict you on such things,' said Drake. 'You know far more about them than I do.'

'On the other hand...' Macharius said. He knew that the inquisitor deferred to him only to set up another point.

'On the other hand, I do know about the way the Imperium is ruled. You cannot make demands of the people you make demands of. You cannot threaten them the way you do. You cannot execute them for failing to meet your expectations. You must make them your allies.'

'So my men must go without ammunition so some contractor can grow rich from graft? My tanks must go without fuel because of the incompetence of some placeman, whose relatives just happen to be high in the Administratum?'

'Some would say your generals grow rich from the plunder of worlds,' Drake said mildly. The fact that he could say such a thing while standing with Macharius and awaiting Sejanus said a lot about his power, his confidence and his familiarity with the general.

'They have earned what they take with their blood and their courage.'

'With the blood of the Emperor's soldiers and the courage of the Emperor's faithful,' countered Drake. 'Not to mention the products of the Emperor's temple-factories and the wealth of the Emperor's worlds.'

'The Imperium gets its rightful tithe. The soldiers share in the spoils of victory.'

'That is not the point,' Drake said.

'Then what is?' Macharius countered.

'Corruption is just a point of view. I could, if I chose to, see it in the way your generals dispose of the spoils of victory. Any fair-minded observer could. You choose to see it only where it works against you.'

'I see it where it is.'

'No doubt. And no doubt you are correct. How do you think your generals would feel if you purged them for taking the spoils you had previously awarded them?'

'You are surely not trying to make a comparison between my generals and corrupt administrators?'

'You have not answered my question,' said Drake. 'Would your generals support you with such enthusiasm? Would they perhaps think they were being persecuted unfairly?'

'Would you stop asking rhetorical questions?' Macharius's voice was mocking, and he mimicked the inquisitor's tone with uncanny precision.

'Obviously they would not,' said Drake, not in the least affected. 'They would be upset. They would think it unfair if you changed the rules so late in the game.'

'We are playing a game now, are we?'

'A very serious one, as you well know, Lord High Commander.'

'Ah, you use my title, that must mean you are getting

ready to slide the blade into my ribs. Metaphorically speaking, of course.'

Drake just looked at him.

'You were about to slowly and painfully belabour your point,' Macharius said. He was smiling, bringing the full force of his charm to bear to take the sting out of his words.

'My point is a very simple one. The men you blame for the corruption are just doing the things that have always been done. They did not set up the system. They grew up with it. They are merely doing what their fathers did before them and their grandfathers before that, and on and on, back perhaps to the time when the Emperor was first immured within his Throne.'

'So I am to forgive them their incompetence and corruption because their fathers and grandfathers were incompetent and corrupt too?'

Drake sighed, a theatrical display of patience. 'No, but you should accept that they are only doing what everyone else does and has always done. You are making enemies you don't need. The people you call corrupt think you are changing the rules simply to suit yourself. They think you are stripping them of their livelihoods and prerogatives for your own self-aggrandisement. They see you reassigning their rights to your own people and think you are worse than they are. They think you are the corrupt one and that you are taking what is theirs.'

'They are wrong.'

'From your point of view that is correct. From theirs...'

'You're saying I should just accept their corruption?'

Macharius sounded a little annoyed now, which was rare for him.

'You should accept the reality we live in. You are making enemies, Macharius, where you don't need to. You sow dragon's teeth where you could be making friends and allies. Provoke those people enough and they will destroy you. They have power.'

'So do I.'

'Yes. At the moment. At this moment you are most likely the most powerful man on the face of creation. You might not always be. Then you will need allies, all the allies you can get. A man who has risen so high has so much further to fall.'

'That sounded almost like a threat,' said Macharius.

'A word of advice is all,' said Drake.

The great lock of the military shuttle slid open with a hiss of equalising air pressure. Wisps of mist rose as the internal atmosphere mingled with that of Emperor's Glory.

A large, stocky figure stood framed in the exit. He raised both his arms in greeting and strode down to meet Macharius. General Sejanus had arrived.

He was a broad, powerful man. His hair was starting to fall out and was combed over. His moustache was even more luxuriant than it had been when I first met him, as were his sideburns. His face was red. His nose was snub. He carried himself with a jaunty air, but you did not doubt for a moment that he could be ferocious when called upon to be so. I had the opportunity to fight alongside him on many occasions and I knew what a deadly combatant he could be.

He walked forward on his own, unaccompanied by any troops or bodyguards. They had all been told to wait within the craft until he had greeted Macharius.

'General Macharius,' he bellowed, and then he laughed. 'And who is that tall, skinny bastard I see with you? Surely it can't be the famous High Inquisitor Drake?'

He embraced Macharius, then the inquisitor, with a startling lack of formality in an officer so senior. He pushed Macharius back to arm's length and held him there in a vice-like grip. Macharius smiled, seemingly as pleased to see Sejanus as Sejanus was to see him. They had been friends and allies for a very long time, since before either of them became famous.

Drake ignored this blast of bonhomie. 'You look well,' he said.

'I can't complain. This one…' he tapped Macharius on the arm with a familiarity few others would have managed, 'keeps me busy, running all over the sector, crushing insurgents here, smashing xenos there. What are you doing here? I cannot believe it is merely to greet me?' The question was as sudden, slashing and direct as one of the campaigns for which he was so famous.

'Apparently he has decided to lecture me on the futility of trying to weed out corruption,' said Macharius. He made a slight warning hand signal with his left hand. Obviously this was not the place to be discussing anything secret. If Sejanus noticed it he gave no sign, but in his way he was just as skilled at maintaining a front as Macharius.

'The administrators count the loot, whine that the Imperium is not getting enough and carry tales back to the toads in the heart worlds, you mean,' said Sejanus. 'They line their own pockets while they do so as well, I expect.'

'I see time and distance have not blunted your pretence of bluff honesty,' said Drake. He did not sound offended. He sounded like an adult listening to the banter of children, faintly amused and a little weary. 'I have often admired the perfection of the act.'

Sejanus reached out and slapped him on the back. The impact was as loud as the snap of gunfire. Drake winced.

'It is good to have you back, Sejanus,' said Macharius. Clearly he was not going to discuss anything important here and now. 'I read your dispatches from the front with interest.'

'Glad you enjoyed them,' said Sejanus. 'Dictated them to my secretary while I was storming a heretic citadel. I trust I made myself look good enough to justify some new decorations?'

'You appeared profoundly heroic,' said Macharius.

'Good. My scribe is doing his job then. I should hope so too. I pay the man enough.' He shot a look at Drake. 'You still writing those reports of yours?'

'I confess I am,' said the inquisitor. 'And I fully intend to write one about this section of our glorious crusade.'

'Just remember to make me look like a hero then,' said Sejanus.

'I shall make you look exactly like you are,' said Drake with some satisfaction.

'I can see I am going to need to write my own memoirs, to make sure my true heroism is revealed then,' said Sejanus. He obviously understood as well. He was a lot sharper than he chose to appear.

'So the Imperium is getting restless about our conquests, and Drake is getting nervous,' said Sejanus. He lounged at his ease in a great overstuffed leather armchair and stared around with considerable appreciation at the furnishings of Macharius's apartments.

There was a lot to appreciate: intricate statues from Silate of Xen showing soldiers in uniforms that were out of fashion when the Emperor had walked among men, three-dimensional holo-paintings of battle scenes depicting Macharius winning his victories on a hundred worlds. I recognised myself in a few of them, an ordinary enough looking face staring out in suspicion and fear, a uniformed man with a shotgun clutched in his hands. The strange thought occurred to me that folk would be looking upon these paintings and seeing me in a thousand years, just as I had looked upon men long dead depicted in paintings in the Museum of Chalcedony Angels on Husk.

'He thinks I am moving too fast. There is intrigue with the local nobles and governors. The Navy is being uncooperative. The Administratum is becoming suspicious.'

Sejanus lifted his glass of brandy and swirled it. 'So we can expect a swirl of intrigue and assassinations.'

'We've always had that. We can just expect it to intensify.' There was silence for a moment, then Macharius spoke.

'How did it go with the Adeptus Astartes?'

I kept my face bland. I could not keep the shock from my face at his next statement, though.

'House Belisarius came through. They are interested,' said Sejanus. 'Representatives will be arriving soon.'

'Good. It would be good if they arrived as spectacularly as possible. It will give the spies something interesting to report back to the High Lords.'

Macharius looked at me. 'You may want to close your mouth now, Lemuel. You look as if you are trying to catch flies in it.'

'You sure he said that?' Anton asked. He sounded as excited as a child who had been told he would get glowberry cake for his Name Day. 'You sure he said the Adeptus Astartes?'

'As certain as I am that I am talking to an idiot,' I said.

'You shouldn't speak about Ivan like that.'

We were on the roof. It was night. The cold stars glittered overhead. Macharius had summoned a new contingent of guards and dismissed me. I looked down. Below us I could see the great geodesic jungle dome Macharius had built for his private hunting parties. Ivan unzipped his fly and pissed down on it. 'Only rain those poor creatures will see on this world,' he said, as if that explained everything. The metal half of his face was unreadable as always, but when he turned his head I could see the human side was frowning.

'What's on your mind?' I asked.

'Macharius and Sejanus would not talk about this in front

of the inquisitor but would in front of you,' he said. 'It doesn't add up.'

'You've developed a nasty, suspicious mind,' I said.

'It comes from having hung around with all these officers and nobles for the past ten years,' said Ivan. 'And from not being stupid.'

'Anton has enough of that for all three of us,' I said.

'He must know you would tell us and maybe even your fancy woman,' Ivan said. I considered the thing, turning it over in my mind. I had not needed to tell Anna. She had already known. So had a lot of other people it seemed. 'Yes.'

'And if you tell us, he must know that Anton will tell his highborn bint.'

'She's not a bint,' Anton said. 'She's a lady.'

'You think he wants word to get out?' I said.

'That he's negotiating in secret with the Space Marines?'

'Did he say which Chapter?' Anton asked. He was still excited by the prospect of Space Marines.

'Yes, Anton,' I said. 'He drew me pictures of their captains as well. In crayon.'

'Can I see them?'

Anton was mocking me now, turning my assumption of his stupidity around on me. I walked over to the edge and took a leak myself. The stream of piss became invisible a long way before it hit the dome. It was a long way to fall. I thought about what Drake had said to Macharius.

'You think it's going to happen then?' Ivan asked.

'I think Sejanus was sent on a secret mission to contact the Adeptus Astartes. That's what all of those private chats with

Belisarius in the past were about. His House has connections with the Adeptus Astartes.'

'It'll be the Space Wolves, then,' said Anton. 'That's who it will be.'

'Most likely, Anton,' I said.

'Why? It's not like Macharius. He avoids contact with the Space Marines if he can. They are the only men in the known galaxy who can steal his thunder.'

'He doesn't tell me these things,' I said. 'I am guessing it's because he must feel he needs their help.'

'Since when has Macharius ever needed anybody's help?'

'Since now I guess.' It was a troubling thought. Macharius was not a man who sought aid from anyone. He was always utterly confident in his own ability to deal with any contingency. That he was reaching out to the Emperor's Angels told us that something deeply worrying was going on.

'Maybe he's looking for allies against the Administratum,' Ivan said. 'Maybe he has his eyes on something bigger.'

'That sounds dangerously like treason, Ivan.'

He answered obliquely. 'You know the Space Marines will intervene when and where they like. They always do. Maybe he just wants to make sure they see him in the right light.'

'What could Macharius offer Space Marines?' Anton asked.

It was a good question. The Chapters of the Adeptus Astartes already had everything they needed. I thought about the Fist and Macharius's anger at its loss. 'I think he wanted to make them a gift of the artefact we picked up on Demetrius.'

'It would explain why he was so worked up about it going

missing. I've never seen him so annoyed about anything.'
Somehow Ivan's metal features looked thoughtful. It was
something about the eyes.

'I thought generals like Macharius were not supposed
to have anything to do with Space Marines. Separation of
powers?' Anton said.

I imagined what would happen when the lords of the
Administratum found out about this, as they surely would
if they had not already. I had not spent ten years watching
Macharius manoeuvre without learning something about
Imperial politics.

'You ever feel like you have just got into a pool full of
piranha-gators? You just don't know how many or where
they are?' Ivan said. 'I'm starting to feel that way.'

I knew what he meant.

'Well,' said Ivan. 'It's getting late, and we've got duty
tomorrow. It's the triumph, you know.'

'As if we could forget.'

CHAPTER ELEVEN

The day of Macharius's triumph dawned.

The crowds roared. Flower petals, paper aquilas and prayer scrolls rained down around us, turning the platform on top of the Baneblade into an altar for the people's offerings to Macharius. They greeted him like a prophet as well as a conqueror, and I wondered how many were starting to believe the rumours we had been hearing ever since we had returned to Emperor's Glory: that Macharius was a saint made invincible by the Emperor's Light and Blessing, fated to reunite humanity under the rule of the Golden Throne.

If ever a man looked the part, it was Macharius that day. Tall and youthful-looking and golden, even though he was old enough to be the grandfather of most of those in the crowd. A wreath of gilded laurel was wound into his hair. His burnished chestplate glittered gold in the sunlight. He looked like he had just stepped out of one of those religious paintings in the cathedral.

Even I would not have been surprised at that moment to see a halo appear around his head. He basked in the adulation of the masses and it seemed to feed something in him. He glowed with enthusiasm and righteous joy. He raised his right hand and waved to the crowd with utter confidence. He smiled with ruthless charm. No sign of the anger and impatience that had been eating away at him since our return from Demetrius showed.

Around the Baneblade, cyber-cherubim fluttered, carrying the portable vision altars that would record this event for posterity and see it broadcast across the world and beyond. Imprints would be dispatched to every army in the field. Remembering my conversation with Anna, I could not help but imagine the gnashing of teeth among the field commanders. There would be those among them who would look upon this triumph with envy and see it as a right that Macharius's mere presence had denied them. More and more of them were coming into the system for a great conclave. Some of them were in orbit above us, even now.

I kept my hand clutched tight on my shotgun and glanced around to make sure that Anton and Ivan and the others were equally alert.

I was in no fit state of mind for triumphal marches. I saw the use of the Baneblade for something other than the crushing of the Emperor's enemies as mildly sacrilegious. I looked out at the crowd and every face seemed that of a potential assassin. I scanned every balcony for snipers.

Every time something glittered in a window above me, I made ready to throw myself forward and knock Macharius down and out of line of sight.

The Avenue of the Emperor was lined with statues of Imperial heroes and saints. It led all the way to the Cathedral of the Emperor's Glory. New stone and plascrete images of Macharius arose on every intersection. Some of them were merely relics of former idols, so old that people had forgotten who they were. They were being resculpted in the image of today's hero. Some of them were new and rose gigantically above us, largest of all, dwarfing the statues around them as the achievements of Macharius dwarfed those of his precursors.

The workmen's platforms were still in place. Normally they would have been filled with labourers plastering and painting and chipping away with chisels or working gold filigree into the statues, but today they were filled with cheering, red-faced people, waving scarves and banners, throwing offerings, chanting the name of Macharius. Perhaps it was the same workmen in their feast day finery, for a planetary holiday had been declared to celebrate the triumph.

The crowd's cries blended together until they filled the air with their vibration. I could feel it rumble in my chest in the same way as I could the vibration of the tank's drives beneath my feet. I must confess that gave me a certain nostalgia for older and simpler days, when Ivan and Anton and the Undertaker had merely been part of the crew of a Baneblade. It made me remember Oily and the lieutenant and

Corporal Hesse and the New Boy and Snake, and all the others who had died along the march to this triumph. The thought did not make my mood any less sour.

Something flashed on a platform above us. I looked up startled, but it was just a man raising a silver drinking flask to his lips and catching the reflected light of the sun. I told myself to relax, that no one wanted to kill Macharius, that these people loved him, for leading the crusade, for returning their world to the Emperor's Light, for restoring the stability and certainty of Imperial rule.

Anna's words wriggled into my mind again. I thought of all the nobles who had ruled this world and the surrounding systems before the Imperium came. How did they really feel about their privileges being usurped, their absolute authority being denied? There had been those who fought to the death against it. There had been others who surrendered reluctantly. There had been others who had been only too willing to embrace the new order that Macharius had brought. Who could tell what was going on behind the smiling masks of their faces?

All of the nobles on all of these worlds were schemers. It was what they did, who they were. Their families had remained in power for millennia because of that. They had been born into a world where they plotted before they were torn from their mother's breasts. They probably conspired against the other babies in the creche to get a bigger share of the milk. Some of them had aligned themselves with Macharius because they had seen which way the wind was blowing, where temporary advantage was to be seized. They might jump the other way if circumstances changed. Things were still fluid. How could they not be?

Macharius had brought more worlds into the Imperium than any man since the time of the Emperor. A new order was being born out here on the edge of the galaxy. Macharius had within his disposal entire systems and subsectors to grant as fiefs, the sort of rewards that made a few inconvenient deaths a negligible consideration for most nobles. I began to understand, to truly understand, what Anna had been getting at.

The seeds of an empire were all here. It would not have been the first time that an Imperial commander had set himself up as an absolute ruler, had splintered away from the Imperium. Such things had been one of the causes of the Great Schism, which Macharius had set himself to mend. From listening to him I understood that the reins of empire were the last thing Macharius intended to seize, but if I was an Imperial bureaucrat lolling in my palace in the distant heart worlds would I believe that? Would I assume that Macharius would not do what I myself would?

And, what if Macharius were lying? He did not confide in me. He did not confide in Drake. He did not confide in anyone, really. He kept his own council. What if all of this was an act? That his charming visage hid a ruthless will and the talent of a master manipulator, I already knew. I had seen plenty of evidence for it. He might be merely biding his time until he had consolidated his rule and then…

I looked at the cheering crowd. I thought of the planetary audience, of those cherubim focusing the mechanical eyes of recorded history on this spot. I thought of the gigantic war machine rumbling across the stars at his command. I thought of the sheer power that Macharius had within his grip. What man would not be changed by such things? It would be inevitable that he came to take such things as his due, to believe himself worthy of adulation and of worship.

I told myself that it did not really matter to me. It was not my role in life to worry about such things. I was just a bodyguard to the Lord High Commander. It was my job to see that his enemies did not kill him, nothing more.

I scanned the crowd looking for threats. I saw nothing. I felt they were there, nonetheless. Macharius waved, eyes unreadable above the glittering smile.

The Baneblade approached the steps of the cathedral. Barriers kept back the press of the crowd, preventing them from being crushed to jelly beneath our tracks. A signal was given, the massive tank rumbled to a halt. Behind us, the line of garlanded vehicles pulled to a halt. Overhead the Valkyries and Vulture gunships soared by.

Under normal circumstances Macharius would simply have leapt down from the side of the vehicle. I had seen him do it before with the casual athleticism of the supremely fit man. Not today, though. A long ramp with a banister of moulded metal angels was wheeled into place. Macharius stepped forward, waved to the crowd and strode down. The rest of us were right behind him. A contingent of his bodyguard, who had been waiting at the foot of the steps, moved to meet him. They were accompanied by a delegation that consisted of the archprelate of the cathedral and his entourage. The clerics smiled unctuously, only too pleased to be taking part in this ceremony and come to the notice of the great man.

Macharius moved to greet them like long-lost comrades. I scanned the faces in the crowds behind the barriers. They were not the same locals we had seen in the streets and on the balconies of hab-blocks. They were garbed with the elaborate formality of the nobility, wearing the richest sparkle-cloths, shimmering with wealth and good health. I reminded myself that these were still relatively minor functionaries. They had only managed to cajole and bribe a place on the steps. The truly influential would be within the cathedral, waiting to see Macharius invested with his honours and to listen to his speech of triumph.

I caught one man staring at me with hot-black eyes that seemed full of hatred. I gave him my most annoying grin, for it was obvious he envied me my place at Macharius's side. Doubtless he was thinking of the use to which he could put the influence granted by being so close to the general's presence. I almost smiled at the irony that a slum boy from Belial should be on the general's side of the barrier and a wealthy nobleman should be on the other. In another time or place our positions would not even have been reversed. I would have been one of those hanging from the statues outside. Then again, that's the thing about events like a crusade; they disrupt the ordered nature of the universe.

We moved up the steps to the arched entrance of the cathedral. The face of some local saint looked down on us from the stonework. I took another glance around. Part of me was glad to get Macharius out from under the sky. There were too many places for snipers to lurk. Part of me was worried. The entrance to the cathedral would be a good choke point for an ambush, and the press of bodies we would soon be moving through could easily hide a killer whose concealed weapon security checks had missed.

As if to confirm my suspicions, someone rushed out from the crowd. They had managed to force their way through the barrier or perhaps be lifted over. I moved to interpose myself between her and Macharius, shotgun held at waist height pointed directly at her. If I pulled the trigger, I would spray half the high notables of the planet behind her with her blood and entrails.

The girl was beautiful and beautifully dressed, long blonde hair, hanging almost to her waist, her face transformed by a look of ecstatic adoration, a garland of flowers held outstretched in her hand like an offering.

'Stop,' I told her. She did not seem to notice the shotgun in my hands. Her eyes were focused on something behind me with a look of religious fervour. She took another step forward. 'Stop or I will shoot.'

I was shouting, but I was not sure she could hear me over the roar of the crowd and the rumble of engines. I did not take my eyes off her. She did not look particularly threatening but then she might have been chosen for that reason.

I felt a hand on my shoulder but I didn't look away. Macharius's voice said in my ear, 'Stand down, Lemuel. She is no threat.'

'She might be an assassin, sir,' I bellowed.

The girl might not have been able to hear me but Macharius's keen senses had no trouble. 'Stand down. That is an order. She is no danger to me.'

I considered disobeying him, but only for a moment. If the girl was an assassin and she killed Macharius, no one would be interested in the fact that Macharius had ordered me to let her by. I would be for the high jump and no mistake. On the other hand, it was Macharius giving the order and he was not a man you disobeyed. I let my shotgun point to the ground and stepped to one side. My eyes never left the girl.

She approached him like one overcome by a mixture of awe and desire. Her mouth was slightly open, she licked her lips with a small pink tongue and her eyes were fixed on Macharius. He bent his head forward as she placed the wreath over his neck. He bowed and swept past, and only then, when the focus of attention had passed, did the rest of the security detail sweep forward, scoop her up and take her away. I did not doubt that she would spend some memorable hours being interrogated. Judging from her expression she would probably think it was worth it.

We passed through the arch of the cathedral, flanked by robed priests of the Imperial cult. The sudden silence was shocking, as was the cool of the shadowy interior after the heat outside. The roar of the crowd became a subdued murmur, cut off by sonic-deadener fields and the thick walls of the towering structure itself. It took my eyes a few panicked moments to adjust. It would have been the perfect time for an assassin to strike, while the guards were blinded by the transition from light to dark. It's how I would have done it myself.

The archprelate had laid an arm on Macharius's sleeve and guided him towards a curved flight of stairs leading up. I do not think he realised how close he came to being clubbed down by Anton and Ivan. They were both as nervous as me. Macharius smiled affably, as if he did not already know the way and was grateful to the archprelate for his guidance. Unlike the prelate, I knew that, since the hospice in Irongrad, Macharius had never entered a building without knowing the layout and how to get out. He never forgot any lesson the universe taught him.

I pushed on ahead, accompanied by the Undertaker. He moved grimly and silently, pushing slightly in front of Macharius on the stairs as they wound upwards, just far enough that no one could get a clear shot at the general around the curve. The stairs had already been scoured by internal security and by Drake's people. We were taking the stairs rather than the archprelate's private elevator because such devices could all too easily become death traps.

We came at last to the great balcony above the cathedral arch. The way was already open, and security men guarded the entrance. I looked at them closely, making sure I recognised their faces. We gave the handsign recognition codes and they responded correctly. I looked at the Undertaker and he nodded, and we stepped out through the curtain fields of silence.

A huge wave of sound passed over us, so loud it seemed

almost deadening. The crowd roared, mistaking the Undertaker, in his uniform, for Macharius, which was the intention. An assassin might be tempted to take a shot at him. If it made the Undertaker nervous, he gave no sign.

We glanced around and saw only our own people on the balconies around the cathedral square. Ten thousand men of Macharius's personal guard were drawn up on the steps now and in the open space leading to it. On all the balconies were armed men in their uniforms. Ratling snipers had lashed themselves to gargoyles and surveyed the crowd through the telescopic sights of their long-barrelled rifles.

The Undertaker glanced at me to see if I had noticed anything he had not. I gave him the all-clear sign. He nodded and stepped back inside to the disappointment of the legions of adoring worshippers who had thought he was Macharius. I took up a position on one side of the entrance, beside a support pillar, partially obscured by one of the huge, draped flags. I could watch the crowd and Macharius's back from here.

Mechanicus cherubim fluttered around the balcony, perched overhead on the gargoyles, engaged in heated exchanges with some of the ratlings. Macharius stepped out onto the balcony. The roar that had greeted the Undertaker and myself was as nothing to the one that came now. The crowd were certain it was him this time and their shouts of adulation could have deafened a daemon on the noisiest floor of the most chaotic hell.

Someone made adjustments on a tech-altar. The noise-deadening fields kicked in. The roar became the background rumble of the sea heard from a beach. Macharius could now talk with his companions if he so wished. All of his attention was focused outwards, though.

CHAPTER TWELVE

Macharius stepped forward to the edge of the balcony and saluted the men of his own guard. They saluted back and, as if that were a signal, the real procession started.

Down the Avenue marched Titans, building-tall, humanoid in shape, the mightiest ground-based war machines ever built. Their void shields made the air around them shimmer. Flags fluttered on their shoulders. On the left were the banners of their legion. On the right, in honour of Macharius, was his personal banner, the lion's head. It was a tribute the Titan Legions rarely granted to mere mortal soldiers. The earth shook as the great war engines approached, and even the mighty roar of the crowd fell silent as they contemplated this evidence of the might of the Imperium. The heads of the Titans as they passed were at the same level as the balcony on which we stood. Their fierce gazes were turned to Macharius and they raised their weapons in salute.

At the exact moment they reached the front of the cathedral there was a sound of thunder from the sky above and thousands of twin-tailed Valkyrie gunships streaked into view, trailing streamers of green and gold smoke, painting the sky with Macharius's colours, leaving the world in no doubt that even the clouds were owned by his forces. They kept moving overhead as the long lines of troops moved down the Avenue.

It was only then that I began to appreciate the true scale of the triumph and exactly how much organisation had gone into making it a reality. I suppose it was understandable. The event was only superficially a celebration of the Imperium's greatest general. The reality was that it was a demonstration of Imperial might and purpose to all of those nobles who had been gathered from across the newly reconquered sector. No one was going to be left in any doubt that the Emperor's rule had returned. All of them would be aware that they were merely looking upon a trivial fraction of the army that moved out there among the stars. Of course, to anyone watching it did not seem trivial.

After the Titans marched the men of the Snow Raiders, Leman Russ tanks to the fore, followed by Chimera armoured personnel carriers and then a thousand selected men marching. They wore their tall white bearskin hats even in the warm weather, and the officers had donned white bearskin cloaks. As they passed the front of the cathedral, they turned with disciplined precision and saluted as one.

Every unit was to parade with just that sharpness today.

'They picked their best drill squads, I see,' murmured Anton from the place he had taken alongside me. He had his sniper rifle in his hand and held it ready. The Undertaker gave him a hard glance but Anton just continued to stand there. He looked nonchalant, as though he were considering lighting up a lho-stick. I would not have put it past him.

Next came the Calistan High Guard. They had mounted cavalrymen and hairless mammoths among their troops. The giant creatures had heavy weapons platforms strapped to their backs. They were notoriously temperamental beasts. One had run amok at the space port killing a hundred loaders only a few days back. I hoped the same thing was not repeated now. They passed without incident.

The Swordbearers of Stula followed. Tall men, garbed in kilts; their officers wore massive battle-blades strapped to their backs, bare-chested save for the leather straps of their scabbard harnesses. The men had bayonets affixed to their lasguns and twirled them in intricate patterns as they marched. Their officers all had shaved heads and long braided beards, and half of their faces were covered in tattoos of rank.

'That's just showing off,' said Anton. Even I was staring at him now. It was only a matter of time before one of the high muckety-mucks noticed him and took him to one side, for one of those conversations that you did not come back from.

The Boilermakers were next. No marching for them. They were a mechanised regiment. All of them were in tanks or

APCs, with the cog-wheel flag of their regiment flying above them. When you looked closely you could see that they were as kitted out with mechanical limbs and organs as Ivan, only in their case their best soldiers had volunteered to have their flesh replaced. They followed some obscure sect of the Machine-God back on their home world, or so I'd heard. 'No marching for those bastards,' said Ivan. He was a little quieter now, so perhaps the Undertaker's glares were having some effect.

It was almost a relief when the 444th Infantry marched past. Their uniforms were Cadian-style tunics in light grey. Their boots gleamed with black polish. Their helmets were spiked.

Next came the Seventh Belial, our old regiment from what seemed like a lifetime ago. They had Baneblades and Leman Russ and Chimeras. Some of them marched just to show they could. I felt almost nostalgic when I saw their grey tunics and rebreather masks. I wondered if we would ever see Belial again. Much to my surprise, Anton said nothing. He just stood there watching misty eyed as the representatives of more and more regiments trooped by.

On and on they came; unit after unit, company after company, all of them looking as smart as if they had just got their first uniforms, and marching with a precision that would have done their drill instructors proud.

Cadian Shock Troopers, in rebreather masks and tri-dome helmets, marched in advance of Darkstorm Fusiliers all in shadowcloaks. Tallarn Desert Raiders, heads swathed in scarves, bodies straight as ramrods, strode along behind bare-armed, tattooed Catachan Jungle Fighters.

After the first few score, other things started to be mingled in with the marching troops. Massive converted vehicle crawlers carried dioramas and symbols of the crusade's triumphs. In an enormous cage was a roaring bipedal gigantosaur from Paleon. It had been kept by the former governor and fed with his enemies in the arena. Macharius had ordered the governor and all his kin sent into the same arena armed with the sharpened sticks they had equipped their former captives with. It had been an edifying and horrific spectacle, but the watching nobles had got the point.

There was the Oracle-Machine, which had been worshipped as a god on Ibal. Men had thought it a remnant of the Dark Age of Technology and followed its pronouncements as if they had come from the Throne of the Emperor itself. Macharius had revealed it was nothing more than a hollowed out shell in which corrupt priests had hidden, making their announcements over a heavily modified vox system.

There were two gigantic xenos who looked like walking trees. They were the last remnants of the Viridar, a sentient jungle for which they had provided nodes of intelligence and communication. They had lost much of their greenish colouration, and I wondered how long they could survive so far from their home world. Their leaves looked brown and their bark-skins were starting to show a sickly white mould that did not look in the slightest bit natural. I had heard that their sap was hallucinogenic and that some of their captors had started tapping it and selling it on the black market.

There were prisoners in chains, of course, tens of thousands of them. They still wore the finery of nobles, but it had not been cleaned in weeks or perhaps months. They had not been allowed to bathe or shave. They looked gaunt and hollow-eyed and mad and desperate. They would be executed after the procession. These were nobles who had opposed Macharius and lost. I am sure the lesson there was not lost on the spectators.

On and on it rumbled, minute after minute, hour after hour. I half expected Macharius to be bored by it, but the smile never shifted from his face and he continued to look on with a mixture of pride and exultation. I suppose being worshipped as a god never grows tiring.

After long hours, the great procession finally ended. It was not because the crusade had run out of prisoners or victories to celebrate or soldiers to honour. There was simply too many of all three. It was because it was time for Macharius to move on to other things.

We stepped down from the balcony and entered the cathedral proper. The assembled planetary nobility greeted Macharius with applause. Some of them rose from the pews and reached out to try and touch the hem of his garments. Some of them he greeted affably, most of them we pushed none too gently back into place. Normally we would have been cuffed for it, common soldiers manhandling nobles, but not on this day and not in this place. We were Macharius's bodyguard and all the normal rules of protocol were suspended in the great man's presence.

Macharius took his place in the elevated area in front of

the altar and accepted the blessing of the archprelate under the gaze of the statues of saints. Some claim to have seen a halo around him then. All I saw were the altar lights playing around him, but I suppose if you looked at them from certain angles you might have seen a holy glow.

Then it was time to leave. We swept out through the rear entrance of the cathedral. There were aircars waiting at all four doors to confuse any potential assassins. Macharius only decided at the last second which one to take. The landing ramp was clear. Valkyries hovered overhead. We clambered into the aircar and rose into the sky, flights of gunships moving into position around us as an escort.

We returned to the palace. Looking out the porthole on the side of the aircar I saw a procession of glittering flyers following us. All of the great nobles and their retinues had been invited to the banquet that followed the triumph. I looked at Anton. He pretended to stifle a yawn. I knew what he meant. It was going to be a long night.

The orchestra played. Music filled the ballroom. The nobles danced. All of them were surrounded by their retinues, bodyguards, personal attendants of every sort, courtesans and companions and pet assassins.

Officers wore full dress uniforms, noblemen their court finery, noblewomen long gowns, narrow at the waist, their great hooped skirts supported by suspensor systems so that they seemed to float just above the ground. Every dress was a statement of power. They each cost as much as supplying a regiment. They glowed with precious materials and fitted their wearers with the same precision as a personal battle-suit. They would be worn only once and discarded, just to show that their owners could afford such things.

Servants moved through the throng bearing trays of drinks and elaborate snacks. Enormous chandeliers housing poison snoopers and surveillance systems looked down like the jewelled eyes of enormous insects.

I wondered how many thousands of people were here. I wondered how much all of this was costing and how many of the poor in the hives of other worlds that money could support. I did so very briefly, for one of the things about being surrounded by enormous wealth is how quickly you come to take it for granted.

Macharius sat on a floating throne. Beside him, on either side, were two of the loveliest women I had ever seen, both high ladies of one of the noble Houses. Both looked at him as if he were some delicacy they intended to sneak from the plate of the other. They both appeared to admire Macharius without noticing the woman on the other side of him. The Lord High Commander was courtly to both and obviously amused by their rivalry. They both sought to get something from him while he played them and their Houses off against each other.

I stood behind Macharius on a raised dais and looked out at the crowd. They were moving through one of the great formal ceremonies so beloved by our aristocrats, one of those rituals so elaborate and courtly that only people with an enormous amount of free time on their hands could master all the intricacies.

As ever Macharius looked completely relaxed and at his ease, but I suspect he was bored. These vast ceremonies were more for the benefit of the locals than they were for him. He would rather have been directing a battle somewhere. Still, in the absence of more physical conflict, he seemed to take some pleasure from social warfare, and here it was visible all around.

One of the ladies leaned forward and whispered something in Macharius's ear. Her mouth was so close Macharius must have felt her breath on his neck. Her rival reached out and touched his arm, letting her fingers rest there moments longer than were strictly necessary to get the general's attention. He turned to look at her, and she looked up at him with wide trusting eyes. Her lips were red and full, and parted invitingly.

Before she could say anything, a great gong sounded, and all were summoned to the feast.

The banqueting hall held thousands of people at hundreds of tables, but there was really only one that mattered and that was the one at which Macharius sat. The whole pecking order of the conquered sector was set out there. The most important governors and planetary nobles were at the table. The closer they were to Macharius, the more important they were. The nearest tables had the nobles of only slightly less importance, and those with relatively small influence in the great scale of things were relegated to the furthest corners of the room.

I stood behind Macharius's chair in my most smartly

formal uniform. I was not there to eat. I was there to look impressive and protect Macharius. The fact that I was allowed to stand at his back with a shotgun in my hands must have impressed a few of the notables because I could see them giving me considering looks. Little did they know, I thought, that Anton and Ivan and I took turns doing this.

Actually, they probably did, as I realised when I came to consider the matter. The planetary aristocracies had their own intelligence systems. They might even have known why we were there, but I doubted that they knew the whole truth of it: that ever since Karsk Macharius had considered us a form of personal, living lucky charm. He had kept at least one of us close to him at all times.

I was not the only one being noticed. I could see the local nobility studying Drake under their eyelashes as well. The less well informed were probably wondering how they could get close to him and find out what influence he had. There were, no doubt, rumours as to his identity circulating behind the lady's fans and out of the corners of men's mouths in every part of the room.

I glanced at the faces of the people closest to Macharius at the table, the ones close enough to speak with him. There was Drake. There was Blight. There was Raymond Belisarius, the factor for the great Navigator House. I wondered where his cousin was right now.

There were hundreds of nobles from the various worlds Macharius had conquered, the most important people politically in the sector. All of them were the heads of various factions, most of them were opposed to each other, and they spent their time glaring daggers at those they thought of as their rivals.

It was like observing a gathering of predators at a savannah waterhole, except that here there were no herbivores, only flesh eaters, all of them looking to tear a chunk off each other. Of all the people present I could not see the expression on Macharius's face. I was standing behind his seat so I could only guess it from the tone of the remarks I heard him addressing to the assembled throng. He spoke of the return of Imperial rule, of the reconstruction of the old order, of a new age of faith and unity to come. The crowd cheered and applauded while all the time thinking about what it could gain.

I thought once again about what Anna had told me. There were very few in the Imperium beyond the reach of its rulers. Possibly only the Space Marines of the Adeptus Astartes, who were a law unto themselves. The great bureaucratic wheels of the Imperium were beginning to turn. The attention of that gigantic entity was being focused on this corner of the universe. How many of those people out there would still applaud Macharius if they knew that it might soon turn against him? How many potential assassins would there be then?

I thought about the generals of the crusade who would soon be arriving. How many of those would be truly loyal to Macharius?

CHAPTER THIRTEEN

We moved through the palace in the wake of Macharius. Overhead, great murals depicting scenes from Imperial history looked down on him. In the massive atrium, a portrait of one-eyed Saint Teresius being nailed to the burning World Tree of Ydrasil by orks brooded overhead. As we passed into the reception chamber, we saw a titanic depiction of the Emperor within his Golden Throne surrounded by a halo of light while primarch angels watched over him. The paintings had been done by the greatest artist on the world Tyranticus, a genius with a liking for wine and theology. He was up there hanging from the roof like a spider in a wire harness even now, brushing away at some tiny corner of the painting, bringing some minuscule cherubim into being with his pigments and brush.

We had other things to think of. The warlords of the crusade were gathered in the conference chamber. They had come to report to their master and be rewarded for their excellence.

The high valves of the great bronze double door were open. We strode through. Multicoloured light from the stained glass windows threw beams down the vast chamber. Angels of glass in armour reminiscent of Space Marines trampled the necks of orks and heretics. After we passed through, the doors closed silently behind us.

The masters of the crusade sat at a huge circular table, as large as a Baneblade and carved from the vitrified remains of a section of the World Tree. An aquila was graven in its surface. Chairs were set out along the wings, only the one at the aquila's head vacant. As Macharius entered, the occupants of the chairs rose at once and saluted smartly. All of them except Inquisitor Drake, who was not part of the military command structure. Macharius returned the greeting and took his seat.

'At ease, gentlemen. Be seated,' he said. 'It is good to see you all again.'

His voice was clipped and commanding, and his face was set as stone.

I took up my position behind Macharius and gave my attention to the newcomers. They were an impressive and terrifying bunch of men.

Immediately to Macharius's right was Sejanus. He lounged back on the great leather-upholstered command chair and looked as if he were going to put his boots on the table. A few times I saw him raise one leg, remember where he was and then put his foot decisively back on the floor. Sejanus, who had obviously been drinking late last night, had bags beneath his eyes and looked at the room with an odd mixture of good humour and pained menace, as if he wanted to order everyone to be quiet but could not because they were all of equal or higher rank.

To the right of Sejanus was General Tarka, resplendent in his hussar general's uniform. You could have cut yourself on the creases of his trousers. His boots were spotless. The brasswork on his sash and buckles was polished mirror-bright. His narrow face was lean and severe. His moustache perfectly framed his mouth as if it did not dare grow one millimetre beyond its assigned place. He wore white gloves, which he inspected through his glittering diamond glass amplification monocle as though checking them for spots of dirt. He looked like the very caricature of the military martinet, one of those dress-up parade ground soldiers who knew nothing about the blood and mud of fighting.

I knew for a fact that he was not. He had fought hand to hand with orks and cut his way out of a heretical ambush with only his pistol and a shard of screen-glass salvaged from the wreckage of his ground car. In a regiment famous for its tradition of duelling, he was the most famous duellist. It was said he had killed over a hundred men in affairs of honour and was not above accepting a challenge now if one was offered to him. His wife was a famous beauty and famous, too, for her affairs, so he still got the opportunity now and again. There were those who said he encouraged her just so he could duel. I doubted it. There is no end to the malice of gossip.

Beyond him sat General Fabius. Fabius looked half asleep, a state accentuated by his drooping eyelids, which ensured that even at his most alert he never looked particularly awake. He had a reputation for liking the good life and for taking the choicest selection of loot, but he was a general of fantastic skill, a specialist in siege warfare, who had taken more cities and hives than anyone alive. He had lost an arm in battle with an ork warlord, and its mechanical replacement was said to be strong enough to crush metal and bone in its grip.

To Fabius's right was Arrian. He seemed a scruffy-looking man until you looked closely at him and realised that his dress uniform was not creased or lined. It was something about the man himself that gave the impression. Perhaps it was the unkempt hair or the way he leaned an elbow on the table and propped his head on his fist. He drummed the fingers of his other hand on the tabletop and twisted his head around on his long neck to focus first on one person then another. Many people thought him mad. Many thought him touched by a holy light. Nobody was sure what he thought. Everyone remembered he had ordered the massacre of a million heretic children on Gamara 12.

Lysander seemed inclined to tell Arrian to stop looking at him. He was a tall man, handsome, more so even than Macharius; but where Macharius was golden-haired and golden-skinned, Lysander was black-haired and pale. He had the narrowest of moustaches, which he was always stroking. He appeared to be admiring his own reflection in the mirrored tabletop, but he looked quite capable of wrestling an ork should one choose to enter the room and do battle right now.

Next to him was Cyrus, the tallest man in the room by far. His features were craggy and stern, and his silver hair fitted his head like a Guardsman's helmet. His eyes were a chilling blue. He gave the impression of great age and great wisdom, although with the juvenat treatments many of the others were almost certainly as old as he was. He was writing something on a pad of papyrus, probably making a note of the fact that Macharius was twenty-two seconds late for the meeting.

By that time I had looked all the way around the table. On Macharius's left sat General Crassus, a man of medium height, who was almost as broad as he was tall. His face was pockmarked and a scar ran from over his right eye to the middle of his cheek. It caused the corner of his mouth to pucker up constantly. It seemed unlikely that a man in his position could not have had the scar removed by medical adepts, so he must have kept it for a reason, to remind himself of something. Crassus had a reputation for annexing more than his fair share of the spoils of war. He kept winning his battles, though, so no one had thought to lodge a charge.

All of the assembled generals looked at Macharius and at each other, assessing potential rivals and their relative strengths. It was as if this table were a battlefield and their opponents were each other. The prize was favoured commands in the next part of the crusade.

Macharius played his underlings off against each other. In some ways, their rivalry was a good thing. It kept them sharp and competitive. In another way it sowed the seeds of the ensuing disaster, for many of the men in that room hated, feared and detested each other. Even though they were nominally in the same army, they regarded each other as the foes and rivals they had on occasion been, back before Macharius had ended the Great Schism. At that moment, though, there was no sign of disunity.

'Gentlemen, let us have your reports as to the progress of Operation Centurion,' said Macharius. He looked at Sejanus.

Sejanus smiled, and his booming voice filled the room. 'Total victory for Battlegroup Sejanus. We have smashed the krull in their home worlds, driven their axe lords deep into the mountain fastnesses. A few guerrillas hold out in the volcanic sectors of Indoland, but they are being hunted down. All of the productive cities are under Imperial control, and output is running at eighty per cent of pre-reclamation norms. I expect it to be at one hundred and five per cent by the time we are done. Without the axe lords tithing productivity for their own personal projects, we can direct the output of the Deep Mines into arms and equipment production far more efficiently.'

He smiled, looked around at all of the other generals and sat down again.

'General Fabius, pray report,' said Macharius. Fabius rose slowly with a slight grunt and looked at Macharius somnolently. 'Battlegroup Fabius reports complete success. The main agri-worlds of the Elaric Combine are occupied by our troops. The remainder have agreed to terms now that they have seen the futility of resistance. The local nobles would rather keep their perks under Imperial rule than see their estates go to their rivals under redistribution law if they are declared outlaws and traitors by the Imperium.'

His eyes were focused on Macharius all the time. He looked like an amiable bear slowly rousing itself from hibernation.

For myself, I was wondering whether anyone here was going to report less than perfect success. To do so would be to cede an advantage to their rivals.

That said, Macharius was known for his ability to get to the truth behind his commanders' reports, and the penalties for false information would be far worse than letting a rival steal a march. General Xander had been demoted and reassigned to supervising a prison world for doing so. No, I thought, in essence these reports would be perfectly truthful, albeit burnished to make their presenters shine.

'General Arrian?'

General Arrian writhed to his feet and surveyed the assembled generals with glittering eyes, as if he thought they might be disguised heretics plotting against him. 'I report utter, crushing Imperial victory over the worms of the Hectacore. The heretics burn. Their ungodly spawn are in re-education camps,' his tone let everyone know what he thought of this particular piece of false mercy, 'their wells and reactor cores are assigned to righteous purpose. Battlegroup Arrian is ready to bring the Emperor's will to more heretics.'

He sat down as abruptly as he had stood. His gaze turned upwards to look at the armoured angels overhead, rather than contemplate the sinners surrounding him. General Fabius suppressed a smile. General Cyrus looked at him with his stony gaze. Macharius did not seem in the slightest bit perturbed.

General Lysander was already rising to his feet. He clicked his heels, saluted, stroked his moustache, contemplated his reflection on the table's surface for a moment and said, with a trace of mocking humour, 'It pains me to report less than total, crushing victory. Battlegroup Lysander can only report complete success. It was enough to merely encircle the assembled forces of the Hegemony of Iskander, cut their lines of supply and then defeat their ground armies in detail. Sadly, there proved no need to imprison the defeated in death camps or burn their children as heretics.'

His mocking gaze met that of Arrian. I half expected them to go for each other's throats. Here were two men who really hated each other. Lysander was one of those Imperial officers who thought honour was important and that there was a proper way to win a war. Personally, I would rather have followed Arrian: at least he had no illusions and did what was necessary to achieve victory whatever the cause.

'Gentlemen, gentlemen,' was all Macharius said. The reproof was delivered in a mildly paternal tone, but I knew him well enough to sense the steely anger beneath. He was not about to tolerate friction between his high commanders. It was a measure of how feared and respected he was that Lysander immediately turned and made a small heel-clicking bow to him and Arrian returned to his study of angels at once.

General Cyrus rose slowly, ponderously. It was like watching a volcano heave itself up from the ocean floor; there was a suggestion of something vast, slow and irresistible in the movement. He paused to let a disapproving glance pass over Lysander, Arrian and Macharius, as if he considered the Lord High Commander not strict enough with his errant followers, sighed and began to lecture us. 'At 12.09.4078.12.00 local time, the forces of the rebellious provinces of Sindar surrendered to the commander of Battlegroup Cyrus. This ended the unfortunate period of rebellion and satisfactorily returned all one hundred billion souls in the subsector to the Emperor's Light.'

I rather liked the phrase "unfortunate period of rebellion". It made it sound as if those worlds had been beyond Imperial rule for only a few months or years and not several millennia. I suppose in the general's mind there was very little difference. And perhaps he had a truer grasp of the way the rulers of the Imperium view time than many of the others in the room.

General Crassus was on his feet before Cyrus had received Macharius's acknowledgement and sat down. 'Battlegroup Crassus reports mission accomplished, sir. All tactical and strategic objectives as covered in the overall campaign plan have been achieved.'

He was back in his chair almost at the same time as General Cyrus was. Macharius looked at the great holo-map on the table.

'You are to be congratulated, gentlemen. You have all done your usual superlative jobs. I expected nothing less, and you have not disappointed me.'

He paused to let that sink in, and you could see all of them puff up with praise while at the same time looking a little disappointed that they personally had not been singled out for more. Macharius smiled.

'Don't worry, gentlemen, there are plenty more worlds for you to conquer. Indeed, there are a virtually limitless number. He indicated the holo-map. It seemed to contract as the point of view pulled back. The huge area already conquered by the crusade shrank to a tiny pattern of light. 'A whole galaxy is out there,' Macharius said. 'There are places not even the Emperor reached.'

Again he paused, just for a moment, to let his audience see what was coming, the way a skilled matador will let the bull see the blade before he kills it. It heightened the moment of drama. I was following the line of his thoughts myself. There were worlds out there that had never seen the Emperor's Light. Macharius intended to bring it to them.

'There are more worlds than one man could conquer in a lifetime, in a hundred lifetimes. There are worlds enough for all of you and then some.'

There was something else in his voice now, a promise. Worlds enough for all of you. I am sure I was not the only man there who read something into that. Did Macharius intend to carve out an empire here at the edge of the galaxy? Were these men to be his satraps? I looked at Drake. He had steepled his fingers on his stomach and his eyes were half closed. He had exactly the same look a great predator has before it springs.

I noticed I was not the only man looking at the inquisitor. The generals, too, were trying to judge his response. I wondered if this was some kind of test Macharius had set up, to see who would stand with him even in the presence of a representative of the distant Imperium.

And perhaps this was as much for Drake's benefit as the generals'. Macharius had a gift for setting men up as if they were pieces on a regicide board, of arranging scenes in a drama that he controlled the outcome of. I found I was holding my breath as I waited to see what would happen next.

Macharius gestured to the huge swirl of stars on the holo-map. A large patch of it became illuminated. 'This, gentlemen, is where we will be going next. This is what we will reclaim for the Emperor. There are thousands of systems, trillions upon trillions of souls, entire civilisations of xenos to be crushed or driven off.'

I saw General Crassus licking his lips. I wondered if he were thinking what I was: that the plunder of such a campaign would be immense, on a scale that had not been seen since the time of the Emperor. Or perhaps he was contemplating saving all those souls.

General Cyrus said, 'It is a huge area, Lord High Commander, enormous. Perhaps too great even for the armies of the crusade.'

'My scouts have been out there among its people. There are human worlds who crave the blessing of the Emperor's

Law. They will side with us. There are thousands of worlds which can be recruiting grounds for new armies, factory worlds to equip those armies, agri-worlds to feed them. There are empty worlds that can be colonised with veteran troops. There will be gigantic new estates created. There will be need of men to rule these new realms.'

And there it was. The promise of empire, of estates that were greater than anything currently extant in the human realms, of new fiefs for those bold enough to take them, lands for veterans. I found myself, insanely, turning over possibilities in my own mind.

A man who had the ear of Macharius might be well rewarded. I did not need a world. I would settle for a hive. I suppressed a laugh at this sudden outbreak of megalo-mania and ambition, but looking at those generals I could see the temptation being waved in front of them. If I could think such thoughts, how much more potent must they be in the minds of those men who had only to stretch out a hand and grab them.

I realised it was not just the generals who were tempted. Drake was staring hard at Macharius. He heard the promise there too. Trillions of souls to be reclaimed for the Emperor, a gigantic expansion of the Imperium. He could be part of it as well. I thought I saw the glitter of ambition in his eyes, quickly suppressed.

'It might be possible,' said Tarka. 'Might. But it would be fatal if our reach exceeded our grasp.'

Was he talking in code now? Did his words have a dou-ble meaning. He was looking at the inquisitor. Macharius's words could easily be interpreted in a treasonous fashion if Drake chose to do so. Perhaps it was a test of where the inquisitor's loyalties truly lay after all these years.

Lysander said, 'If we strike quickly and hard it is possible. We could overrun these sectors before they knew what hit them. Amass a big enough hammer and you can crack any nut with one swing.'

'The scale of your ambition is breathtaking,' said Drake, and at his words the generals' faces froze. They waited to hear what he had to say. 'I have seen no additional requisitions for men and materiel put through to the Munitorum, though.'

'The campaign can be funded by the worlds we have already conquered,' said Macharius. 'And supplied by the worlds we have added to the Imperium, and will add. The crusade will be self-sustaining and self-funding.'

'And your authority for this?' Drake asked.

'I was tasked with returning worlds into the Emperor's Light. I will do so, and I will not slack.'

'Very good,' said Drake. 'I shall see that the scale of your ambitions are reported to the appropriate authorities.'

'By all means do so. Be sure to add that my ambitions are in the service of the Imperium and not of myself.'

'I will certainly report your words accurately,' said Drake. 'But in my enthusiasm I have interrupted your council. Pray, gentlemen, return to your planning.'

Macharius stood and walked over to where the inquisitor sat. He stood looming over him. There was a smile on his face, but his shadow fell upon the other man. I can still remember the sense of ominous forces gathering about the two of them even now. There was a tension in the air. The two of them seemed to have come to a fork in the road they had walked along for so long.

At that moment, the door burst open and something huge erupted into the room.

Chapter Fourteen

The guards on the door could not have stopped them even if they had wanted to, and they did not want to. They were on their knees in positions of deference, overcome at once with wonder and awe.

The newcomers were big men in ceramite armour. Let me rephrase that. They were huge men in ceramite armour, and they seemed even bigger. They moved with deadly, feral grace, and they confronted the highest warlords of the Imperium as if they had every right to simply burst into their council chambers.

All of the assembled generals gawped at them. Even Inquisitor Drake for once looked surprised, and I could not fault him for it. It is not every day the Emperor's Angels step out of legend and into your life. Only Macharius kept his poise and made a gracious gesture of welcome.

The strangers growled and advanced upon him. I considered my action for a second. It was probably going to be suicidal to draw a shotgun on a Space Wolf, but if they had come for Macharius I did not see what else I could do. I was his bodyguard after all. I moved to put myself between the Lord High Commander and the Space Marine, convinced it was most likely going to be the last thing I did.

I found myself looking up into the face of an armoured giant. He showed long fangs that were in no way reassuring and grinned as though I were not pointing a shotgun directly at his head. I swallowed but I held my ground. Eyes that caught the light like those of a dog studied me for a moment. The pupils contracted. He sniffed the air, wrinkled his nose as if he caught wind of something he didn't like.

'Did I fart?' I said. It sounds ludicrous but at that exact moment I could not think of anything else to say. The giant's booming laughter washed over me.

'By the Allfather, you don't lack courage, son of man,' he said. 'Now point your shooting stick somewhere else before I take it off you and ram it up your arse.'

Macharius's hand fell on my shoulder. 'Do as he says, Lemuel.'

I took a step back then, and so I was in the perfect place to observe the meeting between the Lord High Commander Solar Macharius and the legendary Ulrik Grimfang, Great Wolf of the Space Wolves Chapter of the Adeptus Astartes.

It was difficult to decide who looked more regal. There was never a man more commanding than Macharius, but

Grimfang was something more than a man. He had been altered by processes developed when the Emperor walked among humankind and still carried within his body the gene-seed of the first primordial Space Marines. He looked more wolf than human, his face long and narrow, one hand replaced by a huge metal claw that reminded me in some ways of the one Macharius had lost.

He narrowed his eyes as he looked at Macharius, and the air fairly crackled between them. I don't know how Macharius managed to hold that superhuman gaze without looking away. I could not have done so. The Wolf walked around him, sniffing the air, all the time, inspecting the Lord High Commander from every angle.

Macharius did not flinch. You can still see the scene depicted on the walls of Macharius's palace on Emperor's Glory by Antiarchus. The choirs of watching angels are a somewhat unhistorical touch, but the rest is more or less accurate. My face was probably a lot paler and more frightened than the artist makes it look. I was fighting to stop myself shaking. Confronting a Space Wolf like that was like coming unexpectedly face to face with a large and hungry sabretooth. Now that the moment had passed, reaction was setting in.

The other generals continued to gape. I can't say as I blame them. Inquisitor Drake was first to recover his poise. He rose to his feet and said, 'Great Wolf, we welcome you to–'

'Sit down and shut up,' Grimfang bellowed. 'I did not come all these light years to listen to your gabble!'

Drake sat down as if poleaxed. I would have done so

myself if I had been near a chair, and I was only caught in the backwash of that fierce command. The Space Wolf stabbed out a finger at Macharius. 'It is this one I have come to see... and to smell.'

I thought for a moment that he was going to bite out Macharius's throat with those great fangs, but then I noticed he had merely placed his head close to Macharius's and was sniffing the air as though catching a scent. After a long, tense moment, he released the Lord High Commander.

'Are you done?' Macharius asked. His voice was cold and just as commanding as Grimfang's.

The two of them eyed each other again, like two wolves about to fight for control of a pack. Macharius obviously did not appreciate having his personal space invaded. They glared at each other for long moments that seemed to pass as glacially as the Ice Winters of Taran.

The Great Wolf began to laugh, checked himself and said, 'So you are the one who has started this new crusade. I heard what you had to say about conquering new worlds for the Imperium. You do not lack ambition, little man.'

Only a Space Wolf would have thought to describe Macharius as a little man. I was busy trying to understand Grimfang's words. He had heard what Macharius had to say? Even if he had been waiting outside, which given his impetuous manner was unlikely, the door was sufficiently thick to make words inaudible to mortal ears. And Grimfang had most likely been striding through the corridors of the palace. Had he really been able to make out the words? Presumably so.

'You object, do you?' Macharius said. His voice held a measure of insolence that I feel certain Grimfang was not used to. He eyed the Lord High Commander as if considering smiting him with his chainsword.

'You will bring war and havoc to thousands of worlds,' said the Space Wolf. 'You will make it rain blood and snow skulls. Billions will die.'

'Do you object?'

'No, little man. How could I object? It is good. There will be glory and conquest and the reaping of souls for the All-father. We have come because we smell battle, strife such as has not been seen in millennia. This is our place and these are our times. We have come to aid the Allfather's crusade and to take our share of the plunder of worlds.'

He reached out and grasped Macharius's arm in a gesture of comradeship.

I saw the look of shock on Drake's face and the look of triumph on Macharius's. The Space Wolves had given his actions the seal of approval of the Adeptus Astartes, one Chapter at least.

'Now, bring us drink!' Grimfang bellowed. 'And meat. We must celebrate this glorious day.'

With a sweep of his mighty arm, he cleared the table. Sejanus shrugged and produced a hip-flask. Servants were dispatched. Raw and bloody grox was brought.

The celebration began.

'Drink, little man,' said Grimfang. He offered me a goblet with his own hands. I was later to learn this was a great honour. Apparently he had been impressed by the way I had got between him and Macharius.

I looked at him. I looked at Macharius, and then I looked back at the goblet. The Space Wolves were gulping down some foul-smelling spirit from the massive brandy glasses that were full to the brim. Even those looked like shotglass tumblers in their hands.

Macharius nodded. I accepted the goblet and took a mouthful. The spirit was so strong it burned. I gulped it down and then drank some more. It was like having half a bottle poured down my throat. If I had drunk any faster I would probably have died. As it was, I was not sure I could feel my legs.

Grimfang slapped me on the back. I am sure he was being as gentle as he could, but the force of the blow almost knocked me face first onto the table. 'You can drink, even if you are not a Son of Russ,' he said.

'If I drink any more I will fall head first into that bucket of amasec over there,' I slurred. My vision was blurry. My throat felt raw. I looked around. The generals were all drinking save for Arrian. Sejanus was playing hook-knife with some massive Space Wolf warrior, a very dangerous game when sober, a good way to lose a finger when drunk.

Grimfang threw his arm around my shoulder, drew me closer like an old drinking comrade and leaned forwards, murmuring into my ear.

'You have the smell of an evil woman on you,' he said. 'An assassin and something worse. Be wary,' he said. He pushed me away again, his face as jovial as a Space Wolf's ever got, leaving me to wonder about the words he had said, or whether I had imagined them.

And that's the last clear memory I have of that evening.

'Kill me now,' I said. The room seemed to be whirling around as if someone had placed a gravitic rotator under my bed. It felt like one of the Adeptus Astartes was banging on my head with a thunder hammer. My throat felt raw. My stomach churned as if I had the Brontovan trots.

'You saw Space Wolves,' said Anton. 'You drank with Space Wolves.'

'You pointed a shotgun at Space Wolves,' said Ivan. 'Your stupidity is impressive.'

'Don't worry. They got their revenge. They decided a bolter shell was too quick, so they tried to kill me with alcohol poisoning. I think they are on the verge of success. Ivan, if I die, you can have my shotgun.'

'I wanted that,' said Anton.

'Ivan, you have my permission to give Anton the shotgun – full bore in the face,' I said. 'Make sure it's loaded with manstopper rounds. You'll need them to breach his thick skull.'

'Hark at the man who tried to outdrink a Space Wolf,' said Anton. 'He is calling me stupid.'

'I wasn't trying to outdrink him,' I said, pausing to throw up in the bucket that Ivan had helpfully placed near my head. 'I just decided it would be more dangerous to refuse than to drink. Of course, I might have been wrong about that.'

'I hope you did not let the side down,' said Anton. 'I would not want them thinking the boys from Belial cannot hold their liquor.'

'Anton,' I said, dry heaving for a bit before continuing. 'Compared to a Space Wolf, a mastodon can't hold its drink. One of them could outdrink an alcoholic ogryn and its inbred cousin, probably its whole alcoholic clan.'

I had flashbacks to last night's drinking session, just images really, because after I had accepted Grimfang's proffered glass my memory of things shattered into a thousand glittering booze-soaked pieces. I recalled the High Command of Macharius's army drinking toasts to the Adeptus Astartes, sensibly using thimble sized shot-glasses of spirit, while the Space Wolves guzzled tankards of the stuff.

I remembered speeches being given and songs being sung, and over everything a looming sense of unreality hovering. It seemed so unlikely that we could be in the presence of these creatures of legend, that they would be present on the crusade. I remembered howling war cries and tales of battle and a skald singing something in an odd chant that told of ancient battles under bloody suns against foes worthy of Wolves.

I remembered Macharius reeling to his feet and speaking of the wars of his youth, not boasting, simply talking about old comrades, now gone and battles long won. I remembered Drake of all people toasting Macharius and their friendship.

Most of all I remembered what Grimfang had whispered, about the way Anna's scent clung to me. The Great Wolf knew about the Imperial assassin. He suspected her. Not without good reason. The question troubling me was how right was he?

I pushed that aside as something to be worried about another day and lay there and groaned until it was time to take up my duties again.

The meeting chamber was large, but the Space Wolves made it feel small. They had a presence out of all proportion to their surroundings, bristling with an energy that was superhuman, studying us with eyes that were as alien as any xenos.

I looked at them and wondered what they had in common with us. They seemed to have stepped out of an earlier age, one more barbaric and heroic. I have spent most of my adult life fighting the Emperor's wars, and I like to think that few things daunt me, but the Space Wolves did. It was not just their size and strangeness. It was the suggestion that at any moment they were capable of erupting into violence and that it came as naturally to them as breathing. They made me nervous just by being what they were. Fine allies, I thought, but not people I would want to spend too much time around when I was sober. Now that I had had time to consider my actions, I wondered at my temerity the previous day.

Macharius, of course, gave no sign of being intimidated. Of all the people in the room, he was the closest to the Adeptus Astartes. It was not hard to imagine that in a different time or different place he might have been one of them.

He had something of their hair-trigger quickness, their supreme self-confidence, their savage capacity for violence. You looked at Macharius and you looked at the Wolves, and you felt their kinship. War was the element they had been born for. A man fights because he has been chosen or because he must. Macharius and those savage demigods would fight because they loved it.

He sat now on his dais and studied the Space Wolves. They studied him back. They did not need thrones to appear regal. Their natural presence made them seem greater than any noble or any general. Ulrik Grimfang had about him the aura of a particularly savage saint. He stood flanked by a Dreadnought, an ancient living war machine, and a selection of his captains. There was just Macharius and Drake and myself. I had no real idea why I was there. There was nothing I could do to protect Macharius from the Adeptus Astartes if they turned violent. Perhaps my willingness to intervene even with the Adeptus Astartes had impressed Macharius. The cynical part of my mind thought that perhaps they wanted to be sure that what I heard was reported to Anna.

Grimfang cast his eyes around the chamber. 'It is sealed,' he said. His harsh, rasping voice carried through the room easily.

'It is sealed,' said Macharius. 'What is spoken here goes no further.'

'That is well for we talk of ancient and sacred things. If what you say is true.'

'Insofar as it is possible to be certain, I believe it to be true,' said Drake. 'We found the Fist of Russ.'

The Great Wolf looked at him with what might have been contempt. 'Insofar as it is possible to be certain?'

'Nothing in this galaxy is certain, save for the Emperor's Grace,' said Drake. 'The Fist has been lost for millennia, stolen by xenos raiders from the Temple of the Storm Wolves on Pelius, sought for thousands of years by the faithful.'

'And now you just happened to find it?' said Grimfang. The irony dripped from his fangs. 'A thing that seers have claimed was no longer to be found in this universe, that all thought lost forever.'

'We had it in our grasp,' said Macharius.

'You had it in your grasp,' Grimfang said. 'That implies you lost it.'

'Our ship made a false jump – we were attacked by the xenos eldar. When we drove them off, the Fist was gone. They have it.'

A frown crossed Grimfang's brow. 'If this truly was a relic of the time of Russ it must be reclaimed.'

'It was ancient and it bore the runes of your order. I can see that just from looking at your armour,' said Drake. He touched his data-slate. A hololithic image of the object hovered in the air. The Space Wolves looked at it. I could sense the intensity of their scrutiny.

'It is of the ancient times,' said the Dreadnought. Its voice was flat, inhuman. It was the sort of voice you would have expected a Titan to have if they could speak. The accents on the words were subtly wrong, as if the speaker had first learned the use of language in a time so ancient that the words were spoken differently. 'I remember that model.

It was fashioned at the time when the primarchs walked among men.'

'It could be faked,' said the Great Wolf. 'There are many such false relics.'

'Nonetheless,' said the Dreadnought. 'If there is even the slightest chance it belonged to the Founder it cannot be allowed to fester in the hands of the eldar.'

Grimfang made a gesture that indicated that so much was obvious.

'Speak on, in the Allfather's name! How did you find this Fist when so many others have failed?'

'The trail was long and dark. We first heard rumours on Celene nearly ten years ago. They told of a lost ship and a mad crew emerging from the warp in a place called Demetrius. I found a codex that described the Fist as a lost artefact of the heroic age of man. We tracked it and we found it.'

'I have heard such tales before,' said Grimfang. 'They have never turned out to be true.'

'You have seen what we had. You must decide for yourself the course of action you will take,' said Macharius.

'If it is a relic it cannot be left in xenos hands,' said the Dreadnought.

'It will be found again,' said Grimfang, coming swiftly to a decision. 'We shall find it.'

'I wish to help,' said Macharius.

'Help? Us?' said Grimfang. He sounded as though he wanted to laugh.

'There is a fleet of xenos, an indeterminate number holding

the system. Even a company of Space Wolves cannot be entirely confident of overcoming them,' said Macharius.

'If it takes more than a company, I have more,' said Grimfang.

'Time is of the essence,' said Macharius. 'The world is isolated by warp storms. The eldar come and go as they will, by what means we do not know. Who knows how long they will be there. I have a ship ready now and I have an army. I have a Navigator who can make the jump. And I have a debt of honour that needs to be repaid.'

I think the mention of the debt of honour swayed them more than the military reasons. It was something they understood. Their whole way of life was built on it.

'Very well,' said Grimfang. 'You may accompany us.'

It should have sounded colossally arrogant; he was *allowing* an Imperial general to accompany his small force, but it did not. It sounded right.

'Anyway, this tale was merely a goat staked out to get our attention. You have other reasons for wishing us here.' He looked directly at Macharius. The Lord High Commander looked back at him.

'The Imperium has been shattered by schism and heresy. It is time to put an end to it and reunite the realms of men under the Emperor's banner.'

'And you are the one to do that, are you, little man?'

'I am the one who has been chosen to perform the task.'

'Others have tried.'

'I have succeeded,' said Macharius. He was not boasting. He was making a statement. 'Everywhere I have fought, I have ended the strife of man against man, world against world, system against system. I have ended the wars of faith and I will add new worlds to the Imperium. I have done this without your aid. I can continue to do it without your aid.'

Grimfang sniffed. He was clearly not used to being talked to in this way. There was suddenly a dangerous tension in his manner. His eyes narrowed and he looked as if he were considering springing on the Lord High Commander. 'And yet we are here, speaking.'

Macharius looked back calmly. 'This will be the greatest war of the newborn millennium. The Adeptus Astartes are already gathered like eagles at the edges of the struggle. They intervene as they like, where they like, when they like. They are a law unto themselves.'

'As they have always been, as they should be,' said Grimfang.

'Indeed,' said Macharius. 'But there are times when greater coordination between our forces might prove useful. There are times when an understanding between us would be helpful. Informally, of course.'

'We do not need to understand you,' said Grimfang.

'I think you do. I think there will come a time when powerful people may come to you, and the other Adeptus Astartes, carrying tales of me. I wanted you to see me for yourself, to judge me for yourself. I want you to know that I am sincere in what I do, that I wish nothing more than to rebuild the Imperium into what it should be. I want there to be no misunderstanding between us.'

Grimfang looked at him. His nose wrinkled. He sniffed the air. His eyes narrowed. I wondered if Macharius had overstepped the mark.

'There are those who have made fortunes from the chaos. There are those who hold power because of it,' Macharius said. 'They do not wish to see an end to the ages of schism.'

An odd smile twisted Grimfang's mouth. Those monstrous fangs became visible. 'You think we might be numbered among those, do you?'

Macharius shook his head, but for a moment I wondered if he really did think that. Was it possible he saw the Space Marines even as potential disruptions in his master plan? 'No,' Macharius said. 'I do not. As I have said, I want you to understand what it is I do and why I am doing it.'

'I think you achieved that goal,' said Grimfang. He sounded as though, in spite of himself, he was impressed by what he saw when he looked upon Macharius.

'There has been an age of chaos,' said Macharius. 'It must be seen to be ended.'

Grimfang nodded. His head was tilted to one side in contemplation. 'And it will be,' said Grimfang. 'I will send a company of Wolves to watch over you. Logan Grimnar will act as a liaison. He is young and needs seasoning.'

He rose and moved to the door. The meeting was quite clearly over.

CHAPTER FIFTEEN

Helicon Blight's vessel, *The Pride of Terra*, was an enormous ship, a city floating in space it seemed when I saw it, a world unto itself in many ways. In orbit over Emperor's Glory, it docked with a number of shuttles which carried elements of Macharius's elite Lion Guard.

Vast hangar doors opened in its side to allow the shuttles entrance, and once we were within, tank after tank – Leman Russ, Baneblade, Shadowsword, Chimera – disembarked into the hold. I stood there watching as massive stowage lifts raised them into huge multi-level holding pens. Other cargo bays had been converted into impromptu barracks.

Macharius himself received quarters fit for a planetary governor, and the inner circle of his personal bodyguard such as Anton, Ivan, the Undertaker and myself were installed near him. There were a thousand battle-hardened troops on call. If we had needed to we could have taken over the ship, although what we would have done then eludes me.

The embarking of Macharius's private army was not a quick business. Many shuttles needed to dock. We had most of the day to wait while it was happening. During that time, Macharius kept in touch with Sejanus over the comm-net, giving crisp orders for the disposition of the crusade's forces long term.

He was taking no chances of things not going as he planned in his absence.

Of course, we had to be there to watch the company of Space Wolves arrive. Anton insisted. We stood on the platform over the docking bay watching their grey-blue Thunderhawks and transit-shuttles arrive. It had taken some quite spectacular feats of bribery on some of the ship's crew to get us there, but we were known to be high in Macharius's favour and that counted for something as well.

It was odd to watch the internal blast doors open and the small fleet of armoured vessels move into the holding chambers and be secured in metal cradles for the flight. It was even odder to watch the Space Wolves at a distance through the stained armourglass windows. In the vast interior of the ship, they lost some of the sense of scale they had close up. In some ways they were just armoured figures moving through routines familiar to all soldiers in transit. They emerged from their vehicles and looked around, studying their surroundings with watchful eyes.

It took me a few seconds to realise what they were doing.

They were making sure they knew where every last piece of cover was. It was as if they expected that at any moment the interior of the loading bay might become a battleground and they were not going to be at a disadvantage on it.

By squad they moved to secure a perimeter. Their leaders did not seem to give any orders that I could see. They moved into their positions as if they already knew what to do, with an ease and a fluidity greater than any I had ever witnessed. In the Guard it would never have been so. There would have been confusion. There would have been sergeants bellowing orders. There would have been squads taking up the wrong positions and officers trying to organise the chaos and sometimes making it worse. With the Space Marines below, there was none of that.

Anton made a sour expression with his mouth. 'What's wrong?' I asked. 'Disappointed they haven't killed anybody? There's time enough yet.'

He shook his head. 'I always wanted to see Space Wolves.'

'And now you have. If you're really unlucky, you'll get to fight alongside them too.'

'Yes but…'

His lips compressed and his jaw went tight as he struggled to find the words to express what he was feeling. He didn't really have to. I knew him well enough to know. This was something he had been dreaming about all his life and had never really expected to happen. And now it had, and his life's long list of things to be looked forward to had been shortened by one.

'Lost for something stupid to say, Anton?' Ivan said. 'That is a first.'

'Ha-bloody-ha.' His voice held a note of frustration as well as disappointment. 'You think we'll get to talk to them?'

'What do you want to talk with them about? You think you'll exchange war stories? I have news for you, Anton, they might not be as impressed as your noble-born girlfriend by your tales of killing orks on Jurasik.'

He was frowning again, and I could tell he was still struggling with concepts that were not easy for a man like him to get to grips with. He really just wanted to make contact with them, to reach out and touch something greater than human, to speak with as close to a demigod as he was ever going to get. There was a religious component to his awe and his tongue-tiedness.

In the end, he simply turned and walked away, marching shoulders straight into the corridors of the vast starship.

'I think you hurt his feelings,' said Ivan, rather mean-spiritedly, I thought.

A few hours before we were due to depart, Helicon Blight himself came to pay his respects. He had greeted Macharius temporarily when welcoming him aboard, but this time he brought an invitation to the bridge of *The Pride of Terra* if Macharius wished to witness the ship depart. The Lord High Commander agreed to do so. I am sure he had seen such things before, but I guessed he wanted to see how Blight's ship differed from others and to gain some insight into the way the rogue trader ran his vessel.

We accompanied the merchant prince to the enormous chamber. It had forward facing armourglass windows through which the blue and green surface of Emperor's Glory was visible. Over all was a massive throne for the trader to sit upon and positions for his Navigator, astropaths and other senior officers on the ship. We were given pride of place beside the command throne. I was impressed by the way Blight took it for himself without offering it to Macharius. I am fairly certain this was the way protocol dictated, but there are those I have encountered who would have broken those rules in order to curry favour with the master of the crusade.

Macharius studied everything with his usual attention, and I followed suit. There were several massive control altars and lesser thrones for astropaths and other officers. Subalterns and messengers moved around the place. Tech-adepts made last moment checks on the altars.

The huge arched doorways swished open and Zarah Belisarius entered. Blight held one hand to his comm-net earbead and then said something quietly. It was picked up by the patch microphone on his throat. A few moments later klaxons sounded and warning lights flashed. With no sense of movement whatsoever we were on our way, the surface of Emperor's Glory seeming to slide past through the viewport.

The Navigator strode up to where Blight stood, nodded to Macharius and looked out over the command deck. Once again I was struck by the fact that we were in a different world here, where Macharius's rank and power counted for less. These people saw the world differently, were powers unto themselves, and I suppose it dawned on me then that once again we were, in a very real sense, in their hands. We would never get home without their good will.

'Lord Blight,' said one of the helmsmen. 'I am picking up an unusual drive echo in our wake. It is possible that a ship has left orbit around Emperor's Glory at the same time and on the same course as us.'

I saw Blight look at Macharius and then the Navigator. Some secret appeared to be communicated between them, although I could not guess what. I wondered if Blight knew about the Space Wolves.

'Thank you, Squires,' said Helicon Blight. 'It is probably just another craft making for the out-system jump point, but if it plots an intercept course or shows any sign of threat, speak at once.'

'Aye, sir,' said the helmsman. Blight swivelled his chair and smiled. 'Not much of interest will happen until we reach the jump point now and I hand over control of the ship to Navigator Belisarius. It's a two-day transit until then. Perhaps you would care to retire to my chambers and take some refreshment.'

At Macharius's agreement, he said, 'Mister Blake, the command deck is yours,' and we departed to his chambers in the company of the rogue trader and the Navigator.

If I had been impressed by Blight's chambers before, I was even more so on the second visit, for it turned out that the room in which we had seen him was merely an antechamber, used for conducting business. His apartments were as large as any in the palace on Emperor's Glory and even more luxurious.

Luxurious divans, upon which Macharius, Zarah Belisarius and Blight lounged, were everywhere. Robed and masked servants brought drinks and food.

Blight raised a glass to good fortune on their voyage, the Lady Belisarius to a safe passage, and Macharius wished them both prosperity. After the formal toasts were completed, Zarah Belisarius said, 'So you seek to make an alliance with the Wolves of Space.'

Macharius smiled at her. 'What makes you think that?'

'We of House Belisarius have ways of hearing about such things. You talked with them on Emperor's Glory. A halo of prophecy and legend already forms around you. What else could you be looking for?'

'Who else is aware of your speculation?' Macharius asked. His voice was very calm, but I had known him long enough to hear the dangerous undercurrents in it. I was not the only one.

'No one I can be certain of except Lord Blight,' said Zarah Belisarius. 'And my cousin Raymond.'

'Let us say I seek an understanding with them,' said Macharius. 'Are you prepared for the passage to Procrastes?'

The fact that he wanted to change the subject was not lost on her. 'Yes. I am ready.' She sounded confident.

'Do you think there is the possibility of anyone being able to follow us?'

'It is a difficult passage, and no ship with a Navigator aboard skilled enough to plot the transit has been in-system this past few months. I have checked,' she said. 'There are not so many great Navigators in the Imperium that I would not learn of their being in the sector. Are you worried about us being followed?'

Macharius shook his head. Zarah Belisarius considered things for a moment. 'Of course, the Space Wolves vessel would be guided by someone competent to make the jump.'

'That possibility does not trouble me. I am more concerned with the eldar when we arrive.'

'If we are attacked I can assure you that *The Pride of Terra* is capable of handling even a fully armed Imperial battleship,' said Blight. 'We will not be arriving crippled like your previous vessel, either. We are prepared for anything. With this ship we could take a planet.'

'Master Blight is correct,' said the Navigator. 'This is an excellent ship for the purpose of your voyage, none better in the sector.'

'Let us hope you are right,' said Macharius. I was surprised to hear him express such doubts. It was unlike him. Then again, he did not appreciate being in any situation where he was not totally and utterly in control.

'You will be talking with the Space Wolves en route?' Blight asked. He was obviously curious. 'You must have much to plan.'

'There will be discussions,' said Macharius, avoiding the question. 'Plans will have to be deferred until we see what awaits us.'

'To the success of your plans, then,' said Blight, raising his glass. They drank to that.

* * *

The Pride of Terra emerged from the warp. We were all relieved. In our heart of hearts I think we had all been dreading the possibility of another misjump. No sooner had we arrived than Macharius made his way to the command deck.

Zarah Belisarius and the rogue trader both watched him approach.

'It is done?' Macharius said.

'Done, and done well. We have arrived at the exact coordinates you gave us. Preliminary divinatory sweeps have revealed traces of wreckage, most likely relics of your previous encounter.'

The Navigator looked pale and drained. She was unsteady as she rose to her feet. 'It was not the easiest of trips,' she said. 'There is something about this system that disturbs the currents of the empyrean. The storm seems to be getting stronger. It would be as well to conclude your business here as quickly as possible and be gone. If the storm intensifies further a safe departure may be impossible.'

'How long do we have?' Macharius asked. I could see he was already beginning to plan his campaign. He wanted to know exactly how much time was left.

'A week, at most,' said the Navigator. 'I would not want to leave it much longer than that.'

'We must head in-system as soon as possible,' said Macharius.

'I have already laid the course,' said Helicon Blight.

One of the deck officers said, 'Lord captain, we are picking up traces of xenos ships. They are on an interception course.'

'Best strap yourselves in,' said Blight. He indicated rows of empty seats around the edge of the command deck. 'It will be a few hours till we are within range, and then things are likely to get hairy.'

'We must be ready to be boarded,' said Macharius. Blight grinned.

'They will not get close enough to board us, Lord High Commander.' Macharius did not answer. He strapped himself in and waited. We all did the same.

It is an odd and eerie thing to sit on the command deck of a warship during a space battle. Nothing much seems to happen. Officers speak to each other in a clipped fashion. Small lights change vectors within holospheres. Occasionally, you feel a ripple of strangeness as the ship changes direction and the artificial gravity compensates. When things are going well there is no sensation at all, really. When things go badly...

Blight sat on his throne and ordered fighters deployed. The only sign his command was obeyed was when a number of small green dots appeared on the holosphere in front of him, moving on collision course with the incoming eldar.

Occasionally one of his officers would reel off a stream of technical chant and he would respond with a one- or two-word command. 'Fire,' or 'Check,' or 'Prepare control.' I had no idea what he meant, but I felt sure something was happening. In the holosphere things changed colour or vanished. Although no signs were given, out there men and xenos were dying, ancient vessels were being vaporised, terrible things were taking place.

Macharius watched everything keenly, interested as ever in any aspect of warfare. I wondered what he made of this strange silent struggle, in which moves were plotted out long in advance between ships incalculable distances apart.

He probably grasped it instinctively as he did everything connected with warfare, but I could tell he was not enjoying himself. The fingers of his right hand drummed on the arms of the chair into which he had been strapped. Possibly, like me, he was waiting for the familiar shudder that would tell when the ship had been hit, or the flicker of lights that would tell that we had lost a generator. There was not much consolation to be had from the thought that if we took a direct hit to the command deck we would never know. We would be walking in the Emperor's Light before we even knew we were dead.

I forced myself to breathe slowly even though I dreaded that each intake of air might be my last. I was all too aware of the sickness in my stomach and the pounding of my heart against my ribs. I told myself that this nauseating fear was a good thing, that at least it was letting me know I was still alive, but it was hard to convince myself of the truth of it. As always, I found myself wishing that we were on the ground, with weapons in our hands and some say over our fates. The simple act of waiting was terrifying.

Eventually, Blight smiled, looked up and clapped his hands. I noticed there was some small difference in the dance of lights in the holosphere. The red dots were retreating, the green ones were returning towards the centre.

'It is done,' said the rogue trader. 'They are in retreat. Victory is ours. We'll be in orbit over the target within twelve hours.'

It seemed that *The Pride of Terra* was every bit as powerful as Blight had claimed. Or perhaps the eldar had retreated for their own reasons and were simply leading us into a trap. I had seen Macharius do similar things many times. I could tell from the expression on his face that he was wondering the same thing.

We would soon see.

It seems the humans have returned. It is not the same ship but one more powerful. It has driven back my fleet and moves arrogantly to take up position in orbit. I wonder as to why there is only one vessel. Is its owner so confident? Or could it be there is no connection between this craft and the one we first encountered.

I reach out and touch the armoured mechanical fist I claimed on the first human ship. I find it oddly fascinating and oddly comforting, a primitive talisman which touches something deep in my soul. It speaks of a world of violence and death and pain. Preliminary tests indicate that it dates to a time around the first manifestations of She Who Thirsts. There are cell fragments within which do not exactly match the basic human genotype. They will bear analysis and may reward us with some smidgeon of knowledge.

I give my attention back to matters at hand. I tell the fleet to fall back and await further instructions, to maintain a safe distance on the far side of the fat moon. I wish to know what these humans are about, and I want them to be ready to strike again once we have taken a proper measure of their strength.

CHAPTER SIXTEEN

We swung into orbit over the captive world of Procrastes. The globe glowed blue and white against the black of space. It looked peaceful, as most worlds do when you see them from space. It was hard to believe that down there, xenos invaders were torturing and enslaving, that soldiers were dying, that weapons of terrifying power were being deployed.

All the long way in past the outlying worlds of the system, Blight's crew had been monitoring communication bleed. They had pieced together more and more information and presented it to Macharius. The invaders were attacking cities by surprise then withdrawing, taking hundreds, sometimes thousands of the population with them, leaving far more tortured and dead.

In the great scheme of things, such numbers were

insignificant even on this backwater world, but the effects of the attacks were disproportionate. They generated fear and alarm. They kept forces tied down, protecting their bases and homes, rather than investigating the attackers and responding. I did not have to be Macharius to understand this much. It was self-evident from the digests of information that Blight and his officers presented.

As we watched the planet spin below us, divinatory engines were building a picture of its surface, locating major cities, pinning down the remaining communication sources, compiling as much information as was possible. Macharius had set up a command centre near the bridge of the ship and relays of officers came and went. It was obvious he was preparing to intervene. Every now and again he would stop and speak to Logan Grimnar, the massive, youthful-looking envoy of the Space Wolves looming over him. Grimnar would growl something into his sealed comm-net channel. Something was clearly developing there.

Macharius seemed particularly interested in one place, a huge valley in the mountains. Long-range images showed a place that looked like it was a sacred site for xenos, with a massive mountain carved to resemble some inhuman face and a cluster of temples in the long cut of the valley beneath. According to his calculations it was the centre of most of the eldar activity.

Drake studied it and said, 'It is an ancient eldar site. I have seen its like before but never so large or so well preserved.'

'This is not an eldar world,' said Macharius. 'Most of those cities are human and almost all of the signal traffic we can decrypt.'

'I doubt the eldar have been here for a long time,' said Drake. 'They vanished from the surface of most worlds millennia ago, leaving only relics, abandoned cities, ruins.'

'What happened to them?'

'No one knows. There was some great catastrophe that destroyed their civilisation.'

'It looks like they have decided to reclaim this world, then,' said Macharius. 'All of the xenos energy signatures we can pick up are centred there.'

'What do you plan on doing about it?' The inquisitor frowned as he studied the map. Macharius had zoomed in to reveal the valley in the mountains, its temples and statues of gigantic alien daemon-gods in greater detail.

'I plan on landing our troops and securing the valley. They do not outnumber us, in fact I suspect there are significantly fewer of them than us.'

Drake shook his head. 'They seek to enslave a world with a few thousand warriors, that is insane.'

'They do not seek to enslave it. They are enslaving a few of the population and tying up what is left of the defences. All of this is a distraction. It must be. They are sowing terror and creating chaos. They do not plan on holding this world or even doing a significant amount of damage to it. They just mean to see that no one interferes with them. They are using speed and momentum and the lack of communications between the world's inhabitants to give the impression that there are many more of them than there actually are.'

'Are you sure?'

'You have studied the report decrypts as much as I, what did you see?'

'Eldar strike forces slaughtering incompetent militia whenever they liked.'

'Yes, but look at the pattern.'

'What pattern?'

'Attacks are always at least a few hours apart.'

'So?'

'With sufficiently swift vehicles, these attacks could be carried out by the same force.'

'That's an interesting guess.'

'It's not a guess. There are multiple attacks, but if you look at the aggregate reports the numbers never exceed more than a few thousand. The eldar commander is using superior mobility to give the impression of a much larger force than exists down there. He is causing as much chaos as possible. His forces are destroying power cores, communications grids, railheads, space-fields. Any attempts to concentrate forces are smashed.'

'I will take your word for it.'

'The valley is central to the continent, capable of being fortified and the one place they could make all their attacks from in the time spans available. Their ships and aircraft always come from there or pass over it.'

'I believe you, but how are the eldar getting away with it?'

'The orbital monitors were destroyed in the initial wave of attacks. The defenders are blind. The attackers are not. Nor are we. I can see what the planetary commanders cannot.

I have a massed armoured force. We can stop these aliens. We can certainly drive them out of the valley.'

'That would be a good thing,' said Drake. There was a note of irony in his voice that Macharius ignored.

'Yes, it would,' he said. 'The eldar headquarters is in that valley. That is where the Fist will be. We can save it from xenos hands and we can bring this world back into the Emperor's Light at the same time.'

Whatever else you said about Macharius, you could not say he lacked ambition or depth of vision. He had seen multiple opportunities here, and he was ready to grasp them. Drake just looked at him, waiting for him to go on.

'We are the only humans in the system who can provide intelligence and coordination to the planetary defence, as well as an armoured spearhead capable of standing against the invaders. When we appear it will seem as if the Emperor himself has sent us to deliver this world from its attackers.'

Or if it did not now, it would look that way by the time Macharius had finished. I understood him well enough to grasp that.

'Are you certain you understand the situation down there correctly?' Drake asked. 'What if you are wrong?'

'Then we will all die. But I am not wrong.'

He spoke with his usual certainty, but I could not help but remember the temple gardens back on Demetrius. He had not been wrong there either, and still we had almost lost our lives.

'We will make contact with the human leaders, and then we will begin.'

* * *

The face of the Tyrant of Kha held a worried expression. It had done ever since he had stepped off the shuttle, surrounded by his retinue. He was clearly afraid and desperate as we ushered him into Macharius's presence. The Tyrant was a middle-aged man, hair black, sprinkled with silver. His moustache was white. His eyebrows were so black I suspected they had been dyed. He looked quizzically at Macharius. Macharius looked back at him. Grimnar stepped into sight from behind a throne. The Tyrant's eyes went wide with shock at the sight of a Space Marine.

'I am the Lord High Commander Solar Macharius,' Macharius said. 'I represent the Imperium of Man. I have come to free you from the scourge of the eldar and bring you the Light of the Emperor's rule.'

The Tyrant looked off to one side, by force of habit glancing at one of his advisors, a good-looking woman only slightly younger than he. Wife or counsellor or both. She made a small hand gesture that might have simply been her fidgeting or might have been a signal. He nodded ever so slightly and looked back at Macharius and said, 'Any aid against this xenos scourge would be welcome.'

He quite pointedly had not mentioned that the Light of the Emperor's rule would be received with similar enthusiasm. I guessed he was quite happy ruling his section of the world in his own name. Of course, as far as he was concerned he might soon be the absolute ruler of nothing unless something was done about the xenos. He was quite clearly prepared to accept aid from Macharius now and deal with the consequences later.

'When did they arrive?' Macharius asked.

'Less than a moon ago. The first we knew was when our vox-grid went dark. It was too thorough to be a simple malfunction. Mere minutes afterwards, raiders hit our outlying cities and knocked out our defence bunkers. Since then they have been attacking our city at will. I have tried to form alliances with my fellow Tyrants in other cities, but the couriers get through only rarely. I was astonished when your emissary managed to establish a link.'

'We will be using it in the future to coordinate the defence. We should be able to give you some warning of incoming attacks. We have established the fact that the xenos are using a valley in the mountains as their primary base, a relic of blasphemous xenos.'

A confused look passed over the Tyrant's face. 'The Valley of the Ancients? That makes no sense. Surely one of the greater city-states would be better.'

It did not suit Macharius to tell him quite how few the xenos were and that they would have difficulty holding down the population of a whole city. 'I believe it was once a site sacred to their deviant race. Perhaps they have some unholy purpose there. In any case, I intend to cleanse them from it.'

The Tyrant nodded. He was obviously not troubled by the fact that the ancient site was under xenos control. The only thing that meant anything to him was probably that his city-state was the closest major population centre to the valley. This meant, as far as he was concerned, that it was bearing the brunt of the attacks.

'You wish to use Kha as a staging post for your attack,' said the Tyrant, who clearly had not got his position by being slow on the uptake.

Macharius nodded.

'That might draw unwelcome attention to us,' said the Tyrant.

'You are already receiving that attention,' said Macharius. 'I will end it.'

'You are very sure of yourself,' said the Tyrant.

'I will drive these xenos off,' said Macharius. 'I will remember those who aided me. I will also remember those who opposed me. The Imperium is the most powerful force in the universe. It rewards those who stand with it. It punishes those who defy it. It protects its allies. It smashes its enemies.'

The Tyrant looked around. I could practically see what he was thinking. The ship was impressive. He had been brought the long way from the docking airlock. He had seen how vast it was. He had no idea of how many other ships there might be. Macharius carried himself with superb confidence, and then there was Grimnar. I could tell the Tyrant was wondering if he was really seeing one of the legendary Space Marines of the Adeptus Astartes. Even if one had not been seen in this sector for millennia, they would not have been forgotten.

'We will of course cooperate in any way possible,' said the Tyrant. 'But our forces are shattered and demoralised, and our resources are scant.'

'We require only a secure place to set down our forces,'

said Macharius, 'and local guides would be useful. Troops who know the mountainous area leading into the valley.'

'Such can be provided,' said the female advisor. I noticed that the Tyrant did not contradict her or object to her speaking. 'My husband can arrange such things. You will need to provide troops to guard what is left of the space-field perimeter in case of attack. My husband cannot guarantee that our troops could hold it in the face of these inhuman enemies.'

'The perimeter will be secured by my personal guard until we have landed our armour.'

'Armour?' the Tyrant said.

'We have brought Baneblades, Shadowswords and other super-heavy tanks. My force is entirely mechanised.'

'And you intend to take it through the mountains to the sacred valleys?'

'The ways look passable. Are there local conditions I should know about?'

The Tyrant considered this for a moment. 'The mountains would be a terrible place to be ambushed. There are local tribes, bandits who have swarmed there since the world was first taken by men. They defied our rule. They could never be entirely hunted down or exterminated.'

'Is that so?' Macharius said. His face and his voice were bland. I guessed he was interested in these bandits. They might prove more useful allies than the Tyrant and his followers. If those thoughts were running through his mind, he gave no sign of it. 'I will bear that in mind.'

'It would be wise to,' said the Tyrant.

* * *

Kha was surrounded by mountains. It lay in a long valley at the roots of the range and the titanic, snow-capped spires looming over it like great white-haired giants. The space-field had been hit hard by the eldar. I could see burned-out vehicles along the perimeter and ruined control towers where they had struck. I could see Leman Russ amid the rubble, weapons facing outwards as they guarded the landing site where the shuttles had landed.

The old familiar roar of tank engines filled the still, cold air. It made me nostalgic thinking of all the other times I had spent hearing that sound. I had been more than two decades listening to the rumble of mighty engines flood the air of dozens of worlds. The acrid smell of engine exhaust hit my nostrils.

I scanned the sky. Large birds, most likely predators of some kind, hung on the thermals amid the peaks. White clouds smudged the clear blue. The air seemed to have some special quality to it; it was so clear I felt like I could see further than I ever had before. I felt a certain curiosity, I must admit, knowing that somewhere over there was a secret valley occupied by the enemies of mankind. I turned and looked back towards the city.

It was not a hive. It was a massive, tangled sprawl of buildings made from old grey stone. Huge statues rose amid the towers. I could see that some of the buildings had been shattered. Their metal spines were showing. Their structures were scorched black in places as though they had been hit by some powerful weapon and burned. There were crowds of locals around the chain-link fences of the field looking in. I studied them through the magnoculars, ostensibly to check for threats to Macharius's safety, in reality out of simple curiosity.

They had the look of refugees mostly. Their clothes were dirty, their faces had a starved appearance; more than that, there was fear there, a haunted quality that made them look frail and fragile. I thought of what I had seen of the eldar, of how they had tortured and maimed for pleasure, and I tried to imagine what it was like to have been driven out of hearth and home by such creatures and to lie awake at night, under a planetary sky, fearing their return.

'See anything interesting, Lemuel?' Macharius asked. He was standing beside me on the field, looking around with the intense interest he always had when he set foot on a new world. He seemed to be testing the air and the gravity as if they contained information vital to victory. Who knows, perhaps for him they did.

'Refugees, sir, unless I miss my guess. I doubt they are any threat to us.'

'It tells us something, though, Lemuel.'

'Does it, sir?'

'It tells us that the Tyrant and his regime are not terribly well organised or they would have set up shelters and encampments for such people.' For Macharius, a problem could always be solved by logistics. Or almost always.

'Perhaps he has, sir. And perhaps those folk just don't want to stay there. Or perhaps they have come simply to take a look at us. To see what we are like. There might not be much other entertainment for them.'

'Is that what you think we are for them, Lemuel? Entertainment? We are protecting them and bringing them the Emperor's Law.'

'Of course, sir. That too.' I wondered if Macharius had ever known what it was like to be poor and have no other entertainment save what you saw in the street. The answer was obvious.

'I will have the quartermaster disburse some ration tabs to the crowd,' he said. 'It won't do any harm to get some of the locals on our side.'

It was typical of him to turn a gesture of charity into a military action. The charity was genuine, I think. But still it was propaganda.

An alien-looking craft, all predatory lines and curves swept over the horizon, ignoring the clouds of anti-aircraft fire that tracked it. I wondered if it was the first of many, but it was only a scout.

Some of our own Lightning fighters scrambled to intercept it. They swept away beyond the mountains and were lost to our sight.

The humans are transporting a force down to the planet's surface. They have already established a beachhead. Observers have noted a large contingent of their primitive but powerful armour. There is a practised precision about what they are doing that suggests competence and experience. These warriors will not be like the planetary defenders, easy prey to our superior tactics and technology. The warriors appear to be wearing the same green uniforms as those on the ship that escaped. Is it possible that their commander, this Macharius, has returned seeking vengeance? I must see some prisoners are taken and interrogated.

In truth, I would welcome his presence. I like my prey to be challenging. It will help stave off boredom while I wait the last few days for the gate to open. I will take any amusement I can find at the moment, no matter how petty.

I toy with ordering a strike against them now. It would mean concentrating my force at one point and attacking them when they most expect it, at a place where they would have plenty of human allies to act as cannon fodder. It would mean revealing the true strength of my force, which is smaller than the humans', although doubtless infinitely superior in morale, firepower and tactical ability.

The alternative is to wait. Time is on my side. The longer I wait, the closer I get to the gate opening and the secrets of the ancients entering my grasp. I doubt the humans will arrive before that happens.

Am I willing to defer gratification for so long? I am. Unlike Sileria and Bael and the others I need not give in to the first impulse that enters my mind. That is what makes me a leader and them followers.

Chapter Seventeen

Long lines of Imperial armour rumbled along the old road from Kha towards the distant mountains. The tracks churned up the ancient stonework, which had not been made to take the weight of super-heavy battle tanks. I found myself wondering what purpose this road had served. Perhaps it had been a trade artery linking this city-state with another. Perhaps it had provided pilgrims with an access route to the holy valleys. Perhaps there were mines up there and this was a trade route. I studied the road looking for clues, but if there were any I never saw them.

I had plenty of time to think about such things because I was standing behind Macharius in the turret of the Bane-blade. He was surveying our surroundings through his magnoculars. He liked to get a feel for the terrain. I worried about the fact that we might see eldar aircraft moving to attack us. On these narrow roads any flyer with sufficiently powerful weapons could wreak terrible havoc. I did not have much fear for the Baneblade. This ancient monster would be proof against most such weapons. But there were other vehicles, packed with troops, which might be vulnerable.

This was good terrain for an ambush. There were many smaller valleys and gulleys leading off from the one that the road ran through. Huge boulders marked the hillside. There were caves up there, and I was sure there were people watching us. I sometimes caught the glitter of the sun on magnocular lenses. I saw signs of stealthy movement that set the hairs on the back of my neck to rising. It might have been some mountain predator, but I did not think so. I thought there were men in those mountains who were watching us pass through their land.

I thought of what the Tyrant had said about bandits. That did not imply any love was lost between the mountain people and the city-dwellers, and they would know where we had come from. I doubted we had anything to fear from hill-bandits unless we were beaten at the Valley of the Ancients. Irregular troops could make our line of retreat very unsafe indeed. I thought of the effects of demolition charges on these mountain roads, of man-made landslides, of all the things a few determined men could do against an armoured convoy.

I wondered what was going through Macharius's mind. Was this what he had expected to find when he set out? I doubted it. How could he have expected to encounter a force of xenos. He had come prepared for some trouble, though, and I was glad. This was not the usual sledgehammer world-conquering army he would have brought to bear during the course of a normal campaign, but there were enough troops to give me some sense of security and the idea that we would achieve our goal.

I was especially glad of that when I thought about the insanity of the eldar we had encountered, their unending, unrelenting malice and cruelty. I found that despite my horror I was looking forward to reaching our objective. I was looking forward to another chance at killing them.

I looked up at the sky. It was reassuring to think that somewhere in space overhead was a company of Space Wolves ready to drop in and reinforce us. I would have been happier with a Chapter, but you can't have everything.

I wondered what they were thinking. Most likely they planned to drop on the site under cover of our attack and reclaim the Fist. It appeared to be what Macharius expected, and he was usually right about such things.

It seems certain the humans are advancing towards the valley. They have ascertained our position and are moving against us with their cumbersome vehicles. Despite the primitive nature of their tanks, it is nonetheless a formidable force, made all the more so by the presence of the warship in orbit.

The swiftness with which the human commander has assembled his forces and launched them through the mountains is impressive. I am afraid that dealing with the slow-witted inhabitants of this world has caused me to underestimate humans in general. I confess I am pleased. There is more pleasure to be had from humbling foes who at least have a comprehension of the basic uses of military force.

I am left with several choices. I can cease harassing the primitive cities and concentrate my forces on this new threat. This will give the humans a respite and a chance to organise against me, and most likely they will swiftly realise they have an advantage. Or I can wait for the humans to reach me here and do battle on a prepared ground of my choosing.

The main thing is to hold the valley for the moment. Timing is becoming critical. Soon the gate will open and I wish to be here when that happens. I do not want to surrender any ground to the humans. It would be foolish to allow the prize to be snatched from my hands at this late hour.

Let them come. I have a few surprises in store for them when they get here.

It grew swiftly cold in the mountains once the sun went down. The temperature dropped perceptibly within minutes. Breath clouded in the cold air. We set up camp, the largest and least vulnerable of our vehicles forming a perimeter around our improvised base, turrets turned to face outwards, engines left running to provide warmth. Our scouts had chosen a valley large enough to contain our entire force. It was easy enough to hold each end of it. Lines of fire covered the approaches. Overhead, I caught sight of a sleek eldar craft silhouetted against the moon. A few of our fighter air cover got on its tail and the battle raged on somewhere into the darkness, moving out of sight behind distant mountains. Thunder rumbled and lightning flashed where the conflict continued.

We sat ourselves around a fire, eating rations out of mess-tins. Macharius and Drake sat like common soldiers. It was not just for the sake of morale. It made them less conspic-uous targets for any sharpshooter seeking officers to kill. They ate the same field rations with the same cheap Impe-rial Guard-issue utensils. Back on Emperor's Glory, they might have the ransom of planetary governors. Here they mucked in with the rest of us.

'In two more days we should reach the valley,' Macharius said. 'We will drive out the xenos and take possession of it in the Emperor's name.'

'You think it will be that easy?' Drake said. There was a troubled expression on his face. More and more of late it had been there in his dealings with Macharius. If I was not talking about an inquisitor I would be tempted to say it looked as if he were having a crisis of faith. In Macharius.

'Easy or not, it is what we must do. I have not come so far to fail now at the last hurdle.'

'Are the maps of the valley the Tyrant gave us accurate enough for our purposes?'

'They match our orbital divinations in so far as they go. The secret underground routes may prove useful, but I am not counting on them.'

'That is wise since they may not be secret any longer. The

eldar have been in possession of the place long enough to find them…'

'But they have not, at least not all of them,' said a strongly accented voice. I looked up and saw a massive bearded man flanked by two members of Macharius's Lion Guard. More soldiers were with him. One of them said, 'Speak to the Lord High Commander when you are spoken to.' He turned to Macharius and said, 'We found him skulking around the edges of the camp, my lord.'

The bearded man laughed. 'You found me because I stood up and let you see me, otherwise I could have walked into your camp and taken food from your plates without being noticed.' The Guard lieutenant turned and looked as though he were about to strike the giant. Macharius raised his hand and said in a level voice, 'You do not have the look of a thief, sir.'

'I take what I want from those who pass through my land without my permission,' said the hill-man. 'It seems only fair. It is more in the nature of a toll.'

'Why did you allow my sentries to see you?'

'I wanted to talk with you, to see what manner of man commands this force. You are moving towards the xenos so that means you are no city-man, certainly not one of Kha. None of them would dare move towards the valley now. The mere thought of those xenos has them shitting in their pants.'

'And yet you are not afraid,' Macharius said. The big man laughed.

'Oh, I am afraid. Any sane man would be of those xenos.

They are not like the peaceful beings our legends spoke of. They live to torture and kill, and they have more ways of going about doing so than a Dakathi village woman. The screams that rise from the Valley of the Ancients let us know that. I have toyed with sending them some of my enemies for their sport, but in the end I found I did not have the stomach for it.'

'You would deal with xenos?' Drake asked. There was a note of soft, purring menace in his voice.

The hill-man studied him, obviously aware of the threat and equally obviously unafraid. He shook his head. 'In the hills we are unkind to our enemies. As unkind as can be. Or so I thought until I saw those eldar. I find at this late hour, and very greatly to my surprise, that there are things I would not do to my worst enemy.' He laughed and shook his head as though he really were surprised to find this thing out about himself.

'You still have not told me why you are here,' said Macharius. Something about his tone suggested that an explanation might well be a thing it was in the hill-man's best interests to provide.

'Our watchers saw you emerge from the city. They saw your ships come down on the field. The people wanted to know who you are and why you have come.'

'We have come from the Imperium of Man to bring the Emperor's Law,' said Macharius. 'We have come to drive back the xenos.'

'You will make war on the eldar?'

'Yes,' said Macharius.

'I will take word of that back to the people of the mountains.'

'Will you aid us?' Macharius asked.

'If you fight against the eldar, we will. If you recognise our ancient claim to these mountains, we will.'

Macharius simply looked at the hill-man. He was turning over possibilities in his mind. I knew he was thinking that he did not know whether the hill-men had a claim to these mountains or not. He took only moments to consider. 'If such claims are just, I will support them.'

The hill-man smiled back at him. 'They are just.'

'That must be decided at a future date after all claims are weighed,' said Macharius. He spoke slowly and clearly, making sure his every word was heard and understood. He was not going to commit himself or the Imperium to anything as small as some hill-man's claim of truth.

'If you are a just man that is enough,' said the hill-man. 'I will carry your word back to the people.' He looked pointedly at the Guardsmen surrounding him. 'With your permission, of course.'

Macharius nodded to them. The hill-man padded off into the night.

'He may be a spy,' said Drake.

'Of course he is a spy,' said Macharius. 'But he has not learned anything here that he could not have from watching us from the hills.'

'On the contrary,' said Drake. 'He has learned who our leader is.'

Macharius nodded. We changed our position. That night

we slept within the hull of the Baneblade. For me, it was like old times. I found being inside the huge tank reassuring. It had been almost ten years since the destruction of *Old Number Ten*.

For the next two days, as we moved through the mountains we were aware of being shadowed by forces of men. They could not keep up with the speed of moving vehicles, but the road was winding and they seemed able to scuttle directly over the high mountain passes. There was always someone watching us, but they never made a hostile move against us. Eldar flyers assaulted our column but were driven off by our fighter cover.

On the last evening before we reached the Valley of the Ancients, the night was split by columns of light and pillars of fire. Macharius had ordered the bombardment to begin on the eldar in the valley and Blight had obeyed. His ship had taken up a geo-stationary position in orbit and lashed the xenos below.

I stood on a ridge overlooking the valley and studied the fury of the attack. Missiles blew massive craters out of the earth. Energy beams turned gigantic eldar statues cherry-red. There were no eldar to be seen through Ivan's magnoculars.

'Blight has probably killed them all,' said Anton. His voice was flat in direct contrast to his cocky and assured manner.

'More likely they have taken refuge in the tombs and shrines below,' I said. 'They are supposed to run for leagues down there. It's what we would be doing. I don't think they are any more stupid than we are.'

'In Anton's case that would not be possible,' Ivan said.

'Ha-bloody-ha!'

'They'll come back out when we get there, no doubt,' said Ivan. The light reflected on the metal of his face, making it look like some daemonic mask.

'Can't say as I am looking forward to facing them,' said Anton. It was probably the first time I had ever heard him admit such a thing. There was something about the xenos which spooked even a man of his limited imagination. I ran the magnoculars over the valley again. Some of the grounded eldar vehicles lay like smashed insect carapaces on the valley floor. It looked like the barrage was not completely worthless.

I felt an elbow nudge me in the ribs. Ivan was pointing at something, and I glanced in the direction indicated. I could see we were not alone on the ridge. There were groups of figures standing amid clusters of boulders, watching the hellish firestorm below. It took me a moment to realise that they were not our troops, but groups of hill-men, come to observe this demonstration of monstrous power. They did not do anything threatening, but it was worrying that they had managed to take up their positions so close without us noticing till the last second.

I tried to tell myself it was because all of our attention had been focused on the valley below, but that was not reassuring. I should not have allowed myself to do that, to concentrate on one thing to the exclusion of all others. Such a lapse could easily get all of us killed.

I turned the magnoculars on the hill-men. They were all

robed and cowled and carried autoguns and lasguns. Their attention was as focused as ours had been on the valley below, but always in the groups at least one of them was on sentry duty and looking in our direction. I doubted that we would be taking any of them unaware. I thought about what they were doing. Maybe they had come to watch the slaughter of the xenos, but it was just as possible that they wanted to witness the effect of the bombardment. It would enable them to judge the weaponry we had available to us and its effectiveness.

In this they would perhaps be foolish. It would not be a wise thing to judge the might of the Imperium by the barrage laid down by a single ship, just as it would be foolish to judge the strength of its armies by the size of the bodyguard Macharius had brought. Then again, these were the only indicators the hill-men would have to work with.

They did not appear hostile. Given the behaviour of the eldar, that was understandable. I doubted the xenos wanted human allies, and it was very unlikely they had done anything to endear themselves to the hill-men. Quite the opposite seemed likely. Not that it mattered. The attack was going to come soon. Sooner, in fact, than I anticipated.

The ground shakes. Buildings glow with a cherry light as the fury of the orbital bombardment descends upon them. There is a certain primeval loveliness to the effect. Nonetheless, I am glad I have ordered my warriors to await the conflict deep beneath the earth or dispersed them through the mountains far from the points of impact. They move quickly and once the bombardment ends will be able to return in force.

They intend to clear the ridges around the valleys and occupy them, so much is obvious. I will let them take the heights for a time. The entrances to the valley are narrow and provide a choke point where I can ensnare my enemies. Once they are in, they will not find it quite so easy to get out.

The trap is set. I will let these presumptuous mon-keigh enter the valley, and once they are within, my forces will emerge from beneath ground and the surrounding mountains and trap them. Our fleet will make sure their warship cannot intervene. This valley will be their graveyard.

I watch the bombardment continue. It is as I suspected. They are not hitting the valley with the full force of their weapons. For whatever reasons they wish to spare the buildings, or perhaps take us alive. There is no other reason so powerful a force would have been dispatched to assault the valley. They could just have bombarded us from orbit. Perhaps they realise how deep this complex runs. There is no way even the most persistent onslaught from orbit could affect us in the depths. Indeed, the great temple I have chosen as my headquarters is strong enough to withstand the bombardment easily. The massive external walls are warmed by the blasts, but the effects are barely felt within at all.

All they can hope to do is keep us underground while they advance. The bombardment will have to cease at some point to allow the human troops to proceed. When that happens we will emerge and slaughter them.

Soon my ships will engage their warship, and this time it will be in earnest. The humans will have no way to retreat off-planet. The time will soon be here when this farce will be ended.

We had no sooner returned to camp than we were told to report to the command vehicle. We raced there and clambered up the side of the Baneblade. Macharius was waiting, looking relaxed.

'We are going to attack tonight,' he said. We all of us looked at him. It was pointless asking why. He was the commanding officer and in no way obliged to explain his decisions. I thought about all the trouble we had gone to setting up camp, building perimeters, setting sentries. We were in a camp which had given every indication of settling down for the night. Doubtless that was what any enemy scouts were intended to think. It even explained why we had been given leave to go off and observe the valley. Our enemies would anticipate that the barrage would rumble on all night and the attack would come at dawn.

Macharius returned to studying his maps. There were three ways into the valley, only one of which was suitable for super-heavy tanks. It was not a situation that Macharius would like. It made his approach too predictable. At some point the bombardment would have to cease and the enemy would know only too well where to mass its firepower to meet us.

I was surprised to hear orders sending masses of the armour to the east, to an approach where the valley's entrance was a choke point through which our largest vehicles could not pass. I wondered briefly whether Macharius had gone insane. I could see the others had too. Maybe he knew something we did not. Maybe he intended to place us on the slopes overlooking the valley where we could fire onto the enemy within. I slid behind the controls of the Baneblade, invoked the rituals and listened to the thunder of the drives as they fired up.

It was going to be a long night.

CHAPTER EIGHTEEN

I was back behind the controls of the Baneblade when we moved off, our force divided into three parts. At least half our number were taking the obvious route, the one accessible even to the heaviest of vehicles, the main road that led into the east of the valley. Two smaller flanking forces were moving up narrow roads in the hillside on either side of the main road. Artillery was to deploy on the heights overlooking the eastern edge of the valley. Air cover was being held ready for the moment when the barrage ended and the enemy emerged.

We headed to the eastern entrance to the valley, and our vehicle was in the fore. The command Baneblade was even more heavily armoured than a normal super-heavy tank, and Macharius always liked to lead from the front. I did not see what good it was going to do. Once we reached the narrow defile we would be like a cork in the neck of a bottle, stoppering the advance of every tank behind us.

Still, it was not for me to doubt Macharius. I concentrated on the path ahead. At first it was wide. Rocks cracked beneath our treads and the Baneblade rocked from side to side on the uneven ground. I turned us into the defile that led into the valley, and the walls of the cliffs closed in around us.

Down the line of the defile was a narrow slit through which an angry sky was visible. It looked barely wide enough for a man to walk through, but that was just me projecting my knowledge of its narrowness.

The lightning of the barrage split the night, turning the sky brilliant momentarily and then leaving everything seem darker, as if the onslaught itself cast a vast shadow over the mountains.

In the distance, I briefly saw a distant peak illuminated by one mighty flash before it turned once more into a massive, ominous bulk.

There was another flash, more brilliant than the last, and the ground shook as if we were in the grip of an earthquake. The Baneblade shivered.

And then all sound seemed to cease. The world was suddenly appallingly quiet after the thunder of the great explosion. I felt the pounding of my heart in my chest. I became aware of the Baneblade's engines once more, and all the normal sounds you hear in the interior of an Imperial battle tank. All of them felt shockingly loud as my mind sought to adjust to the comparative quiet.

I looked again, and it came to me that the mouth of the defile had suddenly widened.

'Increase speed to maximum, Lemuel,' said Macharius. I did as I was told.

Objects started to ping off the front of the Baneblade, making a grating sound. Something slowed us, and I realised we were encountering physical resistance as we smashed through large boulders and chunks of rock and broken statues, some of which we were grinding to dust beneath our treads.

I concentrated on holding our line. I could hear Macharius responding to incoming reports over the comm-net, and it dawned on me what he must have done. The bombardment had been concentrated near the cliffs overlooking the valley entrance. Under cover of it, siege engineers had been rushed forwards and planted demolition charges. The charges had detonated, opening the bottlenecks and leaving only rubble, which could be pushed aside by a sufficiently powerful vehicle such as a Baneblade.

We had gained an entrance to the Valley of the Ancients. I wondered how much good it would do us. Suddenly, contrails of fire lit the night. Thunderhawk gunships were dropping like meteors from orbit to aid us. The Space Wolves rode trails of plasma down from the sky in search of battle. Their course would take them somewhere into the middle of the valley.

It was as I had suspected – they were using our attack to cover their own.

* * *

The bombardment has stopped. That means the attack will soon begin. I smile, thinking about the trap I have prepared for these arrogant interlopers. Soon they will learn the meaning of terror. Soon I will feast upon their delicious agony.

I notice the changes in the topography of the map. My opponent is clever. He has used explosives to blast a clear path into the valley at what should have been a choke point. He has outfoxed himself. My plan does not rely on choke points. It relies on letting my foe into the Valley of the Ancients, on leading him on and letting him think he is victorious, only to crush him at the moment when he believes victory is within his grasp.

It has always been my greatest pleasure to lead my foes on like this. There is something that appeals to the vanity of every commander, to think that he is crushing his enemy; so few of them realise that they are not as clever as they think.

It is a mighty force my enemy has assembled. I can see the blocks that represent massive armoured vehicles moving into the valley and taking up position on its edges. They are getting ready to pour a hail of fire onto what they think are defenceless targets. I have left enough of my force within the valley to lend plausibility to this interpretation of the data. In truth, I do not have enough warriors left here to oppose my enemies directly, although I have a contingency plan in mind should things go wrong. All we really need to do is withdraw beneath ground into the subterranean labyrinth that runs so far beneath the temple complex.

I order my warriors to open fire on the incoming enemies. We must put up at least a token show of resistance in order to draw them in. They will be expecting some opposition and some opposition they will have.

I feel a surge of glee when I contemplate the punishment I will inflict upon these arrogant vermin. I will have their commander within my grasp. I have given orders to ensure that he is preserved so that I may feast upon his life force as it slowly drains away under my torture implements. Such a consummation is to be devoutly wished for.

The ground vibrates. The roar of weapons fills the air, audible even through my helmet. It is a reminder that battles are not followed merely in the mind, that all of those symbols dancing in the air in front of me represent real objects, real people, real bodies being reduced to pulped flesh and jellied bone.

Part of me wishes to rush out there into the chaos of battle and reap lives. I tell myself that there will be time enough for that later, that I must content myself with more intellectual pleasures at the moment.

I notice something new. On the display, flickers of yellow light are descending upon the valley from above. This is not at all what I expected; not cumbersome armour and fast-moving air support but something else.

The flickers descend with awesome speed. Their descent is aimed at exactly this temple, as if they knew where my headquarters was and intended to take it.

I contemplate the possibility of treachery and dismiss it immediately. None of my warriors could possibly have had anything to do with these human apes. Could prisoners have escaped? Impossible! Perhaps some of the primitives above have scouted out our positions. There are tribes in those hills who spy on us. Even so, how could they know where I was? It is most likely pure chance. Nonetheless, it could prove fatal.

In the time it has taken me to assemble these thoughts, the attackers have completed their descent and I can detect the stutter of weapons on the roof of the temple complex. I hear screams and howled war cries. It looks as though I will get my wish after all; there will be some physical combat. I smile and unlimber my weapons. It will be a pleasure.

Looking down into the valley I saw the gods. Some of them glowed from the heat absorbed from orbital las-hits. They shimmered in the gloom. There were dozens more of them, carved from stone. In the darkness they were massive presences, humanoid, gigantic; something from a time before men had walked this world, when it had belonged to others, not as we.

The largest statues stood on a massive plinth in the centre of the valley, at the exact central point. To the north, a vast face had been carved into the side of the mountain. It looked down on everything, a blank, inhuman, mocking mask. Sheer cliffs surrounded the valley. In alcoves carved in their rock faces, more alien gods stood. Three massive temple buildings, curved in the eldar fashion, dominated the north-west, north-east and southern parts of the valley.

I could see that the gods were not human and had not

been carved by human hands. They were the gods of our enemies.

At least there were similarities between them and the tall, spindly and dynamic creatures emerging from the mouths of the temples in which they had sheltered. The statues suggested their grace and beauty; what they lacked, though, was their evil. These gods were benevolent – their postures and expressions, even visible only for seconds, suggested that. You could not picture them torturing their foes for pleasure. They were the deities of a peaceful people, not the cruel monsters we faced this night. Those things were as different from the people who had made the stone gods as dark from light. Something terrible had happened somewhere to effect this transformation.

Such thoughts flickered through my mind as I watched the eldar prepare to fight us. Their vehicles were fast and light, and they moved through the air. Some of them looked like ships that might once have sailed upon the sea. Some of them were gigantic, organic-looking war machines that reminded me of Imperial Walkers. With the speed of lightning and the precision of a cast thunderbolt, they arced towards the main entrance to the valley, where our force was ready to meet them.

Sporadic fire began to light the valley, and the statues became ever more visible in the light of rocket flare and muzzle flash. The Space Wolves had dropped onto the roof of the eastern temple. I could see the flash of weapons fire from there. Thunderhawks were moving down the valley, strafing as they went.

That eastern valley entrance became a killing ground where xenos weapons unleashed bursts of fire. The main battle tanks in the lead took them and endured, surviving the initial onslaught. A wave of lighter xenos vehicles surged into them, deploying alien infantry who attempted to break into the vehicles over which they swarmed. I shuddered when I thought of facing those deadly creatures in the confines of a tank. It did not matter that the restricted space would reduce their advantage of speed and mobility. The idea of being trapped in a tight space with one of the eldar filled my soul with horror.

Macharius gave the order to open fire. From the heights on the east of the valley, a withering wave of fire smashed into the eldar. They did not have the durability of Baneblades. Those opening salvoes from lascannons carved huge holes in their ranks, smashed vehicles, tossed bodies into the sky and sent them sprawling dead in blast craters. The spearhead of our column broke out into the valley. More and more of our troops followed us in and spread out to engage the enemy. As the frontage of our formation increased, so did the overwhelming amount of firepower we could deploy.

It gave us an advantage. The main force moved down into the valley firing as it came. Our artillery laid down a curtain of fire from the heights. Our own vehicles rumbled forward, blasting away. Some of the eldar dived into the temples, taking cover there.

The rest of the xenos retreated swiftly towards the far northern end of the valley, beneath the gaze of that great carved face, skimming swiftly above the ground with a speed we could not hope to match. I half expected them to turn at bay, but they did not, Instead they raced out over narrow paths where we could not hope to follow them through or became airborne and vanished into the night.

I heard cheering over the comm-net at how easy our victory had proven. Once again, Macharius had triumphed. I glanced over at him and I noticed he was frowning. I wondered whether he was disappointed because it had been so easy or whether some new problem had suggested itself to his keen mind.

Looking down into the valley, I saw nothing but broken vehicles, broken buildings and broken bodies. The eldar had vanished like daemons into the night, leaving behind only the glowing statues of gods they had once worshipped and which they had now abandoned.

Our assailants are sweeping across the roof of the temple complex, driving my warriors out of their prepared positions and actually killing them. I can hear the surprised reports over our communications channels. This was not what my people expected at all. Instead of slow, fallible humans, they have encountered something far more dangerous.

I suspect I know what that is. I have only a few more moments to wait before I can confirm it.

It seems that there will be a worthwhile challenge involved in this after all, that there will be some glory to be gained. Fortunately, it does not interfere with the implementation of my master plan. I always intended to abandon this command bunker and retreat beneath ground to join my reserves there. This merely complicates the matter. I am not too troubled. One should never expect one's plans to survive contact with the enemy. That is a maxim that any commander should live by.

I hear the sound of a controlled explosion. I hear the sound of crystalline armour shattering. I hear the sound of an eldar dying. I catch the scent of something more than human. I look up and I see a massive armoured figure entering the room. It is too big to be a normal man; it bears some resemblance to one but also to a savage war-beast. In one hand it holds a chainsword, in the other a primitive weapon called a bolter. It raises the weapon and points it at me. I throw myself to one side and the shot passes through the air where I was. It howls with a mixture of rage and frustration, an animal cry that lets me know this is one of the so-called Wolves of Space. In truth, it is worthy of the predatory cognomen. Its features suggest the lupine, its mouth is disfigured by bestial fangs; its eyes reflect the light like those of a dog.

The shell embeds itself in the breast of one of my lieutenants and explodes a microsecond later. In that time I have covered the ground towards the Space Marine, for that is what this creature is. I slash at it with the razor-sharp claws of my gauntlet but somehow it avoids me. I'm impressed. It has been a long, long time since anything has managed to do that. It speaks well for the reflex speed of this augmented humanoid.

It lashes out at me with the chainsword. I leap over the blade, feeling the faint vibration in the air as it passes beneath my feet. I reach out and slash the human's cheek. This time I make contact and the venom in my gauntlets takes effect. I can see that the Space Marine is not as affected as he should be. Something in his system is already starting to compensate for the effects of the poison, but, for a fatal instant, he is slowed down just enough for me to pull out his eyes.

Even then he does not react as a normal human would. He continues to sweep the air before him with his blade, hoping to strike me as part of the pattern. I drop to the floor beneath his area of attack and sweep his legs out from underneath him. I roll one side to avoid the blade as it falls, biting chunks out of the stone of the floor. I turn, put my gun against his head and trigger it. Flesh shreds, reinforced bone resists, brain explodes outwards. I flip myself back onto my feet and glance around, taking in the scene.

More and more of the Space Marines are pouring into the room, more and more of my warriors are moving to meet them. An enormous melee swirls through the chamber. At the moment it looks as though my people can win, but who knows how many more of the human warriors are waiting out there. This is a distraction I cannot afford at this stage of the battle.

Smoke starts to fill the room as equipment catches fire and grenades take effect. The clouds seem too thick and dense for the amount of flame. Some of those thrown missiles are producing the smoke, and it does not take me long to understand why. The Space Marines are capable of finding my people in the obscuring mist. Obviously they are using senses other than sight.

I order one of my squads to fight a holding action while the remainder retreat beneath the earth. I make sure I am in the vanguard. It is senseless for a commander to put himself in the way of danger when there is a battle to be won.

Behind me the sounds of combat fade. I race down the long ramp into the cold darkness beneath the temple complex. I feel the faintest tinge of anger begin to colour my mood. Things have not gone as exactly as I expected. Still, at least I am alive to correct my mistakes. Let the humans enjoy this small victory. In the end it all plays into my hands.

Dawn showed we were completely in possession of the valley. The only signs the eldar had ever been here were their wrecked vehicles. They lay like broken-backed beetles, sparkling in the sun, the flicker of strange energy discharges dancing over their shattered hulls. Our own tanks had once again formed a perimeter, facing outwards, ready to confront any foes. I knew the hill-men were up there watching us, and I strongly suspected the eldar would be there too.

Macharius and Drake stood atop the hull of the command Baneblade. Storm troopers and Macharius's own personal guard surrounded them as they surveyed the battlefield.

'So, Macharius, once again you are victorious,' said Drake. There was no irony in his voice.

'I would not be so certain if I were you,' said Macharius. I glanced over at him once more. It was not like him to express any doubt whatsoever, particularly not when he could be overheard. I came to the immediate conclusion that he wished to be, and that he wanted us to be on our guard.

'The eldar have fled,' said Drake. 'We are left in possession of the field, or rather the valley.'

'Any foe who can flee so swiftly can return just as quickly,' said Macharius. 'The xenos commander saw that the advantage lay with us and did what was needed to neutralise that advantage.'

'Surely he fled because he knew he could not win?'

Macharius shook his head. 'He just wanted to minimise his losses. He knew that we had as many circumstances in our favour as we were ever going to have, and he simply chose not to face us on our own terms. By fleeing now, he ensures he can return at a time of his choosing with most of his force intact. In this case the advantage lies with the most mobile force, and they are far more mobile than we are. The best thing we can do is get ready for their return. Also there are an indeterminate number of eldar in the tunnels beneath us. A coordinated attack from the two factions will be devastating.'

'You are certain that they will attack again?'

'They are here for a reason. If they have not yet found what they were looking for, they will be back.'

'I sense strange energies in this valley. They are growing minute by minute and hour by hour.'

Again Macharius looked troubled. He glanced across at the temple around which the Space Wolves were encamped.

There was one objective that was secure at least. 'The eldar will not give up without a greater battle than this one. I wouldn't, and I have a sense of their commander's mind now. He will not give up either.'

'We should investigate the valley, then, to see if we can find what we came for while there is still time,' said Drake.

It seems I have escaped from the Space Wolves. They have seized my old command bunker and are securing the perimeter. It almost makes me laugh.

In the days we have been here we have had enough time to map a large part of this labyrinth. It fits the ancient building schemata used by our ancestors, so our predictive systems have no difficulty in providing us with guidance through the maze. I have enough troops down here to open up a second front when the time comes. My basic plan of trapping my enemies in the valley is still a good one. But I can foresee some difficulties arising in the not too distant future.

The humans need to be kept from the gate until it is opened and I can pass through and find what I seek. The presence of the Space Wolves is also an unforeseen complication. Given the nature of their senses they may well be able to hunt my people through the labyrinth. We need to be prepared for this.

I run my mind back over the initial stages of the battle. I wonder if perhaps I was not too quick to abandon my prepared defensive position. After all, I have no real idea of how many of the Space Marines are up there. I was merely taken aback by the suddenness of their appearance. Is it possible that I panicked? I dismiss the idea. In any case, it does not matter now. The Space Marines are providing the rest of the humans with the opportunity to advance into the valley and seize the central temple complex.

Everything will have to wait until I implement phase two of my plan. I glance around at this ancient chamber with its murals depicting the insipid faces of forgotten gods, and I look at the surviving members of my personal guard. Their faces are masked, but I can sense them watching me, judging me, trying to decide whether I should be replaced. Let them try! They shall discover exactly how deadly I can be. It is only a matter of time before those gibbering apes on the surface find that out as well.

Grimnar and a squad of his Space Wolves stood watch over the entrance to the northernmost temple complex. It was obvious now what the Space Marines had been doing during the attack. They had secured the entrance to the part of the valley Macharius most wanted to hold. As ever the Lord High Commander's plans had plans within them.

'Did you get the Fist?' Macharius asked as he clambered down from the Baneblade and marched up the steps of the temple.

Grimnar shook his head. 'We have not found it yet, and the eldar have scuttled into the depths below. We will soon hunt them down.'

Within the walls of the temple a massive ramp led down into the vast underground complex. All around us tech-adepts and soldiers were manhandling massive bits of technical equipment into place. It seemed that this was going to be our new field headquarters. Heavy weapons were being set up on the roof, along with communications dishes and divination arrays.

He turned and said, 'Have you made contact with *The Pride of Terra*?' to a communications adept.

'No, sir,' the adept responded. 'Not since the reports of the attacks came. It's all static, as if it's being jammed or as if…'

The adept clearly did not want to say what was on his mind so Macharius finished his sentence for him. 'As if the ship has been destroyed.'

'We have lost contact with *The Pride of Terra*?' Drake asked as he entered the chamber.

'It was attacked by eldar ships,' said Macharius. That was a very ominous thought indeed. We might be stranded here on this alien world without orbital support.

'At least if we are stranded here, so are the eldar,' said Macharius. He was trying to make the best of the situation.

'Unless they have some way of travelling we don't know about,' said Grimnar.

Macharius looked at him. 'Do you have something you would like to share with us, Space Wolf?'

The Adeptus Astartes showed his teeth in a grin that was anything but reassuring. I wondered if his Chapter were like orks. With them a smile is a gesture of menace, like a wild beast showing its fangs.

'There are tales in the sagas of them coming and going in a strange fashion. I have heard tell that the xenos travel strangely through underpaths of the universe, fault lines in space-time that they alone know of.'

'I have heard similar theories,' said Drake as though reluctant to admit to such knowledge.

'I am more concerned with what we seek,' said Macharius eventually. 'The Fist of Demetrius.'

'You have not found it?' Drake asked.

'I have caught its scent dimly,' said Grimnar, 'as though it had been here and removed.'

'Perhaps they want to pollute it with their foul presence.'

'Perhaps they are here for an entirely different reason,' said Macharius. 'It is not safe to assume that their motivations are anything like our own. The main thing is to keep them from getting it.'

'Perhaps what we need is a prisoner,' said Grimnar. He looked at Drake. 'You are a psyker... You could question it.'

'Perhaps,' said Drake. He did not sound at all keen on the idea.

'We'll see what we can do about that,' said Grimnar.

'Let's take a look at what we came for first,' said Macharius. He indicated the ramp that led away into the shadowy gloom below us.

CHAPTER NINETEEN

We moved cautiously down into the labyrinth. The entrance was flanked by two massive statues depicting semi-naked eldar, one female, one male. Their faces both possessed an androgynous beauty. Their lobeless, pointed ears and almond-shaped eyes distinguished them from humans as much as their taller, much more slender forms. They looked like skinny people who had been stretched on a rack, and yet somehow were still beautiful.

Anton and Ivan and I moved along in advance of Macharius, and we were wary. The Undertaker looked as though he were out for a stroll. The green-tunicked soldiers of the Lion Guard looked nervous. Space Wolves ranged ahead of us and behind us. Their keen senses would be able to detect a threat long before we could. Their presence was reassuring.

There could be many of the xenos lurking in the shadows,

waiting to catch interlopers unawares. After the Space Wolves had cleared the area, the route had been checked out by companies of infantrymen, agents of Macharius's security detail and Drake's storm troopers, and still it did not feel quite right. We had seen how swift and agile those eldar were, and I did not doubt they would be able to hide in places that were inaccessible to men.

The complex was huge, a veritable labyrinth buried within the rock of the surrounding mountains. All of the tunnels appeared to interconnect with the different temples. It felt as if the whole complex were an iceberg in the oceans of Jotungarth: nine-tenths of it was beneath the ground. The corridors went on for kilometres, opening into huge vaults and enormous pools of steaming, sulphurous water.

There were signs in xenos hieroglyphics and in the local variant of Imperial Gothic script. There were bridges over vast canyons. Crossing them looking down, you could see reddishly glowing magma so far below that the pools looked like pinpricks. Preliminary scanning had indicated that there were sealed chambers and secret rooms and passages.

The interior of the labyrinth was cool and shadowy. Statues lined the walls. Some of them were smeared with colour as if dyed by recent offerings. I wondered what was going on. It seemed unlikely that those cruel eldar would worship these benevolent deities. Could it have been the humans who had previously held the valley?

Everywhere there were statues of the alien gods. The statues depicted more and more deities. The further we went into the temple, the more lewd and strange looking they became, as if the sculptors had started with an ideal of purity and fell into a reverie of lust as the years went on. It was disquieting. Some of the beings at the back of the temple looked like they might be worshipped by the xenos we had fought, if those creatures were capable of worshipping anything. Or perhaps I was simply projecting my human attitudes onto minds too alien to comprehend.

I studied the galleries above us, looking for anything unusual. I saw only men in the uniform of the Lion Guard keeping watch. I did not relax any. I kept my grip tight on the shotgun. If we were going to meet any eldar I wanted to be ready for violence.

Macharius studied our surroundings carefully as we marched. I was not sure what he was looking for. He seemed fascinated by the eldar statues and images, and he gazed in wonder on the gigantic vaults in the temple depths. Some of the statues to be found in them were ceiling high and as big as those out in the valley. I marvelled at the amount of work that had gone into their creation. They were fantastically beautiful, and the level of detail was just as great on the largest as on the smallest. Drake noticed my gaze and guessed my thoughts. 'The eldar live longer than humans,' he said. 'Their artisans are very patient and very skilled, and they tend to have a singularity of vision.'

I looked at the statues and I thought about the eldar we had fought. 'It does not seem possible that these were made by the same people as wait for us outside the valleys.'

Drake laughed. 'It does not seem possible that the same

species could worship the Emperor and yet also worship daemons, but it is true. Evil does not preclude intelligence or artistic talent. Sometimes it seems to encourage it.'

I shrugged and opened my mouth to speak, then closed it again. Macharius noticed and so did Drake. 'You were going to say something, Lemuel,' said the Lord High Commander. 'Spit it out.'

I tried to put my finger on my reservations about what we were seeing. I looked up at the gigantic, joyous and benevolent figure gazing down on me. I thought about the spindly, malevolent beings we had fought. 'The eldar out there are insane, and utterly focused and single-minded about fighting and torture and death. All the evidence we have seen points to this. It's like they have cut everything else out of themselves. The statues we see here cover every facet of experience: happiness, sadness, joy, laughter, sorrow. We see none of that in them.'

'I doubt you see much comedy on a battlefield, Lemuel,' said Drake. I thought about Ivan and Anton and others I had known, and the way joking kept them sane in the face of horror, but I did not say anything. 'We are seeing only one aspect of the eldar we face.'

'I see what Lemuel is getting at,' said Macharius. 'It does not seem like the same beings made these statues as flayed those people.'

Drake smiled his superior smile. 'Heretics do terrible things too. Does that mean humanity can't produce artists?'

'Are you saying heretics are the same as normal citizens of the Imperium?' Macharius countered.

'No, they are deranged.'

'Is it not possible the eldar out there are deranged in the same way?'

'We don't know, and the only way we will find out is by interrogating one.'

'I doubt your methods of questioning would make them significantly less grim,' said Macharius.

'I think that would be a good thing,' said Drake. There was a trace of black humour in the statement. Before Macharius could reply, Grimnar suddenly froze. 'There are eldar close,' he said. 'Be wary.'

The words were no sooner out of his mouth than we saw long, lean shapes slinking out of the shadows, weapons ready. They unleashed a volley of shots. They flickered through the air all around us, somehow not touching us. At first I wondered whether they were really such poor shots, and then I noticed the nimbus of light which played around Drake's head.

I glanced around and saw men lying on the ground, their faces pale rictuses of agony. Drake's shield had deflected the eldar's shots away from those immediately surrounding Macharius but had cost the lives of other bodyguards. When I looked up, the eldar were gone. So were Grimnar and his Wolves.

'What has become of the Space Wolves?' I asked.

'They have gone hunting,' said Macharius.

'Let's hope they do not find themselves the prey instead,' said Drake.

* * *

We fight a war in this underground maze. I have set my warriors to ambushing the humans in an effort to discourage them from spending time here, and in order to keep them away from the gate. It does not seem to be working terribly well. I suspect that is only to be expected given the way things have gone so far. The universe clearly does not wish to present me with any easy triumphs.

We have set traps en route to the lairs we have chosen, and we keep moving in an effort to confuse those who hunt for us. In the meantime I have worked to re-establish communication both with our forces on the surface and in orbit. So far, things up there are going better than things down here.

Our ships have engaged the enemy warship and it looks as though there is very much the possibility of victory this time. Our captains know what to expect and have not been taken off guard. On the surface, in the mountains, the army that had been tied down besieging the human cities is assembling alongside those forces I dispersed to avoid the orbital bombardment. It is only a matter of hours before they are in position to swoop down on the humans and punish their temerity.

For now, I must see to it that my forces below ground are preserved. The gate will be opening soon and that means I must be prepared to act quickly when the opportunity presents itself. I give my attention to one of the humans I have captured. It looks at me, eyes wide with fear. I am hungry and it has been some time since I have had any nourishment. I pull out my toolkit and prepare to feed.

* * *

'This place feels odd,' said Drake as we entered the deepest part of the labyrinth. 'Strange psychic currents swirl in the air here. This is the centre of the psychic disturbance.'

'I will take your word for that, my friend,' said Macharius.

'You would be well advised to, Lord High Commander.'

'Your teams claim there were signs the eldar had been here in strength.'

'We found flayed corpses and the bodies of those who had died under torture. It seemed reasonable to believe the eldar made use of this place.'

'Why do they do it?' Macharius asked. He sounded genuinely baffled. 'Why do they indulge in such a despicable practice?'

'Because they are deviant xenos scum,' said Drake. There was no real anger or horror in his voice. He was simply stating a self-evident truth.

'I have met other xenos. They did not feel the urge to be so cruel. At least not so consistently.'

'The eldar are known for their decadence. Some factions more than others.'

'It would appear we have met one of the crueller ones,' said Macharius.

'How would we know? We have so little to compare them to.'

Macharius shrugged. I looked at Drake. I realised I was seeing an unusual thing; the inquisitor was uneasy. It was not like him to admit ignorance on any subject.

We came at last to an odd, arched structure in the wall. It looked as if it were a gate or a doorway but made of solid stone. Drake took out some sort of portable divinatory engine and turned it on. He studied the results and said, 'It's solid. There is nothing behind this. This gate leads nowhere.'

'Why put it here then?' Macharius asked. 'It is strange to have a representation of such a thing at this spot. You would expect a tunnel, something leading deeper into the earth, another chamber. Why place a gate here?'

Drake looked at his scanner, then at the gate and said, 'I don't know, but energies roil at this spot, and I sense something dark and strange beyond it.'

Macharius raised an eyebrow. 'I thought you said there was nothing behind it, merely solid stone. Is there something buried there?'

Drake looked baffled. 'It is solid. If we blasted the stonework away we would find nothing, and yet I sense...' His voice trailed off into silence and he said, 'It would not be a good idea to try and destroy the stonework here. It is permeated with psychic energies, and they are getting stronger.'

'Has it any connection to the eldar presence?'

'I strongly suspect some things,' the inquisitor said.

'What are they?'

'I think this place was laid out according to some alien geomantic principle. It was intended to channel energies and achieve some goal.'

'You could not be a little more specific?'

'I am not any sort of psychic engineer. The ancient eldar were supposed to be, though. A lot of their so-called civilisation was built on such principles. I think this whole valley is an engine of some sort, and whatever is in it is coming awake.'

'It would seem best to assume that whatever is happening here is not intended for our benefit.'

'That would be wise,' said Drake.

Macharius turned to the men guarding the gateway arch. 'Remain here, and if anything unusual occurs report it at once.'

'At once, sir,' said the soldiers. We turned and made our way back to the surface.

CHAPTER TWENTY

I have the reports from my commanders on the surface. It seems that everything is in place and that the warship in orbit has been drawn out of position to engage my fleet. The signal from the gate tells me that the opening must occur soon. It is almost time to give the order to attack.

And yet something stops me. I am not even sure what it is. Perhaps I simply want to savour the moment, to bask in those last few heartbeats before my plan of attack is implemented and that which was merely a possibility in my mind becomes wedded to reality. Perhaps I am afraid that it will all go wrong as so much has gone wrong during the course of this conflict. I have developed considerable respect for the human commander, which feels like an obscenity when I contemplate it but nonetheless is true. I would not have thought it possible that one of those hairless apes could have caused me so much trouble.

I give myself a few seconds, and then I speak the words that will send my forces into the attack and trap the humans in the Valley of the Ancients forever.

One by one my commanders report back. The assault has begun.

After we returned to the surface, Macharius dismissed us. As the afternoon sun rose over the mountains, Anton, Ivan and I hiked to the northern edge of the valley, directly beneath the great stone face.

Looking up at it from this angle it lost any of its resemblance to humanity, stopped being a face and was just a jumble of lines and stone protrusions. It was like the other cliffs surrounding us, the intelligence that had shaped it in no way evident.

All around us were a mass of boulders, some the size of a pillow, some the size of an armoured vehicle. There was lots of jagged scree. Green moss marked everything. Twin gulleys ran away from the bottom of the rock face. It was set on a separate peak that protruded into the north of the valley like the prow of a great stone ship.

The air was chill and clear, and our breath came out in clouds, like the exhausts of the vehicles in cold climates.

I studied the rocks. There was no sign that a large force of xenos had passed this way last night. There was no sign of tracks or wheeled vehicles. It was as though all the eldar vehicles moved without making contact with the ground. They must have been fiercely manoeuvrable as well. The rocks provided quite an obstacle course for any craft trying to move through them.

I looked up the gulleys and saw green-tunicked Lion Guards at work, laying mines, setting up wire and booby traps and gun emplacements among the rocks. If the eldar came back, they would be noticed and slowed by them. I took a seat on one of the smaller boulders, broke out a ration pack and began to eat. The others did likewise.

Anton let out a long, satisfied sigh. 'I love work,' he said. 'I could watch people doing it all day.'

Anton munched some jerky and looked at the hills through the scope of his sniper rifle. Ivan propped himself up, back against a large boulder so that he had cover, and took out a small toolset. With a hooked implement he began to work at the hinge of his jaw. It was a disturbing sight. It's a strange world when you can get used to looking at torn apart bodies but the sight of a friend repairing his augmetics is off-putting when you eat.

I pulled out a set of magnoculars and looked down the valley. The end of the valley under the face was somewhat higher than the central part, and I had a good view of the temple complexes, the surrounding cliffs and statues. I wondered how many of the bloody things there were.

I watched the green-tunicked Lion Guard set the perimeter. Elite bodyguard or no, their officers set them to digging trenches and setting up earthworks. Our most powerful vehicles were dug in as strongpoints at critical areas for the defence. Our tanks were laid out like a wall, anchored on the main temple complex. Some of our artillery had been brought in from the eastern heights and set up within our lines. Macharius had given very specific instructions for the deployment. It seemed he had something on his mind.

'I don't like this at all,' said Ivan. He shaded his eyes. I could tell from the angle of his neck he was studying the heights to the north-west and the south. He pulled out the magnoculars he had taken from the heretic colonel on Jurasik well over a decade ago and studied the heights. I knew exactly what he meant.

'Too easy to catch us, the way we caught the eldar,' I said.

'Precisely,' said Ivan.

'To be fair,' said Anton, 'I think Macharius probably noticed that too. He does know a bit about generalship. Or are you suggesting that maybe we should start taking advice from the pair of you?'

'He could always call down an orbital bombardment to clear those ridges.' Ivan looked thoughtful as he let his magnoculars drop to dangle on the end of their cords. 'If there is still a ship up there.'

'Blight's boys got it right the first time,' I said. 'I am not sure I want to risk them managing a repeat performance.'

'I know what you mean,' said Ivan. 'Any mistake and they hit the valley and us along with it.'

We shared the ground soldiers' mistrust of those who fought their wars from high orbit.

In the camp, Lion Guards with spades and entrenching tools flattened earth that had been cleared by vehicles with bulldozer attachments. They were raising ramparts between the temple complexes, creating an improvised fortress out of rubble and dirt and barbed wire. I was not sure how much it would slow creatures as agile as the eldar had proven to be, but it was better than nothing.

Some of the Leman Russ crews were sunning themselves on the side of their battle tanks. Others were making field repairs with the sort of loving care I could remember Corporal Hesse lavishing on *Old Number Ten*, the Baneblade on which we had started our careers.

More vehicles were flattening an area around the plinth atop which huge eldar deities cavorted. An officer looked up into the sky and studied an opening in the clouds as if he expected to see a supply shuttle coming in right away.

'Supply drops from orbit,' said Ivan sourly. 'What could possibly go wrong there.' He glanced at the ridge lines to the north-west and south again. He was thinking about how difficult it would be to bring shuttles down in the teeth of fire from the surrounding hills if the eldar could take command of those heights. If there were still a ship up there to make the drops.

'By the Emperor,' Anton said, 'you two are in a sour mood. We've already driven those torturing eldar bastards out of this place. We've got tanks. We've got Macharius. We've got a company of Space Wolves. What more do you want – a couple of Chapters of Space Marines?'

'I would not say no,' I said. 'I don't like this place. I don't like those statues. I don't like the fact we've got a few of the xenos buried beneath those temples. I would bet a bullet to a battle tank that some of them are sharpening their flaying knives in preparation for an evening's entertainment.'

'If they show their ugly faces we'll blow them away,' said Anton. His voice was gruff but his expression was worried. I could tell he was thinking about what might happen if the eldar below us emerged in the night. The ruined temples were surrounded by men and vehicles and barbed wire, but we knew how fast and agile the xenos were and they spooked us.

Our covering batteries on the eastern heights opened fire. There was the distinctive roar of Basilisks. All motion in the valley seemed to stop for a moment. It was as if every single eye were suddenly turned in the direction the guns were aiming at. The observers had obviously spotted something. I glanced up the gulley. Our sentries were alert but there was no sign of any enemy coming down on us.

'I don't like the look of this at all,' Ivan said. He gestured upslope. Xenos landships were starting to appear on the ridges to the north-west of the valley. Wind billowed in their sails, their wings flexed like those of living things.

'Looks like the eldar are back,' said Anton.

'Looks like they brought a few friends,' I said. It was true, too. Hundreds of landships were there and other things, hovering monstrous scuttling things, large as tanks with long, lashing limbs that reminded me of tentacles mixed with the pincers of scorpions. Their vehicles were silent. Their weapons opened up in counter-battery fire. Suddenly a flight of their attack craft soared overhead to engage with our batteries on the eastern heights. They spiralled in like great evil bats and their weapons tore into our guns, silencing them. More eldar vehicles appeared on the ridgeline amid the twisted wreckage of the artillery.

'We'd better get back,' I said. I was uneasy. The eldar had simply reversed positions with Macharius. We were trapped in the valley and they surrounded us.

We had just risen when I heard the sounds of weapons opening up nearby. Down in the gulley, a wave of eldar were moving. Xenos flickered between the rocks, closing with a speed that was inhuman, overrunning the outlying positions. The mines did not stop them. Only a few activated. Duds, perhaps, I thought, or maybe something about our opponents prevented them from detonating. It was not my job to figure this out. I lengthened my stride and clutched my shotgun close.

'I think it's time we reported for duty with Macharius,' said Anton. Agonised screams drifted on the wind, mingled with mad, mocking laughter.

'Pull back,' shouted the Guard officer.

Looking at the monstrous thing scuttling in our direction I felt very inclined to run. It was enormous, and there was something alive about it. Something so huge had to be a vehicle of sorts, but this one had the strange, semi-living look of a great deal of the eldar technology we had seen.

Just in case we had any doubts we had been spotted, shots started to ping off the rocks around us. At least the Lion Guard were in good cover, which probably saved a few lives.

'First squad, cover us. The rest fall back. By unit and in good order.' The officer was using his parade ground voice now. It was pointless using anything else. I saw heads turn as the members of the first squad looked back in our direction. Their commander had just pronounced their death sentence and they knew it.

In their heads they were doing the same calculations I would be making in their position. They were working out the odds of getting back to the camp if they turned and fled now. The fact that they would be shot for deserting their posts and disobeying an order would only be a small part of the reckoning. When death taps you on the shoulder even a few more minutes of life suddenly becomes very appealing.

Against the urge for self-preservation other things warred. Working against that impulse to flee were other ones, some of them coldly rational, some of them steeped in primal emotions. There was the knowledge that if they turned and fled all of us would most likely die anyway as the enemy swept over us from behind. If they stayed they would have a chance to take some of the foe with them, and their lives might at least buy the lives of their comrades. It's hard to communicate the sort of loyalty that gets built up towards your fellows in an Imperial Guard company, but it exists nonetheless. You see men lay down their lives for each other more often than you would think and more often than a cynic would believe.

And they were proud too, of themselves and of their unit. They would stand their ground and die because they were the sort of men who could, or at least they wanted to be. They were brave, they believed in Macharius and they believed in the Emperor. They could die as cowards or walk into His Light as martyrs. One had meaning. One had not. In either case they would die.

I could see all of this pass through their minds in less time than it takes to tell. I read it in the way slumped shoulders squared and lasguns were suddenly raised to the firing position. One or two of them saluted. The one or two who wavered, seeing their companions' resolve to stay, gave bitter smiles and hunkered down to sell their own lives dearly.

It's at moments like this that the quality of a single man can make a difference. All it takes is one soldier deciding to flee to provoke a rout. One soldier determined to hold his ground can keep an army pinned in place if he is the right soldier at the right time. These men were the right men. It made me proud and sad at the same time, even as I turned to move off down the hill with Anton and Ivan. Behind me lasguns fired.

The slope was dark and strewn with obstacles. Ahead of us I could see the walls of our camp. I think every man present had the same idea in his mind that I had, the sensation that doom was swiftly approaching in a particularly nasty and messy form.

Behind us, the covering force were selling their lives dearly and doing their best to avoid being taken prisoner. They saved us. In the teeth of their covering fire, the eldar could not be sure of exactly how large a force they faced so they held back until the monster arrived.

Casting a glance over my shoulder, prompted by some ancient instinct, I saw a scuttling form loom, a gigantic arachnid figure with clicking claws. It reminded me of a Titan, although it was smaller and there was an obscene suggestion of something living and evil about it. There were men in the grip of those claws, screaming and shouting and still firing their lasguns. Looking at the gigantic beast and one of those tiny-looking figures, I swear I caught sight of something horrible.

The man seemed to be shrinking, dwindling, like a deflating balloon filled with blood. I don't mean that the blood was being squeezed out of him, either. I had an image in mind of hundreds of tiny sucker mouths, leech-like, draining all life from him, all vitality. The man's screams became thinner, more wretched, more filled with pain; and then the strangest thing of all happened. His flesh just crumbled, as if all life, all fluid, all animation had been drained out of it. It turned to dust, like an ancient corpse suddenly exposed to light and air when its sarcophagus is opened. I was filled with an ominous sense that not just the man's body had been devoured, but his soul.

A barrage of shots hit the great monster, exploding against its side, blasting great holes out of it. The beast thrashed as though it were in pain, but it did not drop the soldiers it held. It gripped them like a drunk holding his last bottle even as the Baneblade and Leman Russ within our camp sent blast after blast stabbing into its body. More of the monsters appeared now and began to lumber down the slope. They were followed by shark-fin sailed landships loaded with eldar.

We moved as fast as we could downslope away from the great stone face carved in the cliffs back towards the lines of our main camp. The eldar on the north-west heights aimed desultory fire at us. It was as if they were not really trying, or simply wanted to terrify us rather than kill us. It suited their crazed humour.

I had a strange crawling sensation between my shoulders. It would only take one of those cruel xenos to suddenly change its mind and my life would be over. If you've been on as many battlefields as I have, you have a fine appreciation for the sort of mischances that can end a man's days.

I noticed the turrets of our sentry vehicles were elevating their weapons to concentrate on the heights behind us.

My knees felt sore as we pounded downslope. I kept my head down and studied the broken ground with care, knowing that tripping up now might be the death of me. I did my best to weave through the low boulders and shards of broken rock, as they would provide at least some cover to the lower half of my body. Driven by a sudden premonition, I threw myself flat behind a rock and risked a look back upslope. I saw the ground crowded with silent, swift-striding eldar soldiers and their equally quietly moving vehicles. Shots were going off all around. They were moving much faster than we were, and I knew that they would soon overtake us. That was the last thing I wanted.

The rocks made a kind of cave. They had tumbled together so that a slab of stone formed a roof over some more. I wriggled in underneath out of sight. I heard heavy breathing and noticed that Ivan and Anton had slipped into place beside me. They had come back for me. It was kind of touching.

'Planning on making a heroic last stand in these rocks?' Ivan asked. 'Just you and the hordes of eldar…'

Anton said, 'Bastard! I thought maybe you had twisted your ankle or something and needed to be carried as usual. There doesn't seem to be anything wrong with you. You're just getting lazy.'

'I thought I would cover your retreat,' I said. 'You were making very good time as you ran away.'

'Get your head down and have some kip while we did all the fighting more like,' Anton said. He was studying the eldar along the ridgeline carefully. Any moment now he was going to unlimber the sniper rifle and start taking potshots. 'As usual.'

'What are you thinking?' Ivan asked. His metal face was impassive, but he knew how desperate our situation was. We were stuck here in this little island of rocks while all around us the eldar moved forward to assault our position. Our force at the gulley mouth beneath the face had already been overrun, and there was no way just the three of us could fight our way back through the xenos.

'I'm thinking we're stuck here with those xenos bastards commanding the heights above us. It's not like Macharius to make a mistake like this.'

'What else could he do? He wanted to hold these temples. We don't have the force for defence in depth.'

'Who would have thought there would be so many of those eldar?' said Anton. He was looking through the scope of the rifle now. I reached out and grabbed his ankle and pulled him back down. The last thing we needed now was the glint of his scope giving us away to some watching eldar. For all we knew some of them on the heights might have noticed us and be reporting our position to their comrades even now. It was not a reassuring thought. Anton dropped back into cover.

'There's more of them than I count,' he said.

'So more than five then,' said Ivan.

'Ha-bloody-ha!'

'He can get to twenty if he uses his toes,' I said.

'If he takes his boots off,' said Ivan.

'When you two have finished your sad attempt at comedy you might want to consider how we're going to get back down the hill without getting shot.'

'They weren't trying to hit us, Anton,' I said. 'If they had been we'd be dead now.'

'Then why–'

Another long scream drifted down the wind. It sounded like a soul in torment. It rang ever higher until it broke on a horrible insane gibbering note, as if the mind of the man screaming had been broken by whatever torture he was enduring.

Anton shot me a scared look.

'I think they wanted to take us alive,' I said. 'Though we might not stay that way for long afterwards.'

'Any time might be too long,' said Ivan.

'What are we going to do?' Ivan asked. As usual, when the chips were down, the other two were looking to me for guidance. I turned our options over and over in my mind. We could not stay here. We had very little water in our canteens, and sooner or later we were bound to be spotted by one of the eldar. If they had not already spotted us and were just letting the suspense build before they took us...

'We wait until it's dark and then we try and sneak through their lines,' I said.

'You mad?' Anton asked.

'You got a better idea? If we stay here, it's only a matter of time before they find us.'

'Our own sentries will shoot us,' Ivan said.

'We'll just need to risk it. It would be better than falling into the hands of those xenos scum.'

'No arguments from me there,' said Ivan. More screams sounded, echoing down the valley. They appeared to be amplified. Maybe the eldar were broadcasting them to break the morale of our men. Maybe it was just something they did for relaxation.

Anton looked me right in the eye. His face was pale. 'If it looks like they are going to take me alive, shoot me…'

'It will be my pleasure,' I said, but the joke did not seem so funny any more.

CHAPTER TWENTY-ONE

A tall shadow fell onto the rocks where we crouched, telling us that one of the alien warriors was standing there. It seemed like all he would need to do was turn his head and see us. I kept the shotgun clutched very tight in my hands, not sure whether I would use it on him or myself. I felt Anton and Ivan tense beside me.

I glanced sideways. Sweat dripped from Anton's pale, narrow face. The scar was visible on his forehead. I felt my muscles coil. Part of me suspected that the xenos might be able to hear the drops of perspiration falling on the rock. After what felt like an aeon, the eldar finally moved off. Even as it did so I wondered if it had seen us and was now toying with us as a felid toys with a nest of vermin.

As the day wore on, the butcher shop stench of the battlefield drifted to my nostrils. I wondered whether eldar corpses smelt like ours when they died. I wondered whether anybody back in our camp had noticed we were not there. I wondered about Anna and about a thousand other things I could do nothing about but which all were suddenly very important to me.

Darkness came very slowly. My stomach felt as though it were full of acid. My heart pounded against my ribs. My mouth was dry. I wanted to empty my bladder but found I could not. All around us, I could hear the strange sounds of the eldar army moving. I noticed the eerie whine of their vehicles moving less than ten strides away. I felt currents of air displaced by the motion swirl of their sails. Sometimes I caught the scent of cinnamon and some sour-sweet perfume, sometimes what smelt like incense, sometimes something that smelt like an accident in an abattoir.

Eventually, the stars glittered coldly overhead like the eyes of watching daemons. The sounds of combat continued in the distance. I decided it was time to risk a glance out.

I looked down into a sea of shadows on the reverse side of the slope. The eldar were still there. I could see their strange landships and something else, something massive and vaguely scorpion-like. I knew it was another of those monstrous life-drinking beasts. I spotted movement as dim, humanoid outlines moved with inhuman speed, their elongated forms suggesting shadows and daemons and things from fever-induced nightmares. Nearby were a few metal poles with crossbars. Flayed forms hung from them. The stench of blood and raw meat and opened bowels hung in the air, the scent of an operating theatre where the patients were sent to be painfully killed rather than to be healed.

I studied the concentration of forces. There were scores of vehicles and thousands of eldar, and those monstrous things with claws, whatever they were.

Something flickered at the corner of my eye and I realised there were other xenos, far closer to us than those in the camp, scouts or pickets. It was pure chance that they had not picked our hiding spot as their own sentry post.

I froze on the spot, hoping that I would not be noticed. A warm form popped up beside me, and I looked around to see Anton. He was scanning the area beneath us through the scope of his sniper rifle. It had a night-sight attachment. Crouched beside him was Ivan. I could catch the faint glimmer of moonlight even on the dirt-smeared metal of his cheeks.

A long straggling line of Lion Guard stretched along the perimeter wall below us. Here and there weapons emplacements bulged. At various gaps in the walls, armoured fighting vehicles were used as makeshift gates.

We had only a few hundred metres to go to reach our camp. Looking at that force it might as well have been a thousand leagues. The ground between the two forces was a killing field.

I dropped down again and the other two fell into position beside me. I kept my ears pricked up, waiting to hear the telltale sound of a weapon barrel against rock or stone slithering against stone. All I heard was my own soft breathing. It was almost drowned out by my drum-beat heart.

'You still want to try for our lines?' Ivan asked. His voice was as flat and emotionless as ever.

'You got a better idea? We've been lucky so far. I wouldn't count on that luck holding a second day.'

Anton let out a long sigh. 'We'd better get it over with then.'

'We climb down out of here and we circle left,' I said. 'It looks like there's a gap in the eldar line in the direction of the eastern heights. We'll head for the gate made by the Baneblade.' I liked the sound of that. Call it superstition but Baneblades always gave me a feeling of security, even after I had one destroyed underneath me.

Ivan shrugged. One direction seemed as good as another to him. Anton nodded. 'I could use a lho-stick,' he said. It had the sound of a man making a last request.

'Yeah, go on,' I said. 'Maybe you'd like to smoke it as we sneak along.'

'I'm not that stupid,' said Anton.

'We could try a few marching songs as well,' Ivan suggested helpfully. '*Gone for a Soldier* or *The Cadian Boot Song*. A few rousing choruses would certainly raise my morale.'

'Maybe you'd like to set off a flare,' I said. 'We could see better that way.'

'A torch is what we really need,' said Ivan.

'I just said I would like a smoke. There's no need to make a meal out of it.'

We fell silent. We had just been spinning it out to put off making a start.

Suddenly the sound of shooting came from off to the east.

Explosions as well. The turrets along the wall had opened up, blasting at the ridge below us.

'Looks like our lads are trying a counter-strike,' Ivan said.

'Good news for us,' I said. 'A bit of a distraction. Emperor watch over you!'

With that I sent myself diving out of cover before I had a chance to think and regret my action. I slithered down the rocks, half crawling, half scrambling, praying to the Emperor that the sounds of that distant attack had gotten the eldar's attention. As soon as I was off the rocky island, I threw myself flat on my belly and wriggled down a narrow gulley.

Off to my right, not twenty strides away, were a group of xenos. They had their backs to me, but for all I knew that meant nothing. They might have sensors on those battle-suits capable of three hundred and sixty degree scanning. Hell, maybe they had senses we did not know about that would let them spot us without ever seeming to look in our direction. Who knew what the alien bastards were capable of?

I forced myself to lie flat for a minute, and I felt something touch my boot. I fought down the urge to kick out, turned and saw Anton lying there. Behind him was Ivan. They had both smeared more dirt on their faces to make them less visible. I listened. The sounds of distant fighting intensified. Heavy artillery tore up the earth. I found something else to worry about. What if they suddenly decided to target the area we were moving across? I could feel the ground vibrate against my cheek.

I wriggled on, trusting the others to follow me. Maybe it was a dried up stream bed. Maybe it was something else, but the gulley we were in ran a long way downhill. I decided to trust my luck and stick with it.

Another hundred strides of wriggling took us under the shadow of one of those gigantic scuttling war machines. The cinnamon smell was stronger and there was a dreamy sort of perfume with a sour under-tang of blood. A massive tail lashed the air, making a lazy whip-crack sound. A long, low, musical tone cut through the sound of gunfire, and I thought for one brief, heart-stopping instant that we had been spotted and an alarm had been given. Of course, it was mere paranoia. The machine, if that is what it was, turned and began to scuttle off in the direction of the fighting.

Flashes of light made shadows dance madly all around us, the muzzle flicker and explosive glare of all those thousands of weapons being used in the cold night air. I froze for a moment, convinced this time that I was visible to every alien eye on the battlefield. The idea that they might have been looking for targets elsewhere never even occurred to me.

I felt something cool beneath my hand as I shifted my weight to a new position. Looking down I saw something smooth and stone-like, too rounded to be completely natural, with a texture a little like bone. It was not as cold as the surrounding rock. When I lifted it and held it closer to my eye, I saw that it had a similar look to the battle-armour the xenos were wearing. It was clearly some sort of device and I had a sudden crazy idea of exactly what sort.

Carefully I raised it and tossed it down the hill, already strongly suspecting it was too late.

'What the…' Anton said.

'Proximity sensor,' I said. 'I'm guessing.'

'We've been spotted?'

'Seems best to assume that.'

Another huge burst of artillery fire lit the night overhead. I glanced over my shoulder. Some of the shadows back there suddenly looked a lot more humanoid. They moved, and not in answer to any flickering of moonbeams through the clouds. There was a whole company of the enemy down there, closing silently. The time for stealth was obviously past.

I rose and moved forward in a crouching run, zigzagging to make myself a harder target, moving through the boulders towards the rampart wall. As I did so another danger became more obvious. It would be just as easy to be killed by our own side. I began to shout, 'For Macharius and the Emperor!' I held my shotgun over my head in the classic pose of surrender. I shouted the day's password, and then it occurred to me that the eldar could easily have tortured that out of any captive.

A flash of our earlier idiotic conversation came to me. I began to bellow out the words of *Gone for a Soldier*, the ancient marching song used by Guard regiments for millennia. A searchlight probed us. Some las-bolts turned surrounding rocks cherry-red. I heard Anton and Ivan singing behind me. The las-fire surrounding us moved on behind us, stabbing through the night towards the pursuing eldar.

Heartbeats later, breath wheezing from my lips I found myself looking up at the frontal armour of a Baneblade that was being used as a gate in the rampart wall. An officer's head leaned over and shouted, 'What the hell are you doing down there?'

'Sergeant Lemuel,' I said. Knowing I would only have one chance to sway him, I added, 'Personal bodyguard to the Lord High Commander.'

'I know your face,' he said. 'I've seen you with Lord Macharius.'

'Then let us up! In the name of the Emperor.'

'What are you doing down there?'

'Can we discuss that once we're inside the perimeter?' I said.

A rope was dropped and I pulled myself up. Anton and Ivan followed. I don't think I have ever been so relieved to put a barrier between myself and pursuit.

We were held under the guns of the sentries. I don't know whether the Lion Guard thought we were spies or suspected some strange xenos trick, but it seemed like hauling us up was the full extent of their willingness to trust us. A messenger was sent to find out what to do with us. I looked out over the wall and thought about the hordes of eldar out there. I cursed and kept very still, determined that I had not escaped their flensing knives only to be shot by some nervous, trigger-happy Guardsman.

Fifteen minutes later, the Undertaker showed up. He took one look at us and said, 'That's them. I'm responsible for taking them to Inquisitor Drake.'

Delivered as it was in his flat-monotone, that sounded just about as menacing as a massed charge by the xenos. Drake was a man who knew a few tricks of torture himself. I wondered if he was going to practise some of them on us.

'Take us to him,' I heard Anton say. His voice was full of false bravado.

'Your capacity to find trouble never ceases to amaze me,' Drake said. As he spoke his glowing hand passed over my brow. We had already been physically examined and pronounced clean. Now he was using his own peculiar powers.

'We did not go looking for it,' I said. 'We just wanted to take a look at the Face.'

'And yet somehow trouble found you,' Drake said. His voice was cold and clear, as always. If he were bothered by me talking back to him he gave no sign of it. Apparently it was a privilege I had earned over the past ten years. 'You go for a walk, you spend an evening behind enemy lines and then you casually wander back into camp. I can see why Macharius thinks you are lucky.'

'There was nothing casual about it, I can assure you,' I said.

'And now as we are being assaulted I have to waste my time examining you because of the value the Lord High Commander places on your continued existence.'

Drake had a gift for talking about you as if you were not there, or some sort of specimen he was examining. I suppose that level of detachment was an advantage in his vocation. He gave a cold smile, shrugged and said, 'I believe you can return to active service with Macharius. I will accompany you. I have matters to discuss with the Lord High Commander.'

The eldar attacks had stopped for the moment. Outside it was quiet except for the occasional scream of the eldar's captives.

We wait in the darkness beneath. The humans know we are here. The fear of us will paralyse them. They know that within their lines of defence a ruthless enemy waits. They are assailed on many sides, from the heights above the valley, from the access points and from below, from within the fortifications they thought would protect them.

I have given the order that teams of warriors are to emerge when the opportunity arises; they are to take prisoners and devour them, and leave the corpses where they can be found by our foes. Humans are weak. They will know fear. They will give in to it.

I have selected a new chamber to act as my headquarters in the labyrinth. It is positioned with easy access to the routes that lead to the gate so that when the time comes I can easily make my way to my ultimate goal.

I have deployed rings of warriors in a defensive perimeter to make sure that none of the Space Marines hunting us can reach me. These are the very best of my soldiers. Each is individually a match for a Space Wolf.

I study my surroundings. They reveal the obsession of my distant forebears with complex carvings. Thousands of masks have been embossed on the wall; each one of them shows the expression on the face of a forgotten god. It is difficult to tell whether they represent the thousand moods of a dozen gods or the dozen moods of a thousand feeble deities. All I can see are faces that show simpering joy, witless grief, dubious happiness and on and on. I block out the distraction.

Outside my chamber I hear a faint sound, slightly worrying, like a body falling. I draw my weapon just in case. It is not possible that an enemy could have reached me here, but perhaps there is a traitor within the ranks of my own guards. It would not be the first time such a thing has happened to an eldar commander.

I look outside and I see a fallen body indeed. The head is twisted at an odd angle that tells me the neck has been broken. I look around for Bael and see that he is not there. He should be. He was in charge of this detachment.

I step outside, ready to strike in any direction. The corridor is empty, although in the distance at either end I can see a guard. I raise my hand and each of them responds in turn.

I walk over to one and ask if he has seen Bael. He says no. It is the same at the other end of the corridor. It is not possible for Bael to have vanished without them seeing him, or is it?

I walk back along the corridor, this time keeping my eyes on the ceiling, and I notice at one point that there is an opening there, some sort of ventilation system. I spring up and inspect it, and I see that it has been recently removed.

Someone has been here. Someone has entered the very

heart of our position without being noticed and managed to kidnap one of my own officers without the sentries seeing it. I realise it can only be one of the Space Wolves that has done this.

I call the sentries and tell them to keep watch. I tell them to be particularly careful in checking the ceilings for ventilation access hatches. I move my command position again, thinking about how worryingly close I came to being captured myself. It seems that these vermin are more dangerous than I had thought.

CHAPTER TWENTY-TWO

The door swung open and Grimnar walked into Macharius's command bunker. He was casually dragging what I assumed was an eldar corpse by the neck. Then I realised it was more than that.

'I have a prisoner for you to interrogate,' he said, looking at Drake. My eyes widened. He had not only come back alive from a labyrinth haunted by xenos, he had brought one of them with him.

'Very good,' said Macharius. The xenos lay limply, but I remembered the other one that had been faking back on the spacecraft. I held my shotgun ready, feeling as jumpy as a felid that had lapped up Frenzon in its milk. Anton and Ivan looked just as nervous. The Undertaker looked blankly on.

I took another look at the eldar. Its armour was rent in various places and spattered with dark stuff that could only be blood. It had been stripped of all obvious weapons, but still I could not help but think it was dangerous. A creature so swift and deadly could never be considered harmless.

Drake licked his lips. A cold smile flickered across his face. There was something else there as well, an expression I can only describe as nervous as well as cruel.

Good, I thought, remembering what the eldar had done to our soldiers. Let's see how they endure suffering. Drake was an inquisitor, trained to get answers in all sorts of ways, some of them very nasty. Normally I would have done a lot to avoid seeing him at work but, like I said, the eldar brought out the worst in us. A small daemon of violence and cruelty sat on my shoulder and whispered that anything done to this creature was justified. I felt obscurely ashamed. I would have liked to think better of myself.

'Take it to my sanctum,' Drake said. 'I want it stripped, scanned and chained down.'

'I want to be there,' said Macharius. 'I have some questions myself.'

He gestured for us to follow. Drake shrugged. With no effort whatsoever, Grimnar dragged the armoured xenos along the floor. Its slithering made an odd sound on the stone, as if a jewelled serpent were scraping against a rock.

Drake had converted a small antechamber into something that was halfway between a study and an alchemical lab. Divinatory engines sat on either side of a long table. Chains of the sort normally used for manacling deserters were brought. Grimnar tore off the xenos's armour and removed its helmet. He was not gentle about the way he broke the seals.

The eldar lay on the table. Its face was oddly sensitive and beautiful. With its eyes closed it was as serene as one of the statues of the gods out there in the valley. The connection between the creatures we fought and the original temple builders was obvious. The prisoner had the same lobeless, pointed ears and the same almond-shaped eyes. Its cheekbones were high. Its lips were thin.

Drake opened a padded case full of vials and syringes. He considered them for a while then shook his head, dismissing them. Possibly he doubted the effects of truth serums intended for humans on the alien form before him. Perhaps he feared they might prove fatal before he could get his answers. He shut his case again and looked at Grimnar, then Macharius, then us.

'Be ready for anything,' he said. The Space Wolf nodded.

'Is there danger to you?' Macharius asked.

'There is always some possibility of spiritual contamination when dealing with xenos,' said Drake. 'But I am an inquisitor. I can cope.'

I wondered if he was as confident as he sounded. He rolled up his sleeves, laved his hands in water and strode forward, placing his fingers on the temples of the eldar. For a long moment, nothing happened, then I noticed a faint nimbus of light playing around each of Drake's fingertips. The chamber seemed to grow colder, and I could feel the hairs on the back of my neck begin to rise.

Suddenly, the eldar sat upright, moving easily against the

weight of its chains. I brought the shotgun up, and Anton and Ivan placed themselves between the xenos and Macharius. The eldar's eyes were open now and it had lost all the serenity that being unconscious had given its appearance. Its eyes were lilac and commanding. Its expression was shockingly evil. Just looking at its countenance made me want to back away.

Drake's hands remained in contact with the xenos's head. It stared into the middle distance, a grimace of frustration twisted its features. The expression was mirrored on Drake's face. Some sort of spiritual struggle was clearly under way.

For a moment I wondered whether the inquisitor had bitten off more than he could chew. Perhaps the mind of the eldar was too powerful and too wicked for him. Perhaps rather than Drake being the dominant partner, he would end up being corrupted or having his mind broken. As the thought occurred to me I turned my head slightly, and as if by accident brought the shotgun to bear on him. No one else seemed to notice, save perhaps Grimnar. They were too caught up in the unfolding drama.

'What is your name?' Drake asked. His voice was as harsh as stone grinding on stone, and it sounded as though he were simply vocalising the last of a series of statements that had already flickered between his mind and that of the eldar.

The eldar made an effort to resist him. Muscles spasmed, tendons became visible in its neck. Its face twitched. Its eyes went wide. It was trying to clamp its lips shut, to bite down on its tongue, to stop itself breathing.

'What is your name?' Drake repeated. His patient tone was at odds with the strain written on his own face. 'You will tell me, you know. It is only a matter of time.'

The eldar's whole body flexed, but it was held down by the chains.

'What is your name? I can keep repeating this all day, and it will only get worse for you.'

Something seemed to break within the eldar. 'Bael.'

'Bael. Good,' Drake said softly. He had won his first and most important victory, although he gave no sign of knowing it.

'You will answer my questions, Bael,' said Drake.

'It matters not,' said the eldar. It was a voice without the slightest trace of humanity in it. Bael's lips were moving and liquid musical sounds were coming out; a moment later crystalline sounds, more mechanical than musical, spoke the words in Imperial Gothic. It was like listening to a machine speak to the accompaniment of distant, lovely, alien singing.

I realised the singing was the actual eldar speech, the words the product of a translation engine. There was little emotion in the eldar's voice, but his face was twisted with hatred. Clearly the xenos was not enjoying experiencing Drake's psychic powers. 'You are doomed anyway, mon-keigh.'

Drake forced his lips into a cold smile. Beads of sweat appeared on his pale forehead. The experience appeared no more pleasant for him than it did for the eldar, and it appeared to cost considerably more effort. 'Why is that, deviant?'

'Because you face the Archon Ashterioth and his legions. You will die slowly, in great pain, to feed him and his warriors.'

Macharius and Drake exchanged a look.

'Feed?' Macharius said. His voice was glacially calm.

'Answer him,' said Drake. There was a hint of the lash in his voice. The eldar's features twisted in a rictus of pain.

'We feast on the agony of lesser species,' said the eldar. 'Your pain is our sustenance.'

His beautiful, inhuman features showed nothing but contempt, but I was starting to think I detected a hint of horror in his eyes. If his kind fed on pain, what must it be like for him to endure the agony of questioning at the hands of Drake? He must feel as if he were being eaten alive by an animal. I pushed the thought to one side. I did not understand his thought processes and I did not want to.

'That certainly explains what you have been doing to our prisoners,' said Drake.

'They are not prisoners. They are not even slaves. They are cattle.' A chill of horror passed down my spine at the words. Bael really saw us this way. To him we were mere beasts, no more important than herd animals are to a farmer. It was worse than that, actually. No farmer would treat his herds the way these eldar treated humans.

'You will be treated in the same way when you are rounded up. Indeed, it will go worse for you because of this.'

Drake smiled coldly. 'You know that is not true. Your brethren will have nothing but contempt for you for falling into our hands. I have reduced you to the status of a beast. You should remember that.'

Clearly Drake was picking more from the eldar's mind than the xenos was saying out loud. I knew he could lift memories and experiences directly from human minds when he brought his powers fully to bear. If he was doing that to Bael, I did not envy him. The alien's mind must be like a pit of snakes.

The eldar screamed, whether in agony or humiliation it was impossible to tell. 'You did not capture me. Your hound did.'

Grimnar laughed. His mirth had a clean, booming quality that it was good to hear amid the unwholesome monotones of the eldar's translation engine.

'We can argue about it all you like,' said Drake. 'But you are the one bound and treated like a beast.'

'I will make you die a thousand painful, agonising deaths. You will beg for the sweet release of oblivion a thousand times, and I will say no.'

'Yes, yes,' said Drake, an adult listening to the threats of a child. 'Of course, you will. In the meantime, you will answer all the questions put to you truthfully and to the best of your ability, otherwise you will not live to carry out your threats.'

'I do not fear death,' Bael said.

'No. You would welcome it now. Still, you will find it difficult to carry out threats with your limbs removed.'

It was the eldar's turn to laugh, at least I assumed that was what the mad, random sound the translation engine emitted was. 'Limbs can be regrown. Bodies can be rebuilt.'

A frown flickered across Drake's face. 'Yes. Of course, they can. Your haemonculi can do that.'

'You can pick the image from my mind, human, but you have no idea what the reality of it is.'

Drake concentrated. 'They could regrow you even from a simple cell, from the genetic helix if they could find it. Fascinating.'

Grimnar tilted his head to one side. 'Is that true?'

'This creature believes it is. More than that it believes, really believes, that the genetic sorcerers can restore its life and memories from as little as that.'

'Then they must be very different from humanity,' said Macharius. 'Such a thing is not possible, memories stored in the genetic helix.'

'We are different, human,' said Bael. 'Different and infinitely superior.'

'Infinitely more arrogant perhaps,' said Macharius. 'Or infinitely more deluded.'

'You will die in agony, human. You will see who is deluded then.'

'Why are you here?' Macharius asked.

'I am here because I follow Lord Ashterioth.'

'And why is he here?'

'He does not tell me his plans.'

'No,' Drake said, 'But you eavesdrop on him. I can see it in your mind. You eavesdrop on his conversations with your listening devices. You decrypt his personal journals. You spy.' He sounded interested. 'And not just for yourself or by yourself. Your lover spies as well. Lady Sileria.'

'It does not sound as if they trust each other very much,' said Macharius.

'The eldar are treacherous creatures,' said Drake.

'We put our own interests first. As you would, if you had intelligence above the apes you are descended from.'

'Why is this Lord Ashterioth here?' Macharius asked. He clearly wanted to know very badly. Bael clamped his lips shut. He did not want to speak. Once again tendons stood out on his neck. His muscles spasmed. This time he succeeded, or so it appeared for a few long moments.

'He seeks something,' said Drake.

'Get out of my head, mon-keigh. Your presence pollutes me.'

'Where is the Fist of Demetrius?'

'The what?' There was a mocking tone in the eldar's voice despite his pain.

'You know it. You see its image in your mind. I have put it there.'

'Ashterioth has it. It fascinates him.'

'Why?' Macharius asked. Grimnar leaned forward, straining to hear. Given his senses, he did not need to. He was as keen as Macharius to learn the eldar's purpose.

The eldar laughed. The sound was mechanical and insane, and there was something mocking in it.

'What would they do with a relic of the primarch?' Grimnar asked. 'It can mean nothing to them.'

Drake frowned. Sweat ran down his forehead. Blood poured from his nose. The eldar made odd gurgling sounds. He was chewing on his tongue.

'He tries to shield himself,' Drake said. 'He tries to escape into death.'

The nimbus of light around his head made his skin seem even more pale than usual. His lean face took on the aspect of a skull. The eldar screamed and went on screaming until his screams abruptly stopped.

'It is dead,' said Grimnar.

'No matter,' said Drake. 'I have seen some of what he tried to hide.'

His voice sounded appalled.

'What is it?' Macharius asked.

'They are not here for the Fist.'

'It would not serve them. Its holy power would not aid the xenos. The Allfather would not allow it,' said Grimnar.

'They want the Fist because they think there will be samples of Russ's tissue in it, part of his genetic rune structure, part of his helix.'

'What good would that do them?' Grimnar asked.

Macharius grasped it before any of us. 'Because they believe they can rebuild a living being from a sample of its tissue.'

'Recreate a primarch,' Grimnar said. His voice held a note of wonder mingled with horror. He was obviously contemplating the possibility of the return of the founder of his Chapter. 'That would be blasphemy. From the primarchs are all the Chapters descended, or so the skalds sing.'

'It would be worse than blasphemy,' said Drake. 'They will sample his tissue and create abominations from it, add it to their own tissue, make monsters with semi-divine power.'

'Why would they want to do that?' I said. 'They despise us.'

No one seemed inclined to take me to task for my outburst. Grimnar answered slowly and calmly.

'The primarchs had more power than any living being, save for the Emperor himself. They believe that they will be able to recreate the secret of that power and be able to graft it to themselves.'

'Is such a thing possible?' Macharius asked.

'I do not know, but the eldar believed it was, and he knew more about their alien techniques than any of us.'

'The eldar with the power of a primarch, even a fraction, would be terrible foes,' said Grimnar.

I thought that was a remarkable understatement. The idea of the cruellest race in the galaxy wielding the power of the most powerful beings who had ever lived, beings powerful enough to awe a Space Marine, was an appalling one.

'We cannot allow that to happen,' said Macharius. 'The Fist must not be allowed to remain in their grasp.'

'Better to destroy it first,' said Grimnar in the voice of a man forced to contemplate the most heinous blasphemy.

'We must get rid of this body. Destroy it utterly,' said Drake. 'Bathe it in acid or burn it with lasguns until not the slightest trace remains.'

It sounded as if he feared the xenos's return as much as he feared the eldar's plan for the Fist. Given what he had done, and given the nature of the creatures, that was understandable.

'You said the eldar were not here for the Fist,' said

Macharius. He was not one to allow himself to be distracted even by so horrible a prospect.

'No, they are here for the gate that exists beneath the temple complex. They are waiting for it to open.'

'Why?' Macharius asked.

'Beyond it lies some relic of their ancestors, a device of enormous power.'

'A weapon?'

'I fear so.'

'Can they really recreate a saint?' Anton asked. We were alone in our chamber now. Macharius had retired with Drake and Grimnar and his senior officers to plot. We had done our duty for the day.

'Drake seems to think so,' I said.

'Surely the Emperor would not allow it.'

'Who knows what the Emperor would allow. The galaxy is strange.'

'But surely Russ would never serve them,' Anton said.

'Perhaps they could change him during the process of rebuilding,' I said. 'You heard what the inquisitor said, who knows what they are capable of.'

'It is blasphemy, the Space Wolf is right,' said Ivan.

Anton looked excited. 'Who would ever have thought when we signed on with the Imperial Guard we would end up among the relics of the time when the Emperor walked among men.'

'Let's hope we don't end up as relics ourselves,' I said. The words were no sooner out of my mouth when alarms sounded. Drake and Macharius and the others emerged from the command room.

'Ready yourself,' Drake said. 'The gate is opening.'

Another alarm sounded. 'And the eldar are attacking,' Macharius said. 'They will be here soon.'

'The timing is not a coincidence,' Drake said.

I did not need him to tell me that.

CHAPTER TWENTY-THREE

I stood on the side of the Baneblade, leaning out from behind the turret, and studied the heights surrounding the valley. It had been a long night. The eldar mounted one attack after another: swift, subtle, constantly probing. There were feints within feints, swift strikes from one side of the valley followed by sudden retreats which coincided with advances from the other.

They never let up their attacks. A strike was always incoming from somewhere. It seemed to be their intention to never let us rest. It was a war of nerves, which they were well equipped to win because they enjoyed it, like cats playing with mice.

Sometimes they fled, or appeared to, and our troops followed them from our lines, only to have the eldar turn on them and cut them down. Other times they retreated slowly, inviting pursuit all the way to the surrounding hills. Macharius forbade it, of course, not wishing our forces to be drawn into a trap, but sometimes his orders were disobeyed in the excitement of the moment, or obeyed too late, and casualties ensued. And worse than casualties...

The sun rose above the mountains. The attacks had suddenly ceased, and we had just enough time to breathe a sigh of relief when the screaming started. It drifted down from the heights, the sound of men begging and pleading for mercy, amplified by some unnatural means so that we could make out every mutter, wheeze and prayer. The strangest thing was that we never heard the voices of the victims' tormentors. Whatever alien technology broadcast our comrades' agony to us, it did not pick up the eldar's words at all.

'They don't have much of a sense of humour, do they?' said Ivan. He was trying to make a joke about it, but there was tension in his voice.

'They are trying to break our morale,' said Anton. 'To make us doubt ourselves and our commanders.'

'Maybe,' I said.

'Maybe?'

'Maybe they just enjoy doing this. Maybe it's how they amuse themselves between fights. Maybe they just want to frighten us. They feed on fear and pain. You heard what Bael said.'

'I am starting to wonder why we came here,' said Anton. He was trying too hard to sound casual. His face was pale and he kept licking his lips. He scanned the slopes with the sniper rifle. He caught sight of something and nodded; he stopped swivelling the barrel, licked his lips and squeezed the trigger ever so gently. Somewhere on the slope, a figure dropped. Anton grunted in satisfaction.

'Got the bastard.' I wondered how he had done it. After all, one of those helmets had almost withstood a direct hit at close range.

I hadn't realised I had spoken aloud until Anton replied. 'You don't aim for the head. There are weak spots in the armour at the joints, at the armpits, at the throat. If you hit them there you hurt them. I'm not saying you'll kill them this way, mind, but you will hurt them. Let's see how they like a taste of their own medicine.'

There was a viciousness in his voice I had never heard before, and a fear greater than anything I had ever seen in him before, although it was still under control. Like any veteran soldier, Anton was used to being scared. He just would not let it get the better of him. It was the viciousness that was worrying me, though. It seemed the longer we faced the eldar, the more they brought out elements of their character in us. I wondered if it were some sort of evil magic, but then I realised it was simply that as fear begets fear, cruelty begets cruelty. The eldar were easy to hate as well as fear.

Was it possible that if we stayed here long enough and survived we would become like them? You hear stories of such things whispered sometimes, of troops who face Chaos worshippers becoming Chaos worshippers in the end. Perhaps evil is contagious, like a disease. If it were so, the eldar across there would definitely be plague carriers.

Well if that were the case, Macharius was a surgeon,

I thought. I hoped he was getting ready to carry out an operation.

The defensive perimeter had been reconfigured. It formed a wedge now, centred on the main temple, which Macharius had chosen to use as his base. Units were being moved within it, to counter the threat of any eldar emerging from the depths. The men moved decisively to obey their instructions, but there was a nervousness to them.

We stood on the roof of the temple and watched the action. Lightning strike fighters raced overhead to strafe the eldar position. Strange bat-winged eldar vehicles rose to meet them, and a dogfight erupted overhead as some of the Imperial fighters peeled off to defend the ground attack planes and the eldar sought to get on their tails. We cheered as the fighter-bombers delivered their payloads of death.

One by one, the fights broke up into individual duels as the craft raced out of sight along the mountain valleys, leaving only jet contrails and the thunderous roar of their engines as evidence they had passed.

At least we had some air cover, I thought, and they were making sorties. One by one, the eldar vehicles returned to their base, wherever that was. No human planes came into sight, and I had no idea whether they survived or not. Such is the soldier's eye view of war. You catch fragments of a bigger picture, but not enough to comprehend it all. See things that pose questions that are never answered. Witness deaths that may be meaningless or heroic, but you never know at the time.

Just as those thoughts went through my mind, I saw another massive wave of eldar swarming over the ramparts, probing into our lines.

'Time to get back inside,' said Anton. 'It looks like our services may soon be needed.'

'Indeed.'

I heard the roar of heavy weapons outside the temple. The sound echoed down the chamber a fraction of a second after I heard the faint noise from Macharius's headset. The battle seemed to have hit a new height of frenzy. Looking at the intricate patterns on the command tables it was impossible to tell who was winning. The eldar had penetrated our outer perimeter. Our lines were collapsing and our men were in retreat. Huge holes in our defences let them punch through. I wondered if, for the first time, I were about to witness Macharius lose a battle. Given the nature of our foes this would be a bad time for it.

Macharius gave clipped orders in response to reports from field commanders. I had no idea what was going on, but he clearly did. As ever he had the whole battlefield held in his mind and was able to build a clear picture of what was going on from mere fragments of information and supposition. The approach of danger did not faze him.

He looked up, glanced at us and said, 'Hold yourself in readiness. The xenos are about to hit this section of the temple.' I wondered how he could be so controlled under the circumstances.

* * *

Victory is mine. We have penetrated their lines. In orbit, my fleet is slowly overwhelming the enemy vessel. My forces sweep through the gaps they have punched in the enemy's defences. They have almost reached the temple complex that this Macharius has made his headquarters. Hopefully they will capture him, and I will be able to have a few words before I feast upon his essence. All the signs point to the fact that the Gate of Ancients is about to open. I have timed everything to perfection, as ever.

Even as the joy of victory burns in my mind, a few small things niggle at me. Where are the Space Marines? Only hours ago they were hunting my force through the corridors, engaged in a bloody war of attrition. Now they are nowhere to be found. Could it be they have sensed the coming defeat and fled the field of battle?

No matter, I will hunt them down later. Now it is time to make my way to the gate. Later there will be time to celebrate this victory properly.

We checked our weapons again. Anton's throat bulged nervously as he swallowed. He was clearly not delighted by the prospect of getting to grips with the eldar again. I could not blame him for it.

Drake looked at us and said, 'Stay close to me.'

'As long as you stay close to him,' Ivan said, nodding in the direction of Macharius. If his tone upset the inquisitor, Drake gave no sign. He merely smiled coldly.

At that moment something ricocheted across the room and took one of the Lion Guard in the throat. He fell gasping, his skin turning pale, his mouth open in a silent scream.

Macharius took one last look at the tactical display and gave a series of orders, with quick, clipped commands. Clearly he intended to go down fighting till the bitter end.

A group of xenos bounded in, with gravity-defying grace. Their shots took out a target every time they aimed. I tipped a table end over end and dived behind it, stuck my head up and aimed my shotgun at where I had last seen one of the eldar. It was not there. Looking up I saw it descending from above me. I rolled onto my back and pulled the trigger of the shotgun. The blast caught the eldar on the chest and lifted it upwards. It had not killed it, though. It swung its weapon to bear on me.

Anton's rifle spoke from nearby and a heavy calibre shell put a huge dent in the xenos's helmet. It did not penetrate it, but I doubted it had done the alien much good. The bullet must have driven part of the armour through the eldar's skull. It twisted head over heels and landed in a sprawl across another map table.

Macharius strode through the carnage, firing his bolt pistol while giving orders into his mouthpiece. He did not let the swirl of melee around him distract him from taking charge of the battle. The screams of the dying, the muzzle-flare of weapons, the presence of death hovering at his shoulder did not break his concentration. If anything they seemed to make him more focused as if something in him drew strength from the carnage all around him.

I glanced around to make sure there were no eldar closing

with him, then gave my attention back to my surroundings. The remaining eldar had gone down while I was looking elsewhere. Macharius stood over the corpse of one, blood covering his armour, brains splattering his shoulderguard. None of it belonged to him.

Macharius surveyed the chamber, took stock of the situation in a moment and then returned to giving orders to our embattled perimeter. I counted dead. Nineteen of the Lion Guard and half a dozen of the tech-adepts were down. I counted five eldar. It was a better ratio than we had managed on the ship. I was not sure why. Maybe we had been ready for them this time. Maybe they had less room to manoeuvre. Or maybe they had simply been overconfident having made their way so far into the temple.

Suddenly Macharius stopped giving orders. He just stood there, looking satisfied. Drake glanced at him. Macharius said, 'The eldar are beaten.'

I looked at the hologrid. The gaps in our lines had closed. The eldar were trapped within them, caught in a killing ground where the massed batteries of our armoured vehicles could catch them. In their lust to kill, in their desire to maim and slay, they had sacrificed their advantage and fought on a battlefield that played to our strengths. I heard the roar of heavy batteries outside.

Looking out I saw Thunderhawk gunships and Avenger strike fighters strafing the eldar. Once again, Macharius had turned around a battle, made an opponent fight where he should not have. He had turned the trap itself into a trap.

Logan Grimnar entered the chamber, looked around and nodded. 'The xenos are well beaten,' he said. 'I can see you have no need of my help here.'

It sounded like high praise indeed coming from him.

No! In the time it has taken for me to get to the gate, the battle has turned. A sick feeling settles in my stomach. The enemy flight was but a ruse to lure my troops into the killing ground between the temples. Their vehicles are being smashed by the superior firepower of the human batteries. The escaping crews are being overwhelmed by the sheer weight of human numbers. Who would have thought that a human would have the wit to turn his weakness into a strength or that an eldar commander would have turned a position of strength into a weakness.

There is nothing left but to flee. The only way out for me is through the Gate of Ancients. There is still a chance that I can claim the prize I came for and turn this situation around. I must take it. I must.

Drake swayed dizzily. He put a hand to his brow. 'The Way is open.'

A messenger raced up to the blood-spattered Lord High Commander. 'General Macharius,' he said. 'Reports from the labyrinth. The eldar attacked our position down there. They have seized the portal entrance.'

'The last attack was a distraction,' Macharius said. He smiled warily. 'The enemy knew the portal was going to open and took advantage of the last big attack to seize it.

Now we need to stop him before he finds whatever it is he is seeking.'

We raced through the vast depths of the temple complex, past the time-worn statues of forgotten alien gods, moving towards a gate that opened on we knew not what. Faint shivering passed through the rock, reverberations from distant explosions where man and xenos fought for their lives in the valley above.

We reached the gate room. Bodies were strewn everywhere, human and eldar. It had been a brutal fight with no quarter given by either side. By the looks of things, the eldar had not even slowed down to perform their ritual torture. They had been in too much of a hurry, and it was obvious why.

Where once there had merely been stone, now there was something else. The whole area within the carved arch shimmered. It was like looking onto the surface of a pool into which many different types of luminescent dye had been poured. The colours moved and swirled. The area where the rock had been seemed fluid. It felt as if you could dive into it, the way you could dive into water.

An officer raced towards Macharius. His green tunic was ripped, his face was marked by a dozen small cuts, his eyes had the haunted look I had come to recognise in the faces of those who had faced the eldar at close quarters.

'Report,' said Macharius. He tilted his head to one side to indicate he was listening. Over his headset, he was still giving orders to our forces outside the temple as they dealt with the xenos attack.

'They came at us out of the tunnels, sir. About twenty of them. We had our weapons ready but they cut us down from behind.' He looked deeply distressed. 'There was one of them… He was so fast, nothing could stop him.'

'You killed some of them,' Macharius said. He counted corpses. 'Most of them, if your numbers are correct.'

I saw at least a dozen eldar corpses. Grimnar sniffed the air. 'About twenty would be correct. The surviving xenos vanished through the gate. Their scent track ends at this wall.' His frown of distaste let us know how unnatural this was. 'They had the Fist with them.'

'They did, Lord High Commander,' said the officer. 'We thought we had them, there were only a few left, but they jumped into the colours and vanished like, like…' Confusion showed on his face. He struggled to find the words to describe what he had witnessed.

'Did you see what happened to them?' Drake asked urgently.

'They seemed to… recede, growing smaller and smaller, vanishing into the distance, although they did not look as though they were moving. It was very strange.'

'The gate is open. Wherever it leads to.' Drake said, looking at Macharius. 'What do we do now? Wait for them to come back through?'

'We don't know how this thing works,' said Grimnar. 'They may not emerge here. They may find their way out somewhere else.'

'This is the only way in or out that we know of,' said Drake. He looked thoughtful and more than a little afraid.

Grimnar sniffed the air and appeared to come to a decision. He sniffed the air once more. 'They have the Fist with them.' He spoke something in a tongue I did not recognise, a guttural, barking language that might have been his native tongue. He nodded his head as though receiving an answer over some sealed channel on the comm-net.

'I cannot allow the Fist of Russ to fall into such foul hands.'

He bounded forwards into the shimmering surface of the wall, and I saw then the strangeness the officer had mentioned. It was as if he were falling away from us, moving at great speed while shrinking in size, down a long tunnel filled with a multicoloured mist. I caught sight of him less and less until finally he vanished. It felt as if I had been watching him for hours but in reality only heartbeats had passed.

'We don't know whether it is possible to survive in there without protective gear,' said Drake. 'Or whether there is any way back. Or what might happen if the gateway closes while we are still within.'

'Lemuel,' Macharius said.

'Sir?'

'Inspect the gate.' He pointed and he could only mean one thing. For a moment only, I considered refusing, but that would have meant being shot. I took a step forward, obeying Macharius almost instinctively, and touched the surface of the gate. I pulled down my rebreather and took another step.

It was cool and I passed through it. It was like stepping into liquid only for a moment, and then I found myself somewhere else, in a long corridor lit by a strange shimmering glow. I could see no source of it, but I could see ancient eldar statues reminiscent of those in the valley.

It was cold. I kept holding my breath, unwilling to breathe in air that might prove poisonous. My heart pounded in my chest. My lungs started to feel as if they would burst. I let out my breath and inhaled. The air tasted strange but it was breathable.

I took another breath and felt nothing. My lungs did not burn. I was not poisoned. I checked the hazard monitor on my wrist. There were no indicators of danger.

I turned to the wall and looked back. Through the polychromatic, oily shimmering I saw the others looking at me. They stood frozen like statues with no sign of motion.

I frowned. There was something odd about what I was seeing, but I could not put my finger on exactly what. It was like looking at a picture, a still life, not at living, breathing people. I paused for a second, at once anxious to move and reluctant to do so. This would be the moment of truth. I tried to step back through the portal. Once again, the cold liquid surface of the gate closed around me. I felt resistance and wondered whether I was trapped in this strange place.

Everything seemed to speed up. Macharius and the others started moving again. 'It's breathable,' I said.

'How would you know?' Anton asked. 'You were only gone a second.'

Something must have shown on my face.

'Time flows differently beyond the gate,' said Drake. 'Unless I am much mistaken.'

'A heartbeat here was at least a minute there,' I said.

Drake nodded as though I had confirmed something he had suspected. 'It is often the case when you step beyond the normal boundaries of our continuum.'

'What?' Anton said. He clearly did not understand, but Drake was in no mood to explain it to him.

A thought struck me. 'Sir, that means that the eldar may be hours ahead of us down the trail in there. Grimnar too.'

Macharius nodded, grasping the point at once. The longer we stood there, the bigger the lead the eldar would have over us. What seemed like minutes to us might be hours or even days in there.

'We go through,' Macharius said. 'Now.'

He was already stepping into the portal. Drake was following. There was nothing else to do but accompany them. I took a long step into cool strangeness.

CHAPTER TWENTY-FOUR

'What is this place?' Macharius asked. We stood on the far side of the portal, watching the remainder of our force very slowly enter the gate. Each slight movement seemed to take minutes. There was a moment of strangeness when they passed through to our side. Their limbs blurred as if their motions were speeding up, and then, to all intents and purposes, they looked normal.

'I think it may be something the eldar built, a pathway into the beyond.'

'Why would the eldar who stole it bring the Fist of Russ here?'

Drake paused. An odd expression flickered across his face. 'This is a roadway through infinity. The eldar use them to pass through space.'

'You saw that in Bael's mind?' Macharius said.

Drake nodded. 'This one was a sacred path once, and it leads to something awesome. Or at least that is what I assume.'

'Or what he wanted you to assume. Is it possible he could have projected false memories into your mind?'

'Certainly,' said Drake. 'I am sure such was his intention. The eldar are clever and deceptive, and I do not trust anything I saw in his thoughts, but it is all we have to go on.'

Macharius laughed. 'There are only two ways we can go, forwards or back.'

'I can sense the presence of the Fist here,' said Drake. 'I know which way they went. There is something odd, though, a sense of a presence I do not like.'

Looking at the nearby statues I saw that one of them had been marked. It showed a crude rune in a similar style to those emblazoned on Grimnar's armour. Just some lines quickly scratched with a blade. It took me a moment to realise what it was, then I pointed it out to Macharius.

'The Space Wolf is leaving us a trail,' said Macharius. 'Let's move out.'

'Leaving us a trail or making sure he could find his own way back,' Anton muttered, so low that only I could hear him. To tell the truth it did not matter. It was still reassuring. At least we had something to go on and a path back if we survived.

We moved along the path, a company of men in green tunics, along with several squads of Drake's storm troopers. I was wondering whether we should send back for reinforcements.

From what I had seen of the eldar, six of them might be able to take us, particularly if they understood this environment and we did not. Macharius did not wait though, and he knew his business.

Of course, there was the distortion of time that passing through the gate caused. By the time help was summoned from outside, days might have passed in here. We had no option but to race ahead if we were ever going to catch up with the xenos and retrieve the Fist of Russ.

The place that we moved through was the spookiest I had ever seen. The air was close and still and oddly perfumed. My skin tingled as I marched as if it had been exposed to some strange drug. Drake's hazard monitors told us there were no chemical or biological agents present, but it was possible that they had malfunctioned, or whatever was there was too subtle for them to detect. It was not a reassuring thought.

The way ahead seemed to be some sort of tunnel. Massive arches inscribed with odd xenos runes held the ceiling in place. There were times when that vanished, though, and we caught sight of odd vistas. Sometimes through crystal we saw the strange stars of alien skies. Sometimes we saw huge shifting masses of colour that reminded me of chemical cloud formations in the skies of hive-worlds I had visited. The path was wide enough for multiple battle tanks to pass abreast. I wondered who had built it and why.

The thought occurred to me that perhaps the Valley of the Ancients was not a sacred temple site, or at least not just one. Perhaps it was the terminus for this pathway. Perhaps the whole structure was intended to anchor the path in our reality. I pushed the thought to one side and moved closer to Macharius and Drake.

The inquisitor looked particularly queasy and I cannot say I blamed him. There was something in the strangeness of our surroundings that was getting on my nerves. Given his power and his sensitivity it must have been a thousand times worse for him.

I noticed that many of the great statues that lined the roadway had been defaced. In places, it looked as if they had fused or melted under the impact of gigantic las-beams. In other places they were oddly altered. Their features had a lewd look to them. Some of them had multiple arms which ended in claws. Others had… exaggerated physical features. The clean lines that had been the mark of so many of the statues outside were disturbed. There was something about these ones that suggested the crazed uncleanness of the followers of Chaos.

So far we'd had no problem following the right trail because there was only one. We had only two directions in which to go, forwards or back towards the exit. I began to notice that in places the stonework seemed eaten away and strange pools of multicoloured light were visible in the gaps. These swirled and shimmered in ways that hurt the eye. At times the clouds swept forward and billowed flat as if they were pressed against a wall of glass so translucent as to be invisible. When we passed these gaps, I felt nauseous and afraid. It was as if an oppressive presence waited just out of sight, ready to pounce, and its mere closeness was enough to set my nerves to jangling.

'I like this not,' said Drake. 'We are close to Chaos. This is a place where the Ruinous Powers have made their will felt.'

'That does not bode well for our quest,' said Macharius.

'I am starting to feel as if nothing does,' said Drake. 'Perhaps this was all a mistake.'

'Come, my friend, now is not the time for such talk, not when we are so close to finding what we seek. Just think, we will soon have one of the Imperium's most sacred relics in our possession.'

'I wonder whether its time here has contaminated it. I sense evil in this place.'

'Surely a relic of such holiness could not be tainted, even by the Ruinous Powers?'

'There is nothing that Chaos cannot turn to its purposes, nothing. So I was taught. So I believe. It is why we must be eternally vigilant, with ourselves most of all.'

Macharius looked around at our surroundings. If he were daunted by being cut off from our world within the toils of this ancient, alien place he gave no sign of it. 'We will do what needs to be done,' he said.

It occurred to me then that we were very far from home, and that there was a very real chance that we would never return. Less than an hour before I had been celebrating an unexpected victory. Now I was almost sick with fear of the unknown. I wondered if the eldar had known about this or whether they were as surprised by it as we were.

This is a strange and terrible place. It is not at all what I expected. The evil that destroyed my ancestors has touched this webway. All of the signs point to one thing. They created this vault thinking that it would preserve them from the power that was devouring their very souls. Instead, it looks as though they entombed themselves within it. There was no escape for them, here or any other place. The only question that remains is whether the evil that destroyed them still lurks within or whether, lacking anything else to devour, it perished from lack of prey.

My followers are nervous. They do not know why we are here. They think that we are fleeing from a battle that could easily have been won. They think that I am afraid of the Space Marines and what they might do to us. So far none of them have had the courage to say anything, but I can tell that it is only a matter of time. Sileria, in particular, blames me for the loss of Bael. It seems they were, as I suspected, lovers. Well, he was no great loss, and I doubt whether she will be either.

I can see why they are edgy. There is something here that plays on the nerves, that makes even those who are used to causing fear, afraid. This place still reverberates with echoes of ancient terror and ancient pain, and delicious as that would normally be, there is something about it, something tainted that breeds suspicion in our minds.

They think I should be on the surface directing the destruction of my enemies. I can see that accusation in the very body language of every eldar with me. They still do not understand how quickly victory was turned to defeat. Or perhaps they think if I had not been so desperate to get to the gate I might have saved the situation.

Perhaps that is nothing less than the truth.

I would have liked nothing better than to direct the destruction of the humans on the planet's surface, but it is much more important that I should be the first to get my hands upon the ancient reality engine.

I console myself with the thought that at least there is no one here to get in our way, to stop us from finally achieving the goal I set myself all of those centuries ago. I know that time flows differently here. It was one of the warnings that the ancient books contained. I shall let my troops rest before we make our final push towards our ultimate destination.

Then we shall see what we shall see.

The roadway curved downwards and things changed once more. It was hard to put a finger on exactly when and how the changes started. All I know is that the sense of being watched by an alien presence increased. Our surroundings appeared ever more distorted. Larger and larger patches of strangely glowing colours appeared in the walls, and it was not good to look too closely at them. I had no idea how long we had marched. My wrist chronometer said it was only a couple of hours, but this was a place where time had no meaning. It was just as likely that we would return to discover no time had passed as to return and find out we had been gone for days or weeks or years.

Perhaps we would turn out to be like those ships' crews who had been lost between the stars for centuries and returned to find out all their descendants were dead. I had heard tales of those who had entered ancient, haunted vaults for what they thought was one night and emerged to discover a century had passed. Had they entered a place like this?

The way ahead started running through larger chambers. It remained a massive roadway, paved and marked with ancient runes. Sometimes, off the road, we would see robed skeletons lying there. Macharius would not allow us to depart from the trail, but the little I saw of them suggested something inhuman to me. They were too long, too thin, and something in the way they sprawled was not the way a human body would have lain.

The roof of the chamber started to shimmer and change, and sometimes pictures came into view there, gigantic images of godlike beings who seemed to be looking down on us, or into the area through which we walked. Sometimes they were scenes or parts of scenes, broken images with no pattern that I could see and only one common theme. In all of them were tall, beautiful creatures, in surroundings similar to the ones in which we were walking through.

They were eldar, like the ones we had fought physically. Their expressions had nothing in common with the cruelty of Bael and his kindred, though. These people looked peaceful and pleasant and full of love. Of course, who am I to judge whether they were or not. We are taught to be wary of the xenos, rightfully so. Perhaps this was just a deception or a trap, but some deep seated instinct told me that this was not the case.

We marched on. I prayed to the Emperor that we would

find the eldar and get this over with. There was something about this pathway that frightened me more than death.

This place has been strangely altered, tainted by She Who Thirsts or her followers. The path looks like many others I have travelled, but I can see that it is frayed, that the very fabric of the powers that make it up is unravelling. It is only a matter of time before the whole structure is swallowed and another of our ancestors' creations is devoured.

Of all the things they made, this is one of the few I would regret the destruction of. The webway allows us to travel between places and worlds, but this is not like that. It is a vault, a secure place, a protected place. It was intended to keep safe things of value to our ancestors. It was intended to be a refuge when their universe went mad. In their weakness, they sought not to confront and overmaster what threatened them but to hide from it. Their own spinelessness betrayed them.

They thought they had dug themselves a hole to hide in, a burrow where they could hide from the predators that pursued them. It is obvious they were wrong. They brought what they sought to avoid with them, and when they sealed the doors behind them, they trapped themselves with it. The irony is enough to make me laugh. My guards do not understand why I do, but they echo my mirth. Even here they look to me for leadership. They are not afraid but nervous.

So far none have audibly expressed any criticism of my leadership, nor are they likely to, for they know that I will not stand for it. Yet I sense their doubts. I have my own. Memories of the last few minutes of the battle on the surface keep coming back to me. Who would have thought mere apes could have fought so well? My followers are inclined to attribute the setback to the presence of those known as the Adeptus Astartes, and there is some truth in that. I am the only one who knows that is not the whole story.

There is an intelligence guiding the humans, commanding them, a mind of subtlety and great tactical gifts. I have seen it in the traps it has laid for our forces. Every time we thought we found a weakness, it was a snare. We have taken far heavier casualties fighting the humans than even the presence of Space Marines would have suggested.

Warrior for warrior, they are the equal of any of my force and the superiors of most, but they represent the merest fraction of the enemy's number. Those with them should never have been able to withstand our swift and merciless attacks. Their weak spirits should have been broken, their slow minds incapable of understanding the speed of our assaults. Yet somehow they not only stood their ground but inflicted devastating losses on us. Many noble bodies will need to be rebuilt after this. Many fragments of flesh reclaimed.

If I return now, without that which I seek, I will be a laughing stock. My enemies will whisper about how I was defeated by an ape. I will lose face and my enemies will not fear me as they should. I begin to suspect that perhaps I have been lured here by those very enemies. Perhaps it is no human mind that guides them but something else.

I push such thoughts to one side. I must concentrate on my goals. I must find the reality engine.

CHAPTER TWENTY-FIVE

We marched and we marched and we marched through that timeless, sunless place, knowing that the eldar and Grimnar were still ahead of us. I looked at my chronometer and found out to my surprise that it had been twelve hours since we had set off. We had already been up for most of a day before that, and had fought and fled. Some of the men looked weary. I could see that Macharius was reluctant to call a halt but understood the need to do so.

He raised his hand and said, 'We cannot march forever. We shall sleep for a few hours and move on, rested and ready to face the Emperor's enemies.'

He himself looked capable of marching on then and there, but like all good leaders he knew it was unwise to push his troops beyond their limits, except when it was absolutely necessary.

The path passed through a large parkland in a huge chamber. We were surrounded by forests of strange looking trees with feathery leaves. I had never seen anything like them before. There was something unnatural about them. I doubted they had ever been planted in the soil of any world colonised by men. They looked a perfect backdrop for the eldar, though.

Macharius divided us into watches and we threw ourselves down, using our packs for pillows. My head no sooner hit the ground than I was asleep and my dreams were weird and haunted.

At first I remembered my early life in the slums of Belial. I saw my father, old and worn out by work. I saw the guild factorums in which Anton and Ivan and I had laboured. I was chased through them by gangsters. They were going to pull off my fingers with red-hot pliers. There was something daemonic in their faces.

Somehow they followed me into the camp where I did my basic training for the Guard, but now they were instructors, always threatening with the pliers if I did not learn fast enough, and I knew I could not.

They were officers howling commands at me in the jungles of Jurasik and the lava flows of Karsk. They pursued me through the airless tunnels of the asteroid fortresses of Mahagan and the dimly lit streets of Hive Skarthius, where skull-masked priests led armies of grey-skinned men.

As the dreams progressed I became aware of changes in my surroundings. I was still being pursued, sometimes through familiar landscapes, then through places that resembled the valley above – but around its edges were the streets of a city, which extended down into the tunnels below.

At first the streets were empty, but as the chase continued they were crowded by those thin-lipped, fine-featured xenos we had seen modelled in the statuary. They watched me being pursued and they made no move to help, although they seemed interested in a vague and distant way.

I dived into the middle of a crowd of them, determined to lose the things that hounded me. Suddenly there were more of the xenos and they no longer noticed me, crowds of them went about their business, got on with their lives. Somehow the urgency of the pursuit fled and I knew I was, for the moment, safe.

I paused and studied my reflection in the mirrored window of a shop, and I saw now that my form was not human but eldar. I was taller and thinner and far better looking. With the strange logic of dreams I did not question the transformation. My own life as a soldier of the Emperor was the dream now. Memories crowded into my head, of my life as an eldar, of a family and a house and an existence that felt as real as my waking career as an Imperial Guardsman.

I looked up and once again my surroundings were changed. I was in the valley above, but now it was entirely occupied by a prosperous city of stone and crystal, of egg-shaped buildings and oval towers with minaret spires. I strode up a long curved walkway and looked down upon the valley. There were temples there, huge and ancient and familiar. The gods looked down on their blessed followers.

Looping over everything was a massive roadway, reminiscent of the one we had walked on to get through the gate. It floated over the buildings and vanished into the surrounding mountains.

I noticed in the streets that there was a preacher, robed in gold and purple and green. He smiled beatifically at passers-by and preached words of love and charity and hope. He told of the coming of a new god that would lead the eldar once more to greatness of soul and spirit, who would provide guidance to the lost, hope to the dejected, peace to the troubled. He would lead the eldar to a life of simple, endless pleasure.

The priest spoke, and folk listened to the sweetness of his voice and words. I listened too, and I was troubled without knowing exactly why. My people were at the height of their greatness. There was no poverty, no hunger, no hatred in our hearts. What could such things mean to us? There was a sense that all problems had been solved. The only things that troubled us were of the spirit; we faced the boredom of a serene, happy existence. There were troubling reports of great wars among the other races, but we took no part in them.

Things shifted once more. Time had passed. The city no longer looked so clean and clear. The lights seemed dimmer. There were more shadows everywhere, but not because of catastrophe. It was because the people of the city wanted it this way. They wanted shadow now. They wanted quiet places where they could move apart and smoke their pipes and lie in each other's arms and pass their time most pleasantly. The priests in gold and purple and green moved among them, smiling approvingly, speaking their words of tolerance and comfort, encouraging the folk in their pursuit of pleasure.

Life was sweet, and desires were to be embraced. Experience of any sort was good. I heard sermons preached that soon the bright golden god would appear and speak his word and the universe would be transformed in the light of his presence. Listening to the words I felt a sense of falseness and was disturbed, but I took another puff from the narcotic hookah and reached out for my lovers and found peace.

More time passed. The people had turned their faces from the old gods and swarmed into the temples of the new god, who was yet to be born. Shrines lay neglected. Offerings went unmade. Life had altered strangely. People ignored their daily business now, lost themselves in sleep and the consumption of narcotics and hallucinogenics.

Few people went about their business by day, but emerged only at night, to revel and indulge in orgies of lovemaking and drug-taking and the consumption of hallucinogenic wine. The priests led the revels now and preached the word of the imminence of their god, and people watched and waited, sensing that soon the world would change forever. In the tunnels below, new statues were erected to the god. It was not like the friendly beings of old.

Not everyone approved. Not everyone took part in the revels. Other preachers appeared, saying that something was amiss, that some great disaster was imminent, that soon there would be a cosmic crisis that would destroy eldar civilisation. Few paid attention. Sometimes those who spoke out were found beaten to death or overdosed on narcotics. Sometimes I saw priests in gold and purple and green standing over their corpses.

Some took their families and belongings and left, taking flight to new planets or setting out for the great world-ships. Some built a great vault, a safe place into which they could retreat within the webways. They began to experiment with devices that would tap the flows of power, let them restructure reality.

Most stayed, too drugged to move, too overwhelmed by the pleasures of life to do anything other than take part in the day-long rituals in the temples of the new god. I sensed a mighty presence looming over everything, biding its time, waiting its moment. I was not alone in this. The sense of presence, of being at the end of something, gave the revels a desperate fury. People turned to darker pleasures. Blood flowed in the streets, and not all the victims of violence were unwilling participants. All sense of proportion, of restraint, departed.

Now, day after day, night after night passed to the beating of great drums, and dancing and revelry to the sound of hellish, discordant piping. Eldar ran naked through the streets, bodies covered in tattoos written in blood, or woven from scars. Sacrifices were made everywhere to the new god as all vestige of sanity seemed to be extinguished. The priests in gold and purple and green cavorted lewdly in the streets, leading the revels, consuming the potions with the greatest enthusiasm, speaking mad words of revelation that eager-eared listeners drank in. The day of embodiment was fast approaching.

The sermons grew ever less restrained, ever more vehement. The priests led the population in ritual chanting, in the defacing of the statues of the old gods, in the creation of newer and less wholesome idols. Under cover of night things began to appear that looked like people but whose limbs ended in claws. They danced in the moonlit streets surrounded by clouds of intoxicating perfumes that drove all those who breathed them in to greater and greater heights of hedonism.

The day arrived. The sky split. On a thousand worlds, the god appeared and looked down on his people and smiled. And they screamed for they saw at last the visage of the being they worshipped, and they were afraid. Their screams lasted but an instant for the newborn god breathed in and their souls were sucked from their bodies and drawn into his maw.

With every soul devoured the god grew in power and strength. It became harder and harder for those who resisted to endure. Starting with the weaker souls, he gained strength until not even the mightiest could stand against the strain. The worst of it was that even as they died and were devoured, their screams of terror turned to screams of ecstasy. Hearing these, those who resisted, resisted no longer and the mad scramble to escape doom became a willing submission to it.

Bodies fell in the street, drained of spirit and animation,

as the daemon-god fed. The streets of the city became filled with corpses. Ships fell from the sky, no longer piloted. Vehicles slewed off roads as their drivers were absorbed into the presence of the newborn deity. In moments, stillness settled on the city as all of its inhabitants died and were transformed into part of the new entity.

Lights still flickered, signs still flashed, but there was no one there to stand witness. An end had come to the city, and I knew that all across the galaxy, on every world the eldar had inhabited, it was the same. A new evil had been born, weaned on the souls of an entire people, a creature of cosmic power and malevolence, a new power of Chaos destined to strive with the others for dominance of the universe.

In my mind I saw thousands of suddenly empty worlds, and I felt the new god's presence. A single titanic word echoed through my mind in the aftermath of its birth, a name: Slaanesh. I woke screaming. I was surrounded by men doing the same.

Macharius stood staring into the distance. His face was grim. He had not been among the sleepers. He looked down at Drake who had been. The inquisitor's face was very pale.

'This is an accursed place,' he said. 'We should leave here. Our souls are in peril.'

'We have not found the Fist, and I would not surrender it to our enemies.'

'It avails us not if we find the Fist and lose our souls. We would merely be bringing a great spiritual peril out into the Imperium.'

Macharius stared at him, hard, obviously considering his words carefully. 'I have come a long way to find the Fist and I will not turn back now. I will not let so sacred a symbol of the Imperium fall into the hands of those eldar scum.'

'They are corrupt and they are suited to this place. We are not. The longer we remain, the more in peril our souls are.'

'I saw nothing save men whose sleep was troubled.'

'If their dreams were like mine, they were more than troubled. Lemuel, what did you dream?'

Both of them looked at me. I told them.

'I saw the same,' said Anton.

'And I,' said Ivan.

Other soldiers chipped in. Their descriptions were similar to ours. They were not exactly alike in detail but in broad strokes were the same. They had witnessed the destruction of worlds and the birth of an evil god. It was the sort of knowledge that Drake could quite probably have had us put to death for possessing, if he'd so desired.

'I will not turn my back on this quest because of a dream, no matter how frightening or how many people had it,' said Macharius.

'The fact that so many men had it is a sign,' said Drake. 'And not a good one. It is a warning.'

'It was a dream.'

'There is something about this place,' said Drake. 'Some echo of distant terrible events resounds through it. The further we go, the stronger those echoes will become.'

'I am not turning back,' said Macharius and it was a simple statement of fact. He was not afraid, and he would not allow us to be either. 'Nor is any man under my command.'

His eagle-keen gaze swept over us, and we all felt the force of it. I stood straighter when he looked at me and so did every man present. All of us believed that if we showed the slightest sign of fear we would be personally betraying him, and none of us wanted to do that. The matter was settled with that one look. Not even Drake had the stomach for argument after that.

'We've rested enough,' said Macharius. 'We must push on.'

CHAPTER TWENTY-SIX

The further we marched, the stranger it became. The walls of the tunnel became lighter and lighter until they were almost translucent. The ghastly multicoloured fog that had marked the entrance to this place was visible through them. Occasionally it cleared, and I saw snatches of scenes that were shockingly familiar.

Sometimes I saw a single figure, an eldar who resembled someone I had seen in my dreams. Once it was one of the ghastly priests of the new god smiling and nodding at me encouragingly. Another time it was the haunted face of one of the xenos who had walked the city streets. I never saw them directly or for very long. I caught sight of them out of the corner of my eye, had the merest flicker of recognition, and then they were gone as if they had never been, disappeared like shadows when a candle is snuffed out.

It was maddening. I could not be sure I was seeing anything. They were as real as the colours you see when you close your eyes and massage your eyelids and just as temporary. I glanced to my left at Anton and I could see he was queasy as well. Sometimes he looked swiftly to his right or left, as though he were trying to catch a glimpse of something that was not there, or which moved too quickly from his line of sight.

He saw I was looking at him and he turned to me and said, 'I don't like this place.'

For once, he was not whining or complaining, simply stating a fact. Normally I would have mocked him, but now I could only agree.

'So you're seeing them too,' said Ivan quietly.

'Seeing what?' I asked.

'The ghosts or dreams, or whatever they are.'

'Maybe.'

Drake dropped back to march along beside us. He was troubled, and it was a measure of exactly how troubled he was that he chose to talk with us. 'They are echoes, imprinted in the very fabric of this place, echoes of the people who were once here, of events that once happened, of things that once were.'

He sounded utterly convinced of that and very afraid. He glanced towards Macharius doubtfully. He clearly believed the Lord High Commander was leading us towards disaster.

'We've been in worse places,' I said. 'Faced worse foes. He's led us through all of it.'

'Where is the foe he can beat here?' said Drake quietly.

'What is there for him to out-think, to outfight. If there was something to defeat, he could, no doubt about it, but what we face here are shadows and memories, and not even our shadows and memories but those of deviant xenos. This is a place of ghosts.'

Despite the quietness of his speech, Macharius heard him. Without turning his head, he said, 'We have an objective and we have an enemy ahead of us. We will face the enemy and we will achieve our objective. Of that, have no doubt.'

'And what then?' Drake asked.

'We shall cross that bridge when we come to it,' said Macharius. 'One thing is certain. We will not give up now.'

The corridors darkened. The road swooped downwards, descending for what felt a very long way. We kept marching. Every now and again we spotted a mark in Fenrisian runes that let us know that Grimnar had been here before us. It was strangely reassuring.

The air became ever more close and still. I found I was sweating and the tunic of my uniform was sticking to me. I was very tired but had no great desire to sleep again. I feared what I might dream, and what I might see in those dreams.

We came to a fork in the road and Macharius chose the right-hand branch. There was a rune there. The roadway continued downwards. I wondered about this. If these paths ran beneath the surface of the planet we were down very deep now, but some instinct told me that we were not, that we were in a place far more alien and strange. There were more forks and the path looped more. I tried to picture the convolutions of the roadways unwinding around me, and I could not; it had become too bizarre and complex. Occasionally, a cold breeze blew out of somewhere, but it never lasted long and did not provide much relief from the heat.

It made me wonder about the eldar. Was this a natural temperature for them? It seemed possible that this heat was normal and comfortable for the builders of this odd labyrinth. But it was equally possible that the heat was the result of a malfunction in some xenos life support systems. There was ample evidence of dissolution and unmaking around us.

In places there were still statues. Many of them had been defaced and some of them looked downright daemonic. A few looked as if their stonework had been melted and remoulded into newer and more crude shapes, and then allowed to cool and settle again. I knew of no way of making stone do this, of course, but that is what it looked like. We trudged on and I began to feel that we were the ghosts, walking wearily through some limbo. Our whole purpose in being here seemed lost in the fog of tiredness and brain-stun.

I took a stimm tablet. As it fizzled away under my tongue I felt the alchemicals begin a losing battle against weariness. My sense of the strangeness of things began to ramp up. I was starting to feel as if somehow we were marching from one reality to another, from the world in which we had walked as men to the world of which I had dreamed.

Multiple shadows lengthened around us, products of many difficult-to-discern light sources. The click of our boot-heels on the stone of the roadway echoed into the distance. I found myself listening for some sign that someone somewhere had heard them and was coming to investigate. None came.

I looked at Drake. His face showed signs of awful strain as if the aura of this place were pressing down on him. He closed his eyes sometimes, and I could see his jaw moving as though he were grinding his teeth together. A faint nimbus of light played around his head as it tracked from side to side. He was still on the psychic trail of the eldar with the Fist, following it hound-like with his uncanny senses.

At that moment, in my weariness, he looked as different from a normal man as one of the xenos. I suspect, at the end of the day, that is how most of us feel about psykers because it is, ultimately, the truth. They *are* different from us. They see things we don't, experience things we cannot, wield powers beyond our understanding. I could not begin to understand how this place must feel to him. I only knew it was bad enough to me.

Of all of us, only the Undertaker appeared untroubled. He kept moving mechanically, with no sign of weariness or emotion. Somehow, he looked right at home, a hollow shell of a man, amid the hollow shell of this alien place. Looking at him, it came to me that there are some mortal men who can be as strange and frightening in their own ways as psykers, and that he was one of them.

Anton took a slug from his canteen and then wiped sweat from his forehead. He looked off into the distance for a moment then said, 'I hope we find those bastards before the water gives out.'

'There are fountains here, we've passed them,' said Ivan.

'Yeah – but do you fancy drinking anything out of them?'

'I will if I have to,' said Ivan. 'And so will you.'

'I dreamed they flowed with blood,' Anton said. I wondered about that because I had dreamed no such thing. I wondered how different the substance of the others' dreams had been from mine.

'You'll drink it if you have to,' Ivan repeated. 'We all will.'

We emerged from the archway and saw what lay below us. It was a vast bowl in which lay the remains of a ruined city. It looked as if an angry god had stamped his foot and smashed it. I thought of the destruction I had seen in my dreams and realised that this was an exact mirror of it. I realised something else. Down there, in the centre of the ruins, was a tower, and at its tip and down its length lights were glowing. The road ran no further.

'It looks as though we have found what we were looking for,' said Macharius. He glanced at Drake. The inquisitor nodded.

At last, what I have so long sought is within my grasp. The Tower of Heaven stands before me and within it is the reality engine the ancients devised. It feels astonishing that I am finally here, having travelled so far and sought for so long. And yet now it is almost done. I will soon know whether the secret exists or not.

It is clear that we are not alone here. At least one of the Space Wolves, possibly more, has followed us and is intent upon doing us harm. Talyn reports that he has seen other human troops passing into the city. They are not a huge force, yet they outnumber my own. Measures must be taken to stop them. I deploy the remainder of my warriors, giving them detailed instructions as to what they must do. They respond sullenly, seemingly unwilling at this final hurdle. I consider executing one or two as examples for the others, but it is pointless. I would simply be doing my enemies' work for them.

Instead, I remind Sileria and the others that we are trapped here, and the only way they are going to get out is if they do what I say. The argument sways them. They know there is no reasoning with the humans. They are beasts after all. They know also that it is in our best interests to fight together, and that I am their strongest warrior. Their chances are greatly increased by doing what I say, and they are at least bright enough to see that.

Once I am sure they understand what needs to be done, I step within the tower and begin to make my way towards my destiny. I still carry the ancient claw. I am unwilling to part with it. It has become a talisman of sorts for me, although whether for good or evil I cannot guess.

I felt a sense of excitement, the sort that you get before you go into combat. It came from the knowledge that one way or another a resolution was in sight, that we would find what we came for or we would find death.

I still felt tired but my head felt momentarily clearer, as if my brain realised it was going to have to make an effort to be alert if I were to live. I've heard tales of men being too tired to defend themselves. I've never encountered one in my career in the Imperial Guard. When the time comes, you fight for your life. Always.

We marched down into the ruins. I recognised something about this place from my dreams. A few of the shattered buildings looked familiar, and some of the open plazas, full of rubble and oddly changed statues. I thought about what I had seen in my dream and wondered whether there had been any truth in it. Was it possible that thousands of worlds had died to provide the energy that birthed a daemon-god? It seemed insane, but then the universe often does.

One thing was certain, something terrible had happened here. The streets were full of skeletons and they had not belonged to human beings. The bones of the limbs were too elongated, the skulls too long and narrow; the eye sockets were of a different shape. When Anton counted, the mouths held more teeth, and they were smaller than any human teeth would be.

Some of the bones no longer looked like bones. They had a glassy, crystalline quality. I was reminded of the way some of the statues had been transmuted. Perhaps the same thing had happened here. I only know that the bones glittered in the eerie light in a way I have never seen before and hope never to see again.

Something had killed all these people and it had done so swiftly and terribly. A lot of the destruction was probably caused after the fact by all the usual small accidents that can happen when there is no one left to supervise a system. Fires that were not extinguished had spread, explosions caused by machines overheating and running out of control. The eldar technology looked nothing like our own, but I was willing to bet that such things could happen.

And yet there was ample evidence to the contrary. There was still illumination. Something kept the hot, humid air circulating. Lights flickered around us, and strange glowing runes shimmered in the air, obviously written in the speech of the eldar. Whether they were warnings or exhortations, I could not say.

We came to a halt when we saw the body. It was fresh. For a moment, in my weary, semi-hallucinating state, I feared that it belonged to Grimnar, but it did not. It was the corpse of one of the eldar whose kindred we had so recently fought. It was armed and armoured, and it looked as though its carapace had exploded from the inside.

'Bolter shell,' said Macharius. 'It looks as though the Space Wolf has been this way.'

'Let us hope he is still alive.' I glanced around at the ruins. There was no sign of anything moving out there. No sound of anything living. In a human city, I would have expected vermin: cockroaches, rats, sewer-gibbons. Here there was nothing. I had a sense that even when the city was alive there probably weren't any. My memories of the dream agreed with that, although I had no idea how much faith to place in that recollection.

I had another image in my mind now, of fierce, silent stealthy warfare, of the Space Marine stalking the eldar through the ruins and being stalked in return, of two equally terrifying opponents locked in a struggle to the death. I wondered if we would come across the Space Wolf's tortured and mutilated corpse somewhere along the way. I prayed not, not just for the sake of the Space Marine but because it would be a terrible omen and a portent of our fate.

Ahead of us, the titanic tower rose into the strange sky. We began to move cautiously towards it, aware now of the presence of danger and preparing ourselves for battle.

In my life I have walked through the ruins of many cities, but none were stranger than this nameless place where so many had died so long ago. It was too warm, and I was drugged and weary and the shotgun felt heavy in my hands. Ahead of us lay that huge and ominous starscraper, where it seemed our fates would be resolved.

The wreckage of vehicles lay around us, looking like glittering broken eggshells. I pictured them flying through the air and simply crashing on the day doom had arrived. It was an image reinforced by the way some of them were embedded into the upper reaches of buildings.

I reached down and picked up a shard. It was made of a crystal of some sort. It had broken the way glass breaks, jagged edged and unevenly layered. It felt more like glass than metal. I could not imagine beating it into shape or machining it, the way I had once machined parts in the guild factorums of Belial when I was a lad.

It saved me. By pure random chance, bending over to pick up the piece of crystal lowered my head at exactly the moment the xenos took a shot at me. Something struck the wall behind me. Before I knew what was happening, reflexes developed in two decades of fighting on scores of worlds took over. I threw myself flat and scurried for the nearest cover. I noticed around me others were doing the same.

Force of habit had me looking for Macharius. With uncanny swiftness, he had ducked inside one of the crystal-line eggshell remains of a vehicle. I began to wriggle towards him on my belly, keeping down, feeling terribly vulnerable as the realisation of what had happened sunk in.

Someone had shot at me. At me. They would have hit me, too, if I had not chosen the precise moment they had triggered their weapon to bend down. If I had done it a heartbeat earlier they would have had time to compensate, particularly given what I had seen of the quickness of eldar reflexes. It was possible they were looking at me now, wait-ing for me to raise my head so they could shoot me.

I had a crawling sensation between my shoulders. I seemed to feel alien eyes glaring at me. I kept moving, not wanting to present a still target, wanting to make sure I was in a position to do my duty if someone attacked Macharius. A shotgun is not a good weapon for a long-range firefight, and for some reason I thought that this was the sort of fight it was going to be.

I heard the faint hum of lasguns discharging as they fired. I heard a loud crack as Anton opened fire with his sniper rifle. I heard nothing else, no screams, no sounds of bodies falling. I still could not bring myself to raise my head from cover and look around. I had a very vivid image of it being reduced to bloody shreds by incoming fire.

I reached the place where Macharius was and glanced around. I could see Drake lying behind a low wall nearby. There was blood on the ground near him, and I wondered whether he had been hit. I raised myself slightly, glanced around and saw nothing except las-bolts flickering at a multitude of hidden targets, and moved over to the inquisitor to see if he needed help. I dropped into position at his side, looked at him. He shook his head.

I could see his hand was bleeding and I noticed a shard of sharp-edged crystal lying near him. He must have cut his hand on it when he took cover. This was a dangerous place to throw yourself down. He was already starting to bandage it. Storm troopers were closing in around him, taking up position to protect him from potential attackers. I sensed a feral hostility behind the visors of their helmets when they looked at me. To them, anyone was a potential threat to their master.

'Cease fire,' Macharius shouted, and we obeyed. The shooting stopped. Everyone held their position, though. No one wanted to be the first to stick his head up and potentially have it removed. We waited and nothing happened. I felt my heart beating within my chest. Perhaps the eldar were still out there waiting to shoot. Perhaps they were long gone.

Macharius gave orders. Squads began to shift position, sweeping through the rubble around us, moving systematically to see if they could find the eldar. I held my breath waiting for the sound of screaming that would tell me they had encountered what they sought.

Nothing came in, save, one by one, reports that the area was clear. I wondered if the eldar had just vanished or were still out there hiding and watching us. Irrationally, I began to feel as if my would-be executioner were waiting for me to stand up again, as if it had somehow singled me out to be its victim. In that spooky place, having narrowly avoided death, weary and buzzed out on the stimm drugs, it seemed all too likely to be the case.

I exchanged looks with Drake. Under his uncanny gaze, I raised myself to one knee and looked around. I hunched my shoulders to make myself a narrower target, and I held the shotgun ready to fire at the slightest sign of movement. As I did so I realised how dangerous the situation was. There were scores of tired, heavily armed men all as nervous as me in the area. All it would take would be one sudden movement, one mistake, and there would be deaths.

Even as that thought occurred to me, Macharius rose into view, weapons held at the ready. He tipped his leonine head to one side as though listening, glanced around casually and emerged from cover with confidence. Just the sight of him doing so was reassuring.

'Well, now,' he said. 'At least we know there are eldar around here. Let's see what we can do to change that.'

CHAPTER TWENTY-SEVEN

Men crunched stimm tabs and stood tense and ready. Macharius studied the terrain around the one surviving, untouched tower and gave orders for our approach. All around, the strange ruins loomed out of the darkness: broken buildings, defaced by the worshippers of daemons; broken remnants of temples to xenos gods, looted and defiled by their enemies; shattered stumps of starscrapers that once must have touched the stone skies of this odd place.

Squad by squad, fire team by fire team, we rolled forward, each standing unit prepared to give covering fire to the ones moving around it. We were doing what we had been trained to do, and we were doing it under the eyes of our highest commander. It settled us down in that alien landscape surrounded by alien artefacts. I think it gave us a sense that we still somehow had some control over our own destiny.

Any soldier who has ever been in the chaos of battle will tell you how illusory that sense is, and yet it is important too. It is one of the things that make us human, this need to feel that somehow, in some way, we have some say in what happens to us, some feeling that we may have influence on our destiny.

No matter how illusory that proves to be.

It is both better and worse than I had hoped. The machine of the ancients stands before me. It is still functioning, but it looks as though it has been warped by the influence of Chaos. This means it may not function in the way it is supposed to, may be twisted to the purposes of She Who Thirsts.

I am faced with a maddening choice: to attempt to use the device and perhaps be destroyed or to turn my back on it and attempt to leave this place through the horde of waiting enemies.

Over the communications channels, I can hear the chatter that tells me how the battle is going. My warriors are selling their lives dearly but, one by one, they are falling to the superior numbers of our bestial enemies. I have not come all this way just to be slain by mon-keigh.

I lay my hands on the control altar and let them flicker over the complex runes of the initiation sequence. Now I will find out if those ancient books lied.

We pushed on deeper into the city, and every step of the way we came under attack. We were fired upon from the balconies overhead by foes who disappeared as swiftly as they attacked. At first we were unsure whether the attacks came from one eldar moving very swiftly or a group of them. It was hard to tell. Fear of the almost invisible foe multiplied their numbers. The advantage lay with them, for they attacked at will and vanished as they pleased, leaving us to count our casualties.

Macharius stood close to Drake, and Drake was surrounded by his bodyguard. They appeared all too willing to throw themselves between the inquisitor and certain death. I stayed as close as I could, and Anton and Ivan likewise. Being within the radius of the inquisitor's shield seemed like the only slight protection available against our merciless foes.

Macharius frowned now. He was not a man who enjoyed the sensation of being powerless, of waiting for death to come to him, but there was very little he could do. We had the numbers, but our foes refused to meet us on terms where those would do any good.

Another burst of fire struck from balconies and side corners, and by the time anyone could react, the shooters were gone. With their superior reflexes and greater speed and mobility, the xenos were mocking us.

It began to get dark. In places, the ever-burning gemstones of the eldar were dull. Their fire was gone. Either the xenos, with their greater understanding of the working of these things had dimmed them, or the systems were replicating the day/night cycle from before the cataclysm that had depopulated the city. In either case, the effect was the same. It gave the eldar more places to hide, made them more difficult to spot. The city was full of darkness, and in the darkness the eldar waited.

Sometimes we heard screams behind us, and reports filtered up the chain. They always signified the same thing. A man had gone missing. Always an outlier of the group. His comrades had turned their head for a moment, or he had lagged slightly behind, and the next moment he was gone, spirited away. Moments later the screams would begin. If squads were sent to investigate, the screams receded away from them as though the victim were being carried and tortured at the same time. The screams were the same hideous, pained yells that had haunted us back in the valley, signifiers that the xenos were feasting on human agony. Invariably, the teams sent to investigate would need to be recalled before they drifted out of sight and into the inevitable trap.

Macharius did what he could. Squads moved up to junctions and swept them carefully to make sure they were clear. Other squads moved by. The men were ordered to remain in close formation, not to let anyone get out of sight. Squads were left on overwatch in locations that commanded sweeping views of the surrounding streets. They saw nothing. It was as if the eldar knew where they were and how to avoid them.

In our long, slow progress towards the tower, it felt as though we were going to be picked off one by one and dragged down into a hell of burning nerve ends and torture. I am sure that was on all our minds.

'I wish the bastards would show themselves,' said Anton. 'Then we'd see how long they'd last.' He slapped the barrel of the sniper rifle meaningfully.

'They're working on our nerves,' I said. 'Trying to demoralise us and slow us down.'

'Why would they do that?' Anton asked.

'Because they have not found what they are looking for yet, and are trying to keep us away, most likely.'

Macharius tilted his head to one side as if I had just worked out something he had not expected me to be able to. Encouraged, I continued to speak. 'They know that if we get there, we have the numbers to overpower them and keep them from what they want.'

'The Fist is in there,' said Drake, pointing to the tower. It was directly ahead of us now.

Macharius nodded. We began to move towards the tower, across the plaza surrounding it. The hundred strides across open ground felt like the longest of my life. Every moment, I expected eldar weapons to send death scything my way. It took an effort of will to keep my pace down to that of the squad, and I suspected it was the same way for every man there. It was probably easier for me than many of them since I was with Macharius and Drake and had little option but to stay with them. The others might have been tempted to lengthen their strides and shorten the distance.

The entrance to the tower loomed before us like the gaping maw of a daemon-god, ready to swallow anyone who went in. I could not help but feel that there was something wicked waiting inside for us, that we had been allowed to cross the open ground and enter the building because it was a well-prepared trap.

Nonetheless, I went through the door first, shotgun held ready. I was in a massive atrium, at the centre of which was what appeared to be a fountain. At its heart was something that had once been some sort of water spirit but was now reshaped with crab-like claws and the leering face of a lascivious daemon. Dangling from one of those claws was an eldar. I looked up. Balcony after balcony rose within the atrium. I could see one of those had been shattered, and it looked perfectly possible that the eldar corpse had fallen through it at the break point and dropped into the daemon woman's outstretched claw. Indeed it looked almost deliberate.

'Grimnar has been here,' said Drake. Macharius narrowed his eyes.

'Down!' he roared, throwing himself to one side. A hail of fire slashed through the air where he had stood and took out one of Drake's storm trooper bodyguards. Another of them screamed in agony. The inquisitor stood in the centre of the hail of shots untouched, a nimbus of light playing around him. Prompted by instinct I rolled over to where he stood. A faint tingling flickered across my skin as I entered the globe of his sphere of protection.

Something dropped from a balcony above us. I had just time to catch sight of the eldar. It had a blade in each hand. It had realised that Drake was immune to its ranged weapons and it intended to finish him close-up. It had probably decided, quite correctly under the circumstances, that he was the greatest threat among its enemies.

I raised the shotgun and snapped off a shot at almost point-blank range. The force of the blast sent the eldar bobbing upwards. Most of its weight must have been neutralised by some sort of suspensor system. Either that or the eldar and its armour were both much lighter than they looked. Still, even wounded, the xenos sent one of its blades flashing towards me. Instinctively, I raised the shotgun and the blade clattered off its barrel. The eldar, wounded, was already arching its back and flipping down into a new landing position. It had a pistol of a strange, long-barrelled sort in its hand.

Another shot rang out. Anton fired his sniper rifle. By all rights he should have hit the eldar, but it was no longer where he had aimed. It was somersaulting away, back through one of the entrances to the chamber, too fast for any of us to catch. A storm of las-bolts and pistol fire erupted around it, but it jinked and weaved so swiftly that I would take oath that nothing hit it. By the time we reached the entrance to the chamber into which it had vanished, it was gone.

Three men were already dead. Another two died soon afterwards of their poisoned wounds. From somewhere in the distance we heard what sounded like mocking laughter but might just have been random static generated by a translation engine.

More and more of our men filtered into the building. They stepped around the corpses and glanced warily into the shadows. Like me, they could see now how it was going to be. We would seek the eldar through this haunted building, unsure who was hunter and who was prey.

Suddenly, close by, I heard a distinctive sound: the explosive impact of a bolter shell on armour. I heard a scream that was not human, and from the shadows Grimnar emerged. He looked like hell. His armour was chipped and dented, and the paintwork had flaked away. Fresh blood had splattered on his face and gauntlets and chestplate. None of it belonged to him. In his hand, he held the severed head of a female eldar. His face looked savage and feral and inhuman. His eyes were slitted. His mouth was twisted in a mirthless grin that was terrifying to see, and yet, from his manner, I had the sense that he was enjoying himself, was doing the thing he had been born to do, performing his duties in the service of his Allfather.

'Well met,' he said.

'Well met,' said Macharius. The Space Wolf lifted the head.

'This is one of the ones who have been dogging your steps. There is only one left now.'

So few, I thought. So few of them had pinned down our entire force and caused ten times that number of casualties. It was a terrifying thought. At least there was one less of them now.

'Where are the rest?' Macharius asked.

'In the tower. Their leader is there.'

'I am surprised you are not,' said Macharius.

'They are tough,' Grimnar said. The tone of his voice was grudging. He did not like making that admission. I realised that the xenos must be truly superhuman for him to describe them in such a way. 'You are here now. We have a better chance together. Some of us must survive to take back the Fist.'

I could see that too was an admission that went against the grain. In my mind's eye, I had seen the Space Wolves as snarling, berserker warriors, throwing themselves into battle with a howled war cry and a reckless disregard for their lives. Odd as it may sound I had not expected anything like this realistic tactical assessment. I don't know why – even astonishingly powerful as they were, Space Marines would not be useful to the Emperor if they were not capable of reading a battlefield.

'You've been inside,' Macharius said. It was not a question. Grimnar nodded.

'There is a vault, and around it are a series of chambers laid out in a spiral pattern, like the interior of the shell of a nautilus.'

I had no idea what he meant but clearly Macharius did. His eyes narrowed. His grip tightened on the hilt of his chainsword. 'Traps? Deadfalls? Ambush sites?'

'There are many balconies and alcoves, many statues and devices of incomprehensible purpose. There are places where they could lurk and take us by surprise.'

Macharius did not like the sound of that. There would be no room for the subtlety of the complex patterns of manoeuvres he favoured. It was going to be a straight rush into the vault, with the enemy waiting for us. They knew we were coming.

Macharius said, 'It works to our advantage as well. To stop us the eldar must face our numbers.'

'I will scout ahead,' said Grimnar.

We moved into the tower. It was as Grimnar had said. As soon as we passed through the entrance the corridor sloped downwards to the left in a long curve. Almost immediately it widened into another huge chamber. The ceiling above us was curved and the walls of the chamber were the same. I immediately thought of the bowels of a huge beast. It was as if we were being digested by the building and passed through its interior.

There were the same great pools of shadowy darkness as outside, the same dim illumination that seemed to come from nowhere in particular. The walls were marked with glowing eldar runes.

There were fountains and mutated statues and things that might have been altars, although it was difficult to tell. We moved forwards and down, following the interior curve of the building. Once again, I felt the alienness of our surroundings. I had no idea of the purpose of many of the things we saw. I had no idea why the interior was laid out this way. Vague hints rose from the half-remembered memories of my dreams – the shape was geomantic, it affected the flows of mystical energy. Or it had done once. If that were true, surely all these alterations would have affected that. Maybe that's why the lights were dimmer and the place had a strange, fusty atmosphere.

* * *

I entered the vault through the doorway and immediately had a sensation of falling. I felt dizzy, and I struggled to understand the reality of my surroundings. It was as if we were emerging from a trapdoor in the floor of the chamber, which was a vast sphere. Gravity seemed to twist through ninety degrees and the walls of the chamber into which we had emerged became the floor. After the brief sensation of falling, I stood upright, dizzy and nauseous, and flexed my knees as I struggled to regain my balance. I walked a little and followed the curve of the floor. I had to fight down the crazed feeling that if I kept walking I would describe a complete circle around the wall of the chamber and return to my starting point, even though that would involve traversing what was currently the ceiling far, far above my head.

Overhead was a dome of translucent stone, through which was visible the shimmering, multicoloured lights of whatever lay beyond this sub-realm of reality. A wisp of light played in the air. It swirled like water in a whirlpool and appeared to drain away even as it spun. We were in a space where the laws of gravity appeared to have been suspended, where cables of crystal, glimmering with light and shadows, rose from each wall towards a central point. Not only that, lateral cables ran amid them, forming a lattice, a web of light and shadow and colour. I reached out and touched one of the cables, and my hand tingled. It was not an unpleasant sensation, a mild shock that made the hair on my head and neck lift. Looking up along it I could see a humanoid figure, a long way above us, climbing along the cables towards a distant point, which would most likely be the central spot in the chamber.

Macharius had already begun to climb, Drake as well. Grimnar was moving ahead of us. I looked around and saw Anton and Ivan. We looked at each other, slung our weapons over our shoulders and started to climb using both hands to pull ourselves up.

Chapter Twenty-Eight

I reach out through the device and I touch infinity. I feel the pulse of creation around me. I sense the flow of cosmic energy. Beyond that I sense something else, the infinite power of Chaos in that universe that runs conterminous with ours. I feel my mind start to buckle under the pressure of the inputs.

This is not how the machine was supposed to work. Or was it? It was intended to make thoughts and dreams real. How does it do that? I begin to concentrate, to fight back against the waves of pleasure and pain that pulse through my brain. I begin to imagine the shape of reality changing around me, responding to my will. I begin to understand what I have found.

This whole sub-universe is malleable. All of the matter here can be, and has been, changed. I visualise the streets of

Commorragh, and they coalesce around me. I picture Sileria writhing naked, and she dances before me in her skin. There is a ghastly, ghostly quality to this, of the not quite real of illusion, but I know that if only I concentrate hard enough, what I wish will take shape. I see what those long gone eldar were working on before they were devoured. They were trying to tap the forbidden power of Chaos to allow them to reshape reality. And they succeeded. Although their success may have contributed to their downfall.

I know that if I work on this I can summon armies to my aid, armies that will worship me like a god, which will allow me to raise myself to heights undreamed of by the inferior intellects around me. I hear the whispered temptations of absolute power and I do not resist them. Who would?

We swarmed up the web of pulsing light towards the strangeness at its centre. Ahead of me I could see Macharius and Drake and Grimnar. The Space Wolf moved with an inhuman speed and grace that no mortal man could match, although Macharius was close. When Grimnar reached the pattern in the centre of the web, he vanished, simply shimmered out as if he had never been. I wondered where he had gone. Macharius paused for a moment then followed. Drake went next. I reached the portal and paused, drawing breath, suddenly very afraid.

It was another gateway, opening into I knew not where. It was not going to be good, I was sure. I felt my heart pounding against my ribs, a small frightened animal pounding against the bars of its cage. In the end it was sheer momentum that decided me. The need to follow Macharius and not remain behind, waiting for who knew what, perhaps for the xenos to return and torture me. Offering up a prayer to the Emperor, I threw myself through the portal and into a world of strangeness.

At first, it was as if I had stepped through into formless nothingness. All around me was only swirling, multicoloured mists of the sort that had been visible through the walls to either side of the roadway we had walked. I wondered if we had passed through some sort of final barrier and into what lay beyond the cosmic structure the xenos had built. Ahead of me, floating, were the others. Ahead of them, in the distance, was a glowing platform. I could see a small figure moving towards it. I tried to move myself but nothing happened. It was like trying to swim in a medium that had no resistance. I could move my limbs but there was nothing for them to gain traction against. I writhed and twisted my body but my wriggling could not move me from the spot.

I noticed my surroundings were starting to change, that the clouds of floating colours were taking on shape and density. I ignored them and drifted through the ether towards our distant goal. I could see it now. There was an altar. It glowed with holy light, a transcendental energy. Near it stood one of the xenos, the tallest and most powerful looking I had yet seen. It carried itself with an aura of utter confidence, and the glance it directed at us held only the purest contempt. In such a way a man might contemplate an insect he was going to squash.

Even as I felt the chilling gaze pass over me, I noticed that the clouds of formless matter were taking on a new shape. They were becoming more solid, acquiring the look of the ruined city we had seen outside or something much worse, an almost infinitely large fortress of xenos build stretching as far as the eye could see. From each building peered out a hundred xenos faces. I wondered what had happened. Was this some sort of transportation device? Had we suddenly been shifted through space and time to some new alien realm? Were we about to be overwhelmed by legions of eldar desperate to rend our flesh and feast on our agony?

The air shimmered, and more and more of the xenos came into being. How had they achieved this? I had heard of teleportation devices but never of them being used on so vast a scale.

The whole thing had the aspect of a dream. If this were a portal to some distant realm we were not all the way through it yet; reality had not yet twisted all the way. Drake seemed to be shouting something at Macharius. Grimnar ignored him and moved towards the xenos. A score of the newly materialised eldar threw themselves in the way. Grimnar's chainsword flickered out and rent through them.

At first they came apart like ghosts, as if their flesh were nothing more than mist. The Space Marine moved forward, chopping through them, and as he did so they became progressively more solid. Not only that, more and more of them kept appearing, out of nowhere. For every one he cut down, two more materialised. They moved swiftly, with eerie grace, fast enough to match even his superhumanly swift movements. The tide of the combat turned. Grimnar found himself on the defensive, beaten back till he stood beside Macharius and Drake. A hail of fire from the warriors mowed down the eldar, and for a moment things seemed stable.

I paused to look around. Gigantic, dark crystalline structures had somehow swung into place all around me, unfolding out of nothingness until they loomed overhead like the castle of some childhood ogre. Again I was struck by the dreamlike quality of all of this. It could not be real. And yet when I reached out my hand, I felt smooth, cool stone beneath it. When I glanced around, I saw hundreds upon hundreds of eldar infantry moving towards me. I knew the moment of my death had arrived. There were far too many of them to be resisted. Still there was something not quite right. The eldar's armour did not have all the details I expected, the hieroglyphs that marked rank or status or role or function, whatever it was they did. The xenos's movements while graceful were repetitive and similar. They all appeared to move in perfect synchronisation.

I clutched the shotgun tighter and noticed there was ground beneath my feet. It was dark and shimmering like the structures around me, and although crystalline it was not slippery but seemed to have been designed to allow traction. I began to move towards the conflict. There was not really anything else to do. I could remain on my own in the strange city taking shape around me, but that would have meant soon being surrounded by hordes of murderous xenos. I saw Anton and Ivan close by. They looked just as lost and confused as I felt, but they were doing what they could always be relied on to do when in trouble. They were following me. The Undertaker was there and various members of Macharius's Lion Guard, too.

More and more units of xenos were coming into view. There were thousands of them and only a comparative handful of us. I knew the time was fast approaching when I was going to have to sell my life as dearly as possible.

Drake seemed to be trying to explain something to the others and I could not work out what he was saying. I found a low barrier wall to use as cover, took up a position behind it and looked at the oncoming horde. Incoming fire whined around my head. I popped up and opened fire, hitting one of the oncoming xenos at almost point-blank range.

I sense the approach of others. Foolish flies have entered the web woven by my godlike consciousness. I will devour them now. I begin to spin a new reality from dreams and visions, summoning a world into being around me, creating legions of lost souls to serve me.

This time I will destroy my foes.

Anton looked at me. He frowned his puzzlement and popped up and aimed a shot. More eldar raced towards us. Our surroundings continued to change as well. They were more solid, more real than they had been even a few moments ago.

I shook my head, wondering whether I was going mad, whether too much fatigue and too much stimm were affecting my brain. I wriggled along on my belly towards where Macharius and Drake were. Grimnar stood watch with them. A massive explosion ripped the ground, throwing us apart. I fell to land beside the Space Wolf. Somehow he had managed to keep his feet. Where the others had been was only a tangle of broken crystal and strange flickering lines. Hails of fire from the eldar splintered the wreckage around us. I lay prone and still for a moment.

Looking up into Grimnar's face, I noticed that his eyes were yellowish, like those of a dog.

'What is happening?' I shouted over the roar of the carnage around us.

'The reality here is mutable. It responds to a sufficiently strong will. The foes we face have been conjured by the eldar.'

I thought about what I was seeing. The way reality continued to swim and shift. An enormous tower collapsed under the impact of an artillery barrage. A plume of dust rose up as if to touch the sky.

'It looks so real,' I said.

'It is real,' said Grimnar. 'In this place, it is real.'

A look almost of dismay flickered across his face. I tried to imagine what all of this strangeness must be like to him. His senses were keener than mine. He could see things I could not, hear them and smell them as well. It could not be pleasant to have the very forms of reality dance and transform before him.

He shook his head and growled, and seemed like his fierce, determined self once more. 'What can we do?' I said.

'I will seek the Fist of Russ,' he said. 'It is out there in all this Chaos.'

Without another word he threw himself over the wall, rolled to his feet, chopped down some eldar soldiers and ran off. I saw the others moving into place to guard Macharius. I doubted that one more soldier would make any difference, so prompted by some inner daemon, I followed along in the wake of the Space Wolf. I was not sure why. If Grimnar could not handle what he met out here, I was not sure I could make any difference. I went anyway.

I raced across a landscape torn by war, chaotic beyond belief, twisted by a kind of madness that was all but incomprehensible. Overhead loomed a city built by maddened eldar. It shimmered and bent and moved as if part of the flickering imagination of a demented god.

I dived into a trench as wide as the tracks of a Baneblade and wriggled along in the direction Grimnar had gone. I could hear the distinctive sound of a bolter being fired and knew I was on the right track still.

I popped my head up and saw the Space Wolf hacking his way through a group of eldar warriors. Limbs flew trailing droplets of blood. A spine, partially severed, unwound through a broken backplate of crystalline armour. A xenos leapt behind the Space Marine. I raised and fired the shotgun. The shell took it in the back at the same time as Grimnar's bolter butt smashed into its helmet, crushing it. I sensed the Space Wolf's eyes on me, then he turned and moved on. I wondered whether it was my imagination or whether he was moving fractionally more slowly to enable me to keep up.

He paused occasionally to sniff the air, then moved swiftly and surely onwards, always moving as though towards a goal. I followed, trusting to the idea that he knew what he was doing. He entered a long hall and moved through it. An eldar dropped down on him, somehow moving faster and with more skill than the others he had faced so far. The two of them exchanged blows so swiftly it was impossible for me to follow. I ran up, not wanting to get too close to the eldar but wanting to be close enough to shoot if the opportunity arose.

The eldar rained down blows on Grimnar. He parried with the barrel of his bolter. Sparks flew where the two weapons connected. The eldar was the swifter of the two. Its blows made it through Grimnar's guard and chipped his armour. Suddenly Grimnar let go his bolter; it dropped still attached to his neck by the strap. He reached out with both hands, grasped the eldar's head and twisted. The xenos's neck snapped even as its weapons drove into Grimnar's side.

The Space Marine stood there, mouth open, gasping like a wolf on a hot day. I could see he was reeling on his feet, jaw muscles working as though he were in great pain. I ran up to him. His eyes had a glazed look, were focused into the distance as if he could see something astonishing a long way off. Slowly, his sight came back into focus, his breathing slowed and he became steadier on his feet. It was as though he had been poisoned and then his body had slowly adapted to the toxin, leaving him immune to its effects. Without a word he strolled on.

I recognised where we were. It was an almost exact replica

of the atrium of the tower we had passed through to get here, a mirror within a mirror. In the centre of the chamber was an altar and on that altar was a gauntlet. Beside it stood a tall, powerful looking xenos.

The Space Wolf raised his bolter and took swift aim at the eldar's head. The air between them shimmered and suddenly more eldar warriors were there. The head of one of them exploded. I realised the enemy commander had brought them into being to stop us. All of them looked exactly the same, and exactly like the figure we had seen by the altar. Grimnar did not hesitate for a moment. He sprang into action, blasting and smashing a path towards the altar, killing as he went. I lobbed a grenade into the mass of xenos, as far from the Space Marine as I could get it. The shockwave pulsed through them, throwing broken figures doll-like across the chamber.

I glanced back and saw Grimnar wrestling with a group of xenos. They had swarmed over him with their uncanny swiftness and were cutting and slashing at him with no regard to their own lives. They seemed utterly and maniacally fearless. Potent though the Space Wolf was, no single being, save perhaps the Emperor himself, could have withstood such an assault. His bolter was wrenched from his hands, and blow after blow rained down on his armoured form. Twist as he might some of them got through, and he fell amid a mass of his alien enemies.

Panic surged through me. I cursed myself for ever following Grimnar. If a Space Marine could go down here what chance did I have to survive? Desperately, I tried to recall where we had first seen the eldar leader. I primed a grenade and threw it at the spot, just as every alien head turned to look at me. The grenade burst in the air, sending a wave of shock and shrapnel tearing through the enemy ranks. The effect was startling. The massed ranks of eldar grew insubstantial and vanished, leaving only one, reeling in the middle next to the altar. I do not know why.

No! The link with the reality engine is broken. It will take too long to restore it. My legions have vanished. My foes close in. I look up, dazed and nauseous, and I see the human responsible. Of one thing I am certain. On him I will have my vengeance.

The sounds of conflict outside fell suddenly silent. A terrible hush filled the air, the sort of quiet you would expect to hear a heartbeat before the end of the world erupted. I wondered what I had done. The only explanation that occurred to me was that the grenade blast had shattered the xenos's concentration, making it impossible to maintain the armies it had summoned in this strange place. I raised the shotgun to my shoulder, aimed directly at the body and pulled the trigger.

The eldar sprang, moving above the blast with one easy, fluid movement. It seemed to be moving more slowly than previously, and it came to me that perhaps it was wounded, or perhaps the disconnection from whatever had allowed it to summon armies had done something to its brain. Nonetheless, I knew it would be more than a match for me if it got within striking distance.

I kept firing, hoping to distract it and prevent it from summoning more eldar to its aid. It came ever closer, holding its blade at the ready. Strange mechanical laughter spilled from the headpiece of its armour.

'I shall feast on your agony, mortal,' it said.

The eldar moved towards me so fast I barely had time to raise the shotgun. It made no difference. A fist blurred past it and hit me somewhere over the heart. It was like a blow from a sledgehammer. I felt as though I could be catapulted backwards, but something restrained me: the arm of the xenos, it was holding me in place. I heard something click and blades extruded from its gloves. I flinched as I felt cloth and flesh tear. A flap of skin lifted from my back as it was flayed by multiple scalpels. A searing heat flared around the wound. Briefly, I wondered whether it was shock or poison, and then realised it did not matter. I tried to pull myself free but the xenos held me in place. At first skin and flesh ripped in response to my movement, but then the alien moved to compensate.

I let the shotgun fall forward and I pulled the trigger. The blast came at an odd angle. The kick broke my wrist. Somehow the eldar swayed backwards and away, but it had been forced to let me go. The blades came clear of my flesh with an odd sucking sound. I gritted my teeth and forced myself to move. I heard that flat, machine-generated laughter behind me.

Something blurred overhead. The eldar was now in front of me as I tried to scramble away. It had somersaulted over me. It held up its gauntlet. I saw my blood on the scalpel blades emerging from its fingertips. It mingled with gobbets of pink stuff which had been attached to my innards not a few moments before. I reached for a grenade left handed. I thought if I could arm it, I could simply hold it and let the explosion get both of us. I knew I was a dead man and that given the slightest opportunity the eldar would torture me. At any moment I expected to feel the nerve-searing pain of neurotoxins anyway. A quick death seemed preferable to that.

The eldar reached out and batted the grenade away. The action was casual and contemptuous. Behind it, I saw something that made me laugh. It paused for a moment.

Macharius stood there, pistol raised, aiming. He pulled the trigger. The eldar was already in motion, diving to one side. The shell took it in the shoulder and sent it reeling. It rolled over, regaining its feet, twisting to bring its own long-barrelled weapon to bear. Macharius shot again, caught the eldar in the chest. Macharius pulled the trigger again. The shell exploded within the chest cavity exposed by the power of the previous shot. Macharius kept firing shell after shell until his magazine was emptied. Clearly he was taking no chances.

I mumbled my thanks, and then I noticed Macharius's face, and how strange his expression was. Something about it reminded me of the Undertaker. His features held the look of a man who had seen too much. He stood there for a long time, looking at the dead eldar. Drake entered and behind him came Anton and Ivan and the Undertaker, along with a few surviving Lion Guard.

My old comrades raced over and began to treat my wounds. They slapped synthi-flesh on the ripped skin and applied adhesive bandages. 'Go look at Grimnar.' I barely managed to force the words out from between my mangled lips.

Grimnar had already started to rise. His awesome powers of recovery were starting to assert themselves. He was functional again despite having taken a beating that would have killed a normal man. Together he and Macharius and Drake moved towards the altar on which lay the Fist of Russ.

I limped along behind them, determined to witness what came next. I had come a long way and I was not going to miss out on it now.

All three of them stood at the altar looking down on the ancient relic. It was indeed a gauntlet, and it looked like it had been made to fit Space Marine armour. If anything it was bigger than Grimnar's. It had similar runes inscribed on it too.

I saw Grimnar and Drake and Macharius exchange looks.

'This is not the Fist of Russ,' said Grimnar. 'It is ancient and it belonged to the Wolves, but not to our primarch.'

'But…' I heard Anton say. All three of those deadly men looked at him, and even he had the wit to fall silent.

'I will see that this is properly disposed of,' said Grimnar, picking up the Fist.

All looked bleak, their faces frozen as if their features had been carved from immutable rock.

'We are done here,' said Macharius. 'There is nothing for us.'

His voice had an odd quality to it, the sound of massive boulders grinding together within the cold ice of a glacier. 'Let us go,' he said.

With the Space Wolf loping along ahead of us, we departed.

We emerged from the portal. It had taken us what seemed like days to march to it, but when we stepped back into the Valley of the Ancients, it looked like only minutes had passed. The officer set to watch it looked up and blinked in amazement. 'Sir,' he said, 'we did not expect you back so soon.'

His eyes ran over us again, and I could see he was adding up the discrepancies between our appearance and what he had expected to see. We were unshaven, our uniforms were torn, we were red-eyed from marching on stimms; some were wounded, including myself. Many casualties would not be returning at all.

'Show me your chronometer,' Macharius said. The officer complied. Macharius shook his head. 'Sixteen minutes,' he said to Drake. 'We've been gone sixteen minutes.'

Drake looked haunted, as he had done ever since we saw the Fist of Demetrius. He nodded as though Macharius had simply confirmed what he had suspected. 'At least we made it out,' he said.

Macharius nodded grimly. 'And it means I have returned in time to ensure the slaughter of the xenos.'

He began to speak into the comm-net with rasping authority, getting reports as to how the situation stood, then rapping out orders for dealing with remnants of the eldar attack. As he did so he kept walking, and we kept moving with him, emerging from the labyrinthine temple into a night scarred by the blaze of battle.

Macharius launched himself into the conflict with the zeal and fury of a true servant of the Emperor. We strode by his side, weapons blazing, striving as always to keep him from harm.

ABOUT THE AUTHOR

William King is the author of the Tyrion & Teclis trilogy and the Macharian Crusade, as well as the much-loved Gotrek & Felix series and the Space Wolf novels. His short stories have appeared in many magazines and compilations, including *White Dwarf*. Bill was born in Stranraer, Scotland, in 1959 and currently lives in Prague.

AN EXTRACT FROM

THE MACHARIAN CRUSADE:

FALL OF MACHARIUS

WILLIAM KING

It was another of those moments where I knew I was dead. I have lost count of how many times they have happened but they never get any easier to take.

It's always the same. My mouth goes dry. My heart races. I feel that sudden sharp surge of fear that is inevitable when your body realises that it is soon going to cease functioning. In this case, the realisation was compounded with the fact that my body was already struggling with wounds and disease. The visions of dancing daemons swirling through my mind didn't really help much either.

I braced myself for the stabbing of a dozen heretic bayonets. I wondered why they were not already charging at us, keen to take revenge for all their comrades we had sent to greet their daemon gods. I could hear the sounds of fighting, of lasguns pulsing, of chainswords splintering bone to white, bloodstained chips. I could hear someone shouting, 'For the Emperor and Macharius!'

The heretics were charging at us, but their eyes were wide with panic. They did not seem intent on stabbing us so much as keen to get past us. A few of them raced by into Dead Man's Trench, while others threw themselves up the parapet. Their officers screamed for them to stand their ground, or at least that is what I assume they were screaming, but none of the fleeing enemy seemed to be paying too much attention to those orders. They were too busy trying to put some distance between themselves and the green-tunicked Lion Guard coming at them from behind.

These troops were new and fresh and deadly looking. Their uniforms were clean and unpatched. Their weapons were being used with brisk efficiency. It was not them I noticed first though – it was the man leading them.

He looked like a great predator, tall and broad-shouldered, golden-haired and golden-skinned. His movements were poised and deadly. He swept through the melee, a human whirlwind of violence, cutting down a man with every stroke of the chainsword he wielded right-handed, while blasting away with the bolt pistol he was holding in his left. There was a poise and deadliness about the Lord High Commander Solar Macharius which he never lost even at the bitter end. He was a perfect killing machine, as completely deadly in his own way as a Space Marine of the Adeptus Astartes.

His coordination was uncanny, his movements eye-blurringly swift. Just when you thought you knew where he was going to step and whom he was going to strike, he surprised you.

The bullet aimed at him passed through the space where he seemed to be going to be. His stroke turned out to be a feint, never hitting where it was expected but burying itself in flesh nonetheless. A man raised his weapon to block the blade and took a bolt pistol shot through the eyes. A man ducked to avoid the killing shot and found himself impaled on the blade instead.

Macharius fought in close combat the way he led armies, swiftly, decisively, with feints within feints, and a defence that consisted of the swiftest attacks. He was a living god of war, perfect in all he did when it came to battle. At least that was the impression he was still capable of giving when he chose to enter the fray in person. Seeing him, fighting beneath the fluttering Lion Banner, you could not help but feel your heart rise and know that victory was certain.

He battled his way over to us, and I noticed that Ivan was by his side, fighting away, a clumsy half-human automaton compared to Macharius, but deadly in his own way. Macharius's gaze swept over me and he nodded encouragingly and then he went by, killing as he went, leading the massive counter-attack he seemed to have organised out of nowhere.

I noticed then that Inquisitor Drake, his permanent shadow, was with him. Pale where Macharius was golden, thin where Macharius was athletic, Drake nonetheless had his own deadliness. His lean form possessed a surprising strength and an incredible resilience. If he was not quite as quick as Macharius, he seemed just as capable of countering all attacks, possibly because he was capable of reading the thoughts of the attackers.

A halo of light played around his head as he unleashed his psychic powers in terrifying bolts of energy. For a moment, his gaze rested on me as well and I shuddered, for his eyes seemed to be boring into my soul, and I felt he could see the contamination there, the doubts I had picked up, the daemons I was guilty of seeing.

Around Drake were the hand-picked storm troopers of his personal guard, their blank, mirrored visors reflecting the grimness of the battlefield on which they fought. Seen in the shimmering armourglass of those helmets, the landscape of Loki looked even more bleak and terrifying.

In a few more heartbeats, they too were by and more and more troops of Macharius's personal guard followed, looking stern and efficient and implacable.

I wondered then if this was another of Macharius's famous feints, whether we had been the bait in yet another trap to draw in his enemies. At that point I was past caring. I slumped down against the earthwork wall of the trench, my back against a couple of stray sandbags and I contemplated the staring eyes of the carpet of dead bodies, Macharius had left in his wake. I wondered whether any of them would spring back into motion, and whether they would come to drag me down into death and I found, at that moment, in time I did not exactly care.

I did not feel at my best when I came to. I found I was looking up at the face of Macharius. He was standing talking with the Undertaker, saying something so quietly that even as close as I was I could not make it out. Over his shoulder the skull moon leered. The lesser moon raced across the sky, a small daemonling perched on it, giggling.

I tried to pull myself upright and I noticed that Anton and Ivan and a number of the other soldiers were there, along with a few high ranking officers. I saw they were inspecting the dead and noting the fact that some of the corpses were dissolving into puddles of greenish slime, while others, in a new twist, seemed only to be lying there, their flesh green and corrupt looking.

Around everything small pot-bellied daemons gambolled, sticking out their tongues, farting and belching, walking alongside the officers with taloned hands behind their backs, their movements and expressions mockeries of the men they were following.

I wondered where Drake was. Why wasn't the inquisitor sorting these little frakkers out? It was his job after all. Part of my mind, the tiny bit that still held a faint crumb of rationality, told me these were hallucinations, that I was feverish, that I was seeing things.

I pulled myself upright, gurgled for water, and noticed that one of the officers with Macharius did not look like the others. His skin had a greenish tinge. His eyes were mocking. There was something about him that reminded me of the daemons. He seemed to be just as inhuman as one of them and he was fumbling in his belt, pulling his pistol free. I shouted a warning and pointed.

Macharius turned and so fast were his reflexes that he was already reacting to my pathetic attempt at a warning and the sight of the attacker he must have just caught from the corner of his eye. Even as the man drew a bead on him he was already in motion, pulling his bolt pistol free from its holster and swivelling at the hip to snap off a shot.

It was touch and go. The laspistol shot seared Macharius's shoulder, melting one of the lion's head epaulets there. Macharius's return took the man in stomach and punched an enormous hole in it, the way bolt-shells do when they explode. I pulled myself upright, and snatched up a laspistol from a corpse. I shot the man again, but he still kept moving, animated by some spirit of destruction, or so it seemed.

Others opened fire until glittering las-beams made a net around him and through his body, and still he kept on coming. A sniper rifle sounded. The officer's head exploded. I heard Anton give a grunt of satisfaction as the would-be assassin toppled and fell. Someone shouted for a medic and men swarmed towards Macharius.

That's another life you owe me, I thought with some satisfaction, somehow managing to forget in that moment all of the times Macharius had saved mine.

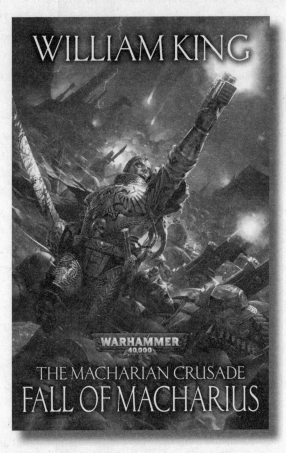